WE DON'T
TALK ABOUT
CAROL

WE DON'T TALK ABOUT CAROL

A Novel

KRISTEN L. BERRY

BANTAM

NEW YORK

Bantam Books
An imprint of Random House
A division of Penguin Random House LLC
1745 Broadway, New York, NY 10019
randomhousebooks.com
penguinrandomhouse.com

Hardcover ISBN 978-0-593-97443-8
Ebook ISBN 978-0-593-97444-5

Printed in the United States of America on acid-free paper

1st Printing

First Edition

BOOK TEAM:
Production editor: Jennifer Rodriguez • Managing editor: Saige Francis
Production manager: Samuel Wetzler • Copy editor: Susan M. S. Brown
Proofreaders: Rebecca Maines, Karina Jha, Andrea Gordon

Book design by Sara Bereta

Interior art: Shiju Graphics/Adobe Stock

The authorized representative in the EU for product safety and compliance is
Penguin Random House Ireland, Morrison Chambers, 32 Nassau Street,
Dublin D02 YH68, Ireland. https://eu-contact.penguin.ie

For the tens of thousands of
Black Americans reported missing every year.
For the thousands more who never stop looking.

WE DON'T
TALK ABOUT
CAROL

PROLOGUE

Twenty-Six Years Ago

I COULDN'T SLEEP. MY YOUNGER SISTER, SASHA, SNORED softly beside me, her exhales making little puff sounds as the breath escaped her lips. I'd lost the battle for equal space in the twin-size four-poster bed hours ago. Her limbs, surprisingly long for her nine years, were splayed; arms in a Y above her head, her legs a figure four. One of her knees pressed sharply into my thigh.

The North Carolina air snaking through the window reminded me of the weather inside our Jack and Jill bathroom back in L.A., when I'd futilely flatiron my stubborn curls ahead of school while Sasha showered.

All Grammy wanted for her sixty-fifth birthday was to have her only family—her son, daughter-in-law, and two grandchildren—under her roof for the week. It seemed like a reasonable ask before I realized that Grammy rarely ran her AC, and that I'd have to share a bed with my snoring, thrashing furnace of a sister.

I scanned the unfamiliar terrain of the smallest bedroom in Grammy's house. A slice of moonlight shone silver across a white dresser. Too restless to sleep, I decided to snoop. I slid from bed as quietly as I could. The old springs groaned as my weight left the mattress, but Sasha's breath kept its metronomic rhythm: *puff-puff-puff.*

I wrapped my fingers around the antique brass handle of the top dresser drawer and pulled it open slowly. It was filled with spools of thread, in various sizes and a Crayola box-worth of colors. The next drawer held paper clothing patterns, yellowed and brittle, tearing at their creases. The other drawers stored tea towels, loose buttons, extra table linens. The bottom drawer was filled with fabric. I picked up the top print, a faded sunny yellow gingham, and unfurled it. It was a summer dress, probably Sasha's size. I frowned, wondering who it belonged to. Maybe Grammy purchased the dress for me or Sasha at some point, but forgot to send it?

I picked up the next bit of fabric. Another dress, this one even smaller, white and embroidered with tiny purple flowers. I was reaching to pick up the rest of the contents from the drawer when my fingers jammed into something hard. I swallowed a yelp, knelt beside the drawer, and felt gingerly around its contents until I found the offending object. It was a small picture frame, ornate and golden but badly tarnished. I shifted into the path of the moonlight to see the photo it held.

It was a sepia-tinged image of a girl around my age, thirteen or so. She appeared to stand on the steps of Grammy's front porch. She wore a dress with a nipped-in waist and a flared skirt that stopped just below her knees. There were similar photos of my father as a child in an old album back in California, posing on that very same porch, frozen in the same faded shades of amber. But I'd never seen this girl before. She had Grammy's coloring, several shades lighter than mine. Like the coffee my mother drank every morning, with a long pour of cream. But I also recognized details of her face in mine: the heavy-lidded stare that prompted my mom to accuse me of having an attitude. The half-cocked, knowing smile.

"Who are you?" I whispered to the photograph.

I carefully returned everything to the drawers, but I slipped the framed photo beneath my pillow before crawling back into bed.

The questions swirling in my mind finally drowned out Sasha's snoring, lulling me into my first and only deep sleep of our visit.

THE NEXT MORNING I FOUND Grammy in the kitchen preparing our breakfast: grits, pork sausage, and scrambled eggs.

"Good mornin', darlin'," she greeted me cheerfully, scattering cubes of sharp cheddar cheese into the eggs. The slight drawl in her speech reminded me of the honey my father added to the tea he made whenever I had a sore throat, its sticky sweetness dripping slowly from the spoon.

"Morning, Grammy," I said, shifting nervously as I pulled the picture frame from behind my back. "Grammy, who's this?"

Her smile stiffened as her eyes scanned the photo. "Oh, baby," she said, her tone as gentle as the touch she used to pull the frame from my fingers. She went over to the yellow refrigerator, stood on her tiptoes, and set the frame facedown on top.

Grammy didn't meet my eyes when she turned to face me, wiping her hands with a dish towel, as though the picture had soiled them. I couldn't be certain, but I thought I noticed a tremble in her fingers.

"Baby," she said finally, her voice kind but firm as the oak tree on her front lawn, "we don't talk about Carol."

ONE

Present Day

"You sure you're going to be able to pack up the house without killing each other?" my husband Malik asked, his warm, rich voice amplified by the rental car's surround sound system.

I snorted as I drove out of the hotel's garage and into sunny, leafy downtown Raleigh. "I can't make any promises."

"There's really no one there who can help?"

"You saw how it was at the funeral. Grammy didn't have any family left, just church friends as old as she was."

"She had family," Malik said. "She had you guys."

I shook my head and felt my springy shoulder-length curls exaggerate the movement. "Our relationship consisted of exchanging birthday cards and calls at Christmas. Not much of a family."

It had all happened so fast. Grammy had always been so spry and independent, it was easy to forget that she was ninety years old. And then last week we got a call that she'd had a stroke, and was in the hospital, unconscious. The next day, she was gone.

She'd told her dearest friends where she kept the folder with all the documents we'd need for this moment, including her will, life insurance policy, information on her prepaid cemetery plot, even a handwritten outline of what her funeral service should entail. All she asked was that my mother—her daughter-in-law, and the closest thing she had to a child now that my father was gone—oversee the process of clearing out and selling her home of over seventy years.

Recognizing what a gargantuan task this would be, and guilt-ridden from spending so little time with Grammy in the years leading up to her death, my sister Sasha and I immediately offered our help. And while I never would have asked him to, Malik, ever the doting and dutiful husband, rearranged his carefully constructed work schedule to join us on a red-eye from L.A. to Raleigh five days ago.

"I shouldn't have left." Malik sighed, the reverberation of the sound through the speakers sending goosebumps down my arms. "I can push my meeting and fly back out there."

Something swelled inside my chest. Malik had spent weeks preparing for the quarterly board meeting of Wealthmate, the financial services start-up he founded. But I knew if I asked him to, he'd reschedule the entire thing. I was staying another five days to help my mother and Sasha with Grammy's house; they'd book their return flights to L.A. when the house was officially on the market.

"Absolutely not," I said. "I know how important this meeting is. We'll be fine here."

"Will you ask Grace or Sasha to help you with your shots?"

"Nah, I've got it," I replied, though the tender flesh below my navel pulsed angrily at the thought.

"I know your mom can be a bit of a drill sergeant, but don't be afraid to take breaks, or to go for a walk around the block if they start getting on your nerves. You know what Dr. Tanaka said about avoiding stress."

My fingers tightened around the steering wheel. *Avoid stress.* What was I supposed to do, lock myself in a spa until one of these

IVF cycles finally worked? "Malik," I said evenly, "I'm well aware. I was the one on the exam table, remember?"

"I know," Malik said in a small, pained way that instantly filled me with guilt for snapping at him. "You've got enough going on without having to listen to me lecture you. I'll let you go. Just promise to call if you need anything. I'll book a flight, hire professional packers, send a rescue team out to extricate you, whatever you need."

"I love that you actually mean that, even though you know I'd never take you up on it," I said, smiling.

"If I offer to take care of you enough, one of these days you might actually let me," he replied.

We hung up and the true crime podcast I was listening to resumed as I continued the drive to Grammy's. She'd lived in South Park, a neighborhood surrounding Shaw, the oldest of the many historically Black colleges and universities in the area. I marveled at how different the landscape looked from L.A. Giant swaths of verdant land appeared untouched, and the ancient trees that towered over homes were so lush they appeared capable of swallowing the structures whole. Unlike the belligerently cheerful L.A. sky, the atmosphere above Raleigh seemed moodier, richly layered, thick with history.

As I pulled into Grammy's driveway, I realized how much her house reminded me of photos I saw of her in her final years: aging yet elegantly kept. Grammy's uncle had built the home back in the 1940s, when it was rare for Black people to own property in the area. The single-story structure was flanked by two-story new-construction houses of a particular style sprinkled throughout the neighborhood. Color-blocked siding and dark fixtures gave them a modern look, but something about the columns and porches whispered hauntingly of plantation homes.

A loud knock on the driver's side window snatched me from my reverie.

"Oh my God, Sasha!" I paused the podcast and lowered the window, frowning at my sister as the still-soupy September air punctured my bubble of artificial cool. "You scared me half to death."

Sasha rested her elbows in the open window, peering at my phone in the cup holder.

"Those podcasts make you so jumpy," she said. "I thought you got out of journalism so you could get away from that shit."

It had been nearly ten years since I'd left the crime beat at the *San Francisco Chronicle.* With a decade of distance, and no responsibility to investigate the stories myself anymore, I found the podcasts oddly satisfying, scratching a very specific itch by unraveling each mystery in forty-five minutes or less.

Rather than try to explain all of this to Sasha, I asked, "Why are you loitering in the yard?"

"Actually . . ." Sasha twisted one of her long dark braids around a finger, an annoyingly childlike gesture for a thirty-five-year-old. "I was hoping you'd let me borrow the car for a sec." I rolled my eyes. "Please? I've gotta get away from Mom for a minute. You don't know what it's like. You get to stay in a hotel; I've been with her this whole time."

"How is that different from living with her in L.A.?"

"Ugh, please?" Sasha whined. "I'll bring coffee when I come back."

"Fine," I said, getting out of the car and dropping the keys into her waiting hand. "But make mine an iced vanilla latte."

"Thanks, Sis!" Sasha cried, wrapping her arms around me. She pulled back, biting her lip. "Think I could borrow a few dollars for the coffee?"

"Oh my God, girl," I grumbled.

It was dark and cool inside Grammy's house, thanks to the shade of the oak trees surrounding the property. A bouquet of cooking oil, jasmine perfume, and Luster's Pink hair lotion lingered in the air. I felt a twinge of regret that I didn't remember if that was what Grammy had smelled like; it had been at least ten years since my last visit.

"Syd? That you?" My mother's voice rang out from the dining

room. Large cardboard boxes stood in front of the long polished wooden table, their mouths hanging open. Mom looked chic in a crisp striped shirt tucked into black jeans, belted at the waist. Her sleek Angela Bassett inspired pixie cut gleamed in the light of the chandelier.

"You look way too nice to be packing up this house," I said.

She shrugged. "Wanted to look presentable in case any more of Grammy's church friends stop by." Her eyes slid down my designer workout gear. "Are you going for a run or something?"

"No," I replied indignantly. I wanted to tell her I was so bloated from all the drugs pushing my ovaries into overdrive that athleisure was all I could stand to wear. "I could be going to brunch in L.A. in these clothes, Mom," I said instead.

"Yeah, well, this isn't L.A." It was true that I only saw my mother in workout clothes when she was on her way to or from a run, despite her having lived in activewear-loving L.A. for more than forty years. Maybe this was a holdover from her own proper Southern upbringing. Mom grew up in suburban Atlanta, the only child of a Morehouse-educated Baptist pastor and a Spelman-educated bookkeeper. They'd long given up on their dreams of having children before learning of my mother's pending arrival. I had vague memories of visiting them in the home my mother grew up in when I was small; they were stiffly loving and frail, and their house had the formal, frozen quality of a fancy dollhouse. They both died before I reached middle school.

My mother pushed a roll of garbage bags into my hands. "Can you take care of the guest room in the back? We've got three piles going here: trash, Goodwill, and keepsake. Don't be too precious about keepsakes, though. We don't want to ship too many things back home."

There was something comforting about seeing Mom return to her characteristically unsentimental form; she'd wept silently throughout Grammy's funeral, one of the few times I'd seen her cry. Mom had been the closest to Grammy of all of us; they'd had a standing monthly phone date since my father died. I was never sure if it was out of a sense of familial duty, or out of longing for her own mother, or if she simply enjoyed their monthly chats.

I carried the roll of garbage bags down the dimly lit hallway to the guest room. It was just as I remembered it from the occasional visits of my childhood—the tiny four-poster bed and matching dresser, the yellowing lace curtains hanging slack against a milky window, like a cataract-clouded eye. The air in the room was thick. I tugged the window open after a brief struggle, feeling layers of paint separate like the parting of parched lips.

I blasted a Stevie Wonder playlist from the tinny speakers of my phone and got to work unpacking the dresser, which seemed largely devoted to sewing supplies. I wondered if sewing was something Grammy had done regularly in recent years, or if the materials were relics from an earlier time. Another pang of guilt hit me. After my father died while I was in college, I came out to see Grammy only a handful of times. There was so much I didn't know about her.

I had just begun emptying the bottom drawer when I spotted a swatch of faded lemon-yellow gingham. Gingerly, I picked up and unfolded the little dress. I'd forgotten all about what I found here when I was a child. My heart thrummed as I slid my fingers to the bottom of the pile and found the hard corner of something rectangular.

I pulled the frame free and stared down at the photo of the girl. I was struck again by the similarity of our features. That wise, sly smile, so much like my own. *Baby,* Grammy had drawled, *we don't talk about Carol.*

I'd known better than to bring up a forbidden topic in my family. I never asked about the girl in the photograph again. Before long, I'd forgotten about her entirely.

The doorbell rang and the eight-note Westminster chime vibrated through the house like a church organ.

"Syd?" My mother's voice was strained, as though she were struggling under the weight of something heavy. "Can you get that?"

"Sure," I called, heading down the creaky wooden hallway. I found a woman around Grammy's age standing on the porch. Her silver hair was pulled back into a neat bun. She wore a peach-colored tunic and matching pants, and a string of gray pearls circled her throat. There was a glass casserole dish in her slim hands. I couldn't help but notice how her crepey skin mirrored the material of her clothes.

"Oh, hi, doll. I didn't interrupt your workout, did I?"

If my skin were capable of blushing, it would have. "You're not interrupting anything. Come in, we're just cleaning up a bit."

I held open the screen door and she walked inside. "You must be one of Effie's grandbabies. Got those same pretty brown eyes." Her accent reminded me of Grammy's, sweet and stretched, the way caramel pulls apart when you break a Twix in half. It was a drawl I seemed to notice only among older folks in Raleigh, as if the accent was slowly fading into memory.

"Thank you, ma'am. I'm Sydney. Let me take that for you." I shifted the picture frame beneath my arm and took the dish from her hands, placing it on the credenza.

"I'm Eloise, an old friend of your gramma's. What you got there?" she asked, pointing at the frame.

"Oh." I looked down at the picture for a moment before handing it to her. "I just found this in the room I'm clearing out."

Eloise inhaled sharply. "Oh lord. Well, that's Carol now, ain't it?"

My heart stuttered. "You knew her?"

She nodded. "I remember the first time I held Carol, just a few days after she was born." Eloise stroked the photograph, as though Carol could feel her touch and be comforted.

"Wait. Carol was Grammy's daughter?" The pieces clicked in my mind—the fact that Carol was posing on Grammy's porch in the picture. The striking similarities in our appearances. The way Grammy had lovingly held on to those tiny dresses. It was so obvious. My kid brain just hadn't put it together.

Eloise nodded solemnly, still staring at the photo.

"Grammy wouldn't talk about her. My father never mentioned her either. What happened to her?"

Eloise gave me a pained look. "Effie wouldn't want me to get into this."

"Please," I said, my curiosity teetering toward desperation. "She was my aunt. You're probably the last person who can tell me anything about her."

Eloise sighed. "Well. I guess I don't really see the harm at this point." She handed the frame back to me. "Effie and Carol had a bad falling out when the girl was around sixteen or seventeen. Carol was a talented singer. Voice like a songbird. She got it in her head she was gonna go to Detroit, get herself signed to Motown. But education was everything to Effie. She was the third generation in her family to get a college education at Shaw. Her great-granddaddy'd been born a slave! But Carol didn't have the patience for school. Effie caught on that Carol was trying to leave high school early and planned to book it to Detroit to try her luck at getting a record deal. They fought about it, and I guess Carol ran off." Eloise shook her head. "That's what your gramma figured anyway."

She murmured that last sentence in the telltale manner of someone eager to share a secret, if only the listener would ask them to.

"Do you have another theory?"

"I don't know. You see, Carol wasn't the only girl that went missing around that time."

"What do you mean?"

Eloise's face clouded over. "There were a couple years back in the sixties when a handful of teenage girls in the neighborhood just vanished. All the missing girls came from houses down by the creek that runs behind this house. Folks in the neighborhood got to calling whoever did it the Creek Killer 'cause of that, even though we never knew for sure they were killed. 'Cause they were never found. But what else could've happened? Folks don't just go disappearing into thin air."

I would have been surprised by her easy candor if it had been the first time someone from Grammy's circle had confided in me in this manner. Thanks to numerous uncomfortably intimate confidences at the repast following Grammy's funeral, I was familiar with the children's marriage troubles, goiter symptoms, and sump pump installation nightmares of people whose last names I didn't know.

"Did they ever catch whoever took them?" I asked.

Eloise sucked her teeth. "Child, please. Police didn't care about a bunch of little Black girls gone missing. They dismissed them, said they must've run away, or were caught up in shady things. But these were good girls. College girls, some of them. I kinda think it might've been easier for Effie to imagine her little girl out in the world pursuing her dreams than think that something awful might've happened to her."

She shook her head as if breaking from a trance. "Listen to me, going on about these old, dark stories. Your gramma would have a fit if she could hear me. Truth is, Carol had talked about running to Detroit, so it's just as possible that's what happened."

Eloise glanced at her delicate silver watch. "I better get back home and stop talking your ear off. I know y'all got work to do. Give my love to your family. Just reheat that casserole for about twenty-five minutes at 350, okay? I wrote my address on that sticky note. Y'all can just bring the dish back over to me when you're finished with it." She gave my arm a squeeze. "You take care now, doll."

Sasha pulled into the driveway as Eloise was leaving, the old woman's steps slow but sure. I watched Sasha greet her with her infectious, toothy smile. She folded Eloise into a warm, tight hug. Sasha had always been that way with strangers, even when we were little, grinning like a maniac in photos with Santa while I appraised him skeptically from the opposite knee.

You could tell we were sisters by looking at us. We had the same rich brown skin, the same strong nose, the same slightly heart-shaped faces, our jaws tapering in toward our chins. But there was a bright openness to Sasha's face when she smiled, compared to my measured, secretive expression. And there was a supple, generous curve to her body, while mine was angular and sinewy. I'd been furious when, despite my nightly prayers, she'd needed to shop for a size DD bra in middle school while I was barely filling my A cups in the tenth grade.

"Um, how cute is she?" Sasha said, breezing past me into the house, a tray of coffees and pastries balanced in her hands. I trailed her to the kitchen.

"There you are, Sash. I was wondering where you'd run off to," Mom said, accepting a cup of coffee from my sister.

"I thought I'd get provisions," Sasha said, passing me my latte. "The shop had this amazing-looking sweet potato coffee cake, so I grabbed a few slices, too."

"That's so sweet of you," Mom said. I bit my tongue to keep from pointing out that my car and money had made Sasha's generosity possible.

"Why are you cradling a picture frame around the house?" Sasha asked, popping a piece of coffee cake into her mouth, oblivious to the crumbs that sprinkled to the floor.

"Oh," I said. I'd forgotten I was still holding it. I flipped it around so they could see her. "Why didn't anyone ever talk about Aunt Carol?"

"Aunt Carol?" Sasha's features melted into a frown as she pulled the picture from my hands. "Dad had a sister? Whoa, Syd, she even looks like you!"

Mom moved to get a closer look. She exhaled slowly, a long whoosh through pursed lips. "I could never get your father to say much about her. When I pressed him on it he said she abandoned him. Just walked away and never so much as called. He said as far as he and his mother were concerned he didn't have a sister, and that was all he had to say on the subject." She shook her head. "You know how well your father held a grudge; guess he had to learn it from someone."

The air in the room grew heavy.

"Grammy's friend thought maybe something bad happened to Carol. That a bunch of girls in the neighborhood went missing around the same time she did."

Mom waved a hand in front of her face. "Sounds like a bunch of old gossip."

"I don't know," I persisted. "Do that many teenage girls really just walk away from their lives and never speak to their families again?"

Mom rolled her eyes. "Sydney, you've got to stop listening to those morbid podcasts of yours. Let's have some respect for your grammy's wishes and let it lie," she said, disappearing back down the hall.

Sasha frowned, sweeping the crumbs she'd scattered across the counter into a pile with her hands. "The girls were all teenagers when they disappeared?"

"Yeah."

"And no one ever found them?"

"Not according to Ms. Eloise."

She looked back down at Carol's picture. "When was the last time someone looked?"

TWO

It took me less than ten minutes to drive from Grammy's house to Eloise's the next day; it was a small, cheerful brick home with white accents and a porch brimming with potted flowers. She answered the door wearing another matching tunic-and-pants set, this time in a serene shade of mint.

"Hi, doll." She motioned toward the clean casserole dish in my hands. "You didn't have to rush that back so fast."

"Oh, it's no trouble. It was delicious, by the way." I tried not to think of the contents I'd hastily scraped into one of the recycled take-out containers Grammy collected in my rush to talk with Eloise again.

One line from our previous conversation played in a haunting loop in my mind: *Police didn't care about a bunch of little Black girls gone missing.* According to the podcasts I listened to, and the crime stories I used to cover back in San Francisco, not much had changed in the years since the girls vanished. I thought about the child Malik and I had been trying to conceive for the past two years. Statistically, if they were to go missing one day, they would be less likely to be found than a white child. The idea made my blood boil.

If I didn't at least ask a few questions about what happened to the Raleigh girls, who would?

"Come on in, it's a hot one out there," Eloise said. "I'll pour you a glass of sun tea."

She ushered me inside and over to a faded chintz sofa in a sunny, tchotchke-cluttered living room. She returned with a glass of tea, a slice of lemon floating on top, and clinking ice. Halved yellow lemons were painted on the glass in a style that struck me as distinctly vintage.

"I was hoping I could ask you a few questions about our conversation yesterday," I said, trying not to notice how hard it was for her to lower herself into an armchair. "I looked online for information about the girls that went missing back when Carol was a teenager, but I couldn't find anything."

Eloise sucked her teeth. "Can't say I'm surprised. They barely made a peep about it in the news even then." She watched as I fished inside my purse for the pad of paper and pen I'd grabbed from the hotel room. "You a reporter, darlin'?"

"Oh no, not for a long time," I replied. "Do you remember the names of any of the girls?"

"Hmmm." Eloise clinked her fingernails against her lemon-printed glass as she searched her memory. "One of the girls had the same name as my favorite singer, Marian Anderson. Anderson wasn't her last name though, was it? I should know; my daughter babysat her for a while. Actually, hold on a sec." She sat her glass down and clutched the armrests of her chair, struggling to rise. "They put a remembrance about the girls in one of the yearbooks. Let me go find it."

"Can I help you, Ms. Eloise?"

She pulled herself upright with a grunt. "Oh, I'm all right. Gotta keep moving, otherwise I might never get back up!" She disappeared for a few minutes and returned with a black book. "1965" was embossed deeply into its cracked and fading leather cover, like a scar.

"Whose yearbook was this?" I asked.

"Oh, that's one of mine," Eloise said, settling herself back in her armchair. "I was the librarian over at Ligon for a long, long time. Pretty sure the page you're looking for is near the back."

I flipped through the black-and-white pages of young men and women in neat dress clothes, perfectly coiffed vintage hairstyles, and dignified smiles. Their ambitions were printed beneath their names: lawyer, linguist, obstetrician, social worker, civil engineer, commercial artist.

"They're all Black kids," I observed aloud.

Eloise nodded. "Schools here were still segregated back then."

I found the page Eloise described, the words "Forever in Our Hearts" printed in looping script at its top. The corners of the page were illustrated with flowers, surrounding the photos of six Black girls. Like those of the other students in the yearbook, the captions below the girls' names included the fields they dreamed of working in one day. But they also included their ages the day they disappeared. Clearly someone thought their disappearances were all connected, because though they'd gone missing over the course of three years, they were included in a single list in the 1965 yearbook:

MARIAN BRADBURY
Ambition: Private Secretary
Last Seen: September 23, 1963, at age 16

BETTIE BROOKS
Ambition: Medical Doctor
Last Seen: March 10, 1964, at age 19

SALLY DUNN
Ambition: Beautician
Last Seen: February 2, 1965, at age 16

LORETTA MORGAN
Ambition: Pharmacist
Last Seen: October 28, 1964, at age 18

CAROL SINGLETON
Ambition: Professional Singer
Last Seen: May 14, 1965, at age 17

GERALDINE WILLIAMS
Ambition: Certified Public Accountant
Last Seen: July 3, 1964, at age 16

The tea in my stomach churned at the sight of my aunt's photograph. Her dark eyes shimmered with life, her gaze bold and confident. She wore a sly smile, as though the photographer had whispered a secret joke they shared just before he snapped the photo.

Carol was only seventeen when she went missing. I remembered that complicated age—how unbearable it was living in my childhood home as my parents' relationship crumbled around us, yet how trapped I felt by my dependence on my parents' support. Working a part-time retail job after school while still enjoying weekend sleepovers with friends. A child. On the brink of young adulthood, but a child just the same.

I took a closer look at the dates beneath the girls' photos.

"Was my aunt the last girl to go missing? Or did it continue after this yearbook was published?"

"Carol was the last, praise Jesus. Assuming she didn't actually run off to Detroit."

"I'm going to take a picture of this page, if you don't mind," I said, reaching for my purse.

"You can hold on to the book, doll," Eloise said with a wave of her slender fingers. "No one's looked at it in years."

"Did anyone have any theories about what happened to the girls, or who might have done something to them?"

"Oh, there was all kinds of talk. Some folks thought it might've been the Klan. But it wasn't really their style, takin' folks without leaving their bodies behind to taunt us. And every neighborhood has a creep or two. You know the type, men who mamas tell their babies to steer clear of. But I never heard any theories that made a whole lotta sense to me."

"You mentioned the girls all lived down by a creek," I said. "Do you know what the creek is called?"

"Hmph," Eloise replied, "not sure I ever thought about it. It's just a little thing, you know. Feel like people only tend to name big bodies of water." She leaned forward in her chair and held her hands out to me. I set down my pen and followed her gesture, placing my hands in hers. "I can see you're not gonna let go of this story anytime soon. And I can understand why you'd wanna learn more about your aunt. But as someone who's known a lot of loss in her life, I can tell you from experience that you shouldn't let the past get in the way of living."

Eloise's voice caught suddenly; she cleared her throat and pressed on. "When I lost my husband in Korea, I lost myself for a while. I never got any real answers about what happened to him. He was just gone. But I had to pick myself up and keep going for my kids." She gave my fingers a squeeze. "These things can have a way of consuming a person. Promise you won't let this consume you?"

I looked down at Eloise's hands. The topography of her skin reminded me of the view from an airplane window, the roads, rivers, and ridges etched into the earth. I gave her fingers a squeeze in return. "I promise to do my best." It wasn't what she wanted to hear, but at least it was honest.

Eloise's soft brown eyes scanned my face for a moment before she released my fingers. "You really are the spitting image of Carol. Or how I imagine she would've looked at your age. How old are you now, doll?"

"Thirty-eight."

Eloise nodded. "Your gramma was very proud of you girls, you know. And . . . don't tell your sister this . . . but she liked to brag about you in particular. Your fancy job, your nice home in L.A., and that handsome husband of yours." Her brow crinkled. "No kids yet?"

My chest tightened protectively, like armor. "Not yet."

Eloise gave a little snort. "And to think my youngest was already in junior high by the time I was your age! Different times, I guess."

I tried to keep my smile steady. I wished people knew how even the most innocent comments could feel like a punch beneath the ribs. They might as well shout, *You're running out of time.*

I glanced at my phone. "I'd better get back to Grammy's. Thank you so much for everything, Ms. Eloise. Would you mind if I called you sometime, if I have any other questions later?"

Eloise's smile was like sunshine. "Doll, you can call me anytime."

THREE

I STOOD BENEATH THE CLINICALLY BRIGHT LIGHTS OF THE hotel bathroom later that night, my plush robe yawning open. I stared at the syringe on the faux marble countertop; it was the second and final shot of the morning, though I had three more injections ahead of me that night. They were all synthetic hormones, all designed to help my ovaries produce as many healthy, evenly mature eggs as possible. My entire life now seemed to revolve around eggs. I couldn't even stand to see them on a breakfast menu anymore.

"There are just so many needles," I'd complained to Malik when I opened our first set of injection supplies a year and a half ago. "I never want to see another needle when this is over. Not even the little ones in those tiny travel mending kits."

Malik set his mug down and raised his right hand in response. "I promise to shield you from all nonessential needles as long as we both shall live."

I stared at myself in the hotel mirror. "You can do this," I told my reflection sternly. Given the angles of the mirrors, it looked as though dozens of Sydneys stared back at me, their expressions grim. "You want this," I reminded them. The Sydneys appeared uncertain.

I ran a washcloth under cold water and pressed it to my belly to numb the area. I cleaned a patch of skin with an alcohol wipe, avoiding the tender flesh of my latest injection site. I took a deep breath and picked up the syringe. Tears sprang to my eyes; I barely felt the sharp little needle slip inside me, but the drug burned as though I'd injected myself with battery acid.

I'd always imagined I would eventually have children. They just existed in the periphery of my thoughts about the future. I figured the desire would simply click into place at some point, like how one day I didn't give a crap about boys, and the next day Aaron Preston tapped my shoulder on the playground, whispered "I think you're pretty," and my heart fluttered in a brand-new way.

Malik and I were on our second date when he started talking about how much he wanted children. We were wandering the Japanese Tea Garden in Golden Gate Park, staring out at a koi pond. It was so serene, like we were miles from the city. Stone paths crisscrossed five acres of lush gardens, leading us beneath blossoming cherry trees and leafy Japanese maples, alongside ponds as still and clear as mirrored glass, and up to the teahouse, where we'd stopped for mochi ice cream. I'd thought he was about to kiss me for the first time when a group of kids ran by, their little feet thundering on the planks of the bridge we stood on. I was annoyed by the interruption, but Malik's eyes were soft as he watched them pass, their harried father following a few steps behind. Malik said he wanted a big family, at least three children. He wanted to be the father his own had barely had the chance to become.

Malik's dad was cutting through the redbrick towers of their apartment complex in Queens, returning from his second job as an MTA transit security officer, when an errant bullet from a nearby gang dispute sliced through his chest, tearing his heart to pieces. Malik was only eight years old; his dad was only thirty-two.

It was one of the many things we'd bonded over, having lost our fathers. Malik carried his father's death like a heavy shroud that dragged behind him throughout his life. I couldn't bring myself to tell him that when my mother called to tell me of my father's fatal car crash, the purest and most immediate emotion I felt was relief.

I always figured that when all the appropriate circumstances fell into place—the right age, the right point in my career, the right man—the desire to have children would follow. Three years into our marriage, when Malik squeezed my hand and said, "Sydney, let's make a family," I'd finally run out of excuses.

Besides, it was a nice idea, providing a future baby with the picture-perfect childhood neither of us had had, creating for them the wholesome and secure home life we'd both wished for. Even if neither of us knew what it took to be those kinds of parents.

Foolishly, I'd expected getting pregnant to be easy, as simple as throwing out my birth control pills and adding a few more nights of sex to our usual routine. When that didn't work, we turned to technology—downloading an app where we could both track the nuances of my cycle and buying a basal temperature thermometer and ovulation testing strips to make sure we were having sex on the days I was most fertile.

Months later, Malik tried to sound casual when he suggested we talk to our doctors about fertility testing. But I could hear the pleading in his voice, see the growing desperation in his eyes, feel that each time my period came, a piece of his dream died. So of course I agreed. We'd come this far; maybe our doctors could find a simple fix, and we could finally move on with our lives.

But after three years of trying, with my body still rejecting the concept of having children despite the intervention of expensive, painful, and schedule-destroying fertility treatments, I wondered if my lifelong apathy toward becoming a mother was nature's way of telling me I wasn't meant to have kids.

I packed my chemistry set of vials and syringes back inside their cooler, placed it in the minifridge, and poured myself a glass of grocery store pinot noir. I felt the naughty satisfaction of a child who'd successfully raided the cookie jar while their parents weren't looking. Some studies showed that drinking could reduce the chances of

IVF success, even before the embryo transfer. Apparently, depending on who you asked, so could consuming processed foods, red meat, or refined sugar; participating in high-intensity workouts; or using nonstick cookware, nail polish, or the hydroquinone cream my dermatologist prescribed to fade my occasional yet persistent acne scars, among many, many other things. If you asked me, trying to avoid all these things was another cause of stress, something else I was meant to dodge.

I crawled between the bed's crisp sheets and lifted my laptop from the nightstand. Armed with a list of the six missing girls' names and the dates they were last seen, I'd been sure I would be able to find more information about them online. I was a former reporter, after all; internet sleuthing had played a crucial role in my job. But scouring countless websites had yielded few clues. None of the Carol Singletons I found was the right one, in Raleigh, Detroit, or anywhere else. There was a disturbing number of Creek Killers, but none from the right time frame, and none that had preyed on Raleigh. I tried searching various terms to learn more about Black girls who went missing in the mid-1960s, but any potential results were buried by the staggering number of Black girls currently missing in America.

I wondered if the information I was looking for had found its way online at all. Maybe it was buried in a library somewhere, a needle in a haystack of microfiche.

Or, I thought, sitting up with a jolt, maybe it was simply hidden behind a paywall-protected archive.

A search for "Raleigh Newspaper Archives" led me to the website of the North Carolina Digital Heritage Center, which had digitized materials from museums, libraries, and countless newspapers from across the state. I typed each of the girls' names into the search bar, and to my surprise, nearly all of them appeared in archived issues of *The Carolina Express*, a weekly newspaper that had been catering to Raleigh's Black community since the 1940s.

Strangely, none of the articles mentioned that the girls had vanished. Instead, the stories chronicled their academic and personal achievements prior to their disappearances—Aunt Carol winning a talent show for her singing ability, Bettie Brooks receiving an academic scholarship from the Alpha Kappa Alpha sorority, Sally Dunn posing with a cosmetology award.

I searched the newspaper's "Crime Beat" but found no mentions of missing girls between 1963 and 1965. The crime section appeared to focus on salacious news items pulled from the police blotter for entertainment purposes: quirky stolen property, pranks by neighborhood kids. It was as though the newspaper covered an alternate universe unspoiled by tragedy.

I returned to Google and tried searching for the names of the other missing girls. Two of the girls' loved ones had turned to true crime websites in an effort to find them. I found posts for Loretta Morgan, who had dreamed of becoming a pharmacist, and Geraldine Williams, who planned on a career as a CPA. Geraldine's page included a rendering of what she might look like if she'd reached age sixty-five. The existence of this image twisted my insides; someone was still holding out hope that she was alive.

The descriptions of their disappearances were eerily similar.

Geraldine was last seen leaving a friend's home on the 5500 block of Branch Street in the South Park neighborhood of Raleigh, North Carolina, at 4:30 p.m. on Friday, July 3, 1964. She planned to go to the grocery store on the walk back to her home on Church Street, a distance of less than a mile, to purchase a few items for the next day's July 4th BBQ. But she never returned to her family's residence and has not been heard from again.

Geraldine was described as a studious, family-oriented, and responsible girl. It was not in her nature to be late, or for her parents to wonder about her whereabouts. Geraldine's parents reported her missing the next morning, after spending the night phoning their daughter's friends and driving along the route between the two homes.

Investigators launched a multiweek search of the Raleigh area, but turned up no sign of Geraldine. Her case is unresolved . . .

Loretta left John W. Ligon Junior-Senior High School at approximately 3:15 p.m. on October 28, 1964, following a meeting of the student council, of which Loretta was treasurer. Loretta was expected back at her home on Carnage Drive before dinner, but she never returned. Another local girl, Geraldine Williams, had been reported missing from the same neighborhood earlier that year, however it was never determined that their cases were connected. Both cases remain unresolved . . .

They were both good girls who just vanished one day.

I thought about what little my mother had been able to pull out of my father about Aunt Carol. How she'd abandoned him by running away; how as far as he and Grammy were concerned, he no longer had a sister. As though runaway teenagers were no longer children, no longer vulnerable to the dangers of the world. No longer worthy of empathy or concern.

I could easily imagine having run away from our tense, unhappy home during my teenage years, if only I'd been brave enough to believe I could have made it on my own, and didn't have Sasha to protect. I wondered if my father considered what might have made Carol's life so unbearable that she felt the only option was to run away and never speak to her family again. If she ran away at all, instead of falling victim to whomever might have taken the other girls.

How could my father and Grammy be so sure that Carol wasn't harmed too, if they never verified that she'd made it to wherever she was running to?

Without much to go on to try to find Carol, I focused my attention on the other girls; maybe starting with them would lead me to finding out more about my aunt. I opened Google Maps to try to pinpoint the creek the girls had all lived along. That's when I realized that while Raleigh was called the City of Oaks, it could easily have been known as the City of Creeks. Miles of streams spread across the city like veins, regularly forking in separate directions and abruptly halting at dead ends.

I plotted out the two partial addresses I knew; Grammy's house, where Carol lived at the time of her disappearance, and the friend's home where Geraldine was last seen, on the 5500 block of Branch Street. Walnut Creek trickled through the tangle of trees behind Grammy's house, a stream so slight I didn't even know it existed. It was the same creek that was visible in some of the photos I found on Branch Street. It wasn't much, but it was the most tangible clue I had so far.

FOUR

I FELL DOWN A DEEP WELL OF SLEEP AT SOME POINT IN
the night, the kind that leaves you feeling exhausted instead of restored. It was still dark outside when I awoke, but the
lamps on the nightstands burned like searchlights. My laptop sat
vigil beside me, though it had died while I slept.

I stood beneath the unforgiving glare of the hotel bathroom
light, applying cooling gel patches to the darkening rings beneath
my red-rimmed eyes.

"What are you doing, Syd?" Even my voice sounded tired. I
was supposed to be connecting with my family during this trip.
I was supposed to be tying up loose ends for a woman who had
loved me from afar my entire life, a woman I'd barely carved out
any time for while she was alive. I was supposed to be making my
body as hospitable as possible for a third IVF attempt. And here I
was chasing ghosts instead.

I told myself to snap out of it. I wasn't a detective. I wasn't even
as knowledgeable as the hosts of the true crime podcasts I listened to.

I stared into my own eyes, recalling the mantra Dr. Domínguez
had suggested when we'd first started therapy together a couple of

years earlier, "This is not your problem to fix, Sydney. This is not your burden to carry."

A FEW HOURS LATER, MOM sent me and Sasha on our first Goodwill run. We loaded up my rental car with the donatable items we'd salvaged so far: an impressive collection of elaborate church hats, ancient yet functional kitchen appliances, pristine serveware that waited patiently in sealed boxes for company that never came.

"I hope I took enough time off from work," I said, pointing the car's air vents toward my armpits, damp from the morning's exertions. "I'm only here for three more days, and there's still so much left to do."

I had thought it was more than sufficient to request nearly two weeks off from work, though having no prior experience in packing up the house of a deceased relative, I was really taking a shot in the dark. I also had to get back in time for my next appointment at the fertility center, though I'd decided not to share that information with my family. I didn't plan to tell anyone about our attempts at conceiving until they actually worked . . . *if* one actually worked.

"It's cool, Syd." There was something endearingly childlike about the way Sasha leaned against the window, staring at the blur of unfamiliar landscape flying by. "You're the one with a full-time job right now. Mom's work is flexible, and I'm . . . you know. I've got extra time."

You've had "extra time" for the past fifteen years, I wanted to say. Though she'd earned a degree in Communications Studies from Loyola Marymount at twenty-two, Sasha had never held a job longer than six months and never seemed to progress in any of the many careers she'd dabbled in. Sometimes I wondered if she deliberately clung to jobs below a living wage as an excuse to continue living in our mother's house.

"So, what happened with that internship at the studio, anyway?" I asked, making an effort to keep my tone light and breezy.

Sasha attempted to match my tone, but I could almost see the drawbridge pulling up, back into herself. "It wasn't the right fit. I want to find something creative. The studio just needed someone to get coffee and run stupid errands for the production team."

I sank my fingernails into the steering wheel. "Isn't that pretty common for entry-level entertainment jobs?" I couldn't stop myself from asking. "You start with menial tasks, but get a foot in the door and work your way up?"

Silence. I stole a glance at Sasha. The light was gone from her eyes; her lips were stitched tightly closed. The moat encircling her was officially impassable.

A familiar weight lowered onto my chest. There was a time when I'd been Sasha's primary confidante. Especially after my parents' always tense relationship turned bitterly volatile. I knew my going away to New York for college would likely have an impact on our relationship. But I didn't expect the distance I felt when I returned for a brief visit that first summer, the clipped answers to all my questions, how when we sat on the same couch to watch a movie, Sasha seemed to squeeze herself against the opposite armrest, as far from me as the furniture would allow.

I was thirty-eight now and had moved through various stages of life—going away for school, progressing in a career, getting married, buying a home, trying for children—while Sasha's life at thirty-five remained largely unchanged from her life when she was twenty-one—carless, frequently jobless, living in our mother's home and depending on her for just about everything. It seemed impossible for us to develop something closer to the friendships I'd seen others build with their adult siblings. There was so much of each other's lives we didn't understand, or relate to.

Sasha finally broke the brittle tension in the car with a snort. "I can't believe you want to talk about job stuff when we just found out we had a whole-ass aunt."

I couldn't help but laugh. "I know. It's so strange."

"Something's been bugging me," she said. "Carol went missing when she was seventeen, right? So she lived in Grammy's house up until then. But the only traces of her are that picture from when she was, like, a preteen, and a couple of dresses from when she was super little?"

I shrugged. "Maybe Grammy got rid of most of Carol's old stuff. It might have been painful to keep reminders of her around."

"I bet that back bedroom was Carol's," Sasha continued, as though she hadn't heard a word I'd said. She twisted a braid around her fingers excitedly. "That four-poster bed? It's definitely girl furniture." She looked at me. "How thoroughly did you search that room?"

Sasha made a beeline for the guest room as soon as we got back to the house, feeling around all the empty drawers I'd cleared out. I watched from the doorway, rubbing my belly; the seatbelt had pressed painfully against that morning's injection site.

"What are you looking for?" I asked.

"You remember how it was," she said, peering behind the dresser. "Everyone had a little hiding place growing up." She looked over at me and caught my rubbing motion before I could stop myself. "You okay?"

"Yeah, I'm fine." I wandered around the room, glancing at empty corners. "There aren't too many places you could hide something in here."

Sasha moved to the bed and lifted the mattress. "I sincerely doubt that's been here since the sixties," I said with a laugh. Sasha flicked on her phone's flashlight and got down on hands and knees, scanning beneath the bed frame. She inspected each nightstand, peering under their drawers, behind their rear panels. She went to the closet and swept its surfaces with her beam of light, pausing when it illuminated a rectangular panel in the ceiling, the kind that likely led to a crawl space for insulation, or a decrepit attic.

The little voice from that morning begged me to put a stop to this fruitless search. "No way, Sash. It's probably full of asbestos up there."

She stood on her tiptoes, balanced one hand on the shelf over the railing, and used the fingertips of the other to pop the panel from its resting place, sliding it slightly to one side.

"Seriously," I objected as she felt around the edge of the opening, "I appreciate your attention to detail, bu—"

Her gasp silenced me. "Syd, help me with this."

The little voice never stood a chance.

I whirled around for something she could stand on. I spotted a small trash can in a corner of the room, removed its plastic liner and placed it upside down by Sasha's feet. With a few extra inches of height, she was able to reach the object that had elicited her gasp: a palm-size notebook covered in pebbled leather the color of eggnog.

Our eyes locked, and a jolt of excitement passed between us.

Sasha climbed down from the trash can, and I stood beside her at the closet door as she thumbed through the pages. While the edges of the lined pages had yellowed, the rest of the pages were remarkably white, save for the looping script in navy ink.

"It's a diary," Sasha said, slowly flipping through the pages again and again. "Look at the dates. 1963, 1964, 1965 . . . it's like they lead right up to when she went missing."

My eyes furiously scanned the pages. "Sash, do you see the name that keeps popping up? Like here, from December 1964: 'By this time next year, it will finally just be me and Michael. With any luck, I'll officially be a Motown artist, and maybe even a married woman.'"

"Yikes," Sasha said, wrinkling her nose. "Wasn't she only like sixteen at the time?"

I took the journal from Sasha's hands. "Michael's name is all over this thing. Look at this, from November 1964: 'I don't know how she learned me and Michael are planning on running away next summer, but she knows.'"

Sasha's eyes widened. "They were going to run away together."

A grin spread across my face, unbidden. "Sasha . . . we've got to find Michael."

Today's Song: "Guess Who," Mary Wells

I wasn't even thinking about boys.

I've only had one thing on my mind since I started 9th grade last fall—get through the next four years and get to Detroit. It's all happening in Motown right now, and I need to be a part of it. I'm destined for it—I feel it in my bones. You should've seen the standing ovation I got for my performance as Dorothy in The Wizard of Oz at school a few weeks ago. You would've thought I was Diahann Carroll up on that stage!

But I've also never been properly courted before. I received piles of roses the nights I played Dorothy, but Michael went through the trouble of finding my locker at school and taping a rose to it every day after the show closed. I might've been able to ignore the first rose, or the second, or third, but a dozen flowers later, it was clear that this wasn't some passing fancy. It's as though Mary Wells' latest song is about him: "someone will wait eternally . . . and it's someone who wants your love desperately . . ."

I finally had to go up to him and ask if he was actually going to talk to me, or if he just planned on leaving me flowers every day 'til graduation. You know what he said? "What makes you think I'm going to stop buying you flowers then?"

I don't think anyone has ever truly cherished me before. And I didn't realize how much I needed to feel that way until I experienced it.

Sure, all the flowers and sweet notes and gentle words are swell, and I don't know when he got to be so handsome. But it's the way he takes care of me that makes me feel like this is love.

Prime example: last weekend, Mama heard that my little brother was playing over in the Snake Pit, that terrible swampy place over by Rochester Heights. Larry has a habit of doing that when no one's looking—wandering along the creek behind our house, looking for crayfish, until he winds up all the way out in the swamp.

So who did Mama send to drag him out of there? Me! As though I'm not also susceptible to snakes or bears or bats or whatever else is lurking in there.

I got on my bicycle and I started out to find him. I was so angry and upset, I started to cry. That's right—I was riding through Raleigh with tears running down my face. What a pathetic sight I must have been.

And then out of nowhere, Michael drove up next to me, like a knight in shining armor. He'd borrowed a friend's car to run some errands and saw me flying furiously down the road. I told him what was happening, and he insisted that I put my bike in his trunk and get inside. He said he'd never let me wander into the swamp. He would handle it for me. He dried my tears with his sleeve, called me his "starling" and kissed my forehead. I thought my heart might just burst.

Michael drove us down there and waded out into the muck, ignoring the fact that he was wearing good shiny shoes and very nice pants. I wondered if he'd be rough or cross with Larry, but when they emerged from the thick trees they were laughing, and Michael had his arm around Larry's filthy shoulders.

Now if that isn't love, what is?

FIVE

That night I sat in bed reading Carol's diary, sifting for clues I could use to identify Michael, when my phone rang.

"Hey, Babygirl." Malik's voice was warm and soft as freshly baked dinner rolls. I felt my shoulders melt a few inches.

"Hey, you," I greeted him. "How was the board meeting? That was today, right?"

I heard the telltale spritz of cleaning solution, followed by the scratch of bristles against tile. Malik was deep cleaning, his go-to coping mechanism when he was stressed.

"They told me I should consider bringing on *a seasoned CEO* again."

"Really? But I thought things were going so well."

"They are . . . for now. But some of the board members think having a CEO with *deep financial experience* will help us scale, and maybe increase our odds of getting acquired." There was a gentle sifting sound, like snowflakes falling on leaves. I could almost feel the bleach powder singeing my nose hairs. "But I have no intention of getting acquired anytime soon. They know that. The second some bank owns us, we'll lose our mission. We'll lose our autonomy, our ability to focus on the features our community actually needs. It'll be all ROI, all the time."

I stroked the spine of Carol's diary in my lap, wishing I could stroke Malik's face instead and set him at ease. "What would happen to you if they brought on a new CEO?"

Malik sighed. "They still want me to be an *integral part of the leadership team.* I'd stay on as founder, executive chair of the board. I'd focus on product innovation, while someone else would focus on growing the business. But to me, those things are so intertwined. I've poured so much of myself into this, Syd. I can't imagine just handing control over to someone else."

My heart sank for Malik. He'd talked about his dream of creating Wealthmate on our very first date. Only one percent of venture capital funding went to Black start-up founders the year Wealthmate closed its Series A round. He launched the business with $10 million and a handful of employees in a co-working space. Since then, Wealthmate had raised an additional $75 million, amassed a team of fifty, and now managed half a billion dollars in assets for its customers. Malik often joked that Wealthmate was the closest thing he had to a child.

I knew Malik couldn't simply say no to the board, though; it was within their power to oust him completely from his own company if they thought he was standing in the way of getting them the biggest return on their investment as quickly as possible.

"Help me take my mind off of all that," he said. "How's everything going over there?"

"It's been so crazy," I said, my words pouring out in an excited rush. I told him all about our discovery of Carol's diary, and my new mission to figure out the identity and whereabouts of the Michael she'd planned on running away with.

"Oh." Malik sounded bewildered. His scrubbing abruptly stopped. "I . . . I was wondering how your grandma's house was coming along. But I mean, yeah, that does sound pretty crazy."

I tried not to read into the subtext of his tone. "Yeah, well, the house is coming along just fine. But finding that diary was way more interesting than our trip to Goodwill."

"Sure," Malik said, drawing out the word.

"What?" I asked, exasperated.

"I don't know, Syd. Are you sure this is good for you?"

The question landed like a sucker punch.

"Malik, I had an aunt I never knew existed. Of course I'm curious about what happened to her. Wouldn't it be weirder if I weren't?"

"I get it. It's just . . . I can't help but think about your last story at the *Chronicle.* I can't forget what it did to you."

Everything in my body stiffened. "It's not the same. This is about my family."

"I know. That makes me worry this might actually be worse."

I sighed and got up from the bed, cradling the phone between my ear and shoulder as I poured a glass of wine. "Things are different now. *I'm* different now."

"Syd—are you drinking?"

A column of anger surged up my body like mercury in a glass thermometer. "I'm having one glass of wine, Malik. One glass of wine is fine this early in the process."

He was quiet for a moment. "I'm not trying to police you, Syd. I just care about you. I feel like I should be there."

The wine tasted bitter on my tongue, guilty and wrong. I remembered that chilly February morning when a white-hot pain shot through my belly, ripping me from sleep. I was six weeks pregnant, following our second IVF attempt. But I instantly knew, even before I realized I was bleeding through my pajamas, that I was losing the baby.

It was Valentine's Day; Malik was in the kitchen slicing strawberries to top the French toast he'd intended on surprising me with in bed. When I told him what was happening, his face crumpled like a building at the moment of detonation, solid concrete disintegrating into dust.

I held his heaving body as he sobbed; the raw, guttural sound of it threatened to dismantle me, too. When I looked out the window over his shoulder to steady myself, the sky was a mercilessly cheerful shade of blue.

All the acid left my voice when I opened my mouth. "I know you're worried about me. But I'm fine, I promise. I'm taking care of myself. And I'll be back in L.A. before you know it."

A text notification chimed just after we hung up. I looked down, expecting to find a kiss emoji from Malik. Instead I found a message from my mother:

Let's go for a run tomorrow. See you at the house at 8.

Not an invitation, but a summons.

MOM DIDN'T BELIEVE IN THERAPY; she believed in running. When I was a child, I used to watch her go out for her early runs, before the sun had fully risen, admiring how her long limbs carried her away from our home. She looked so free.

One morning in the summer between seventh and eighth grade, I decided to join her, greeting her by the front door in my faded gym uniform, my sneakers weary from a full school year's worth of use. I tried to ignore how she eyed me stiffly from the last step of the staircase, where she'd frozen upon spotting me. It was clear she was weighing whether she would allow me to join her. Whether she wanted me to join her.

"All right, Little Bit," she said finally, breezing toward the door, "let's see if you can keep up."

My natural speed and endurance surprised us both. That weekend she took me to be fitted for proper running shoes, and those morning laps around our neighborhood became our private ritual.

Sasha was jealous when she learned about my morning runs with Mom. I think she imagined us giggling and gossiping as we zigzagged through Baldwin Hills, sharing secrets she would never learn, forming a bond she could never penetrate. But our runs were largely quiet, the sound of our rubber soles slapping the sidewalk occasionally interrupted by a comment about my running form, a question about an upcoming exam, or a brief lecture on the importance of sunscreen.

Over the years, running had become my go-to self-care practice as well, but it was among the many activities I was forbidden from enjoying until after the egg retrieval.

When I pulled into Grammy's driveway at 7:58 the next morning, my mother was already on the front porch, stretching. You'd be forgiven for thinking she had a background in the military instead of a career in dermatology.

"Morning, hon," she said, jogging down the porch steps and bouncing in place in front of me. "Ready to go?"

My stomach somersaulted. "Actually . . . do you mind if we walk instead of run today? My IT band has been acting up again," I lied.

Mom sighed. "Sydney, I've told you . . . you have to be more diligent about foam rolling."

After a half block of frustrated silence from having her running plans upended, she asked, "So, are you doing all right, Syd?"

"Yeah, I'm fine."

She gave a quick nod, as though mentally checking a box. "And everything's still going well with you and Malik?"

Malik and I had been together for nearly a dozen largely happy years at that point, yet while I'd given her no reason to doubt us, Mom would periodically ask me this question, as though searching for cracks in our foundation. Like she expected the floor to eventually fall out from under us. I tried to view this as a lingering insecurity from her relationship with my father, and not a condemnation of my marriage.

"We're doing great. You know Malik. He's as sweet as ever."

We broke apart to make room for two small children walking hand in hand, backpacks covering half their bodies. It was the sort of sight Malik would have fawned over, if he were with us.

"And how's work going?" Mom asked. "I saw that boss of yours in the *L.A. Times* a few weeks back. She seems impressive. Kind of kooky, but impressive."

I gave the laugh equivalent of an eye roll. "What's with the twenty questions, Mom? Have you been watching Oprah's *Super Soul Sunday* again or something?"

"I just . . . I want to make sure you're okay. You've seemed kind of distracted lately. I want to make sure you're not . . . I don't want you to have another . . . episode."

Episode. I swallowed the word; it burned as it forced its way down. Why was everyone suddenly so worried about something that happened a decade ago?

"So we're talking about that now?" I asked coolly. "I thought we were still pretending nothing happened."

Mom was quiet for a moment, as if stung by my words. "Just . . . tell me if you start to feel bad, okay?"

"Sure thing, Mom." She would have grounded me for the level of sarcasm in my voice if I were a child.

We finished the walk in silence. It reminded me of the old days.

WHEN WE RETURNED TO GRAMMY'S house, I took the lingering frustration from my conversation with my mother out on the floor of Carol's former room, mopping every inch with boiling water and all-natural, pregnancy-safe floor cleaner.

Of course I'd love to have one of those *Gilmore Girls*–style mother-daughter relationships, where even as an adult I'd feel comfortable curling up in my mother's arms and confiding in her about the challenges of marriage or the physical and emotional demands of IVF. But Rory and Lorelai had that level of closeness only because Lorelai nurtured it for years. It was unreasonable for my mother to expect me to suddenly open up to her about the most tender parts of my life simply because she decided to grill me about them out of nowhere.

She hadn't earned the right.

When I was growing up, our neighborhood runs were the only time my mother and I really spent alone together. Her presence in our house was ephemeral—she would drop us off at school on her way to her dermatology practice, would frequently return home after we had dinner, worked most Saturdays, and would spend the majority of Sundays wrapped up in her own projects: tending to her herb garden in our backyard, reading on the chaise lounge in her bedroom, taking tennis lessons. Even when she was at home, it was as though she were somewhere else, somewhere removed from us.

In the early days, it was our father to whom Sasha and I would run if a classmate was mean to us, or if we wanted an audience for a play premiering in the living room, or if we needed birthday cupcakes to share with the class. There were practical explanations for this—as a retired NFL wide receiver and part owner of a handful of local supper clubs, he had a schedule that was much more flexible than our mother's. But even to a child, it was excruciatingly obvious that he simply enjoyed our company more than she did.

The effort of bringing the dull, ancient hardwood to a shine slowly began to calm my agitated nerves. As I refilled the bucket with cleaning solution, I allowed myself to acknowledge that, with the hindsight of adulthood, a part of me could appreciate how tight my mother held on to her interests and independence.

In their most candid moments, all the moms I knew admitted how, even when their partners were heavily involved, they'd found themselves taking on the majority of the childcare, chores, logistics, admin, and emotional labor of their households, despite contributing a significant if not outsize portion of the household income. How the role of motherhood seemed to consume them—their energy, their passions, their savings, their bodies, their identities.

Despite how loving and thoughtful Malik was, and how desperately he wanted children, given the increasing demands of Wealthmate, I could easily see myself falling into that same trap.

Malik had created Wealthmate to address the financial literacy gap in the Black community, making resources like high-yield savings accounts, retirement planning, and financial advisers accessible and inclusive. Whenever I thought about his work my heart filled with pride, before it promptly sank from the comparable vapidness of my own work. I spent my days as the head of PR for a trendy activewear and fitness accessories brand. While it was the kind of job that made eyes light up with envy at dinner parties, I was hardly helping to save the world.

I couldn't shake the feeling that if one of our careers were to be deprioritized for the sake of our family, it would surely be mine. And given that I didn't even like my job all that much, and that it brought in less money than his, while it went against my fiercely independent, feminist beliefs to admit it, wouldn't that be the logical choice?

And if our career situations were reversed, wouldn't Malik relish the opportunity to step into the role of the playful, ever-present parent my father had when I was young?

My tear ducts burned as I poured the filthy black-brown mop water down the toilet of the powder room. What did it say about me that this was what I worried about—my prideful grasp on my lukewarm career—before I'd even proven that my body was capable of having children, or that such sacrifices would even need to be made?

Maybe I was no different from my mother after all.

SIX

Eloise's daughter, Yvonne, agreed to meet at a coffee shop near her law firm the next morning, my last full day in Raleigh.

I invented a work emergency to explain why I'd be late getting to Grammy's. My mother would've had a conniption if she knew I was disrespecting Grammy's privacy by discussing my missing aunt with strangers. *What happens in this house stays in this house* was a common refrain of both my parents; I didn't know who learned it from whom. But even now that I was an adult, it felt illicit to disobey it.

Yvonne had kept her maiden name and still lived in the area, so it had been easy to track her down. I found her photo on the firm's website so I'd know who to look for, but I would've recognized her instantly—she shared the coloring, build, and bone structure of her mother. Her emerald shift and matching blazer even reminded me of Eloise's adorably coordinated outfits.

"I have to get back to the office in half an hour," Yvonne said brusquely as we settled at a table beside a window.

"That's okay, I'll be quick," I said, pulling my phone from my bag. "Do you mind if I record our conversation?" She eyed my phone warily. "It's just for my own notes."

"All right." Yvonne wrapped her fingers around her coffee cup. Her wedding ring caught the sunlight filtering through the oak trees outside the window, casting a kaleidoscope of color across the table. It was a dated style, heavy and ornate, like the ring my mother used to wear. I took in the ribbons of silver in Yvonne's slicked back bun, the creases forming in the delicate skin of her hands. She actually appeared to be a few years older than my mother. My heart sank.

"Ms. Eloise probably told you, but I just learned about Carol a few days ago—that she was my aunt." Yvonne gave a slight nod. "Were you two close in age?"

Yvonne shook her head. "I used to babysit for Carol and your father, Larry, for a while. I was about . . . six years older than Carol, nine years older than your father." Her gaze met mine. "I was really sorry to hear about Larry's accident. I used to watch him play as often as I could."

Yvonne's smartwatch lit with a notification, snatching her focus. I knew I should keep our conversation on track; our time together was limited. But I couldn't help myself.

"What was he like then? As a kid?"

"He was such a character," she said, a hint of a laugh in her voice. "A real ham. Always telling jokes, pulling faces, singing ridiculous little songs he'd made up. Anything to make people laugh."

I remembered how silly my father could be when Sasha and I were small. He wouldn't hesitate to let us climb on his back and pretend he was our pet pony, or play with our stuffed animals, giving each a distinctive accent and personality, moving their soft limbs with the dexterity of a seasoned puppeteer. My chest tightened at the memory.

"What was Carol like?" I asked.

Yvonne's smile faded. "Oh, she was a sassy little thing. Willful. She resented having a babysitter; she thought of herself as more mature than she really was. She was sweet with Larry, though. Doted on him like he was her baby doll. Their mother often had to work afternoons and nights at the hospital, so Carol was used to having extra responsibilities around the house. Making sure Larry finished his homework, heating up dinner, getting them both to bed on time."

The description of my father and Carol reminded me so much of my relationship with Sasha. Carol and I were both three **years older** than our siblings, and both seemed to take a protective, **almost pa**rental approach to our roles as big sisters. My father was only **four**teen when Carol went missing. I couldn't imagine abandoning Sasha at that age, running away and never speaking to her again. Given how close they were, I found it hard to believe that Carol would do this to my father, either.

If I'd done that to Sasha, she'd probably refuse to utter my name again, too. Though, I realized with a pang of guilt, given the way Sasha had treated me after I went away to school, maybe she felt I'd abandoned her anyway.

"Ms. Eloise told me that several girls went missing from your neighborhood around the same time as Carol," I said. "She mentioned you also used to babysit for the first girl that went missing, Marian. That must've been so scary."

Yvonne shrugged. "I mean . . . I guess we really weren't scared at first. It wasn't immediately clear if anything bad happened to Marian. You have to understand—this was back when if a girl found herself pregnant, her parents might send her away to have the baby. I knew a girl or two like that when I was in school."

She stirred her coffee again, though I noticed she hadn't yet taken a sip. "When the next girl went missing the following year, people started talking a bit more. She was in college, officially an adult, so you could try to explain it away. But when two more girls went missing later that year, that's when people really started to worry. That's when the rumors started about the Creek Killer."

"Did it change the way people in the neighborhood lived their lives, knowing there might be a killer on the loose?"

Yvonne nodded. "I was studying law at Howard while a lot of this was going on. But I remember coming down to Raleigh for a visit, and everything just . . . felt different. Tense. I remember driving down Mama's street and noticing that everyone had their doors and windows shut tight in the middle of the day, in the middle of summer. Mama even took to sleeping with a knife in her bedside table. All this despite the fact that none of the girls were taken from their homes. I was a bit older than all the girls who'd gone missing, but Mama forbade me from walking anywhere alone because we knew some of the girls were last seen walking back home from places right in the neighborhood, on their way to or from friends' houses, or school."

Yvonne took a long breath. "It was already such a turbulent time, so all of this just added insult to injury."

I frowned. "What do you mean?"

She shot me an exasperated glare. "Well, this was all happening at the height of the Civil Rights Movement, of course. The first girl went missing a week after those four girls were killed in the church bombing in Alabama. Your aunt disappeared shortly after Bloody Sunday. There were sit-ins happening at the white lunch counters right here, downtown. Schools were being forcibly integrated all over the state. The Klan would hold marches right along this street, in full regalia."

She pointed out the window beside us. It was as though I could see them, bitter cowards hiding beneath white sheets.

"Did people think the disappearances might have been racially motivated?"

"No. We figured whoever was doing this—*if* someone was doing this—they must've been part of the community. I mean, a lot of girls disappeared in broad daylight. This person was able to move through the neighborhood undetected. Maybe the girls knew them."

She gave me a long look. "I have to be honest though, Sydney; I don't think whatever happened to those girls happened to Carol. She'd been threatening to run away since the days I babysat for her. And from what I understand, she told everyone who'd listen about her plans to run off to Detroit."

"Maybe," I said, though I remained unconvinced. "I tried looking for old police reports or articles about the missing girls online, but I couldn't find anything. It's hard to tell if the police took all this seriously."

"There were searches," Yvonne said, shrugging. "Especially for the girls whose parents insisted their children would never run away. Looking back on it now, from a lawyer's perspective, I can see how difficult their cases were. There were no crime scenes. No bodies. No witnesses. Besides the fact the girls all lived by the creek, and were similar in age, nothing else seemed to link them. There wasn't much to go on." She glanced at her watch.

"Just one more thing," I said quickly. "When we were cleaning out Grammy's house we found a diary that belonged to Carol. She talked about dating someone named Michael, said they were planning to run away together. Do you have any idea who that could be?"

Surprise flashed across Yvonne's face. "Your grandma was quite strict; I'm pretty sure Carol wasn't allowed to date until after high school."

"Was there a Michael in the neighborhood that might have been her guy?"

"I mean, it's just such a common name. No one in particular comes to mind. There were probably three Michaels in my graduating class alone." She sighed wearily. "I'm sorry; I feel like I'm not giving you what you're looking for."

She reached into the open mouth of her purse, retrieving her phone. "You should talk to Geraldine's and Sally's folks. They've been searching for answers about their missing girls all this time. They haven't found much, but they can at least tell you more about their sisters." She swiped her finger against the phone's screen. "Geraldine's sister Barbara, and Sally's brother Stanley. I'm friends with them on Facebook." She showed me their profiles and I jotted down their information.

Just as I finished my notes a photo of a smiling young woman popped up on the screen. "Sorry, that's my daughter," Yvonne said, tapping the decline button. "Probably just confirming what she and her girlfriend can bring to dinner tonight."

"She lives in Raleigh too?"

"Just over in Durham, super close." She glanced at the ring on my left hand. "Do you have kids?"

There was that familiar jab below my ribs. "Not yet," I replied. "I love that so much of your family is right here, so close to home. My family has always been so small and scattered; now that Grammy's gone, it's just me, my mom, and my sister out in L.A."

Yvonne stood then and gave me a small, almost pitying smile. "Maybe that's why you're so determined to find out what happened to Carol."

A FOR SALE SIGN HAD sprouted in Grammy's front lawn by the time I returned to her place. I stared at the house for a while, memorizing its features as I gripped the steering wheel of my rental.

The aggressively contemporary houses that stood on either side of Grammy's modest home seemed to cast it in shadow even at that early hour, swallowing it into the darkness of the past. I wondered whether the new owners would lovingly restore Grammy's house or simply raze it to erect a cookie-cutter construction of their own.

I snapped a few photos of the house on my phone for posterity's sake, though I knew they would probably languish forever in my phone's memory, never to be revisited.

My return flight to L.A. was scheduled for the following afternoon. When I'd booked the tickets two weeks prior, I expected to be relieved to come home. Now, though, the idea of boarding the plane made me melancholy. Grammy was the last of my grandparents, and the last of my extended family; before learning of Carol, I'd thought both my parents were only children. Now that Grammy was gone, we no longer had direct ties to this city, this part of the country that held so much history for half of my bloodline. I was just beginning to color in the faint outline of the place and people I'd sketched during my occasional childhood visits. I was barely starting to unravel Carol's story.

The sound of my footsteps on the polished wooden floorboards reverberated against all that was no longer there. The house somehow appeared both larger and smaller without Grammy's things, more spacious, yet empty of all its former warmth and richness.

I found Mom and Sasha in the kitchen, Mom leaning against the counter and Sasha perched on its top, their heads bent toward their phones.

"Hey, Syd," Sasha greeted me. "I'm trying to convince Mom that we should do something touristy since there's literally nothing more we can do in this house."

"I'm open to it," Mom said, a hint of defensiveness in her voice. She scrolled through her phone. "Just trying to find the right thing."

"There are a bunch of museums near my hotel," I offered, wondering if I could conjure an excuse to head back to my room early and return to googling. I still had the following morning before my flight; it would be my last chance to research what happened to the girls while I was actually in the city they disappeared from.

"Ugh," Sasha scoffed, wrinkling her nose. "We've been stuck inside this entire time."

"All right." I sighed, pulling my phone from my bag. "Let me see if I can find a low-key hiking trail for us or something. It's a nice day out."

I typed "Best Raleigh Walking Trails" into Google and scanned the numerous results. I gasped when my eyes landed on "Walnut Creek Wetland Park." Walnut Creek was the stream that seemed to connect at least two of the potential victims of the Creek Killer.

Mom raised her eyebrows at me. "Find something, Syd?"

"Yeah . . . I see a bunch of recommendations for the Walnut Creek Wetland Park. It's super close; there's an educational center and like fifty-eight acres of trails and greenery."

"Nicely done, Sis," Sasha said, hopping off the counter. "Let's do it."

LESS THAN AN HOUR LATER, the three of us stood on the long porch spanning the entire backside of the wetlands education center, staring out into a seemingly endless expanse of trees, a rainbow of green. The center itself had a clean, organic design, as though it had bloomed on its own from the wetlands below us. The chirping of birds seemed to mimic the squeaking of the rocking chairs lining the porch. The air was somehow both cool and humid, reinforcing the rainforest feeling the view evoked.

"How is all of this here?" Sasha asked.

I flipped through the brochure I'd picked up inside. "This says that Black communities have lived in this area since the eighteen hundreds, when they used to farm the nearby land. Rochester Heights, one of the neighborhoods bordering the park, was developed for Black residents on Black-owned land. It was constantly getting flooded from the wetlands, caused partially by construction in northern neighborhoods that displaced the water."

"I'd bet you a hundred bucks it wasn't Black folks building in those northern neighborhoods," Sasha muttered.

"Apparently people treated this place like a dumping ground for decades," I read on. "Cleanup crews found everything from refrigerators to old washing machines when they were developing this center. The city actually used to dump sewage here."

"Ew," Sasha moaned softly; her expression turned wary.

"The center regularly hosts volunteer days to continue the cleanup of Walnut Creek, which runs through the park . . ." My morning coffee roiled in my stomach.

"C'mon," Mom said with a nudge, "let's stretch our legs."

The trail she chose was smoothly paved but thickly wooded, despite being mere feet from the road. The greenery that surrounded us and blocked a surprising amount of light was not limited to the tall treetops; it sprouted from the ground in felt-like moss. It snaked its way up the skeletons of trees in quivering vines. It dripped from thin branches that stretched toward us, occasionally brushing against our shoulders like phantom fingers. The foliage cast everything around us in a yellow-green glow, as if we were staring through aquarium glass. The air even smelled green—crisp and earthy and primal.

The traffic on the hiking trails and biking paths in L.A. rivaled that of our notoriously congested streets. Here, however, we'd walked for nearly half an hour without seeing another soul. The sound of the occasional passing car from the nearby roadway was all but drowned out by the melody of birdsong, chirping cicadas, wind-rustled leaves, and the gentle babbling of a nearby stream.

Eventually we paused on a small bridge so Sasha could take pictures. I rested my elbows on the railing and gazed at a large pool of still brown water from which countless trees grew, their true heights secreted by the water, its murky depths unknowable.

The sensation that struck me reminded me of the weight of a lead apron at the dentist's office. Gravity's hold on me was suddenly stronger, pulling me more forcefully toward Earth's center.

I gripped the railing as the heavy feeling entered my body, filling my chest. It was the feeling of knowing something deep within the fibers of my body before I had any facts to support it. It was the feeling of knowing something terrible but undeniable.

I let out a low groan. "I know," Mom said from behind me, her eyes toward the opposite expanse of marsh. But her voice was happy, content. "It's so peaceful."

Sasha sidled up to me. "What is it, Syd?" Her voice was soft, so Mom wouldn't hear.

"This is gonna sound weird," I said, in a near whisper, "but wouldn't this be the perfect place to hide a body?"

SEVEN

THE MELANCHOLY CLOUD THAT HOVERED OVER ME HAD not dissipated by the time I boarded the plane the following afternoon. I wished I could have stayed another week, at least. I needed time—time to talk to more of the locals who knew Aunt Carol, time to sift through the scattered details I'd gathered so far, time to formulate a plan. Time I wouldn't have back in L.A., between work and countless fertility appointments and the relentless obligations of adulthood.

I pulled my laptop from my bag, opened a new document, and began to spill everything I'd learned onto the blank page. I longed to create one of those walls detectives assemble on TV—photos and maps and hand-scrawled notes pinned to a giant piece of corkboard. I yearned to transform the jumbled contents of my mind into something tangible, to find trends and yoke them together with taut lines of red string.

Then I imagined the look of horror on Malik's face, walking into the guest-bedroom-slash-office we'd earmarked for a baby's room, only to find the type of collage commonly used by fictional geniuses on the brink of madness.

I flipped through the photos on my phone and the notes in my notebook to create a time line of the disappearances. I began to compile a to-do list for myself: *Contact Geraldine's and Sally's siblings; Research creeks and wetlands; Try to get police records; Find Michael.* I paid for the plane's spotty Wi-Fi, logged in to Facebook, and messaged Barbara, Geraldine's sister, and Stanley, Sally's brother, asking if they'd be willing to speak with me.

I raced against the countdown of my computer's dwindling battery, having foolishly stashed my charger in my checked bag. When the battery finally gave out, I closed the laptop's cool metal lid and stared through the window at the slice of Earth below. We were passing over an endless stretch of terra-cotta mountain. It was rugged, dry, and lonely, though hauntingly beautiful in the bronzed glow of the late afternoon sun.

I'd spent my entire life in cities, where it seemed impossible to be truly alone. Reminders of this fact were everywhere: the voices that wafted through thin apartment walls, the countless neighbors I'd see on my morning runs, the families I'd nod to on hiking trails in Malibu. Up in the air, however, it was clear that there were many places where you could become lost. Or lose yourself.

While I tried not to, I couldn't stop thinking about Yvonne's description of my father as a boy, and how I'd watched him slowly lose that loving, lighthearted version of himself over the course of my childhood.

Many of my early memories of my father took place in the kitchen. My father loved to cook, and Sasha and I were his favorite taste testers. Mornings were his domain, and he'd prepare us elaborate breakfasts before school: dinosaur-shaped pancakes, cheesy grits with fried eggs on top.

He was also the parent who ensured our holidays were punctuated by home-cooked treats. I couldn't see a cinnamon roll without having to tamp down the memory of the Christmas morning when he made a dozen of them from scratch, each glistening with a sweet orange glaze. I must've been around nine years old at the time; Sasha and I devoured two of them shortly after opening presents, still in our matching Christmas pajamas, licking the sugary glaze from our fingers. He'd tapped an icing-covered spoon against the tip of my mother's nose; before she had time to react, he licked the icing away, grinning wickedly. She broke into the type of laugh we rarely heard from her, high-pitched and girlish, as Sasha and I gleefully cried, "Ewww!"

I liked to think of my father as two different people. There was the early version Sasha and I knew when we were little, the silly, loving dad we spent so much time with. The later version was moody, quick-tempered, and unpredictable, and just as removed as our mother.

I began mourning the loss of my dad long before my father died.

Even when I was little, I wondered what had attracted my charming, fun-loving dad to my stoic, uptight mother. Eventually I asked my father how they met. He told the story so vividly it lived in my mind like a scene from a movie I'd committed to memory.

If you lived in Los Angeles in the late seventies and early eighties, you knew about "Lightning" Larry Singleton, the L.A. Rams wide receiver as famous for his electrifying plays as for his high-voltage smile. Everyone, that is, except my mother, who'd recently relocated from suburban Atlanta for a coveted dermatology position at UCLA Medical Center, a rare feat for a woman or a Black person at the time, much less a Black woman.

On a miserably hot July Sunday, my mother stood at a movie theater concession stand waiting for her unbuttered popcorn when an employee set a cup of soda in front of her.

"I didn't order this," she protested.

"It's from that gentleman," the kid said sheepishly, angling his head in the direction of a tall, athletically built man grinning at her. Grace gave him a clipped smile and willed the boy pouring her popcorn to quicken his pace. She'd come to the movies to escape her sweltering apartment, not be chatted up by random strangers.

Larry went to the movies to distract himself from the fact that NFL training camp was starting the next day, and it would be the first time in ten years that he wouldn't be a part of it. A catastrophic collision with two Steelers linebackers the previous season had shattered Larry's right leg in multiple places, forcing him into retirement at thirty. He'd have a slight limp for the rest of his life.

Grace didn't know it at the time, but Larry was flailing in the ocean of his future, having been unceremoniously tossed overboard from the only career he'd ever wanted, and had ever envisioned himself capable of pursuing. Six months later, a former teammate would throw him a life preserver in the form of the Jacaranda, a restaurant and jazz lounge in development that was in need of one more investor.

"I took a gamble on the Dr Pepper," Larry said, sidling up beside Grace. "Coke would've been the safer choice, but you seem too original for that."

Grace rolled her eyes. "Did you really just quote the Dr Pepper commercial to me?"

Larry looked thoughtful. "Did I?"

"You know how it goes: 'Peppers are an interesting breed, an original taste is what we need.' "

"Huh. Guess it was a pretty effective ad."

The kid behind the counter returned with Grace's popcorn. "Well, thank you for the drink," she said to Larry. She began to walk away, and he fell into step beside her.

"What are you seeing?" he asked.

Grace stifled a sigh. "*Caddyshack.*"

"Me too." Larry touched Grace's forearm, his face a mask of concern. "You do know it's a comedy, right?"

"Of course I know it's a comedy."

Larry shrugged as a smile returned to his face. "Just wanted to make sure. Doesn't really seem like your thing, laughing."

Grace pulled her arm away. "Oh, I like to laugh. But only when something's actually funny."

Larry mimed being wounded in the chest, and Grace chuckled in spite of herself.

That was their thing—Grace was serious to a fault, and Larry's silliness brought lightness to her life.

"I loved that your mother wasn't afraid to challenge me," he'd said. "She wasn't afraid to tell it like it is."

That statement would later haunt me, when many of their arguments seemed to begin with a perceived challenge from my mother. But I guess that's what often happens in relationships; it's the things that initially attract you to someone, the things that make them different from you, that eventually become the very things that repel you.

THE NEXT DAY, BACK IN L.A., Malik suggested we head out on a Saturday lunch date. As we followed the host to our table at a breezy rooftop restaurant, my phone pinged; it was a Facebook message. It's a miracle I didn't step on Malik's heels as I read it:

> Hi Sydney,
> Are you free Monday? Barbara and I are friends, and we're planning to get lunch that day. We'd be happy to jump on a call with you.
> Peace,
> Stanley

I tried to stay present with Malik as we sat, took in the coastal view, and perused the menu. I even managed to make a joke about the fifty-dollar espresso martini you could customize by having your photo of choice "printed" into the foam with food dye. But by the time our food arrived, my mind frothed with questions for Stanley and Barbara. I was sure they had theories about what happened to the girls. I wondered if they'd ever gotten a creepy feeling while standing in the wetlands.

"Uh, Syd?" Malik's brows were raised slightly, as though he were trying to decide whether to be amused or annoyed.

"Sorry—I totally spaced. What were you saying?"

He gave me a small smile and set his fork down. "What's on your mind, Babygirl?"

It felt as though a small bird was trapped behind my rib cage. I hadn't planned to tell Malik about my latest research. I thought of the concern in his voice during that phone call in Raleigh. *Are you sure this is good for you?*

"Syd?" he asked, his smile straining.

"Eloise's daughter put me in touch with the family members of a couple of the other missing girls," I said, as nonchalantly as possible. "They agreed to talk to me on Monday."

Confusion rippled across Malik's forehead. "What, like an interview?"

"Nothing as formal as that," I said, trying to ignore the cold bead of nervous sweat sliding down the inside of my dress. "I'm just curious. Eloise and her daughter didn't seem to know much about what might have happened to the girls. But their family members must have some idea. They at least have to know what the investigation was like, and whether police really made an effort to find them."

The ice in my glass made a tinkling sound as it shifted in its bath of sparkling water. "I know you're not supposed to compare tragedies," I continued. "But I can't stop thinking . . . that last *Chronicle* story I wrote, about Hannah McEwan and her siblings . . . as awful as that all was, at least they were found. There was some sort of closure for their family. But the Raleigh girls . . . it feels like so many of them were just forgotten. I mean, the fact I didn't know Carol existed . . . it's like they're being erased."

Malik just stared at me, waiting to be convinced. "There was so much pressure on police to find the McEwan kids," I said. "And there's always so much press coverage of missing white kids from *good* families. I looked it up: Black people make up like fourteen percent of the population of this country, but around forty percent of America's missing kids are Black. Yet very few news stories covering missing kids are of Black children. It's just so fucked up."

Malik nodded slowly. "It is fucked up. It's awful. It's just . . . this is a massive, systemic problem, Syd. Why do you think it's up to you to solve it?"

Indignation shot through my body. "Why did you think it was

up to you to solve the financial literacy gap?" I countered. Malik's eyes widened in surprise. I took a deep breath and softened my tone. "Malik, you do realize that these stats would apply to our future child too, right? If something happened to them, wouldn't you want everyone to do everything in their power to find them?"

A cloud of anguish darkened Malik's expression. I extended a hand toward him, and he folded his into mine. "You know as well as I do that if we just wait around for someone else to do something, nothing will happen. Nothing will change," I said. "I can't ask Grammy about Aunt Carol, because she's dead. The people who know anything about what happened to those girls are dying of old age, Malik. I used to investigate stories like this for a living. If I don't try to at least look into what happened, who will?"

Malik was still wincing, as though battling a dull but persistent pain. "I didn't mean to imply you aren't capable of making an impact, Sydney. If anyone can make something happen, it's you. I just . . . I wish it didn't have to be you. I mean, is this the right time for you to take on something like this?"

"I don't think there's ever a right time for this kind of thing," I said. "I mean, we've been trying to start a family for years. And if we are able to have a baby, that definitely wouldn't be the right time to get into all of this. If I don't do this now, when will I? Besides, I'm just talking about making a few calls and doing a little internet research."

Malik nodded, his expression softening. "Just promise me that if this all starts to feel like too much, you'll tell me. Okay?"

I squeezed his hand. "I promise."

EIGHT

WHEN I DIALED IN TO THE VIDEO CALL AT 8:30 SHARP Monday morning, Barbara and Stanley were already on camera, waiting for me. They sat side by side at a blond wood table. Above their heads was a wall decal of golden script that read: "Bless the food before us, the family beside us, and the love between us."

I was set up in my car on the side of the street, phone against my dashboard, between my prework fertility and therapy appointments. The crooks of my arms ached; it felt like I'd been punched by fists instead of punctured by needles during my morning blood work. I covered the angry red skin with long sleeves despite the late September heat.

"Oh, look at you!" Barbara cried. "Such a pretty girl! Look at those beautiful curls. You've never had a relaxer—not with hair like that—have you? I'm so jealous. I used to have long, thick hair like yours, but I got addicted to the creamy crack!"

Barbara's taut skin made determining her age impossible by sight alone—she could have easily been anywhere between fifty-five and seventy-five. She wore a watercolor print blouse and a matching statement necklace. Her soft brown bob was perfectly smooth and shiny, as though she'd just returned from her weekly press and curl.

Stanley appeared to be a few years older, with deep creases carved into his rich brown skin. His laugh lines were deeper than his frown lines. He wore a garnet polo shirt and a flat cap over close-cropped curls more white than gray. They both looked like they would have hugged me tight if they'd greeted me in person, the kind of hug you'd want to linger in.

"No, you're right," I said, laughing. This was a pleasant surprise; I'd expected a much more somber start to our conversation. "My mom wouldn't let me get a relaxer, no matter how much I begged."

"You should thank your mama for that. I could kick myself for letting my daughter relax hers—"

"Barb," Stanley said with a soft chuckle, placing a hand over Barbara's, "I'm sure Sydney didn't go through the trouble of looking us up on Facebook to chat about hair. You'll have to forgive Barb here," he told me. "She just loves meeting new people. And talking is her favorite hobby. So this is catnip for her."

Barbara swatted Stanley's shoulder so playfully that I wondered if they were romantically involved. "Thanks so much for agreeing to chat with me," I said.

"Well, we know what it's like to look for a missing loved one," Barbara replied. She frowned and fiddled with her necklace. "I can't believe you're just now learning about your aunt Carol."

I felt a flicker of shame on behalf of my family, looking at the situation through the eyes of two people who'd fought for years to keep their sisters' memories alive. "It sounds like my father and grandmother assumed she ran off. I think it was too painful for them to talk about."

"Oh yes," Barbara said, her expression serious. "If Carol Singleton was your aunt by blood, that must mean Larry was your father?"

I didn't know why it continued to surprise me that unearthing Carol's story would also force me to exhume my father's.

"Your father and I actually went to junior prom together," Barbara said gleefully. "As dates!"

My brain struggled to absorb this information. Barbara appeared to be the antithesis of my mother. Yes, they were both classically attractive, neat and well groomed in their own ways. But their outward personalities couldn't have been more different. Barbara was bold and effervescent, while my mother was reserved and opaque.

The more I thought about it, though, the more this made some sense. After all, my father could be bold and effervescent at times, and reserved and opaque at others.

"You've rendered the girl speechless," Stanley said, cutting the tension with a chuckle.

"I'm sorry, sugar. I didn't mean to catch you off guard. We weren't serious or anything. We only dated for a couple months, right around prom."

I knew Barbara was expecting me to ask questions, but my mind was a blank slate. I fumbled around for something light and easy. "What was he like then?"

"Well, your father was so handsome. He was a star on the football team, so tall and athletic. A lot of us girls had crushes on him. When he first asked me out, I felt like the luckiest girl in the world."

My mind latched on to *first*. "Did something change?"

Barbara blinked. "What's that, sugar?"

"You said when he first asked you out, you felt lucky. Did something change?"

"Oh." Barbara looked down, spinning the beads on a bracelet that matched her necklace. "I mean, not really."

The sensation that tickled my nerve endings was similar to the one that compelled me to pick at a fresh scab, even if the skin beneath it was still pink and raw. "It's okay. You can tell me." Barbara squirmed. "I know my father was . . . complicated."

Barbara's expression melted into something between a smile and a grimace. "I knew Larry since middle school," she began. "In those early days he was a real jokester, the life of the party long before any of us actually started going to parties. He'd changed a bit by the time we went to junior prom together. Which isn't all that strange, really—a lot of folks change during those years. And then there was everything he went through with his sister. I related to that, of course. My sister Geri—Geraldine—disappeared a year before Carol. I thought maybe that's why he'd asked me out, because we'd understand that part of each other. But he never wanted to talk about it."

I felt a twinge of sadness; if Grammy refused to talk about Carol, and my father refused to confide in Barbara, I doubt he allowed himself to open up to anyone about what he was going through.

"There was something enigmatic about Larry. He was popular, what with football and all. But he was quiet. He didn't speak up much in class, or at the lunch table, but when he did, he'd surprise you by saying something wickedly funny. Those little moments when he'd share something felt like precious gifts. It made you feel special, that he chose you to share them with. It made you want to try to get to a point where he'd feel comfortable sharing with you all the time." She shook her head. "He didn't really let people get that close to him, though. Myself included."

Barbara studied her bracelet again. "There was another boy who liked me, Kevin Jones. One day Larry was walking down the hall and saw me and Kevin talking by the lockers. I don't know if he thought we were standing too close, or if it was something in the way we were looking at each other, but Larry marched over and grabbed me by the arm, hard, and pulled me into an empty classroom."

I saw the muscles of her throat shift as she swallowed. "He left a bruise on my arm, where he grabbed me. He accused me of stepping out on him, said I wasn't allowed to speak to Kevin anymore." Barbara lifted her chin. "I've never allowed any man to tell me what to do. Not even then. I broke up with him on the spot."

Barbara must have registered pain in my expression, because her eyes met mine and widened. "I'm sorry, sugar—that was probably too much. Listen, sometimes people aren't sure how they're supposed to act in relationships at that age. Just because he was that way with me doesn't mean it was how he always was."

I gave Barbara a somber smile. "Unfortunately, some things don't change."

A notification appeared on my phone, obstructing Barbara's and Stanley's faces. My therapy appointment was coming up in half an hour. I had to steer our conversation back on track.

"So my father never talked to you about Carol?" I asked.

Barbara shook her head. "I don't think he talked to anyone about Carol." She looked over at Stanley. "Stan met her once, though."

My breath caught. "What?"

Stanley nodded slowly. "I met Carol at Shaw, at a party."

My brow furrowed at the mention of the historically Black college near Grammy's house. "She was at Shaw? But she was only in high school when she disappeared."

Stanley shrugged. "It wasn't all that unusual. A lot of Ligon kids wound up attending Shaw, and the schools are only a mile apart. I'd sometimes run into my sister Sally at parties, to both our embarrassment. I'm actually surprised I didn't see her the night I met Carol; after they both went missing, I found out they were friends."

A realization shot through my nervous system with a jolt— Carol mentioned a girl named Sally in her diary. Was she the same Sally who went missing three months before Carol?

"Think the party was my sophomore year," Stanley said. "I was fixing myself a drink and your aunt was trying to open a beer with her bare hands, except it was the kind you need an opener for. Her palms were all red from the effort. I showed her how to open it using the edge of the table."

He laughed, a rich rolling sound. "I could tell she was embarrassed, but she tried to cover it up. Said something like she usually drank champagne. You know, the kind of thing only an underage girl would say."

"She must've really left an impression on you, if you're able to remember her so clearly from one interaction," I said, smiling to keep my comment from sounding accusatory. "How'd you know it was my aunt you met that night?"

"Well, I saw her right before she went missing. A lot of us with missing girls in our families stayed in touch. We'd share any updates or theories we had, few as they were. It was Barb here who told me there might be another missing girl."

"My parents were close with Stan's," Barbara said. "They joined us for dinner one night and Stan came over from Shaw. I told them folks at school were talking about how no one had seen Carol for a while. I showed them her picture, and Stan recognized her from the party."

"Did you know Carol from school?" I asked.

Barbara shook her head. "I was a few grades behind her. I just knew she was Larry's older sister. I'd see them walking to school together, or sitting next to each other in church with their mama." She turned back to Stanley. "Wasn't Carol in some kind of dustup at that party?"

"That's right," Stanley said. "Carol was there with a guy a year ahead of me in school, can't remember his name. They were standing out on the back porch when all of a sudden, this other girl marched into the house and made a beeline for Carol. They were all in each other's faces; for a minute there, we all thought we were going to need to break up a fight! But then Carol turned and ran out of the house."

"Huh . . . What did you think was going on?" I asked. "Some sort of love triangle?"

Stanley's brows pinched. "No . . . If I remember correctly, the other girl was the sister of the young man Carol was with."

"Did you tell the police what you saw? I wonder if it could've been connected to her disappearance somehow."

He lowered his gaze to his open palms, as though seeking an answer in their grooves. "There really wasn't anything to say. Police weren't looking for her, since her family hadn't filed a missing person report. Not that filing a report did the rest of us much good. But that memory of her stuck with me. I remember hoping she'd made it to Detroit like everyone said she'd wanted. I hoped I'd turn on Ed Sullivan one night and see her smiling on that stage."

"Was there anything you remember about the argument at the party in particular? Did you hear any bits of conversation?"

The lines between Stanley's brows deepened. "Oh, I don't know. It was such a long time ago."

"Wait," Barbara said, patting Stanley's hand. "There was something you told me about that fight, back then. I wrote about it in my diary. My mom bought it for me after Geri went missing, so I could get all of my feelings out. And then I started using it to keep track of everything I learned about the missing girls."

Barbara moved off-screen for a moment, returning with an old journal, its pink cover faded and fraying. Turquoise reading glasses perched on the bridge of her nose. "I went back through my diary after you reached out to us, Sydney." She flipped to a bookmarked page and scanned it with her finger. Her eyes rose to meet mine, the lenses of her glasses exaggerating their size. "Does the name Michael Hall mean anything to you?"

My stomach plummeted. "Hall? As in Eloise Hall? And her daughter, Yvonne?"

"That's right!" Barbara said. "Their family was friends with your father's family. They used to sit together at church."

My mind spun. Yvonne's brother was the Michael from Carol's journal? Yvonne fought with Carol shortly before her disappearance, and she didn't think this was worth telling me about? She had made it sound as though she'd had little direct interaction with Carol since her babysitting days.

I'd specifically asked Yvonne if she knew anyone named Michael who Carol might have dated. *I mean, it's just such a common name,* she'd said dismissively. *No one in particular comes to mind.*

Perhaps she hadn't thought it necessary to mention her brother's name because she couldn't imagine him dating my aunt.

Or maybe she omitted his name from our conversation on purpose, because she knew that he had.

Another notification obscured my phone screen. It was 9:15; I was officially late for therapy.

"I-I'm so sorry. I have to go," I said.

Barbara held up a finger. "Just one more thing. Years back, I managed to get copies of some of the police files from a detective who was retiring from the force. My daughter helped me—what do you call it Stan, computerize?"

"Digitize."

"That's right, she digitized them for me. There's not much there, but I can send them to you, if you'd like?"

I felt a sudden flush of hope.

Today's Song: "It's All Right," The Impressions

Well, I'm grounded. But boy, was it worth it!

Michael invited me to join him and his friends at a Shaw party last night—my first college party. He encouraged me to bring a friend along, so of course I brought Sally. She tapped on my window at 9pm sharp, and I climbed outside—no easy feat in a party dress!

It was only an eight-minute bike ride from home, but it might as well have been another world. There were no adults, the music was loud, and the alcohol was flowing. Couples were necking in corners and swaying on the makeshift dance floor. It felt like freedom!

"It's All Right," the new song by The Impressions, was playing on the radio when Sally and I walked in, and suddenly, everything did feel alright. Michael danced up to us, moving his hips to the music and singing along, handing us each an open beer.

We had so much fun! I was tempted to stay all night—Mama was working a late shift at the hospital so she wouldn't be home til early in the morning. But I didn't feel right about leaving Larry on his own overnight. He may be eleven years old, but he gets bad nightmares sometimes and likes to come into my room when he's scared. I kept thinking about him waking up and realizing he was all alone in the house. I couldn't stand it, so I split. Sally wasn't ready to leave, so she found some friends who promised they'd get her home safe.

Unfortunately for me, when I got back home, I saw that the lights were on in the kitchen, and Mama was standing at the window, looking dead at me. Busted.

I guess Larry had woken up in the middle of the night,

realized I was gone and called Mama, scared the monster in his dreams had taken me.

Mama called me selfish, said I didn't care about my brother. Me, the person who helps him with his homework most nights, cheers him on at his peewee football games, and gives him advice on how to properly talk to girls.

But I know what she's really mad about—that people at work might be gossiping that her son was home alone and her teenage daughter was misbehaving. She's mad that we might have tarnished her perfect attendance record at the hospital, and her sterling reputation as a mother of two perfect little angels.

She made me pick a switch from the tree out front and whipped my behind, giving me her usual speech about how it hurt her more than it hurt me (blah, blah, blah).

But I didn't cry or shout—I wouldn't give Mama the satisfaction. Instead I just got up, pulled my skirt down and told her she was a hypocrite. I'd stayed by myself with Larry _plenty_ of times when I was his age. I doubled the length of my grounding by talking back, but I don't care.

Larry felt _so_ bad for getting me in trouble, but it's not his fault, it's Mama's. One minute I'm mature enough to be treated like an adult at eleven, and the next minute I'm too young to be trusted on my own at fifteen. It's not fair.

Thank goodness Mama had to work again today—at least she's out of the house.

Larry and I spent the day playing Clue in the living room. Pretty big departure from last night, but we had a lot of fun. Even though clever Larry won almost every time! He made up silly voices for all the characters, and I couldn't stop laughing.

I don't have to be grounded to spend time with Larry—I love my little brother. Mama just isn't around enough to see it.

NINE

Every other month or so, Mom invited me to Sunday dinner at her house. I dreaded those invitations. Occasionally a prior commitment would provide me with a convenient reason to politely decline. But I regularly found myself making the fifteen-minute drive from the Culver City townhouse I shared with Malik to the View Park home where my mother and Sasha lived.

The house was meant to be a fresh start for our mother following our father's death. She moved into it alone; I had recently moved from New York to San Francisco for my job at the *Chronicle*, and Sasha lived twenty minutes away in a residence hall at Loyola Marymount. The house had two bedrooms, two bathrooms, a little nook for an office—the perfect amount of space for a fifty-something woman carving out a new life for herself. Except that Sasha moved into the guest room after her freshman year. And though she was now in her mid-thirties, she had no plans to leave.

I took my time gathering the grocery bags from the trunk of my car, savoring a few deep breaths of sultry early October air. My mother, who had gladly left cooking duties to my father while we were growing up, usually ordered in from a neighborhood restaurant. Sasha typically took care of dessert, taking Mom's credit card and buying the supplies needed to bake a new recipe, while I played bartender.

"What will we be sipping on tonight, Sis?" Sasha asked as I walked into the gleaming white and steel kitchen our mother had painstakingly renovated a few years prior. She rested her chin on my shoulder as I arranged the bottles and herbs I'd brought on the quartz countertop.

"Thai basil mojitos, since Mom ordered Thai food. They're great with or without rum."

"Mmm-hmm," Sasha said, spinning around and lifting herself into a seat on the counter, nearly crushing the bag of basil. I went to the cavernous farmhouse sink to give the herbs a rinse. "Will you be imbibing tonight?" she asked.

"Nah." I kept my eyes on the bright green leaves in my hands as I spoke. "Malik and I are only drinking on Fridays right now," I lied. "We're on a bit of a health kick."

"Mmm-hmm," Sasha repeated, picking up the bottle of rum and inspecting the label as Mom walked into the kitchen carrying bags bulging with styrofoam containers. "I swear you just make up these sober-curious excuses to hide that you're trying to get pregnant."

Her words were a punch to my tender gut.

"Hush, child," Mom said, swatting my sister's leg to coax her from the counter like a disobedient house cat. "Please change out of those ratty sweatpants and set the table."

"Fine," Sasha grumbled as she jumped down from the counter, every bit thirty-five going on thirteen. "Paper or real?" she asked as she moved toward her room.

"Paper—let's use those cute new ones you found at that store last weekend."

My chest tightened with jealousy at their easy intimacy, their casual shorthand. I wouldn't have moved back in with my mother after getting a taste of collegiate freedom if she'd begged me to. But I was nagged by the suspicion that she never would have allowed me to move in with her if I'd asked.

I thought of those runs we used to go on together when I was younger, our clipped conversations about my grades, her lectures urging me toward a professional path similar to her own. While I don't remember her explicitly coddling Sasha, I also don't recall her pushing her toward adulthood with the same force as she pushed me.

My mother, distant and solitary for most of our childhood, now seemed to do everything with Sasha, from their weekly trips to the grocery store to weekend excursions to Catalina or Palm Springs. Their lives had grown as intertwined as two trees planted too close to each other, their roots so tangled it seemed impossible to separate them without damaging both.

"So," my mother said, once we were seated around the dining table, spooning the fragrant food onto our plates, "are children something you and Malik are interested in?"

Sasha snorted, spilling a few grains of jasmine rice on the table. "Wow, Mom, could you sound any more clinical?"

"Malik and I love kids," I replied evenly. "Nothing's off the table."

Sasha chuckled. "Wow, Syd, could you sound any more like a publicist?"

"I know you said your job has great benefits," Mom continued. "Do they cover egg freezing? I've heard that's something a lot of the big tech companies are starting to provide."

"Where is all of this sudden concern for my fertility coming from, Mom?" I asked, punctuating my question with a laugh. I'd meant for it to sound lighthearted, but it came out shrill. "If Malik and I have news we'd like to share about children, we'll be sure to let you both know."

Mom and Sasha exchanged a glance.

"Anyway," I said, "any updates on the job front, Sash?" This was a risky move, like pulling a structurally significant block from a wobbly Jenga tower.

She shrugged, loudly slurping tom yum goong from her spoon. "I've got an interview next week at one of the studios."

"That's great! What's the role?"

"Development intern."

"Oh. It's another internship?"

Sasha shot me a look as sharp as a shiv. Her teenage resentment of me had thawed slightly over the years; she was even warm toward me as long as I respected the unspoken rules of our détente: no pointed questions about her stunted career or whether she ever intended to move out of our mother's house.

Her resentment shouldn't have surprised me, in retrospect. I'd spent so many years shielding her as much as possible from our parents' scarier fights, distracting her by turning up the volume on the TV to mask their raised voices, making room in my bed so she could climb in when she was frightened. In my attempts to insulate her from the ugliness, I'd stripped her of the ability to learn how to navigate it without the safety of my presence. It was as though I'd set her on a bike atop a steep hill and pushed her, without the practice of first riding on a flat surface, aided by the stabilizing presence of training wheels.

"It sounds like this one offers some interesting hands-on experience," Mom said, a reproachful edge to her voice. "You'd be helping to evaluate script submissions, right, Sasha?"

"Exactly." I could tell by the jut of her chin that she was debating whether to continue sulking or change the subject. I was relieved when she asked, "Any updates on the case of our missing aunt?"

I saw my mother narrow her eyes disapprovingly at Sasha—had they always communicated so much with their eyes?—but chose to ignore it.

"Not really. I've been trying to track down Michael Hall ever since Barbara and Stanley told me that he was with Carol at that party. But I haven't had any luck yet."

I'd assumed it would be easy to find Michael's information online. But since he had a pretty common name, and I didn't know his current whereabouts, I was having no success locating him. I tried finding him by searching for his sister and mother online, since those creepy online directories that scrape and compile publicly available personal data often include links to family members, but none of their pages had information on Michael.

If I didn't find anything by Monday, I'd have to call Eloise for more information on her son. It didn't seem wise to try Yvonne again, since she seemed to have intentionally omitted her brother and the fight she'd had with Carol from our coffee shop conversation.

Mom held a forkful of larb salad in the air as she regarded me. "Does Malik approve of all this?"

"I don't need his approval, Mom. But yes, Malik is very supportive." As I said this, I recalled his words to me back when I was in Raleigh. *Are you sure this is good for you?*

"Learning about Carol has made me realize how much we don't know about our own family," Sasha said. "I mean, we don't even know who Dad's father was. And I don't know about any of your family that came before your parents, Mom. Do you realize this means I could accidentally match with, like, a cousin on a dating app?"

"Are you on a dating app?" I asked. I hadn't known Sasha to actively date anyone since the boyfriend she briefly had her freshman year of college.

"No," she said, pouting. "But the point is, I could be, you know?"

I glanced at Mom for a hint at her feelings about Sasha's prolonged singledom, but she kept her gaze steadfastly, almost pointedly, directed toward her plate. Sasha's love life—and Mom's, for that matter—were among the forbidden topics in their house.

I wanted to tell them they didn't have to look beyond the dinner table to find strangers lurking in our family tree.

I WAS IN THE KITCHEN packing up my mojito supplies when Sasha walked in and began tidying the messy counter where she'd apparently made that night's dessert—fluffy Thai iced tea cupcakes topped with condensed milk buttercream frosting. There was so much baking-related detritus that I didn't notice the shiny teal stand mixer until I saw Sasha remove its frosting-coated paddle attachments. Teal was an unusual choice for our mother, who favored classic neutrals for most things, especially pricey appliances.

"Nice mixer," I said. "Is it new?"

"It is!" Sasha said, petting it like a new puppy. "Mom knew I'd been saving for one, and when it went on sale a few weeks ago she gave me the rest of the money I needed to buy it. Look," she said, gesturing at the bakeware and utensils beside her, "we got all this to match!"

A cold ache spread through my chest at the sight of the cheerfully hued bakeware, tangible evidence that Sasha's roots in our mother's home were growing deeper and stronger with each passing year.

For a while when we were growing up, *House Hunters* was my and Sasha's comfort show. We'd watch it for hours, debating over which homes were the best choices, and daydreaming about the cities we'd live in one day. While I'd always been laser-focused on moving to New York after high school, the cities Sasha listed varied with each conversation.

"I don't think I want one big house," Sasha said more than once. "I want apartments all over the world. Paris, Tokyo, Miami. I'll be traveling constantly when I'm a film director, so it'll be convenient having places scattered all over."

I regularly distracted Sasha with made-up *House Hunters* scenarios during our parents' fights. "You're moving to Barcelona," I'd say, willing us both to ignore the alarmingly loud voices seeping through the walls. "Would you take the apartment in the middle of the city with the tiny, outdated kitchen and bathroom; the huge apartment in a sleepy neighborhood twenty minutes outside of downtown; or the spacious bedroom in an apartment surrounded by restaurants and shops, but one that you share with two roommates?"

"Easy," Sasha would say. "The tiny one in the middle of town. I'd be too busy enjoying life in Barcelona to need a fancy kitchen or bathroom anyway."

We'd pause to picture Sasha in her charming Spanish apartment until a particularly loud shout yanked us back to reality.

"We won't be here forever," I'd say solemnly. "We're going to get out. We just have to wait a little longer."

Sasha would smile bravely. "I know," she'd say.

But instead of the jet-setting lifestyle Sasha had once envisioned for herself, beyond the school year she'd spent in a dorm room in her hometown, Sasha had never lived outside of our parents' houses. The thought made me deeply, painfully sad.

I couldn't keep tiptoeing around her feelings, pretending that watching her let her life and dreams slip away wasn't breaking my heart.

"Sash," I said quietly, in case Mom could hear from her room, "are you planning on staying here forever?"

As expected, Sasha heaved a long-suffering sigh. She gathered the dirty baking utensils into the bowl of the mixer and brought the bowl to the sink, brushing roughly past me in the process. "Why do you even care? We see you, like, once a month? If you don't make up an excuse to flake on dinner? How is my staying here impacting you in any way?"

Her words stung, but I ignored the pain. I had to make the conversation worth the discomfort. "It impacts me because I love you, Sash. I want to see you happy. I mean, you're thirty-five now. Don't you want to be going on dates, or hanging out with friends, or traveling the world instead of spending all this time with Mom?"

"Who says I'm not happy, Syd? Just because I'm not living the life you think I should have?" She turned off the tap with a forceful smack. "Pretty bold of you to make assumptions about my happiness; you barely even know me anymore. When's the last time we had a real conversation, when you asked me a question because you were genuinely curious instead of trying to point out some flaw in how I choose to live my life?"

"I . . . I try to talk to you all the time, Sash," I said, though the truth of her words made my face burn. "When I do, it feels like you shut down. Like you shut me out."

Sasha scoffed. "You're one to talk. 'If Malik and I have news we'd like to share about children, we'll be sure to let you both know.'" Her tone was mocking as she parroted my words from dinner. "Super open and vulnerable, Sis."

The soft, sympathetic feelings I'd felt for her only a moment before began to harden. "Fine," I said, throwing my hands up. "Let's say you're actually happy living like this. What's your end-game here? Mom's almost seventy. She should be retiring soon. Are you planning to live off her 401(k)? Tag along with her to a retirement home?"

"Ah, so that's what you're really worried about," Sasha said, her face contorting into a sneer. "You don't actually care about my happiness. You're just worried that one day I'll be a problem for your bank account."

"That's not fair," I said, my voice wavering. But the thought had crossed my mind: if our mother could no longer support Sasha, what would become of a woman Sasha's age who'd never paid her own rent, or set up her own utilities, or budgeted for her own groceries? What sort of future was she setting herself up for, or condemning herself to? What sort of future was my mother enabling for her by allowing her to stay?

I also couldn't help but feel that I'd failed her somehow along the way. What sort of big sister lets this happen? Could I have done more to prevent it?

"Whatever. Just spare me the unsolicited lectures or phony concern, okay?" She dried her hands on a dish towel and tossed it crumpled onto the island as she left the room. "In case you haven't noticed, no one's asking for your help."

TEN

The moment I shut my car door, I released the scream I'd somehow managed to suppress since arriving at my mother's house. I pressed my fingers to my eyes, but hot tears of frustration slipped through them anyway.

I had been so hopeful when our mother bought that house. I'd thought it symbolized a new chapter for the three of us; maybe, with my father gone, we could finally create the warm, open, and easy family dynamic I'd always craved. But our monthly dinners were disheartening reminders that while my father's death had removed the threat of violence from our home, it did little to bring the rest of us closer together.

I would never have said it aloud, not even to Dr. Dominguéz, but I'd felt like my father's crash was an act of divine intervention. My parents didn't seem to view divorce as an option, no matter how miserable their marriage became. Maintaining their public power couple persona seemed more important than dealing with the dismal reality of our home life.

The crash was a far more humane ending to my parents' relationship than the one I'd feared was coming. After all, my father's blood alcohol level was five times the legal limit when his Corvette smashed into the jacaranda his supper clubs were named for; he may not have even been fully conscious when it happened. The tree had covered the mangled black fiberglass with a blanket of purple petals, as if attempting to shroud my father's body from view.

In movies, the angry alcoholic father typically emerges on screen fully formed, as though he were born with a bottle of Johnnie Walker in one hand, the fingers of the other curled into a permanent fist. It wasn't like that with my father. His devolution was as gradual as watching a glacier melt.

At first I knew the angry version of my dad only as a raised voice I occasionally heard on the other side of the wall between my bedroom and my parents'. It was easy to separate that loud, scary voice from the playful, loving person who made our breakfasts before school.

By the time I reached the fifth grade, my parents' arguments had grown louder, and I was able to make out more of what they argued about. Though by that point it was impossible to tell what had caused the rift to form between them in the first place, or who was in the right.

Was Dad squandering their money by buying a Corvette on a whim, or was my mother being unnecessarily frugal with the money he'd saved from his NFL days? Was Dad being irresponsible by staying out at his restaurants too late, or was he simply trying to avoid fights with Mom? Was he drinking too much, or simply relaxing in the safety of his own study? Was he being lazy by sleeping past breakfast on school days on occasion, or was it only fair since he was the one who put dinner on the table if her dermatology appointments ran late?

Their arguments were nearly constant, though for years I would confuse their temporary cease-fires for actual peace. By middle school I realized there was a pattern to their fights; if you paid close attention, you could predict them like the weather.

I thought of my father's sunny, playful side as his baseline, the side he displayed to diners at the Jacaranda, or to fellow parents who asked him for autographs during parent-teacher conferences. Over a period of time—days, weeks, or months—his mood would grow increasingly overcast. He'd become more sullen and withdrawn, retreating for hours to his study, or avoiding home altogether, returning in the middle of the night only to sleep. Entire bottles of scotch would appear empty in the recycling bin overnight, or he'd return home with slurred words and unsteady steps. He would become short-tempered with us, especially Mom. The tension in the house would darken and expand, the way the air becomes thick and staticky before a thunderstorm.

At that point, anything could set him off. One morning when I was in the eighth grade my father slept through breakfast, so I prepared bowls of cereal for me and Sasha. I lost track of time, and we had to run out of the door to meet our school bus; I left our bowls in the sink instead of rinsing and placing them in the dishwasher like we'd been taught. When we returned home after school, we could hear our father's shouts before I even unlocked the door.

"Larry, enough already." Our mother's voice wafted from the kitchen as I ushered Sasha upstairs to her room. Mom sounded exhausted, like they'd been at this for hours. I crept into the hallway to monitor their argument, like usual. As far as I was aware, their fights were never physical, yet they somehow felt incredibly violent. It wasn't just the vile things he called our mother, or the volatility in his voice, like his rage was a vicious animal in a subpar cage. It was that the contempt they had for each other was so palpable that violence felt inevitable. I took it upon myself to stay alert during their arguments, in case I needed to intercede.

"... everything I do for this family," my father slurred over the sound of running water, "everything you all expect me to do. All I ask is that you keep the space I'm expected to cook our meals in clean, and you can't even do that?"

The guilt that gripped me was sudden and paralyzing. It reminded me of the horribly lifelike replica of the drowning mammoth I'd seen during a recent field trip to the La Brea Tar Pits. The thick black tar had swallowed him up to his chest; he trumpeted futilely as he died while his partner and despondent calf watched from the edge of the murderous pit.

I'd known better than to leave our bowls in the sink. It was my fault, but Mom was getting yelled at for it.

"Larry, we're human; it's not like this happens all the time," Mom said in that calm tone that we all knew drove our father insane. But I felt a ping of gratitude at her choice of words: "we're human," lumping herself into the dirty dishes incident, protecting me and Sasha. "Besides," she continued, "they wouldn't have left dishes in the sink at all if you hadn't been too hungover to fix them breakfast again."

No! I wanted to shout. I didn't understand why she often did this, goading him when she knew how he'd react.

The sound of ceramic shattering against the stainless steel sink filled the house. I never had my father's dinosaur-shaped pancakes again; after that day, he stopped making breakfast for me and Sasha altogether.

The morning after a particularly bad argument, a bouquet of flowers would materialize on the kitchen island. I never actually heard him say the words "I'm sorry"—not to my mother, and certainly never to me. Then, like clockwork, the cycle would begin again.

I told all my future boyfriends I was allergic to apology flowers.

By the time I reached high school, my father's mood was overcast for the majority of his time at home, and a sudden storm could develop at any moment. I'd wondered if it had something to do with the fact that the Jacaranda chain was beginning to fail; they'd had to close all but the original location. But I'd grown bored of his tantrums, and resentful of having to tiptoe around him when he was in his darker moods. I began to think he was all bark and no bite.

And then one weekend in my junior year of high school, Mom, Sasha, and I went to San Diego. Sasha's birthday fell on a Saturday in January during her obsession with becoming a marine biologist, and in an uncharacteristic move, my mother took the day off to drive the three of us to San Diego for an overnight trip. On Sunday morning we awoke early to board a whale-watching cruise. We actually saw a humpback breach from the ocean like you see in the movies, splashing the entire boat with mist.

We returned home shortly before dinnertime. While it wasn't particularly late, the sun had set long ago, and we found my father sitting in near-total darkness at the kitchen table, a half-empty bottle of Johnnie Walker and a full tumbler of amber liquid in front of him.

"Where were you?" he asked, craggy-voiced.

My mother clicked on the light; my father's eyes narrowed and blinked. His expression was set in a menacing scowl, but his cheeks were streaked with tears. Something about those tears unsettled me most of all.

"We were in San Diego, Larry," my mother said evenly. "For Sasha's birthday? I told you we were going."

"When?" My father's voice went shrill. "When did you tell me?"

"Two nights ago."

My father shook his head. He had the tendency to forget things when he was drunk. He'd once eaten an entire dinner, fallen asleep in his study, and emerged hours later asking where his meal was.

He tapped a fingernail against the cut-crystal tumbler, *clink-clink-clink*. "You think you can leave me?" he growled.

"Larry, we didn't leave you—you told me you couldn't come, you had to work."

His movement was surprisingly quick for someone so clearly intoxicated. He hurled the tumbler across the room with such force that the scotch remained inside the glass until it collided with the wall beside my mother's head. It exploded into a million pieces that rained onto the floor like hail.

The legs of his chair scratched the floor as he rose to his feet and marched toward us. Without thinking, I gently pushed Sasha behind me and took a step ahead of my mother. My father's rage had been almost exclusively directed toward my mother throughout my childhood, so when his eyes locked on mine, it was the first time I'd felt its full heat. It was like the sun's surface, bubbling red, barely stable. But beneath that heat was an unfathomable sadness.

His lip curled in a snarl as his gaze shifted back to my mother, who remained as calm and still as though she were carved from marble. "Perfect!" he boomed; I felt Sasha cower from the noise behind me. "You've poisoned them against me, perfect." His shoe crunched on glass as he took a step toward us; my heart leapt into my throat, but I held my ground. I was tired of cowering in his presence. I wanted him to know I saw him for the pathetic bully he was.

He stood close enough that I could smell the sickly sweet scotch on his breath. That scent would forever turn my stomach. He continued to sneer at us, though fresh tears slipped down his face.

"The way you all look at me," he said, voice cracking. "You all hate me that much? Life with me is that awful? Maybe I should go ahead and end it then. That what you want? Maybe I should put everyone out of our misery and end us all."

He marched out of the room toward the study, shoulder-checking Mom along the way, trailing wet pieces of crystal as he went. We'd find shards of it embedded in our feet for days.

As soon as the door to the study slammed, I whirled to face my mother. Her face was stoic as always, but panic simmered in her eyes.

"Mom," I whispered, "we have to get out of here."

She scoffed. "We're not going anywhere, Sydney. Your father is all talk."

I looked at Sasha, who stood with her back to the dripping wall, weeping silently. I moved beside her, bits of crystal popping beneath my feet, and took her hand. "Mom. Please," I said. "We have to do something. We at least have to report it to the pol—"

Mom's finger was in my face before I could finish my sentence. "Sydney, we are not to speak of this again. To anyone. 'What happens in this house stays in this house,' remember? The last thing we need is the neighbors all up in our business after they see a police car in our driveway."

You could imagine how my mother later felt about the media circus that followed my father's death, and my decision to go into journalism, profiting from publicizing the private lives of strangers.

"Mom," Sasha whispered between gulps of breath, "I'm scared."

Mom's dark brown eyes went cold and flat as black ice.

"Why should you be scared?" she spat. "None of this concerns you. You two go up to bed. Just . . . I don't know, lock your bedroom doors tonight if it makes you feel better. I bet you twenty dollars there will be a supermarket flower arrangement on that table by the time you come down for breakfast."

She held her head remarkably high as she crunched over broken glass on the way to the broom closet.

The next morning, the air in the kitchen was thick with the scent of Stargazer lilies.

At the time, I thought my father's behavior that night was a natural progression of his ongoing alcohol-fueled deterioration. After learning about Carol, though, I wondered if his outsize reaction to our temporary disappearance had more to do with the unprocessed agony of believing his beloved sister abandoned him all those years ago.

ELEVEN

I TRIED TO STAY FOCUSED AND ENGAGED DURING MY BACK-to-back meetings on Monday morning, but as soon as I had thirty free minutes, I found an empty conference room and shut myself inside.

I still hadn't been able to track Michael down online, despite googling for two additional hours on my phone in bed the night before, too wound up from my fight with Sasha to sleep. I knew what I needed to do; I just hoped the well hadn't been poisoned. I navigated to my phone's contact list, searched for her name, and hit call, listening to my own shaking breath over the trill of the dial tone. She picked up on the third ring.

"Hi, Ms. Eloise—it's Sydney, Effie's granddaughter."

"Oh, hi, doll!" Her honeyed voice transported me back to her cozy living room, the faded chintz sofa, the taste of freshly brewed sun tea. "What can I do for you?"

"I don't know if you know the Dunn family—Sally Dunn went missing a few months before Carol? I was talking with her brother, Stanley, and he told me he met Carol at a party at Shaw."

There was a pause. I pictured Eloise's forehead creasing with confusion. "At Shaw? That can't be right. Carol was only in high school."

"I know . . . it sounds like she actually might have hung out with a slightly older crowd." My throat caught as I swallowed; I regretted not bringing my thermos of water into the conference room. "Stanley mentioned that your son was at the same party. He didn't happen to attend Shaw, did he?"

I might have thought the call had dropped, if not for the faint melody of the *Jeopardy!* theme song somewhere in the background. Finally, Eloise said, "What makes you ask about my Michael, doll?"

"It's a long shot, I know," I replied, throwing in a self-deprecating laugh for good measure. "I just thought, if he did go to Shaw, maybe he saw Carol hanging around campus? I figured he'd recognize her, since you were so close with her mom. I'm trying to piece together who was in her circle around the time she went missing. Maybe he saw something, knew who she spent time with."

I could hear Eloise drumming her fingers on the surface of something solid. "Yvonne said you might ask for Michael's number."

My stomach dropped. Why would Yvonne mention Michael to her mother when she hadn't even mentioned him to me by name?

I swallowed, unsure of what to say. Then I remembered the old reporting trick—silence could be a useful trap; most people can't bear to leave it unfilled.

I felt a small surge of satisfaction when, after a few beats, Eloise said, "Honestly, though, I don't know what she's so worried about."

"I'm sure I'm totally grasping at straws here," I demurred. "There are just so few people I can reach out to who might have known her then. I figured it was worth a try."

Eloise breathed heavily into the phone; the sound tickled my ear. "To tell you the truth, I think becoming a lawyer has made my daughter a little paranoid." She laughed, and the sound instantly relaxed my tensed muscles. "You got a pen, doll?"

I called the number as soon as I hung up with Eloise. The leather office chair creaked like old bones when I rose to my feet; the adrenaline pulsing through my veins made it impossible to remain seated.

An automated greeting sounded after just two rings; I'd been sent straight to voicemail. Should I leave a message, or just keep calling back?

After the tone, I found myself speaking into the receiver. "Hi, Michael, my name is Sydney Singleton. This is a long shot, but I'm trying to find out more about my aunt, Carol Singleton." My pulse raced as I improvised. I dialed up the helplessness in my voice as I went on. "I actually didn't know she existed until a few weeks ago. I know your mother and my grandmother were close . . . I figure you probably knew Carol. If there's anything you can share about her, any little story or memory . . . it would mean the world to me." I left my number and ended the call.

I gripped my phone tight as I scanned my memory of the voicemail for any potential errors, wondering if I'd made the right choice in leaving a voicemail at all. I was so startled when my phone rang that I knocked into one of the leather chairs; it clanged loudly against the conference table. I answered the call without bothering to look at the caller ID.

"Hello?"

"Hi, Sydney, this is Dionne calling from Dr. Tanaka's office. It's time to schedule your trigger shot."

Health classes and after-school specials had made me terrified of an accidental pregnancy long before I'd started having sex. In my case, though, conception proved as painstaking as landing a rocket on Mars.

The trigger shot, which would propel my body into ovulation, needed to be self-administered exactly thirty-six hours before the extraction of my eggs. Malik would need to provide a sperm sample that same day, and the following morning for good measure. Then our genetic material would be forced to do under bright light and microscope what seemed impossible to accomplish in the warm darkness of my body.

This wasn't our first egg retrieval. At the start of our IVF odyssey, we were able to extract eleven of my eggs. Six were fertilized, and four became embryos. But after genetic testing, only two were found to be viable candidates for implantation. Our first IVF attempt failed, and the second resulted in that awful Valentine's Day miscarriage. We needed more embryos in order to try again. And as all of the literature on the topic insisted on reminding me, my odds of providing the quality and quantity of eggs we'd need plummeted with each passing day.

THAT NIGHT, MALIK AND I sprawled on our leather living room sectional, legs intertwined, watching a long-running legal drama that we'd invested too much time in to abandon.

Malik grabbed the remote and paused the show. "Bathroom break," he said, pressing his lips to my forehead. I reached for my phone and checked my email. My eyes sifted through the digital junk mail until I spotted a message from Barbara titled "POLICE RECORDS."

I gasped and pushed myself upright. It was a link to a digital folder. Inside were hundreds of files, images, and PDFs, all with indecipherable computer-generated names, and in no apparent order. I clicked on a few files at random. There were copies of hand-scrawled notes, images of nondescript slices of neighborhood, and scans of official-looking documents, the importance of which was not immediately clear. I looked quickly for patterns. Noticeably absent were files for Carol, since no police report was ever made for her. My heart twisted at this; was Grammy really so angry with Carol for supposedly running away, for being a rebellious teenager, that she never even bothered looking for her?

It would take hours to sort through and analyze all the files. I felt more than overwhelmed; I felt ashamed of my own hubris. Embarrassed by the conversations I'd forced with Eloise, Barbara, and Stanley, the painful memories I'd made them exhume. What made me think I was qualified to solve a series of cases that had gone cold sixty years ago?

Malik padded back into the living room, pausing to take in my newly alert posture. "What's up?"

"Barbara sent me the police records," I murmured, still scrolling, as though a pattern would magically emerge. "They're a mess."

Malik sat beside me, regarding my phone as though it were likely to catch fire. "Did you want to stop watching so you can focus on that?"

"No, no," I said, setting my phone facedown beside Malik's on the coffee table. "I'll take a closer look tomorrow."

I don't know how the episode of our show ended. I spent the rest of the hour staring at the back of my phone, preoccupied by the clues it might contain, and how I might uncover them. It had been ten years since I'd last investigated a missing person case; I couldn't remember where to begin.

I HADN'T PLANNED ON BECOMING a crime reporter; I thought I'd be an investigative journalist, exposing corrupt politicians and unscrupulous corporations. But they didn't hand those jobs to kids fresh out of college. Instead, after months of trying to land a reporting job in New York, I expanded my search and secured a still-coveted position as a general assignment reporter at the *San Francisco Chronicle.*

I quickly impressed the editors with my unflinching coverage of the crime stories that landed on my desk, and I was surprised by how much I enjoyed working on them. There was something thrilling about sitting in the galleries of courtrooms during trials and arraignments, and finding clever ways of getting the suspect's friends and loved ones to open up to me. I thrived on the competitive nature of the work, on trying to find a piece of information or a compelling interview subject the other local news outlets had missed, or potentially uncovering a clue the police weren't even aware of. I had to remain steadfastly impartial in my coverage, but I relished the opportunity to position all the puzzle pieces I'd gathered strategically on the page, where the reader could easily complete the job of connecting them. When I was offered a promotion to officially join the crime team four years later, I couldn't say no.

I didn't analyze my chosen profession much at the time; I enjoyed writing and loved a good mystery, so journalism always seemed like a logical path. In retrospect, though, I wondered if there had been a deeper motivation for my choice. Maybe for someone who grew up in a household that favored suppression and obfuscation, choosing a career dedicated to publicly uncovering the truth was the ultimate form of rebellion. Maybe, given that my father died a mystery, there was something cathartic about untangling the mysteries of others.

The McEwan kids and their father had been missing for three days when my editor assigned me to their story. The most widely circulated picture of the family had been taken at Hannah McEwan's birthday party earlier that year. Hannah sat at the head of a long wooden table behind a large, expertly frosted cake. Flames danced on the tips of eleven candles. The cone-shaped hat she wore smooshed her blond bangs, partially obscuring her piercing blue eyes. Her smile was strained, as though the person behind the camera was taking too long to shoot. Eight-year-old Nathaniel perched on his knees on the chair beside his sister, his dimpled grin bright and carefree. Their mother, Lisa, laughed as she balanced a squirming three-year-old Emma on her hip. The children's father, William, smiled stoically behind Hannah's chair. His hands, which gripped either side of the chair's tall back, looked enormous in comparison to his daughter's head.

A quick Google search of Lisa McEwan led me to a blog where she chronicled a carefully curated, pastel-filtered version of her life as a Bay Area mom. There was a photo of Lisa and the kids sitting around an artfully assembled charcuterie board on a pristine gingham blanket, beneath the headline LIVEN UP LUNCHTIME WITH A PICNIC IN THE PARK. There was a picture of Hannah helping her mom bake vegan, gluten-free, low-sugar Halloween cookies, above suggestions for "Healthyish Halloween Treats."

I noticed that unlike the forced grin in the birthday party picture, Hannah seemed to smile unabashedly in all of the blog photos.

I knew there were a dozen innocent reasons to explain this difference. But there was also a notable absence in the blog photos: her father, William.

William had been a prominent software engineer during the late nineties tech bubble, but the company he helped build collapsed when the bubble burst, and his career never recovered. During my reporting, I learned he'd made a series of bad investments in recent years, and had taken out a second mortgage on their home in coveted, just-shy-of-suburban Noe Valley only a few months before the disappearance. Lisa's sister told me Lisa had been planning to file for divorce shortly before William, the children, and the family minivan went missing.

I stayed up for hours after Malik had gone to bed in our apartment in grittier, trendier Hayes Valley, bent over my laptop, searching Lisa's blog for clues. Spurred by the thought that if I clicked on just one more link, or scoured one more post, I might find the clue that would unravel everything. I stared at those pictures so long I began to have vivid dreams of Hannah in the rare moments when I actually slept. In them, she was always trying to show me something, pointing into a blackness my eyes were unable to pierce, or whispering a phrase too hushed for me to decipher.

Something broke inside me when a young woman earning her pilot license spotted the shattered remains of the McEwans' minivan in Mount Tam State Park. The vehicle had careened off a notoriously dangerous, winding stretch of road and tumbled down a six-hundred-foot embankment. There were no survivors.

There was also no sign that William had tried to prevent the van from plummeting over the cliff's edge. In fact, it was determined that the scuff marks a quarter mile down the road were caused not by his attempt at braking but by the sudden, rapid acceleration of the van's tires.

I couldn't stop thinking about Hannah, who'd been launched from the passenger seat on impact. Did her father's stomping on the gas and abrupt turning of the wheel surprise her? Or had her father long threatened that he might do something like this one day, the way my father had?

Years later, in therapy, whenever Dr. Dominguéz referred to my "childhood trauma," I'd dismiss it. "It's hard to think of my childhood as traumatic when I think of what those McEwan kids went through," I'd say.

But Dr. Dominguéz would shake her head and reply, "Just because your father didn't make good on his threats doesn't make the threats themselves any less traumatic."

I COLLAPSED INTO A DEEP sleep beside Malik shortly after 10:00 P.M. that night, but after a bathroom break around 1:00 A.M., sleep proved elusive. My mind was annoyingly alert. I tried not to think about what would happen if this egg retrieval was unsuccessful, or if this IVF cycle didn't take. And thanks to my trying not to think about it, it became all I could think of.

I turned over in bed, hoping the change in position would help calm my mind. I occasionally allowed myself to wonder how my life might look if we set aside our baby journey. Certain areas of my life had been on pause over the three years we'd been trying to conceive.

The enviable fertility benefits and generous parental leave offerings at my company made the idea of finding another job so illogical, I never even considered it. Plus, I had an impressive title, a healthy salary, and all the free activewear I could want. But it wasn't fulfilling. It didn't feel important or meaningful, the way journalism had before I had to walk away from it. I wondered what career I might pursue if I wasn't tethered by the perks of my current role.

Malik snuffled in his sleep. His arm instinctually reached out for me, warm and pleasantly heavy. A flood of tenderness rushed through me. All I had to do was think of Malik to grind any ruminations about a possible life without children to a halt. I knew he would give anything to pass the genes of the father he'd barely known down to a child of his own. I'd never be able to take that away from him.

I glanced over Malik's shoulder at the digital clock on his nightstand: 2:17 A.M. I wasn't going to fall back asleep at that rate.

I carefully climbed out of bed, gathered my laptop and a notebook, and curled up in the armchair in the corner of the room. The digital folder of police records was open on my screen. The feeling of overwhelm that descended on me when I'd first opened the folder threatened to return, but I exhaled deeply, as though attempting to blow it away. "Just start somewhere, Sydney," I whispered to myself.

I decided to go through each file and enter any relevant details into a spreadsheet, eventually creating a searchable document to make it easier to spot any patterns in the cases and jotting any potentially interesting details into my notebook.

I'm not sure when I fell asleep; the next thing I knew, Malik was leaning over me in the armchair, his hand on my shoulder, his breath warm on my cheek. "Sydney, what are you doing over here?"

Behind him, through the sliding glass door that led to our tiny patio, the sun was just beginning to rise. A pale yellow glow filled the room, giving Malik an angelic quality as he hovered above me. But his face was etched with a familiar expression of concern.

I yawned as I stretched my legs, stiff from being curled in the armchair for hours. "I couldn't sleep. I thought I might as well get a little work done."

He pulled the notebook from my lap and blanched when he saw what was on the page.

"What is it?" I asked, feeling preemptively embarrassed as I retrieved the notebook from his grasp and looked down at the paper.

I'd clearly dropped the pen I was using midscrawl—a long blue slash ran diagonally across the bottom third of the page. But my chest seized when I saw what was written above it.

I must have been delirious at the time, because I had no memory of writing it. But Carol's name filled the lines on the page, over and over again. Like I was a student punished by having to write my lesson across a chalkboard. I'd written in cursive, with no spaces between the words, so her name was an unbroken chain across each line:

CarolCarolCarolCarolCarolCarolCarolCarolCarolCarol
CarolCarolCarolCarolCarol

The writing grew increasingly illegible as the rows went on, as though I'd nodded off as I wrote it, my hand a phantom limb.

TWELVE

THE NIGHT BEFORE MY EGG RETRIEVAL, MALIK INSISTED on making dinner. When he called me into the dining room, I found the table decorated with candles, their golden flames dancing in the gentle breeze of the air-conditioning.

The room smelled divine. He'd already plated our meal: pan-seared scallops in lemon-butter sauce, Parmesan risotto, roasted broccolini. It was the same dinner he'd prepared the first time he cooked for me, the night he asked me to be his girlfriend.

"You might be the last romantic man of our generation," I said before kissing him. I gestured toward the tumblers beside our plates, each filled with bright red liquid, a single sphere of ice, and a spiral of orange rind. "What are those?"

"Virgin Negronis," he said proudly.

I was technically the one told to refrain from alcohol, coffee, and running in the period immediately leading up to and following the egg retrieval. But Malik adopted the same rules, so I wouldn't feel alone.

I kissed him again, and he wrapped his arms around me. Feeling the strength and solidity of his body pressed against mine reminded me of something else that was forbidden: sex. The side effects of all the shots helped lessen its appeal to me. My swollen ovaries left me feeling bloated and heavy. The skin around my stomach was tender from all the injections. And I was often too tired by bedtime to feel the urge to touch or be touched by my husband.

Malik's fingertips feathered their way from behind my left earlobe down to my clavicle, sending a current of desire through my body. I shuddered and pulled away with a laugh. "Don't go starting something we can't finish."

Halfway through dinner I rose to refill our water glasses. When I returned from the kitchen Malik was staring off into space, his brow furrowed.

As I regarded Malik then, I noticed the dark half-moons beneath his eyes. The rich mahogany color of his skin had faded, like a grand old table in need of a good polish. An uncharacteristic slump curled his broad shoulders.

I racked my memory; had he looked this way when we spoke before work that morning? While we ate dinner in front of the TV the night before? Guilt bloomed in my gut when I realized I couldn't answer these simple questions.

"Hey," I said, setting down our glasses and caressing his shoulder. Energy and brightness returned to his features, as though he'd flipped a light switch, though the dark circles and ashen complexion remained. "What's wrong?"

He passed a hand over his face. "Ugh, I didn't want to talk about it. You've got enough on your plate." He glanced up to see me looking at him persistently, urging him to continue. "One of our closest competitors just got hit with millions in regulatory fines," he said. "They were on track to IPO, and this is definitely going to delay that."

I nodded as I processed the news, returning to my seat. "Which means your investors are probably nervous that something similar can happen at Wealthmate."

"Exactly," Malik replied. He speared a scallop with his fork and slid it absentmindedly around his plate. "We've spent the past few days combing through everything we're doing to make sure we're not at risk. And we're looking to raise additional funds soon, so the timing of this extra scrutiny is terrible. It also adds weight to the argument of bringing on a CEO who understands the weeds of the finance side of things better than I do."

Malik set his fork down on his plate, the scallop still impaled on its tines, bleeding butter. "Maybe they're right. The past few days have been really intense. It would've been helpful to have someone else at the top to bounce ideas off of, poke holes in my recommendations, make sure I'm thinking through all sides of every scenario. Someone who can argue for the regulatory side as strongly as I argue for the product side." He exhaled slowly, like a just-punctured tire. "Maybe it's time for me to take a step back."

The guilt in my gut curdled. This had been going on for days?

"I'm so sorry, Malik. I can't believe I didn't know about all of this. Why didn't you tell me?"

Malik winced. "I didn't want to say anything until after the retrieval. You know what the books say about the impact of stress on IVF success."

A grumble of frustration erupted from my throat. "I'm not made of glass, Malik. And you can't bubble-wrap me until a baby comes. I need you to tell me if something is going on. Nothing will stress me out more than feeling like you're keeping me in the dark."

There was a nearly imperceptible flutter across Malik's brow, like an involuntary twitch. But I knew him well enough to understand its message: *You're one to talk.*

His brow was right. I pushed my lingering irritation aside and went into solution mode. "What about bringing on a co-CEO? That way you wouldn't have to forfeit your role altogether."

Malik shook his head. "I've never seen it work. It always creates confusion for the team. At the end of the day, you need one captain steering the ship." He shrugged, as though the issue were a cloak he could let slip from his shoulders. "Anyway, this isn't something we're going to solve tonight." He drained his mocktail and tilted the empty glass in my direction. "Your turn."

"My turn?"

"What's really on your mind lately? You haven't talked about your aunt or your research in a while. I'm sure that's for my benefit." My face grew hot. Malik smiled. "Yeah, I noticed."

I stared into the mouth of my mocktail glass, wishing for the cold, clean, dulling effect of gin. "Honestly? I'm starting to feel kind of silly about the whole thing. I have no idea what I'm doing."

"Even with all your reporting experience?"

I shrugged. "That was different. It wasn't my job to develop theories about what happened, or figure out who the suspects were. I just had to report the facts."

I sipped my drink. "It really hit me when I got all those police files from Barbara. There are so many of them, and most of the time I don't really understand what I'm looking at, or looking for. Plus, there's zero information on Carol, since Grammy never even filed a missing person report for her. Can you imagine that? Disappearing at seventeen and your own mother doesn't even try looking for you?" I stroked my glass. "I'm sure Grammy felt she had her reasons, but I just couldn't imagine turning my back on my child that way."

Malik looked thoughtful for a moment. "I still feel like I should be encouraging you to drop this whole thing, but remember when you made me watch that true crime documentary a while back, about the serial killer? And how some of the details that helped unravel the case came from people in, like, true crime chat rooms? What do they call those people?"

"Citizen detectives."

"Right. Have you looked into any of those? Maybe there are some true crime fanatics in North Carolina who've heard stories about the missing girls, or could kind of help ask around, or something."

A knot I didn't know existed loosened in my neck. "Malik . . .

that's an amazing idea. I can't believe I hadn't thought of it before. They're always talking about citizen detectives on the podcasts I listen to."

Malik smiled somberly. "See? Sometimes it's helpful to have someone to bounce ideas off of."

THE EGG RETRIEVAL PROCESS WAS more invasive than the implantation that would follow a few weeks later, assuming we'd have viable embryos. Fortunately, the sedative that snaked from an IV into my veins spared me from the awareness of the needle piercing my ovaries. The entire process took less than thirty minutes. They were able to get eight eggs, but we wouldn't know if any of them would become viable embryos for weeks.

I felt hot and woozy as Malik and I walked to the elevator that would take us from Dr. Tanaka's office to the garage. "Can we take a walk around the block before we get back into the car?" I asked. "I think I need some air."

I inhaled deeply when we emerged onto the Beverly Hills sidewalk. The L.A. autumn heat had abated slightly; a hint of ocean air whispered from the west, blowing free the curls that clung to the damp skin at the back of my neck.

Malik brought my hand to his lips. "How about I make you breakfast in bed when we get back, and we watch movies for the rest of the day?"

I wrapped an arm around his waist as we continued our slow stroll. "I love you," I said.

I closed my eyes for a moment, and when I opened them again, something clawed at the edge of my vision. It gave me the same sense of dread I occasionally felt when I walked into a darkened room at home, and for just a moment, I mistook a pile of clothes for a stranger lurking in the shadows.

We were walking past Louis Vuitton on Rodeo. The entire building was wrapped in mirrored glass, but it contained a pattern that garbled the images it reflected. It was my own reflection that caught me off guard. There was something wrong with it; something about the shape of the hair, the suggestion of a full skirt when I was dressed in joggers. The gait didn't quite match mine.

When I turned to look head-on at the mirror, it was clear I was looking at a distorted image of myself. But for the briefest of moments, I thought I saw Carol's reflection walking beside me.

March 18, 1964

We're going to do it—me and Michael are going to run away together! 🖤

Why should we wait? To make my Mama happy? I'm convinced she's never been happy a day in her life. Even if I did exactly what she wanted, and gave up singing outside of church and went to college and got into medical school and married a judge (after graduation) and became the first negro female pediatrician in Raleigh, I still don't think she'd be happy.

And even if she was, why do I need to sacrifice my dreams to make her happy? Why do I have to change who I am to make her love me? I don't have to change anything for Michael. His love for me is unconditional. I love Michael, and I love music, and I don't see what a diploma has to do with either.

Of course, a diploma is important to Michael, since he wants to be a lawyer and all. But he's planning to transfer his credits to a school near our new home. He's keen on going to law school in California, but I'm confident I can convince him to go to school near Detroit instead. He knows how important my Motown dream is to me; there's no way he'd try and take that away.

I'll miss Larry, of course. And he'll probably be sore with me for a while for leaving. But maybe the fact that I'm leaving with Michael will soften the blow.

Michael is sooo good with Larry. He's joined me to watch several of Larry's peewee football games, and when I've had to miss them for theater or choir practice, he's even gone without me to make sure Larry has someone cheering for him in the stands. 🖤

Larry walks around the house repeating things Michael's said like an adorable little parrot. "Michael said this," and "Michael said that." I have to keep reminding him that Mama can't know Michael and I are together.

I think all of this is finally making Larry realize how ridiculously strict our mother is. "I don't understand what she has against him," he lamented last week. "If she spent any time with him she'd see how great a guy he is." My heart nearly melted. It's clear how much he idolizes Michael, and how much Michael adores Larry. It makes me wonder if they've both craved a big brother–little brother relationship all these years, and have finally found their sibling soul mates.

"She doesn't have anything against Michael personally," I consoled him. "She doesn't want me dating anybody."

"But Michael isn't just anybody," he said. I gave him a big squeeze.

It will all be okay, one day. When I'm a big Motown star, I'll buy Michael and me a house big enough to give Larry his own room, and he can stay with us as often and for as long as he wants.

Yes, Larry will be upset that I ran away at first. But he'll grow to understand why I had to leave, eventually.

THIRTEEN

I AWOKE THE NEXT MORNING FROM A DREAM THAT DID not want to release me; I could feel my consciousness struggling to escape it.

It was dark in my dream, dusk or dawn. The sky and the tepid, chest-high water I stood in were the same inky shade of blue. The water lapped softly against me, as if rocking me gently to sleep. Though I stood alone in a large body of water, I felt strangely calm. My feet were submerged in some sort of sea vegetation, hidden from view by the opacity of the water. In the distance, I could just make out the shadowy mounds of a coastline. I lifted a foot to move toward the slice of land, but, just like the dream itself, the sea vegetation held me in its grasp. I felt its cold, slimy leaves slither up my ankles, grasping like long fingers. The harder I pulled, the tighter it held me.

My dream-scream died on my lips when my eyelids burst open, revealing the familiar landscape of my bedroom. Malik stood at the foot of the bed, fiddling with the cord of my electric heating pad.

"Sorry to wake you, Babygirl," he said, grimacing in apology. "You got tangled up while you were sleeping."

I blinked, my mind struggling to function through the hazy hangover of sleep. "What time is it?"

"Just after eight." Malik freed my ankles from the cord and rubbed at the ridges it had dug into my skin. I hugged the velvety pad against my abdomen. The cramps were less intense than when I'd fallen asleep, but it still felt as though an invisible giant was using my belly as a stress ball.

Malik was going back to the fertility clinic to provide another sperm sample. "I'll pick up a wireless heating pad for you and grab brunch on my way home," he said. "Are you craving something sweet or savory?"

I smiled. "Savory, please."

"You got it," he said, bending down to kiss me. "See you soon."

I extricated myself from our bedding and walked into the bathroom, keeping my eyes averted from my reflection; I'd tried to avoid mirrors ever since that unsettling moment on Rodeo.

I stopped myself before reaching for my toothbrush and closed my fingers around the edge of the countertop instead. "It was just your imagination," I told myself. I forced my eyes to meet the pair in the reflection. My own dark brown eyes. My own dark brown curls, spilling out of my black silk headscarf like water leaking through a failing dam.

"You're okay," I said, urging myself to believe it.

I went to my dresser, where the framed photo of a preteen Carol I'd taken from my grandmother's house now lived, sandwiched between the boxes that stored my jewelry and sunglasses.

I studied her image. While we looked eerily similar, there were distinct differences between us. There was something delicate about her nose, while mine was broader and more prominent. Our eyebrows were placed in slightly different positions, mine farther away from my eyes. Her skin was a paler shade of brown. My natural curls tumbled wild and free from my scalp, while hers appeared ironed straight, with curved bangs and upturned ends as though she slept in foam rollers. But if we'd lived in the same time and place, acquaintances would have easily confused us for each other.

My gaze lingered on her precocious smile, the way her hand rested on her hip, the way her chin was slightly raised. Her entire countenance seemed to say, *Try me. I dare you.* I wondered if the confidence she radiated was one she truly felt, or if it was a mask she wore to hide her softer parts.

I imagined that her early maturity and feigned worldliness were tools she used to distract herself and others from the fact that she was just a child. A child who, like me, grew up a little too fast, ignoring her own desires for familial love and protection in order to prioritize the emotional safety of her younger sibling. A child who, unable to find the warmth and care she craved at home, sought it elsewhere.

Maybe all of Carol's mischievous behavior was actually an effort to finally earn the attention of Grammy, whose affection she craved most.

My heart ached at the thought that if Carol's running away had been her final attempt at getting Grammy's attention, it had backfired spectacularly. Not only had Grammy made no effort to find her daughter; she'd spent the rest of her days denying that Carol had existed at all.

I carried the photo and my heating pad into the guest bedroom-slash-office down the hall, the room that would become our baby's if the fertility treatments worked. It was sparsely furnished and rarely used, as Malik and I did our best to leave our work at our offices.

I still didn't have much in the way of clues. According to police records, a few people claimed to have seen Geraldine and Sally enter a dark, early 1950s sedan on the days of their disappearances. One person speculated that the car was a Chevy 210—one of the most popular vehicles on the road at the time, according to Google—but neither of the people who made these reports was sure of what they'd seen. And police never seemed to treat these as leads worthy of chasing.

I turned my attention to the forums and websites frequented by true crime fanatics and internet sleuths. Entering these sites was like stepping back in time, thanks to their clunky navigation, antiquated fonts, and colorful backgrounds. But some of the posts about unsolved murders and disappearances received hundreds of comments, and thousands of views.

I scanned the headlines of the first few entries in a forum called "Murdered and Missing":

NASHVILLE SIBLINGS VANISHED SIX YEARS APART IN THE '80S
647 Comments. 4,231 Views

BRENDA LEWIS DISAPPEARED FROM HER RHODE ISLAND TOWN
IN 1976. TWO DAYS LATER, HER HUSBAND WENT MISSING
215 Comments. 1,502 Views

I attempted to tap my rusty crime reporter skills as I drafted a post of my own:

SIX BLACK GIRLS WENT MISSING FROM RALEIGH IN THE MID-1960S.
WHY HAVEN'T THEY BEEN FOUND?

I described what I knew so far about the girls and their disappearances. I re-created the grid of photos, names, and ambitions from the back of the yearbook Eloise gave me, adding the details I'd pieced together from the police reports about their last known whereabouts. I copied and pasted the post into the forums of the most popular true crime sites I could find, along with a new email address I created for people to submit their tips.

I was pleasantly surprised by how quickly and easily I was able to assemble the post. It turned out that while my reporting skills hadn't been used in quite some time, they weren't the least bit rusty after all.

When I finished, I leaned back in the office chair and gazed at my aunt's photo.

"No matter what happens," I said, clutching my heating pad against my raging belly, "you're not a secret anymore, Aunt Carol."

ON MONDAY MORNING, I SAT on a butterscotch leather couch in one of the lounges at my office. I needed a location with a wall to my back so I could freely scroll through the true crime message boards without worrying about someone seeing my screen. There were already dozens of comments on my posts, though none seemed particularly helpful.

A Slack notification popped up on my laptop screen. It was from my boss, our CEO:

Hey Syd, is there a briefing doc for this Fast Company call?

"Shit," I hissed under my breath. I glanced at the time. It was 10:52; she was speaking with a reporter at 11:00, taking the call from home. She always expected to receive a document with background information and suggested talking points at least an hour ahead of an interview. I scrambled to find the draft the PR agency had sent me to review hours earlier. I quickly skimmed it to make sure there weren't any glaring errors before sending it to her.

So sorry about the delay! The doc is attached; I'll be on the call to facilitate intros and take notes.

I could feel the icy irritation in her clipped *thx.*

My cellphone vibrated with a call from a number I didn't recognize. I assumed it was the reporter; maybe she was having trouble finding the dial-in. I picked up the call as I gathered my things and scanned the office for an empty conference room.

"Hello, this is Sydney," I said, trying to keep my voice calm despite the chaos tumbling in my brain.

"Wow," a male voice exhaled. "You sound just like her."

The blood froze in my veins.

"Michael?" I scrambled into a small conference room and sealed myself inside.

The clock on the wall read 10:59. *Shit.*

"I'm impressed you were able to track me down," he said jovially.

"I had a little help along the way." The clock struck 11:00. My stomach churned. "I hate to do this, but I'm running into a meeting. Could I call you back in half an hour?"

"No problem. I'll still be doing office hours, which my students usually neglect to take advantage of." He laughed again. A professor, I realized. My mind conjured an image of a bespectacled man surrounded by stacks of books, suede patches on his thickly knit sweater. It was incongruous with the shadowy, suspicious placeholder that had loomed large in my mind since Raleigh.

"Thank you so much," I said, dropping my things onto the white laminate table and reaching for the speaker phone.

I could barely focus during the *Fast Company* interview. Fortunately it was a softball story about trends in the wellness consumer goods space. I found myself watching the spinning second hand on the clock. My stomach twisted further as every minute passed; what if Michael got cold feet before I was able to call him back? What if his sister was able to convince him not to talk to me while I was sitting on this conference call?

I'd wanted to take a few minutes to gather myself before talking to Michael, but I was so wound up that I chucked all preparation to the side and dialed the second the interview was over. He greeted me after just one ring.

"So," Michael began after the requisite pleasantries, "you asked if I knew Carol Singleton." He took a long, deep breath. "I loved your aunt Carol, Sydney. Very much."

My stomach flipped. My hunch had been right; he was the Michael from Carol's diary. And it sounded like his feelings were just as strong as hers.

Something kept me from admitting to finding her diary; I wanted him to focus on sharing what he remembered of Carol instead of asking what she'd written about him. "Did you two date?" I asked, feigning ignorance.

"Well . . . sort of," Michael said. His voice had gone syrupy. He coughed, then I heard him take a drink of something. I wondered if it was water, tea, or a steadying sip of whiskey.

"See, I was a little older than Carol," Michael said. "Three years older. Which, if we were both adults, wouldn't have mattered to anyone. But when we were kids . . . well, her mother didn't approve."

He took another sip. "I haven't allowed myself to think about her in years. But when you called and left that voicemail, and your voice sounded so much like hers . . ." His voice grew thick again.

"I'm sorry to stir up these painful memories for you," I said. This was always the part I hated about my journalism days: forcing open the tender wounds of strangers.

"No," Michael replied, resolute. "I'm sorry to hear her own family kept her memory buried all this time; to think you didn't even know she'd existed until recently. Though, honestly, I can't say I'm surprised."

I wished I could see his face as he spoke, watch his expression change as the past flooded back to him.

"You see, your grandma Effie was a very proud woman. She was raising two kids on her own. In retrospect, Effie must have struggled so much, working multiple nursing shifts to provide for the family, keeping the house up, keeping two kids out of trouble. I'm a father myself now, so when I look back at things, I see it all in a different light. But at the time, I just thought Effie was plain ol' mean. Especially when it came to Carol. Probably because Carol was such a strong-willed free spirit." Michael gave an amused grunt. "It was as though Effie gave birth to her total opposite."

My mind swam with questions, but fortunately Michael didn't seem to need me to ask any of them; the story spilled out of him like grains from a punctured bag of rice.

"I'd known Carol since we were both young; our mothers had been close for years. She was just this little thing running around the house whenever my mom dragged me over to their place for a visit. I'd never given her a second thought. During my senior year of high school, Carol was a freshman. Just before Christmas, the school put on a production of *The Wizard of Oz*. Carol was cast as Dorothy, which was quite a feat—typically that lead role would go to a junior or senior. Just goes to show you how talented and determined she was."

A soft laugh escaped his lips. "When she wandered around that slice of stage-prop farmland, belting out 'Somewhere over the Rainbow' in that blue dress . . . well, I think I fell in love with her right then. The way she commanded the auditorium, all that confidence, and the richness of her voice hitting you right in your feelings . . . I was a goner."

I remembered Carol's diary entry about this, how Michael wooed her for days after the performance by taping roses to her locker door. *I don't think anyone has ever truly cherished me before*, she'd said. *And I didn't realize how much I needed to feel that way until I experienced it.*

"I started walking her home from school every day after that," Michael said. "It was the only time we could be alone. Her mama would be away at work, and her little brother—your father— wouldn't be home for a while longer. At first we'd take the most direct route to her house, walking at a normal pace. But as we got to know each other better, we started to stretch those walks as long as possible, wandering through the neighborhood. Little old ladies would speed past us on the sidewalks." Michael laughed again, and I found myself joining along.

"She'd tell me all about her favorite musicians. Mary Wells was her idol. You know Mary . . ." He sang a snippet of a song, endearingly off-key. "*There's nothing you could say, to tear me away from my guy.* Carol felt she and Mary were kindred spirits. Mary was young and tenacious—supposedly she walked right up to Berry Gordy in a club in Detroit and finagled an audition on the spot." Michael exhaled a *hmph*, as though an idea just occurred to him. "She told me Mary grew up not knowing her daddy, too," he added.

"Anyway, one day, we'd just got to her driveway, and I was about to kiss her on the cheek when the front door flew open. Effie stood there with one hand on her hip—just like Carol would—and the other hand grasping the doorframe to keep herself from flying at me. *Ooof*," he said, his voice shuddering, "she called me by every one of my names. 'Michael Eugene Hall Jr., get your narrow behind away from my daughter!'" Michael chuckled. "I was sure by the time I got home, my mother would be sitting there by the phone ready to give me an earful. But she just patted me on the shoulder, smiling like she was trying not to laugh at the whole thing, and said, 'Best to stick to girls your own age, Michael.'"

"I have a feeling you didn't take your mom's advice," I said.

"I couldn't help myself," Michael replied. "I'd never met someone with so much spirit, so much life inside her. So we started sneaking around. She'd spend time with me up the road at Shaw whenever she could. We'd talk for hours, about our dreams for the future, my frustrations at school, her difficulties with her mama, what life would be like when we left Raleigh."

"Did you both plan to go to Detroit?" I asked.

Michael sighed. "Well, that was our main point of contention. Carol was dead set on moving there. But an uncle of mine was a lawyer with a firm in Oakland, and he wanted to carve out a role for me. I'd done a couple internships during the summers there. They had a bunch of Black lawyers, and there was this amazing energy to the place. And Oakland in the sixties, my God . . . especially for a boy from Raleigh, seeing all those beautiful Black people with their proud Afros and slick outfits walking around in the California sunshine. . . . I had to be there.

"At first, when leaving felt theoretical and way off in the future, we could just agree to disagree on the subject," he continued. "But by the time Carol was a junior in high school, things started to speed up. She was fed up with her mama's strict ways. Carol said that Mary Wells had signed her deal with Motown at seventeen, and she dreamed of doing the same. I was trying to convince her to run away with me to California. I wanted to transfer to a school out there and intern at my uncle's firm while studying for my law degree. I told her that she'd be within driving distance of L.A., and all the record companies and studios down there, even though I knew how long of a drive that actually was."

I heard the sound of a fingernail clinking on glass through the phone. Now I definitely pictured a crystal tumbler of amber liquid in Michael's hand. I tried not to think about my father's predilection for scotch.

"Honestly, though, I was just being selfish," Michael said. "I wanted her, and I wanted my vision for the future, and I didn't want to compromise. She was so desperate to get out of her mama's house that at one point I got her to agree to come to California with me. But as we approached the date we were supposed to leave, she started to have second thoughts. She didn't want to be the kind of woman who threw her dreams away for a man, no matter how much she loved him. We fought about it the last time I saw her. At first, when I stopped hearing from her, I thought she was just done with me."

I couldn't stop myself from sighing in frustration; here was yet another person who claimed to love Carol but gave up on her completely the moment they assumed she'd left them.

"I've been going through all the old police records," I said. "There are missing person reports for a bunch of the girls. I can't believe Grammy didn't file a police report for Carol. Even if she was mad at her for taking off."

There was a long pause on the line. "Even if Effie never filed a report, surely you found mine?"

All the heat seemed to evaporate from my body. Michael filed a missing person report for Carol? If that was true, what happened to it? Why wasn't it in the digital police records?

"No," I told him. "There's no report on record for Carol."

"Huh," he said. "I wasn't too keen on the police at the time— Black teenage boys have long been the disproportionate victims of police brutality, mind you—but I was desperate. After three days of not hearing from her, I stopped by her house when I knew her mother would be at work so I could talk to Larry. He's the one who told me she'd ran." Michael must have leaned back in his chair; the sound of springs creaking under new weight filtered through the phone. "Sydney—I never stopped looking for your aunt. Hell, I moved to Detroit to try to find her."

"Wait," I said, confused. "You're in Detroit?"

Michael laughed, but it was a mournful sound. "I was miserable in Oakland without her. I didn't know how to get ahold of her, so I decided to come out myself. I went to all the live music spots, thinking I'd catch her onstage, or enjoying a show out in the crowd. I went through the phone book and dialed the handful of Carol Singletons listed. I even hired a private detective to try and track her down. I did everything I could think of to find her. Pathetic, right?"

"No . . . it's actually really romantic. Like something out of a movie."

"I've never been able to forget about Carol. I even still have her old trunk of things she kept at my apartment at Shaw. I haven't been able to part with it, after all this time." Michael took a sharp breath, as though surprised by something. "Oh my goodness, Sydney, I've been blabbering on so long, I'm going to be late to teach my next class."

There was a sound of rustling papers, as though he was shoving a stack of graded blue books into a satchel. "Listen, if you ever find yourself in Detroit, I'd be happy to share Carol's things with you. Haven't opened that trunk in years. Still smarts to think about her, if I'm honest. But to have a member of Carol's bloodline in my home . . . I imagine it's the closest I'll get to seeing her again."

FOURTEEN

That night, I insisted on making dinner. It was the first time in a long while that I researched a new recipe, made a special trip to the grocery store instead of scrounging for ingredients we had on hand, and set the dining table instead of the coffee table.

Malik's eyes sparkled when he saw the thick bone-in pork chops, herb garlic asparagus, and mashed sweet potatoes whipped with butter and baking spices.

"How was your day?" I asked as I poured him a virgin Moscow mule.

"Busy," Malik answered, easily slicing through the juicy meat with his knife. "We were finally able to launch some of the new products delayed by that regulatory fire drill, and the press coverage so far has been really positive."

"That's amazing, sweetheart."

Malik tilted his head from side to side, his face scrunched with uncertainty. "We'll see. A bit of good press won't completely distract our investors from our competitor's mess, but it can't hurt. How about you? What was the highlight of your day?"

The memory of my misstep with the *Fast Company* interview washed over me, but I shook it away. "I actually heard back from Michael. It turns out, not only were he and Carol secretly dating for years, he actually filed a missing person report for her when she disappeared. Seems like he was the only person in her life who cared enough to look for her."

"Whoa," Malik said, his brows lifting in surprise. "Wait, I thought you said there wasn't a report for Carol in your files?"

"There isn't. That's where things get really weird. After I hung up with Michael, I went back through all the police records again. I decided to take a closer look at Sally's records, since she and Carol were friends, and they went missing within three months of each other. In the middle of a call log with tips about Sally, there's this one cryptic line: 'Y. Hall cancels report on C.S., citing conversation on 5/25/65.' May twenty-fifth was eleven days after Carol went missing. And 'Y. Hall' has to be Yvonne Hall. Malik—I think Michael's sister retracted Carol's missing person report but never told Michael about it."

Malik's brows rose even farther. "Why would she do that?"

"I don't know. It must have something to do with that fight they had at Shaw shortly before Carol disappeared. Yvonne's being way too cagey for me to ask her about it, but I bet Michael would tell me what they were fighting about."

"Do you think Yvonne had something to do with Carol's disappearance?"

I shrugged. "She has to be connected. I mean, why would she be so secretive if she had nothing to hide? Michael was really open with me on the phone today; I feel like I can get more out of him. Apparently he's even kept a trunk of Carol's belongings all this time at his house in Detroit, and he offered to share it with me, if I'm ever out there." I paused, tracing fissures into my sweet potatoes with my fork. "I was thinking about flying out there this weekend."

Malik made an incredulous sound. "Sydney—you can't be serious. Isn't this the same guy you thought had something to do with your aunt's disappearance, like, two days ago? And now you want to fly all the way to Detroit to meet him at his house?"

"His story makes sense to me," I said, shrugging. "Anyway, why would he want to talk to me if he had something to do with Carol's disappearance? It would have been so easy for him to have just ignored my call."

"I don't know." Malik sighed.

"Malik, I don't think Grammy even tried to look for Carol. And I know my father was only fourteen at the time, but I don't think he ever tried to find her either, even after he grew up. Someone in this family has to try. I have to do something."

I gritted my teeth. I wanted to be annoyed by Malik's overprotectiveness. But if I were honest with myself, I could see he had a good reason to worry.

In the days following the discovery of the McEwan crash site, I repeatedly thought I spotted Hannah in various places throughout the city. In the feminine care aisle at Target, I did a double take at a bored blond girl thumbing an iPhone while her mother compared boxes of tampons. I nearly dropped my cappuccino when another blond child ran past me in the Ferry Building Marketplace. My head whipped around, eyes scanning the faces of the shoppers and tourists, searching for her pursuer. But the girl came to a stop at Miette Patisserie and turned back to grin at the parents who trailed behind her, pointing at a glossy pink macaron behind a glass case.

I knew it was impossible, of course. Hannah's body and the bodies of her siblings had been positively identified at the crash site.

At least, at first I knew it was impossible. But at some point, my mind began to question whether this was fact.

"Malik . . . I think I need this," I admitted. "This part of the IVF cycle really sucks. I feel like a walking science experiment. It's like I'm not a person anymore. I'm just a womb, an incubator. My schedule isn't mine, my diet isn't mine, my body damn sure isn't mine. And there are no guarantees, just all these shots, and all this waiting—"

My voice cracked, surprising us both. I was annoyed by my tears, yet another thing beyond my control. Malik reached for my hand; I blotted my eyes with the other.

"This might sound crazy, but looking into what happened to Carol and the girls . . . I've felt more like myself these last few weeks than I have in a long, long time," I continued. "It feels so good to have something I can do right now, something I can work toward that isn't dictated by doctors. Something that's mine. Where I can make a real difference. And I'm still so good at it, Malik. Look at all I've been able to learn already; imagine what more I can uncover if I go to Detroit and talk to Michael face-to-face. We're not expecting to hear back from the clinic for a while, so leaving for a weekend wouldn't disrupt anything."

Malik stroked my fingers; his eyes were filled with sympathy tears. "I didn't know you were feeling this way."

"I don't think I fully realized I was feeling this way either," I said, sniffling.

"I haven't fully appreciated how hard all this must be on you," he said. "Not completely. I know I offer to go to just about every appointment with you, but you're the one who actually has to go. To rearrange your schedule constantly, and feel every symptom, and be on the receiving end of all those injections."

He squeezed my hand tenderly. "I've always loved how passionate you are," he continued. "How you throw yourself into a project that interests you. It made me feel like you understood why I was so consumed with Wealthmate back when most of my friends didn't get it. I don't think I really considered how IVF has impacted the time and energy you would typically put toward all the things you're passionate about."

A current of emotion surged through me, tickling my already raw tear ducts. I hadn't realized how much I longed to hear Malik say those words, to show that he recognized the sacrifices I was making for us, for our potential family.

"You should go to Detroit, if it's this important to you," he said.

"But I don't want you to go alone. And I'm slammed with work right now; I have at least eighteen hours' worth of shit I need to get done this weekend."

The answer occurred to me out of nowhere, fully formed. But it would require another uncomfortable conversation I wasn't ready to have.

"What if Sasha came with me?"

AN HOUR LATER, WITH ANOTHER thirty minutes to kill before my scheduled shots, I applied a sheet mask and tried to focus on a new episode of *The Unforgotten*, my favorite true crime podcast. But my thoughts kept returning to my conversation with Malik at dinner, and the cause of his concerns—the McEwan case.

For weeks after the mangled van was discovered, I managed to hide my growing suspicion that Hannah's father had manufactured the crash site, and that he was still on the run with a frightened Hannah in tow. I somehow kept up with my work and social obligations, subbing the late nights I'd once spent combing through Lisa McEwan's blog with hours spent searching the internet, old news stories, and true crime blogs for past examples of people faking their own deaths, building my case.

That is, until one Sunday when Malik and I waited in line for brunch at a trendy Potrero Hill restaurant that didn't accept reservations. As we stood on the sidewalk beside a dozen others and hungrily waited for our names to be called, a sleek silver Audi driven by a scowling white man rolled by. In the backseat was a crying blond girl, and every cell in my body believed it was Hannah. I began screaming at the top of my lungs, pointing frantically at the car. Everyone waiting on the sidewalk and on the other side of the restaurant's massive picture windows gawked at me as I pleaded with Malik to call the police, shouting that Hannah was alive, that we could save her.

I didn't understand why everyone just stood there, staring at me. I didn't understand why Malik begged me to calm down, his eyes as wide and frightened as those of a startled deer. I was relieved when

I finally heard sirens approaching, believing the police were arriving to take my statement. But I was confused when an ambulance pulled to a stop beside the restaurant instead, and I began to scream louder when the paramedics coaxed me toward the gaping back doors of the idling vehicle. I don't remember when they eventually sedated me; I just remember seeing the tears streaming down Malik's face before everything faded to black.

Trying to recall details of the first few days I spent in the Acute and Emergency Services division of the UCSF Medical Center's Psychiatry Department was like trying to see through the viewfinder of a camera with a fingerprint-smudged lens; everything was smeared and blurry. It was probably due to the cocktail of antipsychotic medications prescribed to me. But I do remember that Malik never left my side. I had a hazy recollection of a few friends' faces in my sterile, beige room. I suspected, and later confirmed, that my mother "couldn't get away" from L.A. to see how I was doing.

I also recalled Dr. Kapoor's steadying presence, her voice like chamomile, her hand warm on my shoulder. Toward the end of my eight-day hospital stay, during yet another talk therapy session, Dr. Kapoor told me that what I experienced was known as "brief psychotic disorder with obvious stressor," a reaction to the stress of the disturbing McEwan case, exacerbated by "repressed childhood trauma."

"Most people who develop BPD only have a single incident, and don't experience any additional symptoms," Dr. Kapoor said, her brown eyes soft.

"And the others?" I asked warily.

Dr. Kapoor folded her long, slim fingers atop her desk. "BPD is officially among the schizophrenia spectrum of illnesses. But given the speed of your recovery, and the circumstances leading up to your symptoms, I don't believe this is something you need to worry about."

I tried to let her words act as a salve for my jangled nerves, and my newfound mistrust in my own mind. But it's difficult to hear the word "schizophrenia" and not feel some level of concern.

For years, I'd blamed my father's increasingly erratic behavior on his excessive alcohol consumption, likely spurred by his insistence on staying in a miserable marriage. But after my brush with BPD, I began to wonder if I'd gotten the cause-and-effect order wrong; maybe his mercurial moods were already present within him, and he used alcohol in a misguided attempt to regulate them. Maybe he secretly struggled with his mental health all along.

As I later learned, some mental health disorders, including schizophrenia, could be hereditary. Maybe he'd unknowingly passed his disorder on to me. And if I had children, maybe I'd pass it on to them, too.

It was a nagging fear I continued to work through with Dr. Dominguéz. "While it's impossible for me to accurately diagnose anyone in absentia, based on what you've told me about your father, I don't believe he exhibited the markers of schizophrenia," she'd said in a recent session. "It's also important to note that the vast, vast majority of people living with schizophrenia are not violent, and never pose a threat to themselves or others."

She'd looked at me as though she wished it were appropriate to hug me. "Based on all my conversations with you, and all the notes from your doctors in San Francisco, I continue to agree with your original diagnosis that your experience will be isolated to a single occurrence. And that continuing to heal your past traumas and address your tendency to repress painful experiences will only make you stronger. There's no reason for you to think that you'll pass something down to your future child."

I wanted to believe her. But once you lose trust in your own mind, it's incredibly difficult to rebuild it.

I never returned to my job at the *Chronicle*. After checking out of UCSF, I spent the rest of my twelve-week mental health leave going to therapy, taking long, meandering hikes through Muir Woods, and applying for lifestyle-focused PR jobs in L.A.; Malik and I were both ready to leave San Francisco. I needed a role where my reporting experience would be appreciated but where the highest stakes involved would be whether we'd gotten as much press coverage for our frivolous, nonessential products as our competitors got for theirs.

After years of pouring so much of myself into reporting, there was something freeing about a role that made it easier to compartmentalize my work and personal lives, and demanded far less of my emotional energy. And yet, tracking down Michael and discovering that his sister had rescinded Michael's missing person report reminded me how deliciously satisfying my journalism career once was. And it was impossible to ignore that while I was good at PR, I was excellent at investigations.

The timer on my phone blared, reminding me to peel my ghoulish sheet mask from my face. I massaged the remaining serum into my skin as I brainstormed how I'd broach my idea with Sasha.

It had been just over a week since our ugly fight in our mother's kitchen. It wasn't unusual for us to go several days without speaking, but given how badly our last conversation had ended, this silence felt charged.

Now that the frustration of that conversation had subsided, I could see where she was coming from. That maybe she was happy with how she was living her life, and how nearly every time I spoke to her, I made it clear that I thought she should change. Even if my heart was in the right place, and even if her continuing to live with our mother at her age didn't seem healthy to me, I could see how much it would hurt to be on the receiving end of my constant disapproval.

I was reminded of a heartbreaking line from Carol's journal, referencing her fraught relationship with Grammy: *Why do I have to change who I am to make her love me?*

I just wish Sasha knew how hard it was to be in my shoes, watching from afar as she let year after year slip away, hiding in our mother's home in this prolonged state of adolescence instead of building and experiencing a life of her own.

Maybe going on this trip and investigating our missing aunt together was exactly what we needed to help us reforge the bond I'd once considered indestructible.

I swallowed my pride and texted her a mea culpa.

Maybe going on this trip was also what I needed to prove to myself once and for all that my brush with BPD was, in fact, an isolated incident. It had been nearly ten years since I'd checked out of UCSF. Ten years of therapy. Ten years without a relapse. I'd be able to recognize any warning signs this time. I'd know if the firm lines of reality began to blur. This time would be different.

FIFTEEN

SASHA CRACKED THE PASSENGER WINDOW OF OUR RENTED SUV open; the early morning air was crisp and clean. I cracked mine too, willing the breeze to bring me fully awake. I wouldn't have felt rested if I'd managed to sleep through every minute of our four-and-a-half-hour red-eye to Detroit.

"I always forget how flat other parts of the country are," I murmured, staring out at the endless expanse of gray freeway.

"Yeah, but look at these trees!" Sasha exclaimed, staring out her window. It was mid-October in Michigan, and the crowns of the trees burned scarlet and amber, in startling contrast to the slate blue sky. "Now I get why people who aren't from L.A. complain about missing seasons," she said.

TV shows and news coverage about Detroit tended to focus on its ruined parts. And sure, as we hurtled downtown we saw some signs of decay. Periodically, as we scanned the residential streets above the freeway, we'd spot the charred remains of a house nestled among those still standing, as though a vengeful god had selected houses at random with a finger of fire.

But the freeway emptied us onto a stretch of road flanked by handsome skyscrapers, including the collection of dark cylinders that appeared in every photo of the city's skyline. The Detroit River lapped at the shoreline behind it. Canada stood just on the other side of the shimmering water, close enough that we could easily read the signs on their largest waterfront buildings. The city seemed lively and energetic, bustling with a pride and sense of possibility that those TV stories seemed to have overlooked.

Our boutique hotel had once been an old firehouse, and the 1920s brick architecture had been beautifully restored. The giant arched doorways through which fire trucks once raced remained intact, though the large red doors now served as shutters for the dramatic picture windows of the restaurant on the hotel's ground floor.

I'd made a point of finding one of the most stunning hotels in the city and including its website in my text to Sasha proposing this trip. I knew an all-expenses-paid travel experience with luxury accommodations would increase her likelihood of accepting my offer. I'd worried that things would be awkward and frigid between us, but I'd forgotten that our childhood had made us both experts at brushing aside and ignoring familial tension. I felt a bit sick at the thought that this trip was my version of sending her a bouquet of Stargazer lilies.

Mercifully, my request for an early check-in was granted, and Sasha and I took turns in the sleek subway-tiled shower before heading back out for the primary mission of our trip—meeting Michael.

As we neared his address, we turned onto a tree-lined boulevard with a wide, lushly lawned median slicing through its center. The Boston-Edison Historic District of Detroit was populated with brick homes built in the early 1900s, many with alluring Tudor details, set back from the street to allow for the kinds of expansive front yards that were rare in most of L.A. Some boasted historical placards for the famous folks who previously called them home: Henry Ford, Joe Louis, Berry Gordy.

Michael's was a lovely two-story gingerbread house, brown

brick trimmed with cream. Even the chime of the doorbell was warm and inviting. Still, my belly was a bundle of nerves. What if I spooked Michael by bringing up my theory that Yvonne had retracted his missing person report and he closed ranks around his family, shutting me out for good? What if we learned nothing from Michael, and this entire trip was a colossal waste of time? I didn't have any time to lose; the fact that we were currently in an IVF waiting phase had been crucial in getting Malik to support this trip. I couldn't imagine him being so amenable if this cycle were to take, if we had a baby on the way.

A teenage girl opened Michael's glossy white door. His granddaughter, perhaps? She had the type of bold haircut I'd never have the confidence to pull off: an asymmetrical pixie with curly bangs that grazed her teal-lined eyes. She introduced herself as Maya and ushered us inside.

"Come in. My dad's so excited to meet you."

The surprise must have registered on my face, because the girl laughed. "I know—he's an old dad." The entryway was bright and airy, with pale wood floors and walls in shades of gray and white, like clouds.

"It smells like heaven in here," Sasha fawned.

Maya laughed again. "Yeah, I hope you're hungry. Dad insisted that Mom make you a feast."

We followed her into an expansive kitchen, where an adorable couple stood behind a giant island covered in platters of food. The man was tall and lanky, with hair and a goatee the color of dust. If his hair were darker, he could have easily passed for a much younger man—his cinnamon skin was smooth and unlined.

He had one arm around the woman standing in front of him, and one arm stretching toward a platter of golden spring rolls. The woman laughed as she swatted at his arm. It was the unabashed giggle of a young girl, though she looked to be somewhere in her fifties, at least twenty years younger than her husband. She pushed a curtain of long, glossy hair out of her face as she spotted us, her smile warm as fresh peach cobbler.

"Oh, hi, girls!" she greeted us, shaking off her partner to offer us vigorous handshakes. "Come in, come in. I'm Rosa. Do you like Filipino food? You don't have any food allergies, do you?"

"We eat everything," Sasha said, eyeing the spread gratefully.

Michael remained frozen behind the island, staring at me with an expression I couldn't quite read.

"I'm Sydney, and this is my sister, Sasha," I said, hoping to shake loose Michael's catatonic stare. When this didn't work, I turned to Rosa. "It's so nice of you to make all this for us."

"It's my pleasure," Rosa said, handing us plates. "It's so sweet of you girls to fly all the way out here to learn more about your aunt. Family is so important to us . . . It must be wild to learn about a completely new branch in your family tree after all this time." She laughed at Michael and waved a hand in front of his face. "Hellooo? What are you doing all the way over there, Mike? Come over and introduce yourself!"

"Sorry," he said, blinking as though waking from a sudden nap. "It's just . . . you look so much like her." I put out my hand to shake his as he made his way across the kitchen but was surprised when he folded me into a tight hug. When he pulled away to look at me his warm, chocolaty eyes were glossy, as though he were on the brink of tears. But then he smiled and his face glowed like a light had been turned on within, and I was instantly reminded that he was Eloise's son.

"I . . . I didn't realize your sister was coming with you," Michael said, glancing at Sasha with his hands still resting on my shoulders. His words were matter-of-fact, though I thought I detected a hint of disappointment in his voice.

"Sasha is just as curious about Carol as I am," I said.

"Plus now we get to explore Detroit together," Sasha added, as Michael lifted his hands from my shoulders to give her a quick embrace.

"We thought you all could enjoy lunch on the deck," Rosa said, walking over to Maya and bumping the girl's narrow hip with her own generous one. "You've got to enjoy days like this while you can in Michigan," she added.

"You aren't joining us?" Sasha asked as we filled our plates with fragrant, vibrantly colored food.

"We're going to see if that bake shop at Eastern Market has any more lemon butter cheesecakes, give you all a little space," Rosa said. She gestured toward Michael, a small opening and closing of her palm. Michael moved toward her, wrapped an arm around her waist, and rested his head gently on top of hers.

I felt something twist in my chest. It wasn't the house that radiated the atmosphere of love and belonging I'd felt as Maya guided us through it; it was the Hall family themselves. This was the kind of warmth a child was meant to grow up in.

Michael, Sasha, and I carried our plates out onto a red cedar deck and sat at a picnic table with a view of the pristinely manicured lawn.

"Your home and family are so lovely, Michael," I said, dipping my fork into thin fried noodles laced with cabbage, carrots, and onions.

"Thank you," he replied, his face illuminating once again with his lantern smile. "I was pushing sixty when I met Rosa; I'd resigned myself to being a lifelong bachelor before she came along." He looked at his house as though admiring it with fresh eyes. "I always told myself that if I ever had kids, I'd give them a better childhood than the one I had. I thought I wasn't going to get that chance."

I tried to keep my expression neutral. With a mother like Eloise, I didn't expect him to have such negative feelings about his upbringing.

"What did you want to do differently for your kids?" I asked.

"Be around, for one thing," he replied with a sad smile. "My father died when I was young, in Korea. Mama struggled with that for years; there was a long while there where my sister had to take on the maternal role in our family." He shook his head quickly, as though casting off the thought. "But you didn't fly out to learn more about my childhood. You want to know more about your aunt."

He turned to me, and let his eyes rest on mine for a moment before he spoke again. "I hope you don't mind, Sydney, but I couldn't help but look you up after you called. I found your Instagram—I was blown away by your resemblance to my starling . . . my Carol."

My Carol. He said the words so tenderly.

"Ohmigod, I know," Sasha said. "She looks more like Syd's sister than I do."

"If they were the same age, they could pass for twins," Michael agreed, studying my face, which was beginning to burn from all the attention.

"What's your favorite memory of Carol?" Sasha asked. I found myself smiling at her, happy I'd brought her along. It was the exact sort of question I would never think to ask. Not facts, but feelings.

Michael steepled his fingers in front of his mouth as he thought and made a soft humming sound when the right memory found him.

"Carol loved to drive. Her mother taught her, said every woman should know how, but never let her take the family car out on her own. Often when we were out together, she'd ask to drive my car. Well, technically my friend's car; he'd let me borrow it from time to time. I could never say no to her. One time she said she wanted to take me on a date. So I came up to her house while her mom was working a night shift, and when I got there Carol insisted on tying a scarf around my eyes and putting me in the passenger seat."

Michael laughed. "It was a terrifying experience. Carol would have made an excellent NASCAR driver. At some point I could tell she'd taken the car off the main road. Finally she stopped, said she'd just be a minute, and got out. When she came to let me out and untied the scarf from my eyes, I saw she'd set up a picnic for us in this field of tall grass. She'd laid out a blanket in the path of the headlights, and let the local soul station playing on the radio be our soundtrack. She said she hated that we could never be truly alone together—a friend was staying with me at Shaw and we obviously couldn't hang out at her house. So she wanted to create an outdoor room for just the two of us."

He glanced behind Sasha's and my shoulders, back at the house. "Don't tell my wife, but it's still the single most romantic thing that ever happened to me." Michael's smile glowed. It was clear how much he'd loved Carol, and how much her loss still pained him.

"You and your sister both described Aunt Carol as being very strong-willed and independent," I ventured carefully. "I imagine that kind of personality might have rubbed some people the wrong way at the time. Did it cause any issues for her, with anyone?"

Michael snorted. "Her mother, mostly. She appreciated those aspects of Carol's personality when it came to her helping around the house, and looking after Larry. But she resented how stubborn Carol was when it came to things like pursuing music over college, or disobeying her orders to stay away from me. She knew Carol was sneaking around. I know they were fighting quite a bit before she went missing. I felt bad about that, being the reason they fought. But if you'd gotten to know Carol, you'd know that there wasn't anything you could do or say once she set her mind to something."

"Speaking of fighting," I said, my adrenaline spiking, "I was talking with Stanley Dunn recently. His sister, Sally, was one of the other girls who went missing around the same time as Carol. He mentioned that he met Carol shortly before her disappearance, at a party at Shaw. He said that Carol was there with you, and that Yvonne showed up, and she and Carol got into an argument."

A grimace spread across Michael's face. "I forgot all about that night. That was very out of character for Yvonne; she's always been quite reserved, so normally a public dispute would've been out of the question. But Yvonne didn't approve of my relationship with your aunt either. Yvonne was a bit of a mama bear with me, and she had a very specific vision for our futures. She didn't want us to struggle with money the way we sometimes had growing up. She dreamed of us both becoming successful lawyers, and maybe even opening our own firm together one day. She thought Carol was a negative influence on me; my grades slipped a bit toward the end of college, and she blamed Carol for it. That's what they argued about; Yvonne was home from Howard for a visit. She intercepted my grades at Mama's house and flipped her lid. She forbade Carol from seeing me."

"Did Carol listen?" Sasha asked.

"In a sense." He sighed. "It was one of the last times I saw her. But I think that's only because in our final conversation, we fought about which city we were running away to. I figured Carol was done with all of us after that, and ran off to chase her dreams alone."

"But you filed a missing person report," I said, "even though you thought she ran away?"

Michael lifted his hands. "I was desperate to find her. I had no way of getting in touch with her to apologize and make things right between us."

"There wasn't any part of you that worried something bad might have happened to her, given that several other girls disappeared around that time?" I asked.

"No," Michael said adamantly. "It's like I tell my law students, 'When you hear hoofbeats, think horses, not zebras.' We were actively talking about running away, Sydney. It's the most logical explanation for what happened to her."

He stared thoughtfully at the pine trees bordering his lawn; they made a gentle swishing sound in the breeze. "You two grew up in a different time," he said. "All that hysteria around 'stranger danger' didn't really start till the eighties. There was no evidence that anything nefarious happened to those girls."

"And you never heard from her, or heard of anyone communicating with her after your last conversation in Raleigh?" I asked.

Michael shook his head somberly. I took a deep breath and pulled my phone from my pocket. "I was going through the police records for the missing girls, and I found something strange," I said. I zoomed in on the call log so the damning line was centered on the screen: Y. HALL CANCELS REPORT ON C.S. . . .

I handed the phone to Michael, and his eyes locked immediately on the relevant text. He seemed to read it again and again, but his expression remained stoic, indecipherable. He handed the phone back to me. "I'm not sure what that means."

Something inside of me deflated. I'd been so sure he would have been just as confused by the note as I was. "The report was canceled eleven days after Carol went missing," I pressed gently. "Did you . . . did your sister happen to know that you filed a report for Carol?"

There was an air of dismissal in Michael's half smile. "My sister was hardly the only 'Y. Hall' in Raleigh at the time. Carol could've even called to cancel the report herself, in an attempt to stay hidden. Maybe she dropped my sister's name as a final 'screw you' to me, and I just never got the message."

I wanted to toss his words back at him — horses, not zebras — but I restrained myself.

"Did you know any of the other girls who went missing around that time?" I asked. He shook his head vaguely, his eyes searching the sky as though trying to remember their names, so I named them: "Marian, Bettie, Geraldine, Loretta, Sally?"

"Can't say that I did. I mean, I was a few years ahead of them all in school."

"Not even Sally? She and Carol were friends. Stanley said she went to parties at Shaw, too."

Michael scrunched his nose. "I'm sorry . . . no. I knew of the girls, and may have seen some of them around, but I didn't know them." He took in the disappointment on my and Sasha's faces. "What I can share, though, is your aunt's trunk. Come on," he said, rising to his feet. "Let's go take a look."

Michael led us back through the house and into his study, where he kept Carol's things. It was a small dark room surrounded by bookshelves bursting with books, photos, and trinkets.

Michael went to an ancient steamer trunk standing on its side in the corner of the room. It looked like a decorative object purchased at a vintage shop, with cracked nut-brown leather and tarnished brass closures.

"This was Carol's," he said, stroking the top of the trunk gently, as one might an old, fragile pet. "She wanted something to store a few of her things in at my place, at Shaw."

He clicked the brass latches open and pulled the two sides apart, revealing a small wardrobe in a faded white-and-brown floral print, with a hanging rod on one side and a series of drawers on the other. There were a few articles of clothing on wooden hangers: a pale blue dress, a yellowed white blouse in delicate dotted swiss, and a kelly green skirt.

"Wow," Sasha exhaled as we knelt in front of it. "It's like a time capsule." She carefully slid the top drawer open; inside was a neat stack of 45s in crinkly old sleeves with holes in the middle to display their labels. Several had MOTOWN written across the top in a blocky rainbow font, bearing names like Mary Wells and the Marvelettes.

"I kept trying to get rid of it, but I just couldn't bear to do it. I've lugged that thing around with me every time I've moved."

He chuckled soberly and slid his hands into the pockets of his jeans. "That's why I asked if you had any plans to come to Detroit, Sydney. It's like I've been the sole archivist of a very small museum all this time, and I've grown too attached to my job."

He rubbed the flank of the trunk lovingly. "If you'd like it, you're welcome to take it with you. I'm sorry I made you come out all this way for it."

My heart swelled. "That would mean so much to me."

"Now, it's pretty heavy, and I wouldn't trust those old leather handles anymore. I've got a hand dolly in the basement. I'll go grab it for you girls," he said, leaving us in the study.

My knees, stiff from my lifelong running habit, began to ache from squatting in front of the trunk. Now that I knew it was ours, I allowed myself to wander around Michael's bookshelves, scanning the innumerable spines, framed diplomas, teaching awards, and photos.

There was a framed photograph beside Michael's degree from Shaw. It was a faded sepia-toned image of a group of young men, some in letterman jackets with block S's for Shaw on the front, leaning against the hood of a car. A dark sedan. A Chevy; its front reminded me of a catfish, its headlights like a pair of wide-set eyes, its grille a silver-toothed grimace.

My heart caught in my throat.

"Here we go," Michael said, materializing in the doorway, wheeling a metal handcart behind him.

"Who are all these guys?" I asked, pointing at the photograph.

Michael came over to me and peered at the image. "Ah, those are my old road dogs from college. That's me and my teammates Perry and Douglas in the letterman jackets; we played basketball together at Shaw. That's Raymond making that goofy face, and Luke in the glasses."

"Is that . . . a Chevy 210?" I asked.

Michael gaped at me in happy surprise. "Do we have a gearhead in our midst? You sure you aren't from Detroit?" He laughed. "That's right, a Chevy 210. Popular ride at the time."

"Whose car was it?"

"Oh, that would be Raymond's. Raymond Green. He wasn't in school with us anymore by that point, but he managed to stick close to campus by offering us rides everywhere—to parties, to the store. It was actually kind of sad."

"Why was it sad?"

"Well, Ray had it tough growing up. His parents died when we were all really young. Car accident, I think. One of his relatives moved into his parents' place to help take care of him. They didn't have a lot of money and he was always running around in old worn clothes that didn't fit right, especially since he was so tall and skinny. Kids used to call him Scarecrow. When he got a little older he got to be a halfway decent athlete, but he wasn't much of a student and regularly got himself in trouble for academic reasons. That's why he lost his scholarship to Shaw after freshman year. But he still wore his letterman jacket to parties, hoping to impress girls who didn't know he wasn't on the team. He just couldn't let it go and move on to something else."

"Are you in touch with him?"

"No." Michael exhaled, his hands retreating to his pockets. "A lot of us avoided the draft just by being college students. But Ray, being a young, healthy college dropout, was a prime candidate. He always talked about how he'd become a Canadian before he'd go to 'Nam. It was pretty easy to get Canadian citizenship if you were a young American back then. When he stopped hanging around, I figured he finally made good on his promise and headed north."

"When was the last time you saw him?"

"A lifetime ago." Michael sighed. "Can't recall exactly. But that picture is special to me because it was right before a lot of us started to head our separate ways. It was a different time. There was no social media, or email addresses, or digital footprints of any kind. It was incredibly easy to lose touch with people."

He began to count the ways on his fingers. "I had friends like me who were eager to leave Raleigh and went off to New York and Chicago and New Orleans. Vietnam took a lot of people I knew. A bunch of folks got really involved in the Civil Rights Movement, and left home to do it." He shook his head. "I haven't thought about so many of them in so long."

"Have you tried reconnecting with some of them on social media since then?" Sasha asked.

"Some of them, here and there." Michael chuckled. "Folks my age aren't always as eager to put our lives online as your generation." He picked up the frame and turned it over, sliding the small latch that held the backing in place. "Let me see if I wrote the date on here; sometimes I'd do that." He looked down at the faded handwriting on the back of the photo. "March 1965."

"Two months before Carol disappeared."

"Suppose so."

Michael placed the frame back on its shelf. I stared at Raymond's face. It was long and narrow like the rest of him, with high cheekbones that made me uncomfortably aware of the skull beneath his flesh.

"You know, a few people thought they saw two of the missing

girls get into a dark sedan on the days of their disappearances," I said. "One even thought it was a Chevy 210."

Michael gave me a look as though I was a small child about to have her bubble burst. "My Maya is obsessed with *Law & Order* reruns. In the span of one hour, an entire mystery is solved, usually with just the smallest bit of evidence. But I can tell you from my years as a lawyer that it rarely works that way. Sometimes a missing person is just someone who wanted to start a new life somewhere else. And sometimes a suspicious vehicle is just a regular old car driving through a neighborhood. Seeing a 210 then would be like seeing a Prius now."

"No, I know," I said halfheartedly. "Still . . . would you mind if I take a quick picture of the photo, just in case?"

Michael smiled at me, a bit wearily, but maybe also a bit impressed by my persistence. "Knock yourself out."

November 20, 1964

Today's Song: "Don't Let Me Be Misunderstood"

Mama knows.

I don't know how she learned me and Michael are planning on running away next summer, but she knows.

Did Larry overhear me and Michael talking, and tell her about it? Did she find this journal?? I'd better find a new hiding spot for it just in case.

Sometimes I think Mama was never a teenage girl. Or if she was, she must've been such a square. Control and discipline are not the same thing as love. Why can't she understand that?

She said I'm already throwing my life away by refusing to go to college, why can't I at least wait til I get my high school degree?

But I pointed out that four girls my age have gone missing from our neighborhood in the past year, three of which before graduating from Ligon. If the rumors are true, if there is a "Creek Killer" stalking girls in Raleigh, isn't that more reason for me to leave? Isn't that more reason not to delay my dreams?

It was probably the worst fight me and Mama ever had. I'm sure the neighbors heard us. . . . Mama must hate that. She sent me to bed without dinner, like a child.

I waited until I heard her go to bed, and then I planned to sneak out to Michael's for the night. I had to get out of that house. Thank goodness I already have a trunk of things at his place for just this occasion.

But just as I was climbing out of my bedroom window, Larry walked in with a plate of dinner that he'd saved for me. I don't think I'll ever forget the look of betrayal on his face.

I told him I would be back in the morning, I just needed to cool off for a bit. He threw the plate across the room and slammed the door behind him. It was a miracle Mama didn't wake. I cleaned up the mess and rode to Michael's.

It's been four days, and Larry's still barely said a word to me. He's still only thirteen, more kid than teenager. He'll get it when he's my age. Unless Mama's different with him, less strict. That's definitely possible—he is a boy, after all.

Michael felt bad that Larry was so upset—he sent me home with a whole box of those new Pop-Tarts Larry loves so much and Mama refuses to spend money on. That softened Larry up a bit, but he still doesn't look at me the way he used to.

Maybe he does know that I'm leaving him soon . . .

SIXTEEN

THAT NIGHT, SASHA AND I SAT AT A RESTAURANT ON THE seventy-first floor of Michigan's tallest building, staring down at the sparkling lights of the city and the shoreline of Windsor, Ontario, beyond. The Detroit River flowed below us, dark and brooding.

"I know you think something awful happened to Carol," Sasha began thoughtfully, "but isn't there a chance she did just run away to start a new life somewhere, like Michael said?"

I absently fingered the bottle of cab franc perched on the table; it was likely the last time I'd be able to imbibe before an embryo would be placed inside me, provided Malik and I had a healthy, fertilized embryo waiting for us. Sasha and I were sharing the bottle of wine, though she'd also ordered a vodka soda with our appetizers and nodded when our server asked if she'd like another when our entrées arrived.

"If five other girls hadn't gone missing around the same time, I might be more hopeful," I replied. "Anyway, it all just feels too strange and meaningful to be a coincidence—Yvonne straight-up lied to me when I asked if she knew any Michaels Carol might have dated. She conveniently neglected to mention that she fought with Carol shortly before she went missing. And seeing that one of Michael's friends drove the exact same car two of the girls were reportedly last seen getting into . . . it's hard to believe it isn't all connected somehow."

"Yeah," Sasha admitted. "It's all pretty weird."

"Also, there's something so severe about running off and never speaking to anyone from your old life again," I went on. "Even if Carol's relationships with Michael and Grammy were so bad that she didn't want them in her life anymore, it sounds like she was too close to Dad to do that to him. And even if she wanted to keep her distance for a little while, I don't get why she wouldn't reach out to him at all, ever, once they were older."

Despite the confidence of my words, I felt my certainty wobble as I said them. I thought about my fight with Sasha in our mother's kitchen, and the icy stalemate that had stretched between us until I reached out to suggest this trip. How long would we have gone without speaking if I hadn't needed her to accompany me to Detroit, to alleviate Malik's concerns? What if our fight had been more vicious, our words more regrettable? Maybe we were also just one bad fight away from becoming strangers.

Sasha nodded slowly, as though she was having trouble believing me, too. "You're probably right." She sipped from her wineglass, holding it delicately by the stem, as though practicing a gesture she'd only seen in movies. I realized we'd never done this before— dined together at a restaurant, just the two of us. I'd never asked her to do this before. I'd been too stubborn, too annoyed by the fact that I'd have to pick up the tab, too resentful that I'd have to stick to our script of approved topics or risk our spending the meal in awkward silence.

Maybe this dinner, and this trip, could be the start of a new tradition for us. Maybe by getting Sasha alone, outside of our mother's house, and spending time beyond our forced family dinners would help us create a new, healthier, more honest relationship. Maybe doing so would even inspire her to leave the nest on her own, without my useless and incessant prodding.

"I wonder how Dad felt when he realized Carol was gone," Sasha said, taking another unsteady sip of wine. A cloud passed over her face then, as though she'd just realized something unpleasant.

"What?" I asked.

She looked at me warily. "It's just . . . it's not the same thing, but . . . I think I can relate a bit to what Dad might have felt. When you went to college."

I could actually feel my defenses rise. Adrenaline flooded my veins, heating the surface of my skin and vaporizing the thin shield of benevolence I'd briefly worn.

"When we were growing up, and things were bad at home, I always felt better because at least we had each other," Sasha continued. "At least I had my big sister. But just as things were getting really bad, you left me."

"Sash . . . I didn't leave you. I graduated from high school and I went to college. That's what people are supposed to do."

Her wineglass empty, Sasha returned to the dwindling reserves of her vodka soda. "You had a million choices right in L.A. Or at least in California. But you had to go to NYU. Literally on the other side of the country. You might as well have gone to Mars."

She set her glass down, hard; I felt the woman at the table beside us turn to look. Sasha's eyes had darkened, and her eyelids sagged. I'd never seen her like this before. I restrained myself from pointing out that she was behaving just like our father.

"What did you want me to do, Sash? Put my life on hold and stay in that house indefinitely? And for what? You and I both daydreamed about living outside of L.A. one day. My moving to New York was always the plan. But even when you were old enough to go anywhere you wanted, you still decided to stay. No one forced you to go to LMU."

Sasha pursed her lips; her dimples flashed incongruently. "Unlike you, I wasn't going to just abandon Mom."

I was surprised by how easily she accessed her anger toward me. It was as if it had always been there, simmering just beneath the surface of her warm smiles and cheerful embraces.

"You want to talk about being abandoned?" I spat. "Try waking up in a psych ward and learning your mom and sister couldn't be bothered to take a one-hour flight to make sure you're okay."

Sasha blinked, briefly stunned. "I—It wasn't my choice not to come, Syd. I didn't have the money to buy a plane ticket, and Mom needed the car to—"

"You make it sound like you were just a kid, like none of those circumstances were within your control," I hissed, struggling to keep my volume low. "You have choices now, Sash. You don't have to leave everything up to Mom anymore. If you just got a real job and got out of that house, you could actually live your life and stop using Mom's decisions as your excuses."

"That's your answer to everything, isn't it?" Sasha scoffed. "To leave. Did you know it's actually common in many cultures to live with your parents well into adulthood? Not everyone treats family like something you're supposed to escape from."

"That may be true, but I bet that even in those cultures, adult children are still expected to work, and contribute to the household finances. But beyond that, it just doesn't feel like you're really living, Sash. It feels like you're hiding. You can have a close relationship with Mom without continuing to exist in the same dynamic you two had when you were a kid."

She shook her weeping willow braids, cloaking her face, as if protecting herself. "You don't get it. After you left, Mom and I were alone in that house with him. But we were there for each other. She was there for me. I'm not just going to leave her now."

I felt my anger abate. "Sasha . . . we were kids. It wasn't our responsibility to protect Mom. It was her responsibility to protect us. You don't owe her your adulthood because she was there for you as a child."

Sasha swallowed hard and stared out the window. "You don't know what it was like."

"What do you mean? I was in it with you for the first seventeen years of my life!"

Her gaze snapped back to me. "What's the worst thing you remember?"

I sighed, suddenly furious with myself for bringing Sasha along on this trip. "This is ugly, Sash. What's the point of comparing old wounds?"

"Humor me."

"Ugh, fine," I exhaled. "That time after we got back from San Diego for your thirteenth birthday trip with Mom. How he threw that glass so close to Mom's head. How he threatened to 'put everyone out of our misery and end us all.'" I stared into the bloodred pool of my wineglass. "That was pretty fucking awful."

When I looked up Sasha was frowning at me, confused. "That's not even the worst thing that happened when we were all together."

Now I was confused. "What are you talking about?"

"That road trip we took to Oregon, back when we still used to travel together. We were in Dad's Jeep; he was driving, Mom was in the passenger seat, and we were in the backseat, sleeping. It was dark out, and we must have been driving back down the coast— I remember waking up and looking out the window and seeing the ocean right on the other side of the road."

I vaguely remembered a family trip to Oregon—wandering the endless aisles at Powell's Books, hiking to a waterfall rushing down a hillside covered in lime green moss—but I didn't remember anything about driving there.

"Mom and Dad were whisper-fighting in the front seat," Sasha continued. "I couldn't hear them well over the music Dad was playing, some romantic R & B song that felt totally out of place with their conversation. And then I realized Dad was crying; they both were. I don't think I'd ever heard Mom cry before, and it scared me. Their voices got just loud enough for me to make out little pieces of their words. Mom was begging him to pull over, to let her drive. Dad started driving faster. That's when I heard him say . . . he was going to drive us all into the ocean."

Sasha played with her near-empty glass, watching the ice disintegrate into the watery remains of her cocktail.

"I turned to wake you up, but you were already awake, staring at the backs of their heads, wide-eyed. You were pulling up the door lock with your fingers, like you were going to eject yourself from the car."

The images hit me like a wave of motion sickness. I could suddenly see everything Sasha described, down to the coastline rushing past the window beside her, the waves frothing like the dark mouth of a rabid dog. But it was as though I were remembering a movie I'd watched once, long ago; the details were choppy, like there was a flaw in the film.

The line between Sasha's full eyebrows deepened. "You don't remember?"

The wine and heavy food sloshed in my gut. Beads of cold sweat gathered at my hairline.

"I thought that's why that story about the father driving his kids off the cliff hit you so hard," Sasha continued, her voice gentle, as though the cloud of anger that had settled around her vanished as quickly as it appeared. "I thought it brought you back to that night in the car with Dad."

I shook my head before shutting my eyes and stilling myself; even that small movement summoned a fresh wave of nausea.

I felt the small cylinder of plastic between my fingertips. The interior lock on the windowsill of our father's Jeep Grand Cherokee. It was cold in the Jeep, too cold. Goosebumps embroidered my limbs; I was still dressed in the T-shirt and shorts I'd worn in the heat of the summer afternoon. But now it was night, and our father was blasting the AC, as usual. He tended to run hot.

My legs were shorter and skinnier then. I must have been twelve? Thirteen?

My father's driving had grown increasingly erratic; he veered sharply toward the coastline, once, twice. Sasha and I screamed. Mom grabbed the steering wheel, fighting to keep the Jeep on the road.

I thought we were seconds from plunging into the sea. I imagined us struggling to escape the sinking vehicle as icy black water rushed inside. I'd watched an episode of *Rescue 911* once about a girl trapped in a car that crashed into a lake. How did she escape? Were you supposed to open a window before or after the vehicle submerged? What if your seatbelt got stuck? What if, like me, you didn't really know how to swim?

I wondered if I'd have the courage to fling myself out of the car. I wondered if I'd survive the impact with the road. I wondered if taking that risk was better than waiting for our father to finally make good on his threats. It certainly seemed better than drowning in the Pacific.

"Syd?" Sasha asked. Her voice was small and distorted, as though she were speaking through an ancient transatlantic phone line.

"Sydney!"

The restaurant disappeared from view as I plunged into blackness.

SEVENTEEN

I STOOD BENEATH THE HOT SPRAY OF THE HOTEL SHOWER until the bathroom was choked with steam. I felt thoroughly numb, as though my consciousness had been stripped from my body and floated formless in the humid air.

All those years spent wondering why the story of Hannah McEwan and her family had unraveled me. Never understanding why the physical sensation of my anxiety and the experiences of my nightmares always mirrored the feeling of drowning. The excavated memory of that awful experience on the Pacific Coast Highway was the puzzle piece I hadn't realized was missing.

All those years of therapy, and the answers to so many of my questions could have been unlocked simply by having the right conversation with my sister.

No wonder reporting on the McEwan story fucked me up. My father hadn't only threatened to commit the same terrible act as Hannah's father; he'd actually attempted it. I'd just buried the awful memory so deep that I couldn't access it. Couldn't understand why I was so determined to discover what really happened to the McEwans.

Why I'd wanted so badly to believe that Hannah had somehow survived.

Perhaps, on some subconscious level, I'd hoped that figuring out what happened to the McEwans could help me understand what happened to my own family, my own father. Maybe this was the real reason I sometimes lost myself in investigating the mysteries of other people's lives; because it dulled the pain of knowing I'd never have real answers for my own.

"Repression is a defense mechanism," Dr. Dominguéz once told me. "When you were a child, growing up in an unstable environment, repressing the situation at home protected you. It helped you focus on the future, and thrive in school, despite everything going on. We have to thank younger Sydney for keeping you safe the only way she knew how. But the issue with repression is that the thing that's hurt within us never heals."

I wondered how different our lives might have been if our father had found a Dr. Dominguéz of his own along the way.

I collapsed onto the queen bed beside Sasha's. The thick white hotel robe held the shower's humidity against my skin. The bun I'd raked my curls into dripped onto the pillow. Sasha had changed into a chic black pajama set with white piping and buttons, a look that had "gift from Mom" written all over it. She set her phone down and rolled onto a hip to look at me.

"How are you feeling?" she asked gingerly.

"Exhausted." I closed my eyes but felt Sasha's gaze piercing my eyelids.

"You've really never fainted before?"

"Mmm-mmm." I took a deep breath, gathering the strength to turn my head to look at her. "Can we please not say anything to Malik about this?"

Sasha's brows pinched. "Why not?"

I sighed and pushed myself up to a sit, hugging my knees. "Okay, I'm not ready to tell Mom about this yet. . . . Malik and I are keeping this to ourselves for now, but . . . we're trying to get pregnant."

"I knew it!" Sasha cried, slapping the bed. "I knew all those excuses for bringing mocktails to dinner were bullshit. But . . . I don't get it. Why all the secrecy?"

My tears came out of nowhere, like a sun-shower. "It's been a lot harder than we expected," I said, trying to swallow the sudden thickness in my voice. "We've been trying for years. We're on our third round of IVF right now. The doctor told me I should try to keep my stress down, to help with the process. Malik didn't want me to come on this trip in the first place. If he hears that I passed out at dinner . . ." I shook my head.

Sasha nodded, but in a slow, shallow way that told me she didn't really understand.

"I don't know, Sasha . . . I'm just not sure I have any business being a mother," I said, my voice wobbling.

"What makes you say that?"

I wiped my eyes with the cuff of my robe, uselessly, because my tears continued to flow. "The last thing I want to do is re-create our childhood for my own kids. But sometimes I feel like I'm doomed to repeat it. Sometimes I worry that I might have the worst of both our parents inside me."

Sasha scrunched her nose at me. "What are you talking about?"

"Okay, even if my therapist is right, and Dad's behavior has nothing to do with some undiagnosed mental illness that he passed down to me, that I could pass on to my child, you can't deny how much I have in common with Mom."

Sasha shook her head. "I still have no idea what you mean."

"I'm selfish!" I cried, much louder than I meant to. "I love my freedom, not being tethered to anything that truly depends on me. When I think about the way Mom was when we were little, spending as much time away from the house as possible . . . Why should I think I'd be any different? I'm just not sure I was born with that loving, maternal gene. Sometimes I think all this trouble I'm having getting pregnant is just nature's way of telling me I'm not supposed to."

I pressed the heels of my hands into my eyelids and tried to calm my staccato, hiccupping breath. "That night in Dad's Jeep is a perfect example of how fucked up my instincts are. Like, what . . . I was just going to leave you? Save myself and leave you in that car to drown? What kind of person does that?"

Sasha sprang up from her bed and dropped onto mine. She burrowed her head into my shoulder, wrapping her arms around me as best she could from that awkward angle.

"You weren't going to leave me, Syd," she said slowly, ensuring I heard every word. "You grabbed my hand and pointed to the lock you were holding. You nodded until I unlocked my door, too. We couldn't talk without them hearing us, but I knew what you were trying to tell me. You were going to squeeze my hand three times before we jumped, just like we'd do before we jumped into a pool or a ball pit. You weren't going to leave me there. If Mom hadn't talked Dad into pulling over and letting her drive, I know we would have jumped together."

She tightened her grip around me. "That's why I felt safer when you were around," she said. "I knew you'd never leave me behind."

I took a deep shuddering breath and rested my head against Sasha's. I knew my hair was probably dripping down her face, but she didn't flinch.

"Look, I know I don't have any real experience with kids or whatever," she continued, "but growing up as your little sister makes me confident that your future kid will be lucky to have you as a mom."

Sasha held me and let me cry myself to sleep. When I woke the next morning, puffy-eyed and stuffy-nosed, she was still curled around me on top of the duvet, tight, like she was trying to hold me together.

WE'D PLANNED TO GO SIGHTSEEING the next morning before heading to the airport, but we were too emotionally exhausted to leave our hotel room. Instead I ordered a room service breakfast so large they had to wheel it in on a preset dining table: warm pastries, eggs scrambled with cheese, bacon, home fries, coffee, and juice. We lounged in our robes, munching while Chip and Joanna Gaines fawned over salvaged shiplap on TV.

"You know," I began, tearing a corner of croissant into tiny pieces, "I can't stop thinking about something you said at dinner last night."

"Ugh . . . forget everything I said at dinner. I was being a tipsy little bitch."

"Maybe," I said with a smile, "but it was also the most honest conversation we've had in years." I brushed the buttery remnants of croissant from my fingertips. "You said the San Diego glass-throwing incident wasn't the worst thing that happened while we were still all together. The way you phrased it . . . it makes me think things must have gotten worse after I left."

Sasha stared into her mug as though willing herself to disappear into it.

"You didn't really tell me much about what things were like after I went to college," I added.

"I guess I didn't really see the point in telling you," she said. "What were you supposed to do all the way in New York?"

I shrugged. "I could've been there for you emotionally even if I couldn't be there physically. And if things got really bad, I could've come back. Or at least sent you a plane ticket." I tried to ignore the hole that opened in my stomach as I prepared to ask the question I dreaded most. "How bad did things get?"

Sasha took a deep breath, as though steeling herself. "I was supposed to be in the car with Dad the night of his crash."

It felt like someone had just pulled the plug on my heart. "What?" I croaked.

"We'd gotten into a fight. He'd stopped reserving his anger for Mom by then." She pulled her knees to her chest until she formed a little terry-cloth ball.

"It was my freshman year at LMU, but I came home for dinner a couple nights a week. I made the mistake of mentioning that I was having a hard time in my Elementary Stats class, and that at the rate I was going, I'd be lucky if I passed." Sasha snorted. "Dad went ballistic."

"Had he been drinking?" I asked.

"When wasn't he drinking? Though, honestly, he didn't need to get drunk to freak out on us anymore."

She sighed and fiddled with the belt of her robe. "Anyway, he just kept going on and on about how much they were spending on our education, and how ungrateful we were. I kept trying to explain that I was exaggerating, that I'd already gotten a tutor to help me. But he just accused me of back talking."

I felt my pulse begin to race; it was as though I was sitting at that table, too. "What did Mom do during all this?"

"She tried to get him to calm down, but of course that just made everything worse. He said we were ganging up on him, as usual. He jumped up from the table and said he was going to the restaurant, and that he was going to take me back to school, where I belonged, along the way. Even though, obviously, LMU was in the opposite direction of the restaurant."

Sasha stopped fiddling with her belt. When she spoke again, her voice was so quiet I could barely hear her over Chip and Joanna's banter. "He had that look in his eyes. You know? That desperate look he had the night he threw that glass, and that night in his Jeep. Like some cornered animal willing to gnaw its own leg off to escape."

Sasha dabbed at a tear with the cuff of her robe. "Dad threatened to drive when he was drunk a lot back then. Like he was testing how much Mom loved him. He'd try to leave, and she'd take his keys and hide them."

"I remember," I said.

"Dad grabbed me by the arm and said we were going. He'd never tried to take one of us with him before. He was crying, and I was crying. I was so scared. I kept thinking about that night he tried to steer us into the ocean. I tried to pull away, but he wouldn't let me go. He held me so tightly that there was a hand-shaped bruise on my arm the next morning."

My stomach lurched as I thought of Barbara's story of the fight she and our father had in high school: *Larry marched over and grabbed me by the arm, hard, and pulled me into an empty class-room,* she'd said. *He left a bruise on my arm where he grabbed me.*

"Mom stood up, grabbed his keys from the side table, and pulled me toward her before shoving his keys into his chest," Sasha continued. "She told him, if you're dead set on going, then just go, but she and I were staying right there. Half an hour later we got the call that he'd crashed into the tree in front of the restaurant."

My tears were coming so quickly that my vision blurred. "Oh my God, Sasha."

"See?" she said, smiling weakly. "Mom saved me."

"How can you say that? It was Mom who put us in danger all those years by allowing us to live in the same house with him."

Sasha shrugged. "Isn't it possible both things might be true?"

Suddenly, memories of the aftermath of the night on the Pacific Coast Highway began to resurface like fossils from an eroding bluff.

Sasha and I had to go to school the next day and our mother greeted us when we walked hand in hand into the kitchen, skittish from the previous night's events.

Mom appeared as emotionless and self-assured as ever, dressed in her usual work uniform of tailored slacks and a stiffly starched dress shirt. "Sit down, girls," she said. "Do you remember why gossip is so dangerous?"

I remembered being confused. Why were we talking about gossip at a time like this?

"Because it can hurt people," Sasha replied quickly.

"How?" Mom prodded.

"It can start a mean rumor that follows that person for a long time," Sasha said.

Mom nodded. "It's like my mother always used to say: rumors are often started by the very people victimized by them. Maybe they say something private to someone they think they can trust. But that person tells someone else. And so on. Like a game of telephone, the story becomes increasingly exaggerated until it barely resembles the truth. But that exaggerated version is the story every-one remembers."

My stomach lurched. I knew where our mother's lecture was headed.

"A rumor about what happened last night . . . well, that could be very bad for your father's reputation. My career, and your father's role at the restaurants . . . they're all built on the strength of our public image. That's why it's very important that we don't talk about private family matters with anyone outside of this family."

I felt certain that my mother had been taught this same speech as a child herself, likely to protect her pastor father. I wondered what about his reputation needed protecting.

My mother's steely gaze landed on me. "What do we say about keeping family business within the family, Sydney?"

I was only thirteen, the same age as Carol in the framed photo-graph in my home, but I already knew the line by heart: "What happens in this house stays in this house."

Throughout our childhoods, Sasha and I had only each other to confide in. After I left for college, she'd stopped confiding in me, too. Now I wondered what else she'd felt she had to keep to herself all those years.

EIGHTEEN

On Sunday afternoons Malik typically went to the gym, and I would go for a run when my doctor allowed it. But the weekend after the Detroit trip, Malik convinced me to take our badly neglected tennis rackets to the court near our townhouse. Neither of us was particularly good—we spent half the time chasing balls that had flown to far corners of our court or into other courts entirely. But it felt freeing to do something that required so much concentration that my mind couldn't wander to Carol or Raymond, or the pending genetic testing results of our embryos.

I loved the rare moments when my racket connected perfectly with the ball, directing it just beyond Malik's long reach. I loved Malik's silly, awkward celebration dances when he hit a perfect shot. I loved how strong my legs felt as I jogged back to our court with a rescued ball, my heart rate pleasantly high, a reminder of how alive I was.

We held hands on the walk home. I briefly daydreamed about pulling him into the shower with me when we got there, until I remembered the awkward realities of this: the tile in our bathroom was slippery; one person was always stuck beyond the shower's warm spray, shivering and cold.

"Whoa, what's that?" Malik asked, snatching me from my thoughts. A huge box stood propped beside our front door.

"Carol's trunk." I exhaled.

Malik and I slid the heavy box through the doorway, down the hall, and into the office. It had been sealed with several layers of tape, requiring a few minutes to hack through enough of it to free the trunk from its cardboard cocoon.

"This is incredible," Malik said, marveling at the trunk the way Sasha and I had when we first saw it. "Like stepping back in time." His phone chimed in his pocket then.

"Ugh, I have to jump in the shower if I'm going to get to Tony's before kickoff." He pressed his lips to my forehead. "I can't wait to hear about what you find."

I sat cross-legged on the rug, staring into the trunk, imagining Carol carefully curating these items to keep at her boyfriend's place. It seemed meaningful that she kept her things in an item so easily movable, instead of asking for a drawer at Michael's apartment. Was this because he simply had no storage space to spare? Or because they were both planning to leave Raleigh soon? Or was it because Carol already had one foot out the door of their relationship?

I was going through her stack of 45s, their dry paper sleeves crinkling against my fingers, when I heard a soft *pop*. I froze for a moment, confused. Had the sound come from inside the trunk? Had it been damaged in transit?

I rose to my knees and peered inside. It took a while for me to realize a corner of the back panel had popped free from the trunk's backing. I reached inside to try to push it back into place, and as my fingers brushed the edge of the panel, I grazed something velvety just behind it.

I reared back in surprise for a moment before bending farther into the trunk, struggling to grasp what was there. Finally, my index finger managed to pull the object forward just enough for me to slide it out.

It was a small bloodred drawstring pouch, the type you might store jewelry in. I jiggled the pouch, sussing out its weight. There was definitely something inside.

My heart thumped; had Carol hidden something in a secret compartment of her trunk?

I opened the pouch and emptied its contents into my palm. A tiny plastic bag filled with tarnished bits of silver spilled out. It appeared to be jewelry of some kind, silver links with various shapes sprinkled throughout, little hearts and circles. I carefully peeled the bag open and shook the bits of silver into my hand.

It was a bracelet with small engraved charms. There was an old-fashioned telephone with a tiny rotary that actually spun. There was a heart with a horseshoe at its center, flanked by the words "Good Luck." There was a tiny book with "My Diary" printed on the front. And there was a miniature oval-shaped locket with the letters "SD" engraved in elaborate script. It was the type of bracelet a teenage girl might wear.

"Who's SD?" I whispered to myself, touching the tiny locket. I used my fingernails to carefully open the locket's clasp; inside were photos of two girls I didn't recognize, two Black girls similar in age to the missing.

"SD, SD, SD," I mouthed to myself. Something whispered at me from my subconscious, a flicker of recognition. I rose from the rug and went to the desk, shaking the mouse until my laptop blinked awake. I scanned my notes from the case. When I found it, my heart lurched:

SALLY DUNN
**Ambition: Beautician
Age at Time of Disappearance: 16
Last Seen: Around 4 p.m. on February 2, 1965,
walking to Faye's Salon of Beauty from her South
Park home. Someone claimed to have witnessed her
getting into the passenger side of a dark sedan, possi-
bly an early 1950s Chevrolet 210 . . .**

Sally Dunn. Stanley's little sister. Carol's friend. I sifted through my digital files until I found the scant police reports about Sally's disappearance, but there was no mention of a bracelet, or anything else Sally might have worn the day she was last seen.

February 2, 1965. Sally was the last girl to go missing before Carol, three months before Carol's disappearance.

I struggled to swallow; my throat was suddenly bone dry.

Was this Sally Dunn's charm bracelet? And if so, why did Carol have it?

December 7, 1964

Today's Song: "Hit the Road Jack," Ray Charles

It was just supposed to be the two of us at Michael's place this weekend, but his friend RayRay was crashing with him <u>again</u>. He's always hanging around now, like a stray puppy.

Michael is too nice for his own good. What are the odds Mama will go out of town again?? We've never gotten to spend two whole days together. It was supposed to be special. We could pretend that we'd already run away and were properly living together.

RayRay walked in just as we were sitting down to "family dinner"—we'd invited Larry to come over for pizza and Cokes on Saturday night. I hoped it would give Larry a taste of what life would be like if he came and stayed with me and Michael in our new home, after we leave.

I don't think it would take much convincing—they're spending more and more time together these days, even when I'm not around! Larry's having a hard time with math, and I'm not much better than he is, so Michael has been meeting him at a sandwich shop after school once a week to help him with his homework. Considering how happy Larry is when he comes home, I have a feeling they don't talk about math the entire time 🙂 I hope the offer to come live with us will help Larry forgive us for running away.

Michael's pity for RayRay better not extend all the way to Detroit. Or California. Michael is pushing more and more for California lately. He keeps pointing out that Motown has an office in Los Angeles now, and they've started signing local artists there. But everyone knows the real Motown is in Detroit.

Anyway, RayRay has got to go. I don't like the way he looks at me when he thinks I can't see him. Like he's a starving coyote, and I'm a juicy cut of steak.

One time, I was changing clothes in Michael's room when I got this weird feeling. I turned around, and Michael's door was open a crack. I know I closed that door. It was dark in the hallway, so I couldn't see anything, but RayRay was definitely out there, leering at me. I told Michael about it, but he just brushed me off. He says that RayRay is harmless, just awkward.

Maybe he's right. But let's just say I wouldn't want to be left alone with him to find out.

NINETEEN

THE LARGEST CONFERENCE ROOM AT MY OFFICE WAS DE-
signed to resemble a lounge, with buttery leather couches
and a shaggy Moroccan rug that shed more white fluff than a Per-
sian cat.

I walked into the room a few minutes before our Monday leadership team meeting to secure my favorite spot, a cloud-like bouclé
armchair in a corner, where no one could peer over my shoulder to
see my laptop screen. Nearly all of us had our MacBooks open in
our laps.

I stared at a photo I'd snapped of the charm bracelet. Would
anyone in Sally's family remember this bracelet after all this time, if
it had belonged to her? I tried to think of any distinctive accessories
Sasha had worn as a teenager, but my mind was blank. The only
way I'd know for sure that the item was hers would be if I had a
photo of her wearing it.

Photo. I suddenly remembered the mentions of a few of the girls
I'd found in the online archives of *The Carolina Express.* Wasn't
Sally featured in one of those stories?

I searched through my notes until I found the screenshots I'd taken. There it was—a picture of Sally winning a cosmetology award, posing with a gleaming trophy. Her hair was impeccably coiffed, ironed straight and fashioned into thick waves cascading just past her jawline. She had the unabashedly joyful smile of a child, showing both rows of her straight white teeth.

I stifled a gasp when I noticed her left wrist, positioned below the trophy she held. A bracelet circled that wrist. And while the resolution of the image wasn't particularly clear, I could make out a few tiny shapes hanging from it. Charms.

Of course, Sally wouldn't have been the only girl her age who wore a charm bracelet. Google informed me that they were very popular at the time. I could try asking Stanley if he or anyone in the family recognized the bracelet. But what if Stanley's family thought that Carol might have had something to do with Sally's disappearance if they learned I'd found the bracelet in her trunk?

I turned my attention back to Raymond. I'd searched for information about him online shortly after returning from Detroit but came up empty. I considered reaching out to Michael to ask him to tell me more about his old friend. But he'd seemed protective of Raymond and unwilling to consider that anything nefarious had happened to Carol. I also imagined how painful it would be to have to consider a former friend as a suspect in the disappearance of your first love. I didn't want to go that route without more evidence.

Stanley thought he was a sophomore at Shaw when he attended the party where he briefly met Carol. If he knew who Michael was, maybe he'd known Raymond, too? They had all grown up in the same city, after all, attending the same schools.

It seemed that no matter what I did next, it would need to involve talking to Stanley. I opened Facebook and typed out a note:

> Hi Stanley—
> I have a random question for you. Did you know a Raymond Green when you were growing up in Raleigh, or while you attended Shaw?

*   *   *

I HAD MY BIWEEKLY ONE-ON-ONE with my boss following our leadership team meeting. It was usually an opportunity to get her feedback on things she hadn't found time to review, since she rarely had feedback for me. But this time, she had a warning.

Though I'd thought I'd done a good job of hiding it, she'd noticed how distracted I'd been during the leadership meeting, how distracted I'd been in general.

"We all go through things sometimes that make it harder to be present at work," she'd said, her face a mask of care and concern. "I just need to know if I can count on you. I need to know your head is still in the game."

I swallowed the lump of panic forming in my throat. I had to get it together. The company's benefits were covering our expensive fertility treatments, and their parental leave offerings were far more generous than anywhere else I'd ever worked. I needed this job.

"I love this company," I said, as earnestly as possible. "I love this job, and I love working with you. You're right—I haven't been as focused lately as I need to be. I'm going to fix that. I promise."

I returned to my desk feeling embarrassed and small, like a chastened child. I'd grown accustomed to my laid-back work environment, and I'd gotten sloppy. I needed to cut way back on the amount of time I spent researching Carol and the missing girls during work hours.

Though my alternatives were limited. Maybe I could do more of it in the early morning hours before work? Evenings were out—Malik would worry that I was spreading myself too thin, replicating the obsessive days that preceded my involuntary trip to the UCSF Medical Center.

I felt a column of anxiety creep from my stomach into my esophagus, cold and wet. If I was struggling to find time to do this research now, what would happen if Malik and I were finally able to conceive? I couldn't imagine doing all of this with an infant at home. The brain space currently dedicated to the missing girls would be colonized by rigorous feeding, sleeping, pumping, and changing schedules, the endless, exhausting minutiae of trying to keep a brand-new human alive. Not to mention the yo-yoing hormones, debilitating sleep deprivation, and the sinking feeling that somehow, despite my best efforts, I was doing everything wrong.

If I didn't get to the bottom of what happened to Carol and the girls soon, I doubted that I ever would.

I closed all the browser windows on my laptop and focused my attention on work.

An hour later, a notification pinged on my phone. It was a response from Stanley; he and Raymond were neighbors as kids, and he'd be happy to tell me everything he knew about him whenever I had time. I nearly asked if he could speak right then. However, remembering my new rule about protecting my work hours, I suggested we chat first thing in the morning, long before I was due in the office.

L.A. WAS A CITY FILLED with creatives, freelancers, and entrepreneurs, adults untethered from the nine-to-five shackles of a traditional office. It was easy to find a coffee shop where I could do my early morning research, blending in with several other earbud-wearing patrons, sipping their coffees and matchas, faces aglow in the light of their laptop screens.

It was only 7:10 when I settled into a quiet corner seat with a turmeric latte and a bowl of overnight oats. I had twenty minutes until my call with Stanley. I decided to try Yvonne's cell; I'd texted her a few times since returning from Detroit to set up a time to chat, but she hadn't responded.

My call went straight to voicemail. Apparently I'd have to take a more aggressive tack. I looked up her phone number at her law office and dialed before I lost my nerve.

Her chipper assistant greeted me after a single ring. "Just a moment, let me see if she's available," he said.

My heart hammered in my throat as I waited.

"I'm sorry," he said a few beats later. "She's tied up right now. Can I take a message?"

"Actually, would you mind sending me to her voicemail?" I swallowed hard as I listened to Yvonne's greeting. "Hi, Yvonne, it's Sydney. I'm sorry to bother you at work, but I can't seem to get through to you on your cell. I'm hoping you can clear a few things up for me. I learned that you had an argument with Carol shortly before she disappeared, and according to a police call log, you retracted a missing person report your brother filed, eleven days after Carol went missing. Perhaps you just forgot to mention all this to me during our last conversation, but I'm sure you can understand why this would be confusing. Call me back when you get a chance . . . or I can just keep trying you at work."

My fingers shook as I ended the call. Had I just threatened to stalk Yvonne? No, no, I assured myself; this was the same heavy-handed persistence that made me an effective crime reporter.

I needed to calm my nerves before talking to Stanley. I decided to check on the true crime message boards. It had been a while since I'd scrolled through the latest comments. There didn't seem to be any salient new clues or promising threads of speculation. Instead, a wildfire of outrage had spread in my absence.

How can SIX teenage girls go missing without any clues or suspects? Either police never really looked for them or there's some kind of conspiracy here.

I've lived in Raleigh all my life and never heard about these missing girls til now. Why isn't Raleigh press all over this???

Where are all the podcasts and documentary shows about missing Black girls?? This story needs to be told.

If this were about six missing white girls, please believe that we'd already know all of their names.

I felt a sudden warmth, like stepping directly into the path of early morning sunshine. People cared. Complete strangers cared about what happened to Marian, Bettie, Geraldine, Loretta, Sally, and Carol, and were infuriated by the lack of information and public concern about their disappearances. All at once, I felt a lot less alone.

But I needed more than solidarity to solve this mystery— I needed witnesses and concrete clues, and outrage that burned beyond the true crime community. I had to get this story in front of a much larger audience, through a source that would give the story the credibility it deserved.

The forum commenter was right—I needed the Raleigh press to cover the missing girls. I navigated to the website of *The News & Observer*, North Carolina's most widely circulated newspaper. My PR career had taught me the importance of targeting the right journalist for every story. Covering the missing girls would require a certain degree of courage; doing so would undoubtedly call the efforts of local law enforcement into question and potentially invite their ire. I also needed to find a reporter trusted with longer-form investigative journalism; a tiny blurb in the crime pages would be too easily overlooked. And I needed to find someone skilled at tugging on the heartstrings of their readers just enough, while maintaining their journalistic integrity.

I scanned the last six months of crime stories. All the headlines that grabbed my attention were written by the same senior reporter. I clicked on her profile. Her long box braids and dimpled cheeks reminded me of Sasha. She'd earned her master's in journalism at the University of North Carolina, but my heart skipped when I saw where she'd attended undergrad: Shaw.

I spent the remaining minutes before my video call drafting the strongest story pitch of my life and emailed it to the reporter with a link to the true crime forum so she could see the growing public demand for answers I'd already garnered. I felt a twinge of jealousy as I hit send, imagining myself on the receiving end of this monumental mystery, knowing I'd be able to research it with the backing and resources of a major newspaper.

I looked again at the reporter's photo. "Please—do me proud, sis," I whispered.

When I logged on to the call with a minute to spare, Stanley was already waiting for me, just as before. He appeared to be sitting in a home office. A series of pennants hung on the wall above his head in the same deep red as his shirt, the words SHAW UNIVERSITY printed across their fronts. It felt like a good omen.

"So, you wanted to talk about Raymond Green," he said. "How'd you even come across that name?"

"I managed to track down Michael, my aunt Carol's old boyfriend, recently. The one she was fighting with at that party where you met her."

Stanley's dark brows, which stood in dramatic contrast to his short white curls, lifted skyward. "You're quite the investigator, huh?"

"Guess it's my old reporter instincts kicking in," I said with a shrug. "I found Carol's diary when I was cleaning out my grandmother's house. Michael and Raymond were friends, and it sounds like Raymond might have hung around Michael and Carol quite a bit. Raymond made Carol . . . well . . ."

"He creeped her out?" Stanley asked, rescuing me from my desperate grasp for a more delicate euphemism.

"Yeah."

Stanley grunted. "Ray had a habit of doing that."

"How long were you two neighbors?"

Stanley leaned back in his chair. "Raymond lived three doors down from me long as I can remember. There were a bunch of kids our age on our street; we'd congregate together on weekends, playing tag, riding bikes, that sorta thing. I think we were in the fourth or fifth grade when his parents died in that car wreck. Terrible thing. Ray was out of school for a while. Our teacher had us make sympathy and get well soon cards that they delivered to his hospital room."

"Wait," I said. "Raymond was in the car when his parents were killed?"

"Oh yeah, he was in the backseat," Stanley said, nodding solemnly. "Got pretty banged up. There was a scar on the side of his head that was visible as long as I knew him."

Stanley sighed and passed a large hand over his face. "I'm not sure how well we all treated him after that. He was this walking reminder that we could be the victims of a tragedy at any moment, too. I don't think we ostracized him or anything. But I'm not sure we went out of our way to invite him to join us in our games of tag anymore."

My heart ached at the thought of a young boy, newly orphaned, sitting alone and lonely in his classroom as the other kids whispered and stared and turned their backs to him on the playground.

"Michael said a family member came to live with Raymond after his parents died," I said.

Stanley gave a snort. "Ms. Mabel. His aunt, I believe. Mean old lady. If you lingered within six feet of their house for more than a minute, she'd come out the front door with a broom in her hand hollering, 'Quit loitering on my lawn, you hoodlums!'" Stanley chuckled to himself for a moment before growing more serious. "Man, I can't imagine what it must have been like being raised by her."

"You said Raymond had a way of creeping people out," I said. "What did you mean by that?"

Stanley was thoughtful for a moment. "He'd always been a quiet kid. But he started to act . . . strange. He had this way of staring at you that made you feel like he was looking through you. He had these huge eyes, all dark and vacant."

I remembered what Carol wrote about "RayRay" in her diary: *I don't like the way he looks at me when he thinks I can't see him. Like he's a starving coyote, and I'm a juicy cut of steak.*

"When he did speak," Stanley continued, "he often said the wrong thing. He'd reference a topic from a conversation that you'd already moved on from minutes ago. Or make jokes that rubbed people the wrong way. Dark jokes with no punch line. I'm sure he was just trying too hard to fit in, but it came out all wrong. The way he dressed didn't help either. He got tall fast. All skin and bones. Ms. Mabel either couldn't afford to get him new clothes or didn't care to, because he kept going to school in old rags that just didn't fit. Kids used to call him some nickname about it . . ."

"Scarecrow," I said, remembering what Michael had told me in Detroit.

Stanley's dark brows twitched in recognition. "That's right. Scarecrow. Anyway, things got a bit better for him in high school. He filled out some, started working out, and got himself on the basketball team, which helped with his popularity. Then, it must have been later on in high school . . . junior year, maybe . . . when Ms. Mabel passed on. Now, I don't know how this happened . . . maybe rules were different back then, or maybe Ray fell through some loophole of age or something, but he just went on living in that house alone. His house became the party house, 'cause there weren't any adults around. That helped with his popularity too. I mean, people were more willing to overlook an awkward personality if you were giving them a place to hang out and drink away from the watchful eyes of their own parents. He also got a car around then and would offer people rides to and from school."

My pulse quickened. "A dark Chevy 210?"

A flash of surprise rippled across Stanley's face. "Yeah. Exactly. A black Chevy 210. I remember because my pop drove a red one." Stanley scratched the white stubble on his chin as he regarded me through the screen. "Sydney, what exactly is piquing your interest in Raymond?"

His tone wasn't accusatory, it was curious. It was as though he was probing to find out if we might be thinking the same thing. I decided to take a chance.

"I was going through the police reports Barbara sent me. A couple witnesses thought they saw both your sister and Barbara's sister getting into a dark sedan at the time of their disappearances. Someone even thought they saw Sally get into the passenger seat of a dark Chevy 210." I paused to take stock of Stanley's reaction, but he just went on scratching his chin, thinking.

"I know it was a really popular car," I said. "But when I was at Michael's, I saw a photo with him and Raymond and some of their friends posing in front of Raymond's car. And when I went back through Carol's diary, and read about how uncomfortable Raymond made her, I just wondered . . . did you ever suspect Raymond of doing something to those girls?"

Stanley heaved a great sigh from somewhere deep and old. "One of the hardest things about Sally's disappearance was how . . . complete it was. Like she'd vanished into thin air. Because there was no real evidence, all we had to go on were our own theories and rumors. So, naturally, one of the first things we did was put together a list of all the neighborhood weirdos, and Raymond was definitely on that list, especially given the car he drove, common though it was."

He swallowed and looked away from his screen for a moment. "Thing is, I've started to think differently about Raymond in my later years. My son Kevin is on the autism spectrum. He's high functioning, did really well in school, and has a good job, but he has a hard time in social situations. Some of his behavior can seem odd to other people. He's had a really tough time making friends." Stanley swallowed again, perhaps in an effort to choke back his emotions.

"When I was young, Raymond was this weird kid no one wanted to spend time with. But now, as an adult, I think . . . he was a socially awkward child who spent his last years of high school with no family, no one to look out for him. If that's all it takes to make people think you're capable of hurting six little girls, then what's to keep people of accusing my Kevin of the same kind of thing?"

Stanley shook his head once more. "I used to wonder if Raymond had something to do with it. But honestly, Sydney . . . it could have been anyone."

I hung up from the video call feeling frustrated. It had hardly been the damning condemnation of Raymond that I'd hoped for. Instead, all Stanley had done was make me feel sorry for Raymond's friendless, parentless childhood.

My phone vibrated against the table. It was a message from Yvonne. My heart clenched as I picked up the phone to read it.

Sydney, If you contact me again, you'll be hearing from my lawyers. And you should know—they're even more ruthless than me.

TWENTY

 ON WEDNESDAY EVENING, MALIK DECIDED WE WERE overdue for a date night.

"Listen, I'm trying to get you pregnant on Friday," he stage-whispered playfully from across the table, using the long parchment menu to shield his face from our fellow diners. "If we were doing this the old-fashioned way, you'd better believe I'd wine and dine your ass first."

I laughed. "Does it count if we're drinking mocktails instead of wine?" I asked, holding up a highball of herbed tonic, miso, and pineapple that was somehow the same price as a real drink.

Malik clinked the strawberry, lavender, and ginger concoction he'd ordered in solidarity against my glass. "It definitely fucking counts."

It felt good to be fun and flirtatious with my husband. I was still trying to shake off Yvonne's icy text. And Malik and I had both been rattled when the fertility center called to inform us that despite extracting eight eggs during the retrieval, we had only one viable embryo for the transfer on Friday.

Malik had tried to maintain his preternaturally hopeful expression, but he couldn't hide the flash of fear in his eyes. Just one embryo, a potential baby girl. Just one chance.

I was nervous, too. Nervous that the transfer wouldn't work, again. Nervous that we'd have to decide if we would try the same thing a fourth time, or try something else, or stop trying at all.

And while it was excruciating to admit it in therapy the day after receiving the news, I was also nervous that it would work.

"Why aren't I more excited?" I'd asked Dr. Dominguéz. "Shouldn't I be excited? I've had friends all my life who couldn't wait to be parents; I've never been that way. I've never daydreamed about my future kids. My eyes don't glaze over the way Malik's do when he sees a dad playing tennis with his kid. Don't you think that means something?"

Dr. Dominguéz uncrossed her legs and leaned forward in her chair. "I would never try to talk you into having children if that was something you didn't want. But I don't get the sense you're telling me you don't want to be a mom. I think you're telling me you're terrified of being a bad mom. And you've been collecting what you believe to be evidence of this, building a narrative you've repeated so often you now believe it to be fact."

"I've never had examples of how a healthy, functioning family is supposed to look," I countered.

"Sydney," Dr. Dominguéz said. Then, pausing on each word to give it time to sink in, "Your history is not your destiny. It's very common for people who grew up in challenging home environments to feel apathetic about becoming parents themselves, out of fear of creating a similar environment for their own children. But you are not your parents. And while it's true that we can learn a lot about the kind of parent we want to be by witnessing positive examples firsthand, the lessons about the kind of parent we don't want to be are equally important. You know so much more than you give yourself credit for."

I'd absorbed this information on some level, but my mind continued to grope for proof that Dr. Dominguéz was wrong.

I tried to shake away these thoughts and focus on Malik, and the beautiful restaurant he'd chosen for our dinner. We were seated on a serene patio beneath a pergola dripping with ivy and market lights. You'd never know we were sitting below the high-rises of Century City, filled with prestigious law firms and talent agencies. It had been a relentlessly hot day, but a cool, sweet breeze now wound its way through the patio, and I was grateful to have Malik's cardigan warming my shoulders.

I couldn't deny it; the whole thing was pretty damn romantic.

"This was a really good idea," I told Malik, sipping my overpriced yet delicious juice. "You've been so busy lately I feel like I've hardly seen you."

He winced, and I immediately wished I'd chosen my words more carefully.

"I know," he admitted. "I'm hoping that if I'm able to fill some of these leadership roles I'll be able to get more of my own time back. But . . . I don't know, we're also under pressure from our investors to make some significant strides before our next funding raise, so I'd be lying if I said my schedule will change anytime soon."

He began to anxiously fumble with the corner of his menu. "I'm starting to worry a little. I want to be able to be present for my kids. And for you. I don't want to become one of those husbands who lives this completely separate life, making occasional cameo appearances with his family."

My heart ached with a peculiar combination of solace and sympathy — Malik worried about what kind of parent he'd be, too?

"Hey," I said, stilling his overactive fingers with my hand. "I know you. You'd never be that kind of husband. Or father."

Malik's eyes met mine, and I was surprised to find they were wet. "My dad never had the opportunity to be present, even before he died," he said. "He didn't work long hours because he was trying to build some tech dynasty. He had to work two jobs just to keep us fed. You and I are far from broke. If my job keeps me from my family, isn't it only out of greed?"

"Malik, there's nothing wrong or greedy about being ambitious." I stroked his fingers. "If it makes you feel better, I've been worrying about this too . . . what kind of parent I would be. I even talked about it with Dr. Dominguéz this week."

He sniffled, and the sound yanked at my heart. "Did she have any advice?"

I scrunched my nose, embarrassed; I'd planned on keeping this information to myself. "She told me to make a list of what I think makes up a good parent. And then every day I'm supposed to take fifteen minutes to reflect on the list, and picture myself emulating that description. She said it will help me believe I'm capable of being that person."

A hint of a smile lifted the corner of Malik's mouth. "What did you put on your list?"

I told him how I'd bought a notebook on my lunch break and sat in a park near my office. How I'd been surprised by how quickly the words flowed out of me when I followed Dr. Dominguéz's suggestion to imagine I was sitting beside myself as a child, asking her how she'd describe her ideal parent. I pressed the nib of my pen against the creamy white paper and jotted down everything I imagined she'd say:

- *Someone who makes their child feel heard, seen, and understood*
- *Someone who makes their child feel safe (physically and emotionally)*
- *Someone who creates an atmosphere where their child can talk openly, without fear of dismissal or retribution*

I couldn't help but notice how many of the things I'd wanted were things Carol yearned for, too.

I recalled the time I stood by the door before my mother's daily run to ask if I could join her. I thought about how after she saw my natural talent, she took me shopping for new sneakers, and running became a healthy long-term habit I adopted for myself.

- *Someone who models the importance of cultivating healthy hobbies*

The park was in a residential neighborhood. I'd glanced at the homes that surrounded me. It was a neighborhood for families. I couldn't help but notice a crayon drawing of a rainbow taped to the window of a cheerful blue bungalow, and a tricycle abandoned in the yard of a forest green craftsman. There was something comforting about the sheer number of families on this street alone, the sheer number of parents trying their best to be good to their kids.

- *Someone who tries their best to be good*

As I scanned what I'd written, I was flooded with a torrent of anxiety. What made me think I was capable of doing all of these things?

I took a deep breath and wrote:

I am more than capable of trying my best.

I'd underlined the sentence three times. I wasn't sure I fully believed it, but it felt nice to think it might be possible.

As I recapped my list for Malik, his face filled with a smile. "I want to pick up a notebook on our way home," he said. "I think I need to make a list of my own."

THAT NIGHT, AFTER MALIK ADMINISTERED my nightly progesterone shot into the increasingly tender flesh of my ass, I sprawled across our bed and opened Instagram. I had several new notifications, which was odd since I couldn't remember the last time I'd posted something. They were all from an account I didn't recognize: MEHesq. Whoever it was had liked a dozen of my old photos, some of which I'd posted years before. They'd left a comment on one of the pictures: "You look so much like Carol here."

I looked again at the username, MEHesq. A memory nagged at my subconscious, like an aggravated tooth. I was transported back into a conference room at work, listening to Michael's voice for the first time as he shared the moment Grammy caught him kissing her daughter.

"She called me by every one of my names," he'd said, laughing. "'Michael Eugene Hall Jr., get your narrow behind away from my daughter!'"

It was Michael. My chest tightened at the thought of losing someone you loved only to be faced with their doppelgänger sixty years later, like a haunting.

I clicked on his profile, but it was empty. He didn't even have a profile photo. Malik's mother's profile was the same way. She'd created an account just to view our posts, see what we've **been up to.** Sometimes I forgot that people who didn't use social **media regu-** larly didn't understand its unspoken rules, including the fact **that** liking someone's old photos could be confused as being aggressively flirtatious. Or creepy.

I opened the true crime message boards. The outcry over the decades-long mystery and questions of whether law enforcement had looked into the girls' disappearances seriously enough had continued to grow.

On a whim, I checked my email. My heart lurched when, amid the numerous messages about upcoming retail sales and new Substack posts, I spotted a response from the reporter at *The News & Observer.*

A yelp of excitement flew from my mouth as I leapt to my feet, though it quickly turned into a cry of pain as I tweaked my injection site.

Malik appeared at the door, his brows lifted in concern. "Everything okay?"

"Yes!" I said breathlessly, one quivering hand holding my phone, the other rubbing at my sore butt cheek. "That Raleigh reporter I reached out to is looking into doing a story about Carol and the girls!" I waved the phone at Malik, who walked over and took it, scanning the message.

"This could be huge," I said. "She writes some of the paper's biggest investigative pieces."

Malik's face glowed with genuine pride. "Sydney, that's amazing!"

"Now she just needs to sell her editor on the story. I have to arm her with everything she needs." My mind began developing a frantic list of things to prepare, things I'd want if I was in the reporter's shoes—names, dates, theories, contact information for the other families. "I can't fuck this up, Malik," I said.

"You're in PR," he said, placing his steadying hands on my shoulders. "Selling stories is what you do."

I took the day of the embryo transfer off from work. After an early morning walk, a fifteen-minute meditation on my Good Parent List, and our pre-procedure breakfast ritual, consisting of scrambled eggs, toast with jam, fresh fruit, and water with lemon, served on the coffee table so we could watch *Love Jones,* my favorite comfort movie, we finally made our way to the clinic.

Unlike the egg retrieval procedure, the embryo transfer didn't require me to be fully sedated, and Malik could stay in the room while it happened.

I slid my fingers against his, interlacing them with mine. "It's okay to be nervous," I said.

He nodded, his thumb stroking the back of my hand. "It's hard not to be," he said. "How are you feeling?"

I inhaled deeply, taking emotional stock. "I actually feel good. Better than the last two times we've done this. Something about this time . . ." I looked into Malik's handsome and hopeful face. "Something about this time feels different."

It did feel different. I felt different. I'd had a dream the night before that I was afraid to share with Malik, in case doing so would keep it from coming true, like verbalizing a wish before blowing out the candles on a birthday cake.

The dream was short, but incredibly vivid. In it, Sasha and I stood in my living room, looking out at my backyard through the open sliding glass doorway. I could feel that it was my living room, my backyard, my home, even though it was a house I'd never seen before. A true house, unlike the townhome Malik and I currently lived in.

The backyard was modestly sized but seemed to have everything we needed—a rectangle of lush grass, a paved, shaded area with a café table and a grill, and a surprisingly chic play set, complete with swings and a slide, constructed of gray-stained teak and white molded plastic.

Sasha and I watched, smiling, as Malik lifted a giggling toddler in a mustard-colored romper onto the top of the slide. She squealed with joy as she slid down. As soon as her tiny Adidas hit the ground, she ran toward me, laughing so hard it was difficult for her to stay upright. The puffs of curls crowning each side of her head bounced as she moved. They were my curls. And she had the same heart-shaped face that Sasha and I shared, her pillowy cheeks sloping inward toward her little chin. And she had Malik's warm, sparkling brown eyes.

I knelt down, and the girl collided into me with the clumsy force of a child fully confident that she would be safely caught. Her body was at once soft and pliant yet incredibly strong; the little arms around my neck pulled me tight against her. I could smell the coconut oil in her hair.

And then I felt her hot breath on my neck when she spoke.

"Hi, Mommy!"

Warm tears were sliding down my face when I awoke. There was something about that dream that felt more realistic than my most lifelike nightmare. It was as if it hadn't been a dream at all, but a brief, Technicolor glimpse of my future. I could almost see the love radiating from my insides as I watched my daughter run to me. I could still feel the warmth and weight of the little girl in my arms.

Watching how happy and loving and secure we were didn't just make me feel that it could be possible; it made me want that life more than I'd ever wanted it before.

The doctor came into the room and showed us a picture of our embryo just before the procedure began. Our only embryo, but possibly the only embryo we'd need. As I stared at the tiny cluster of cells, I surprised myself by whispering, "I can't wait to meet you, little girl."

TWENTY-ONE

IN THE DAYS FOLLOWING THE TRANSFER, I FELT AS THOUGH I was enduring the worst PMS of my life: I was tired, crampy, and incredibly irritable, my every nerve on edge.

Malik asked about my symptoms with a frequency and specificity that bordered on obsessive. "Are your breasts tender?" he asked as we sat on the couch on Sunday evening watching our favorite soapy legal drama.

"Malik, please stop checking for pregnancy symptoms." I sighed. "It doesn't help."

"Sorry," he said sheepishly. "I'm terrible at waiting."

To be fair, the two-week period between the embryo transfer and the blood test at the clinic was torturous. It was easy to spend that time overanalyzing every twinge of sensation, scouring your memory to recall how you felt during the same phase of your last IVF cycle, and taking store-bought pregnancy tests though the doctors told you not to.

Instead, I funneled my nervous energy into compulsively hitting refresh on *The News & Observer*'s crime page and going on long walks—one of the few physician-approved physical activities I could take part in post-transfer. I was taking a leisurely walk back to the office after picking up lunch when I visited the crime page for the thousandth time and finally saw it: RALEIGH RESIDENTS STILL SEARCHING FOR SIX BLACK TEENS MISSING SINCE THE '60S.

I scanned the article hungrily, unable to process it piece by piece until I understood its gist. All the facts were there—the names and disappearance dates of the missing, the disproportionate number of missing Black children dating back decades. There was a clipped quote from law enforcement: "there are no active investigations . . . all viable leads have been exhausted . . ." But the article also packed the emotional punch I'd been hoping for. There was a photo of Marian's elderly mother, wiping away tears as she stood in her beloved daughter's bedroom, preserved all these years in case she miraculously returned. There were quotes from Stanley and Barbara about the agony of tirelessly searching for answers for six decades. And the article ended by sharing a tip line readers should contact if they had any information pertaining to the girls' disappearances.

I wished that tip line funneled people directly to me instead of the Raleigh P.D.

I had to get back to the office; my next meeting was starting soon. I decided I could break my rule against doing anything related to the case during work hours, just this once. There was no way I'd be able to wait until I got home to read the article more closely and begin sifting through the dozens of comments already left on its page. But just as I went to put my phone back in my purse, it vibrated in my hand.

"Hi, Barbara," I answered. "Did you see the article? I was just reading it."

"Hey, sugar," she replied. I heard a soft clinking sound, as though she were anxiously playing with a set of bangles on her wrist. "I read it just now. The reporter did a fine job, a very fine job."

I frowned at her unusually tepid tone. "It sounds like you were hoping for more than 'fine.'"

Barbara sighed. "I'm sure it's unfair of me; I was just thinking that maybe she would've been able to uncover something we didn't already know. Or point everyone in the direction of who did it. Especially 'cause, well . . . I was more forthcoming with her than I've been with anyone about who I suspect may have done it."

I stopped dead in my tracks. "What? Who?"

"Stanley told me about your chat about Raymond Green, and it brought up a lot of old feelings for me," Barbara said. "Feelings I've been trying to ignore for a long, long time."

I gasped so loudly that a passing pedestrian turned to stare at me. I quickened my pace, wishing I was back at the office so I could duck into a conference room and take proper notes.

"Stanley always tries to see the best in people," Barbara continued. "Especially after watching his boy struggle with folks making assumptions about him just 'cause of his autism. But the thing is, Kevin is nothing like Raymond was. Sure, Kevin is a little socially awkward, but you can tell what a good, gentle soul he is. Now Raymond . . . Raymond had a darkness about him. Everyone felt it. The way he'd look at you . . . People said there was an emptiness to his stare. But it wasn't empty as if he wasn't really looking at you. It was as if he was lost in thought about all the evil things he wanted to do to you."

I was suddenly a lot less hungry for the expensive take-out salad I carried. "Did you think he might have had something to do with the missing girls?"

"It's just a *feeling* I've always had," Barbara replied, stretching the word like taffy.

"Because of the way he'd look at people?"

"The way he'd look at girls. Wasn't just that, though, or the fact that the creek ran right through his backyard." Barbara sighed. My heart sputtered; Raymond lived along the creek, too?

"Stanley wouldn't understand this," Barbara continued, "but you're a woman, so I'm sure you know. Haven't you ever been around a guy who made you feel . . . unsafe? Maybe there was someone at your school who all the girls knew not to be left alone with?"

My mind flipped through a Rolodex I hadn't realized I'd kept—Mr. McKay, the smiley former neighbor Mom told us to stay away from, who'd stand on his porch with his hands deep in his pockets, watching us playing in our front yard. Tommy, an acquaintance at NYU who was fine when he was sober but would get too handsy on the dance floor if he'd been drinking. Mr. Nowak, my ninth-grade math teacher, who'd massage the shoulders of certain girls in class, pretending to look over their worksheets as he peered below the necklines of their sweaters.

"Yeah," I said, "I know the kind of guy you mean."

"Stanley told you about the parties at Raymond's house, right?"

"He did."

"I was too young to go, but my sister Geri sometimes would." Barbara made an amused chirp. "Geri was *not* the partying type, but some of her friends were what we used to call 'fast.' I used to eavesdrop on their conversations when they'd come over. Sometimes I'd write down what they said in my diary, like I was writing for a gossip rag or somethin'."

"One day a couple of Geri's friends were over, and I was sitting out in the hallway listening in. Cathy was the fastest girl in their group, always trying to drag Geri out to some party. So of course they found themselves at some of Raymond's. They were discussing a party they'd gone to the night before. Geri and her other friend—can't recall her name—were both upset with Cathy, 'cause she insisted on staying past the other girls' curfews. But the girls had a pact against splitting up, 'cause by that point there were already two girls missing, Marian and Bettie."

There was no way I was going to remember all of these names without writing them down. I reached into my tote bag and pulled out the notebook I'd purchased for my Good Parent List, the only source of paper I had on me.

"Geri and her friend were giving Cathy a hard time about staying behind at the party," Barbara went on, "and Cathy kept going on about how she could take care of herself. Started bragging about how she got away from Scarecrow when he started messing with her—Scarecrow's what some of the kids used to call Raymond. Did Stanley tell you about that?"

"He did."

"Cathy noticed Raymond staring before she went to find the restroom at some point, but he was all the way on the other side of the room, so she didn't think much of it. When she went to leave the restroom, Raymond was standing right outside the door. She tried to excuse herself and move past him, but he blocked her way, backing her into the bathroom. He'd gotten big and muscular from all the basketball he played. She told him to stop, to let her leave, but he just got closer, telling her how beautiful she was, like he actually called himself flirting. He tried to kiss her and she slapped him. She was afraid he might get mad at her and try to retaliate, but he just laughed and walked out of the room."

I sighed with relief.

"A while later, Cathy was out in the yard, admiring the hydrangeas at the back of the property. Suddenly she was aware of someone standing close behind her. That's when a male voice whispered into her ear, 'Beautiful, aren't they?' When she agreed, Raymond moved over to the bush and wrapped his fingers around the stem of a wilting blue flower. He looked her directly in the eye as he ran his hand up its stem; the ball of petals popped off cleanly and landed at her feet. 'But they need a good deadheading,' he told her."

A chill traveled up my body despite the warmth of the early November sun. Barbara's bangles clinked in the background.

"Cathy didn't take it all that seriously," Barbara said. "Raymond had a dark sense of humor. But after Geri went missing, I couldn't help but wonder if he had hurt those girls. I mean, isn't it strange that when people stopped seeing him around girls stopped going missing?"

My pulse began to race. Barbara and I were clearly on the same page about Raymond. But I couldn't let myself get carried away. After all, papers print concrete facts, not theories.

"Did Stanley tell you that I went to Detroit to talk to Michael Hall?" I asked. "He thinks Raymond went to Canada to avoid the draft."

Barbara harrumphed. "Isn't that convenient."

My phone buzzed in my hand; my next meeting began in fifteen minutes. My boss's recent words returned to me: *I just need to know if I can count on you,* she'd warned. *I need to know your head is still in the game.*

"Do you know if police looked into Raymond?" I asked, officially breaking into a speed walk. "I didn't see any mention of him in the files you sent me."

Barbara sighed. "I don't know. They talked to a bunch of people in the neighborhood. But I don't think they looked at him seriously. I told them they should, and I know I wasn't the only one. But none of us had any real proof to back up our hunches."

I heard Barbara's bangles in the background again.

"Is his house still there?" I asked.

"Oh no, it's long gone. Someone had it demolished; pretty sure they were planning to build on the land, but never got around to it or ran out of cash to do it. I'd ride my bike over there after school almost every day while they were tearing it down. I kept expecting them to find something. I kept wondering if maybe my sister had been there all this time."

"What's on the property now?"

"Last I saw it was still a vacant lot. Think that land is kinda swampy, due to the proximity to the creek. Not sure folks are eager to build on it."

Clink. Clink. Clink.

"I put all of this away years ago," she said. "When you get attached to a theory, but have nothing to prove it, after enough time passes, you just have to let it go," she said. "But when Stanley told me you asked about Raymond, completely on your own, without anybody mentioning him to you, it made me wonder . . . what if I'd been right all along?"

IT TOOK EVERY SHRED OF willpower within me, but I managed to wait until I got home that evening to close myself in our guest-bedroom-slash-office, pull up Google Maps, and search for Raymond's old address.

Malik was away for a work dinner, wooing a chief operating officer candidate out from Brooklyn. Apparently, this was more easily achieved over expensive sushi and ocean views at Nobu.

Of course, now all I wanted for dinner was sushi. But as soon as the embryo transfer was complete, I was instructed to stay away from all items potentially dangerous to a gestating baby as a precautionary measure: raw fish, soft cheeses, hot yoga, my retinol serum.

Just one embryo, my mind whispered, as it had done incessantly since the call from the fertility clinic. *Just one chance.*

I shook off the voice, took a bite of the fish tacos I'd settled for, and clicked the computer awake. I didn't expect Malik home until after ten, giving me plenty of time to research Raymond and do my nightly reflection on my Good Parent List. I connected my phone to the Bluetooth speaker on the desk, turned on the playlist I'd made from all the songs Carol listed at the top of her diary entries, and got to work.

I pulled up my notes from my conversation with Stanley to find the address of the home he grew up in, three doors down from Raymond: 5540 Branch Street. The street view showed a small one-story structure that had undergone a facelift in recent years. I panned slightly to the left and right until I found what must have been Raymond's old property. It was a narrow plot of land, though its depth was obscured by a thick tangle of overgrown grass, trees, and shrubbery.

As my focus moved toward the right edge of the property, I noticed a small break in the trees before the neighbor's neatly manicured lawn began. My breath caught in my throat when I spotted the telltale shimmer of water.

There it was—the creek. It appeared to be just a sliver of a thing, but it was difficult to accurately gauge its size given the volume of trees that grew from its banks. Their thin trunks tilted toward the water, their branches stretching toward their brothers across the creek, as though attempting to shield the water from view. A flimsy chain-link fence separated the sidewalk from the marshy land.

I tried to zoom in for a closer look, but the image exploded into an indiscriminate sea of pixels. I sighed in frustration, wishing for the hundredth time that week that I was back in Raleigh.

On a whim, I plugged Raymond's address into the search bar of the folder of police documents. My pulse quickened when a single result popped up. I opened the file, a PDF scan of an officer's typed notes.

8-14-64

Interviewed R.G. at 5546 Branch Street, after two tips suggesting invest. of 'The Orphan.'

Approx. 20 minutes.

Shifty kid, either avoided eye contact completely or stared aggressively at interviewer.

Said he worked at The Crown Barber Shop on E. Hargett Street the afternoon of Fri., 7-3-64. Later confirmed by Mr. Crown, recalling how busy the shop was. Everyone wanted a fresh cut ahead of the 4th.

Story corroborated by several of Mr. Crown's customers that afternoon.

I read the brief passage over and over. July 3, 1964. I knew that date. I scanned my notes until I found it. It was the day Geraldine Williams, Barbara's older sister, went missing. I reread the details of her disappearance and a chill raced up my back. Police *had* looked into Raymond for Geraldine's disappearance. And she was last seen at a home on Raymond's street. But he had an alibi, at a busy barbershop, with multiple witnesses attesting to his whereabouts.

Barbara and her family must have missed this brief, cryptic mention within the police files. If I hadn't looked up Raymond's old address, I never would have found it either.

Did this mean Raymond was actually innocent? He didn't strike me as the type of person several people would lie for in order to create an alibi. Maybe the cops' time line was off, and Geraldine was abducted several hours after she was last seen, possibly after Raymond got off work. Or maybe Raymond took a break at some point, long enough for him to snatch Geraldine off the street. Or maybe he had nothing to do with any of the girls' disappearances at all.

I groaned in frustration. Was I just going around in circles?

I typed "Orphan" into the search bar of the document folder to see if I could find the tips the officer mentioned. Two hits turned up in a single document.

"You should check out that orphan kid on Branch," said the first tip from an anonymous source. *"He's always leering at my daughter and her friends. I think he lives all alone in that house, and throws raucous parties with high school girls, even though I believe he's in college now."*

"I'm telling you, that orphan kid is no good," another anonymous tipper was quoted as having said. *"Tooling around in that car of his, shouting obscenities at girls, smoking grass on the front porch of that dilapidated house. If anyone in this neighborhood is doing something to our girls, it's him."*

I found myself feeling surprisingly defensive of Raymond at that moment. The reasons behind the tips—catcalling girls, joyriding around town, and smoking weed—were a far cry from the usual red flags I heard about serial killers on my true crime podcasts. I thought about how lonely he must have felt after his aunt died, living by himself in an empty house, cast out by his community.

But then I recalled Barbara's story, and Carol's haunting diary entry: *let's just say I wouldn't want to be left alone with him . . .*

I knew exactly what I would do if I were in Raleigh. I would ask Barbara and Stanley to put me in touch with other people who might have known Raymond at the time. I would knock on doors, look up old phone numbers, visit every address that appeared in police records, walk every inch of Raymond's old property myself.

I had to go back.

Of course, a thorough search of his old property—the kind that might actually uncover evidence, or even human remains—would require a warrant and the presence of law enforcement.

That's when it dawned on me that I hadn't tried reaching out to the police. It took only a few minutes to track down the email addresses for several detectives at the Raleigh Police Department's Homicide Division, on a page seeking information on multiple cold cases. I carefully drafted a single email that could be shared with each of them and included all the information I'd provided to the reporter, as well as a link to the article I'd helped secure. And this time, I included a summary of everything Barbara had shared about Raymond.

When I was done, I glanced at the time: 10:17. I'd managed to blow through the entire evening without ever opening my therapy journal.

What was wrong with me? Why had I prioritized my Raymond research over my Good Parent List?

Why am I not more excited? Shouldn't I be excited?

I carefully tidied the desk, turned off the Bluetooth speaker, put away all the physical evidence of my digital sleuthing, and shut the door behind me. It wasn't as easy to close the cavern of guilt in my gut, which seemed to have a gravitational pull all its own.

As the door clicked closed, I thought I heard a sound from down the hall. I froze, still clutching the office doorknob.

Was it just my imagination, or was there music coming from the bedroom Malik and I shared?

Goosebumps scurried up my arms. Malik wasn't home yet; surely I would have heard him come in, and he definitely would have peeked inside the office to say hello.

I crept toward the closed bedroom door. From the crack below it, I could see that the room was pitch-black.

My mind wasn't playing tricks on me—there was definitely music coming from inside the room.

I breathed deeply but silently, racking my brain for a logical explanation. There was something familiar about the woman's soulful, plaintive voice, and the vintage-sounding organ that added a hint of gospel to the melody. But I couldn't quite place it.

Ignoring my screaming instincts, I swung the door open and flipped on the lights.

The music was coming from the Bluetooth speaker on our dresser. Malik had purchased and connected several of them so we could play music throughout the townhouse.

My heart still thrumming, I pulled my phone from my pocket and navigated to the app that controlled the speakers. Apparently, I'd been playing Carol's music in both the office and the bedroom all night. Though it was weird that it was playing in just those rooms, and not the entire house. Maybe it was a leftover setting from the last time someone used the app?

I tried to laugh at myself and hit pause on Mary Wells. Why did old love songs sound so eerie when played in the wrong context?

When I looked down at the title of the song, a shudder rippled through my body.

It was called "Guess Who."

TWENTY-TWO

MALIK DIDN'T FIGHT ME WHEN I TOLD HIM I WANTED TO go to Raleigh over Veterans Day weekend. Perhaps this was because the Detroit trip had gone so well; he still didn't know I'd fainted at dinner with Sasha. Perhaps he was reassured by the fact that I'd spend the bulk of the trip with Barbara; I wouldn't be there alone. Perhaps it was due to misplaced guilt; he and several team members were planning to work through the weekend to ensure an upcoming product launched on time. Or perhaps it was because he recognized that if I was out of town, he'd be less likely to drive me insane with his continued questions about potential pregnancy symptoms.

We still had a week until our official pregnancy test at the fertility center, and the wait was maddening. I distracted myself by packing and repacking for Raleigh. Whenever I thought about zipping the suitcase shut for good and returning to Malik, I imagined the searching look on his face when he'd inevitably ask, "How are you feeling?" for the umpteenth time that day. I'd suddenly become inspired to find a new item to fold into my bag.

The final addition to my luggage came on Friday afternoon, after Malik arrived home a couple hours earlier than expected, startling me as I stood in the bathroom gelling down my edges while listening to the latest episode of *The Unforgotten.*

"What are you doing back so soon?" I asked, picking up the brush I'd dropped to the floor in surprise and hitting pause on the podcast. "I thought you weren't going to pick me up for the airport till three."

"Yeah, I know," he said, his expression cowed as he leaned against the doorframe. "I thought we could have lunch before we head to the airport. I'm going to miss you while you're away."

I fought the urge to roll my eyes as I turned back toward my reflection to finish my hair. God, I was irritable. "I'm only going to be gone for a weekend," I said.

"I know, I know," he replied. His gaze rose to meet mine in the mirror. "So, how are you feeling?"

I shooed him out of the bathroom with a promise that I'd meet him downstairs shortly. But as I headed down to him, I found myself in desperate need of just a few more moments of solitude. I ducked into our guest-bedroom-slash-office and shut the door softly behind me.

My eyes fell on Carol's trunk. I gently pried its tarnished brass latches open and inhaled the smell of its contents. It reminded me of the slightly musty scent of a used bookstore, but there was also a lingering sweetness that made me wonder if notes of Carol's perfume were trapped in its faded floral lining.

With no plan or purpose in mind, I pulled open one of its cloth-covered drawers and fished out the decrepit plastic bag containing the bracelet I'd found. The charms shifted against my fingertips as I stared at them through the gauzy film of their ancient casing. I'm not sure why, but I took the bracelet to our bedroom, tucked it into a small velvet jewelry box, and slipped it into the leather tote waiting on top of my suitcase. Maybe it would act as a talisman to guide me during my journey, or at least a physical reminder of the myriad questions that hovered over the case like fog.

* * *

THE GENTLE MELODY OF MY iPhone's alarm the next morning might as well have been an air-raid siren. I shot out of bed, or at least tried to, but found myself restrained by my bedding, aggressively tucked beneath the mattress by the hotel's housekeeping staff.

My heart raced as I groped to silence my phone and fumbled for the light switch, filling the room with sickly yellow light. It took a moment for me to remember that I was in Raleigh. I pulled myself farther upright in bed and rubbed my eyes, which were parched and grainy from lack of sleep and the frosty, recycled hotel room air.

I'd set my alarm for seven, which meant it felt like four, since I was still on L.A. time. Barbara was scheduled to pick me up at eight, having eagerly agreed to take me on a macabre tour of the city.

As I stretched my sleep-stiff limbs, my arm grazed my right breast, and I winced. I touched both breasts gingerly; they were uncomfortably swollen and tender to the touch. I thought about texting Malik—it was a potential sign of pregnancy—but decided against it. I didn't want to send him down a Google tailspin.

I moved into the bathroom to get ready for the day. I was so lost in thought, my body on autopilot as I performed the ritual of relieving myself, that it took my brain a moment to register the small red splotches on the tissue I held. I was spotting.

My stomach somersaulted. The sight of blood immediately brought me back to my Valentine's Day miscarriage. But this was far less blood. I tried to remind myself that light bleeding at this stage could mean nothing, but I also knew it could mean the end of everything.

I thought of the little girl from my dream, and my chest tightened.

I sent a message to my fertility nurse to tell her what was happening. My phone buzzed in my hand immediately, but it was a text from Barbara: "Be there in 5!"

There was nothing I could do but wait for the nurse's reply; at least if I waited with Barbara, I could keep my restless mind occupied. I packed a few of the precautionary menstrual pads I kept with me into my tote bag for the day and tried to refocus on the busy day ahead.

Barbara was downstairs waiting for me in a champagne-colored sedan, nodding to whatever song played on the radio. I tapped lightly on her passenger window, and the sound of Chaka Khan's "Ain't Nobody" wafted into the cool air.

"Hi, sugar," Barbara greeted me, waving excitedly. "Come on in!" Her cheer was like a balm to my rattled nerves.

She navigated us onto a road flanked by painted brick buildings that had clearly stood for quite some time. They were all just a few stories high and housed shops and restaurants on the ground floor.

"Folks used to call this area Black Main Street back in the day," Barbara said. "There used to be a beautiful Black-owned hotel with a fancy ballroom. Mama and Pop used to get dressed up to see bands play. They saw Duke Ellington in the flesh!"

Barbara had barely finished her sentence when a series of stately burgundy brick buildings with cream trim appeared in front of us. A banner affixed to a wrought-iron fence welcomed us to "Bear Country."

"That's Shaw, right?" I asked.

"That's right," Barbara said, nodding. "It was one of the first places in the South where a Black person could get a higher education. SNCC was actually born there. That's the Student Nonviolent Coordinating Committee, sugar. They organized all kinds of sit-ins and peaceful protests against segregation." She lifted her chin proudly. "I was actually one of a handful of students chosen to integrate an accelerated math program at the all-white high school, my senior year."

I looked at Barbara, taking in the smooth brown skin of her face. While I was well aware of the blatant racism my parents experienced, especially growing up in the Jim Crow South, it was still hard to believe how recent it all was. It shouldn't have been a surprise, though, given how racism continued to infect the lives of my generation. The way the flash of red and blue lights behind our car didn't make Malik worry about a pricey ticket, but about the possibility of a routine traffic stop going terribly, fatally wrong. The way some of my college classmates assumed I was only admitted into my school because of nonexistent affirmative action quotas. How the staff at the high-end boutiques in Beverly Hills sometimes followed me around the store like a second shadow, and I occasionally found myself buying something just to demonstrate that people who looked like me could afford to do so.

Eventually Barbara steered us into a residential neighborhood. The houses were more modest than those on Grammy's street, and many appeared to be in various stages of disrepair. I didn't see any of the tall new builds that smacked of gentrification. The clusters of men that lingered on the front porches of the homes turned to watch as we drove by, as though sussing out whether we belonged or posed some sort of threat.

As I took in the landscape rolling by my window, I noticed a squat burgundy sign blooming from a patch of grass.

"Walnut Creek Trail!" I said, reading it. "That leads to the Walnut Creek Wetlands area, right?"

Barbara looked impressed. "You sure you haven't spent much time in Raleigh?"

"Just a lot of time on Google Maps."

She pulled over and put the car in park. "We're here." She sighed, tilting her head toward her window. "Raymond's old plot."

I leaned forward to peer past her. There it was, the same view I'd pulled up online, only larger, crisper, real. A narrow tract of land, choked by overgrown greenery, sloping gently toward a silver stream.

I extricated myself from my seatbelt and exited the car, flooded with such a rush of adrenaline that I nearly forgot to close the door behind me. I stopped at the curb and stared into the thick layers of foliage, a kaleidoscope of green. It was nearly as difficult to see the details of the land when I was here as it had been on my computer back in L.A.

I took a step toward the thicket of overgrowth, but Barbara grabbed me by the arm. "It's not safe," she warned. "There could be snakes, ticks, lord knows what else."

I stared longingly at the land. I wanted to crawl through the tiny forest, feel the grass beneath my boots. I had only forty-eight hours in Raleigh; I couldn't afford to waste it chasing dead ends.

I moved toward the creek edge of the property. The flimsy fence barricading the creek was more rust than metal. The water didn't appear very deep; I could nearly see the entirety of the rocks that jutted from its surface. The creek made a gentle sound as it meandered through those rocks, as if whispering to me.

From this angle, I had a slightly better view of Raymond's old property. It went farther back than I expected. I thought I spotted a flash of blue beyond all the green, the color the sky would have been on a clear day. I raked the ground with my gaze until I spotted a large stick. I hoisted it up and parted the bushes closest to me to get a better view.

"Barbara"—I gasped—"look. Just to the right of the stick."

I heard a sharp breath behind my shoulder. "The hydrangeas," Barbara exhaled. There appeared to be hundreds of them, growing thick on top of one another. Some of the blooms were brown and wilted, like the one Raymond had deadheaded in Barbara's story, but many were a powdery blue, vibrant against the plant's green leaves. The hydrangeas seemed to cover the entire back edge of the property, like a giant funeral spray. I was desperate to know if they were a horticultural miracle, having survived untended for so long, or if they thrived thanks to the nutrients they'd feasted on from whatever was buried below.

BARBARA HAD GENEROUSLY OFFERED TO assemble some of the loved ones of the missing girls, as well as a few of her and Stanley's friends who'd lived in the neighborhood when the girls began to vanish. It would be helpful to hear what they thought might have happened to their daughters, sisters, cousins, and friends, and, I hoped, to learn more about the people who might have been involved in their disappearances.

As we arranged cocktail napkins, disposable plates, a charcuterie board, and a large pitcher of lemonade on Barbara's coffee table, I stole glances at the framed photographs scattered throughout her living room. I couldn't help but smile at an image on her fireplace mantel. In it, Barbara stood between a young man and woman, likely in their late twenties or early thirties. The backdrop was a blur of ocean and sky, the type of vantage point you could achieve only aboard a large boat. The picture captured them at a particularly windy moment; Barbara and the young woman were trying to hold their hair out of their faces, and the young man's tropical print shirt flapped like a flag. They were all laughing so hard I could almost hear it.

"Are those your kids?" I asked. Barbara turned to glance at the photo.

"Yes! Those are my babies. Ebony and Cory. That's when they surprised me with a cruise for my sixtieth birthday. Ain't that sweet?"

"They must be good kids."

"They're the best," Barbara said, shifting a tray of cookies slightly farther from the table's edge. Then she chuckled. "Well, that wasn't always the case, but all kids have their growing pains. Hard to believe that my Ebony is about to be a mother herself!" Barbara straightened and looked at me appraisingly, her eyes resting on my wedding ring. "How about you, sugar? Planning on having kids?"

Maybe it was because I still hadn't heard from my fertility nurse, or because of my yo-yoing hormones, or because the warm chocolate chip cookies on the coffee table smelled like a happy home. But all of a sudden, I began to cry.

"I'm sorry," I said, attempting to plug my leaking eyes with my fingertips. "I don't know where this is coming from."

"Shhhhh," Barbara said, wrapping an arm around my shoulders and steering me toward her cream-colored couch. The tenderness of her touch only made the tears come faster. "It's okay, sugar. I'm sorry I asked. My kids are always chastising me for asking people sensitive questions I have no business knowing the answers to."

"No, it's all right," I said, my voice pitiful even to my own ears.

I accepted a handful of cocktail napkins from Barbara and dabbed my eyes. "My husband and I . . . we've been trying. For years, actually. It's been really hard."

Barbara *tsked* herself as she gently rubbed my back. "And here I go throwing salt in the wound, askin' you about it."

"You'd think I wouldn't be so sensitive about it after all this time." I took a deep, calming breath. "Actually," I said, "if we're going to talk about personal stuff, do you mind if I ask you something?"

"Shoot."

"How did you know you were ready to be a mom?"

Barbara laughed. "Oh, I don't know that I ever felt ready," she said. "I'm not sure if anyone really does. You can't imagine all the ways your life is going to change."

Her hand moved in a soft clockwise motion against my back. "I have to ask though. You said you and your husband have been trying to get pregnant for a while. But you're still wrestling with whether you're ready to have kids?"

My tears flowed faster. "All these years, trying to get pregnant . . . it's given me too much time to think. It's forced me to imagine what a life without children of my own would look like, because—let's be honest—at this point, that could be a real possibility."

I wrapped my arms around my middle, as though covering the ears of the little girl that might have been growing inside me. "Sometimes, when I think about that life, I think it might actually suit me better. I mean, look at me . . . flying across the country on the spur of the moment to play amateur sleuth. I couldn't do things like this if I had kids."

The image of the little girl running into my waiting arms floated past my consciousness. I found myself smiling at the memory of her warm, surprisingly strong embrace.

"Lately, I've grown kind of attached to having a little g— I mean, a child of my own," I said. "But I can't stop wondering what kind of mom I'd be. If I'd be what that child deserves."

Barbara shook her head. "Back when I got married, I didn't know any married couples who didn't have kids unless they were physically unable to. Things have changed a bit now, of course. My son, Cory? He and his partner don't wanna get married, ever, and they don't wanna have kids."

She took my hands in hers. "Sometimes I get a bit jealous of your generation. All the options you have, all the ways you can choose to live your lives. All that choice sounds like such a luxury. But I'm beginning to realize it must be a burden, too. There's so much pressure to make the right decisions, and concern over what people will think about them. Hell, even my choosing to get a divorce at forty-seven felt reckless!"

Barbara laughed. "I don't think most people know for sure that they're ready to have kids. They just make a commitment and trust they'll figure things out along the way. And you will figure things out, Sydney. Look at all the energy you're puttin' into finding out what happened to Carol, and Geri, and the girls. If you care this much about kids you never met, imagine how much you'll care for your own children."

Her words cleared something away in my mind, like sunshine burning through a morning marine layer.

"When my son told me that he and his partner decided not to have children, I asked him, 'How can you be sure you won't regret it?'" Barbara chuckled wryly. "I tell you, this kid is so wise. He said the decisions we make in life might not be as important as what we choose to do with them." She squeezed my hand. "I know it's scary, but sometimes in life the only way forward is to take a leap, and not look back."

TWENTY-THREE

As the guests began to arrive, Barbara's house filled with the same muted festivity I had witnessed at the repast following Grammy's funeral. Old friends caught up on the events of the preceding years over light bites and beverages, though their conversations were shrouded by the solemnity of the occasion that brought them together.

Everyone seemed to know one another, or at least knew someone else in the room they could talk to. Knowing no one, I lingered beside Barbara, who graciously introduced me to people as they arrived.

There were the family members of missing girls: Loretta's niece, Bettie's older brother, Marian's mother, whose tearjerking photo was included alongside *The News & Observer* article. And there were friends and loved ones who knew them: Sally's boyfriend, Bettie's roommate at Shaw, and Cathy, the girl—now a woman roughly my mother's age—whose ear Raymond had whispered into by the hydrangeas.

"Oh my God," one woman said when her eyes landed on me,

just as Barbara was about to introduce us. A hand shot to her red lacquered mouth. "You look so much like Carol."

"You knew my aunt?"

She nodded slowly. "We were best friends for a while. We'd grown apart by the time she was gone. You know how high school friendships can be. She was so busy with theater and choir and her little college boyfriend, she barely had time for her old friends anymore."

"Michael?" I asked.

The look of surprise returned to her face. "What?"

"Her college boyfriend. Michael Hall?"

"You knew about that? She'd always tried to keep their relationship a secret from everyone."

"Sydney is an excellent investigator," Barbara interjected, her tone warm and slightly proprietary, like that of a proud mom.

"Are y'all talking about Michael Hall?" asked a woman with a sleek salt-and-pepper bob, joining our circle. "I had such a crush on that boy! He was my sister's math tutor for a minute. I'd find every excuse I could to go into the kitchen while they were studying and strut past the table, as if he'd pay any attention to my little behind."

The women all laughed knowingly, as though remembering their own feeble attempts at flirting with Michael. Except for one woman, with coppery shoulder-length curls. Her lips were pinched shut, as though preventing a secret from battling its way out of her mouth.

"Who's your sister?" I asked the bobbed woman.

She smiled solemnly. "Marian," she answered. "She was the first of the girls to go missing."

Huh. Michael tutored Marian? He'd said he didn't know any of the missing girls besides Carol. Maybe he'd forgotten? It had happened sixty years ago, after all. But wouldn't her eventual disappearance have burned his connection to her into his brain?

"Everyone had a crush on Michael," a woman with purple cat-eye glasses said. "He was just so handsome." She shook her head. "I just never understood why he hung around that creepy kid."

"You mean Scarecrow?" Carol's friend asked.

"Mmm-hmm," said a woman with purple glasses. "I mean, I can understand why he'd want to align himself with someone like Michael. But what did Michael see in him?"

The woman with the copper curls shifted uncomfortably, fiddling with the strap of her purse.

"I talked with Michael recently," I offered. "He made it sound as though he and his friends took pity on Raymond, that they felt bad about how people treated him."

"Guess Michael's a kinder person than me," Purple Glasses said with a snort. "Pretty sure people only treated Scarecrow the way they did on account of what a creep he was."

"Did you have a weird experience with Raymond?" I asked.

Purple Glasses clucked her tongue. "Child, there were too many to count. Like when his assigned seat was behind mine in one of our classes, and I kept catching him leaning in close, smelling my hair."

The women all gave a collective groan.

"Sometimes he'd follow me to my next class, even though he wasn't in it," she continued. "He'd walk directly behind me, so there was barely any space between us. If I turned to confront him, he'd just stand there and stare at me, with this weird little smile on his face."

"He had a crush on a friend of mine once," Carol's friend spoke up. She caught the urgency in my glance and shook her head. "Not Carol," she clarified, "but someone else in our friend group. Carol's boyfriend courted her by taping a rose to her locker every morning. I guess that inspired Raymond to do something similar. But instead of roses, he slipped a piece of paper into the girl's locker every day for weeks, with a heart drawn in red crayon."

We all stared at Carol's friend blankly. A hand-drawn heart didn't sound so bad.

"It wasn't a cute Valentine's Day heart," she explained. "It was a detailed anatomical drawing, with all the veins and valves sticking out."

The women released another chorus of groans.

"Sydney!" Barbara called from somewhere across the room. I

scanned the crowd, finally spotting her beside the kitchen island. Stanley had arrived at some point. Barbara rested a hand on his shoulder, a familiar gesture, and I found myself wondering again if they might be more than friends.

"Sydney, there you are!" Barbara called, waving me over. The somber atmosphere in the house had shifted; the gathering was beginning to feel more like a party. Stanley and I hugged. "Sorry I'm late," he said. "I wanted to bring my cousin Dorothy, but she didn't get off work till three."

"It's so nice to meet you," the woman beside Stanley said, extending a hand in my direction. "I've heard so many great things about you from my cuz here."

As I took her hand, I noticed the bracelet hanging from her wrist. A vintage-looking silver charm bracelet. I'd seen two of the charms before: an old-fashioned telephone with a tiny rotary, and an oval-shaped locket with an engraving in elaborate script. Only the bracelet in my tote bag was engraved with the letters "SD." Possibly for Sally Dunn. Stanley's missing little sister.

My stomach lurched. Barbara frowned at me. "Sydney? You okay? Looks like you saw a ghost!"

"Your . . . your bracelet," I stammered, still holding Dorothy's hand.

"Yeah," Dorothy said, "it's super old-fashioned, I know. But I've had it forever. A few of us had them growing up, my older sister, and my cousin Sally. We were all super close."

I swallowed the bile that rose in my throat. "I . . . I found a bracelet that looks just like it."

I finally dropped Dorothy's hand and reached into my tote bag. All of my earlier concerns fluttered around me like a swarm of flies: would revealing the bracelet call Carol's innocence into question? Was I pointing a finger at Michael or Raymond without sufficient evidence? But I ignored them; the presence of a matching bracelet made it impossible for me to keep the secret any longer.

I fished the velvet jewelry box out of my tote with unsteady fingers, pulled from it the ancient plastic bag, and held it out to Dorothy.

She squinted at the bag, struggling to see the contents through its decades old film. Her eyes grew wide when the recognition clicked into place.

Dorothy's shriek sliced through the party like a hot knife.

TWENTY-FOUR

"It's Sally's!" Dorothy cried. Her hands trembled as if I'd dropped a hot coal in her palm. "Look, the locket has her initials, just like my locket has mine."

"Sydney," Stanley rasped, his eyes wide, "how do you have my sister's bracelet?"

Dorothy's scream had silenced the party; everyone in Barbara's house was staring at me, eager for my response.

"I found it," I said shakily. "In Carol's trunk."

"The trunk Michael Hall had all these years?" Stanley clarified. Accusatory whispers drifted through the room like an icy breeze.

"It was hidden behind a panel. I'm pretty sure Michael didn't even know it existed." Shame coated my esophagus. Was I defending Michael by throwing my own missing aunt under the bus?

I turned to Dorothy; her face had gone ashen. "You, your sister, and Sally all had the same bracelet?" I asked.

She regarded me skeptically, as though I might have stolen the bracelet right from Sally's wrist. Finally, she nodded. "We saved up and bought them at a shop over on Hargett Street. They were popular with kids our age; you could personalize them with engravings and charms. We thought of them as friendship bracelets, symbols of how close we all were. We kept pictures of each other in the lockets. See," she said, opening the locket with "SD" engraved on its front. "That's me, and that's my big sister. My sister and Sally are still in mine. We never took them off." She began to weep. "It just . . . it makes no sense that Carol would have it . . . or Michael."

As Dorothy broke into full sobs, and Barbara and Stanley bent to comfort her, I noticed the woman with the coppery curls dig her phone from her purse, glance at its screen, and make her way toward the door. I'm sure it was supposed to look as though she'd just received a text prompting her to leave, but it also looked like the move of someone who'd just invented an excuse for an early exit. I couldn't let her leave without talking to me. It almost seemed as though she was uncomfortable with everyone's glowing descriptions of Michael.

"I'll be right back," I said, following the woman through Barbara's increasingly crowded living room and catching her just as she set foot on the driveway.

"Excuse me, ma'am?" She jumped a little before turning to face me. "I'm sorry to bother you; I realized I didn't have a chance to introduce myself. I'm Sydney Singleton, visiting from L.A. My aunt Carol was one of the girls who went missing. Barbara helped put this event together because I'm trying to piece together what might have happened to her, and all the other missing girls."

The woman looked at me for a long moment, like she was deciding whether to engage or run. I gave her my most hopeful smile and extended a hand. I'd learned from my reporting days that it's harder to escape someone who's aggressively friendly than it is someone who's just plain aggressive. "It's nice to meet you," I added.

She sighed before finally shaking my hand. "You too. I'm Joyce."

"Did you know any of the missing girls?"

Joyce shifted in her cardigan. "Not personally, no. But I knew of them. Everyone in the neighborhood did."

"I could be totally wrong about this," I began gingerly, "but I thought you might have had a bit of a reaction to those stories about Michael and Raymond."

Her brow twitched.

"Did something happen to you?" I asked.

Joyce huffed. "You heard them in there. Seems like every girl in town had a Raymond story."

"It's true," I replied. "But I have a feeling you might be one of the few with a Michael story."

I was taking a chance; it was only a hunch. I held my breath for a painfully long moment, until her eyes locked on mine with a level of intensity that could only mean I'd landed on something true.

"Michael was dating my aunt when she disappeared," I said. "Anything you could share . . . I would be so grateful."

Joyce crossed her arms over her chest. Her body language told me she had no intention of telling me anything. But she didn't walk away.

"I'm just not sure Michael was the golden boy everyone seems to think he was," she said at last, studying her shoes.

My heart skipped. "Why is that?"

Joyce's gaze remained downcast. "Most of my strange experiences were with Raymond, like everyone else. We were on the same bus route before he got his car. He'd often sit right next to me, walking past rows of empty seats. He'd sit so close I could actually feel the heat coming off him. He'd stare at me the whole ride to school."

I felt slightly sick as I listened to her story, as though I could feel Raymond's stare on my own skin.

"But the worst was when we were all at Shaw," Joyce continued. "I was at a party with some friends. It was getting late, and a girl I knew said she was getting a ride home with a few people and convinced me to come with her. She didn't want me to walk home alone. 'Course when we got outside, I realized the car we were walking toward was Raymond's."

She shook her head and sighed. "I didn't want to make a scene, and there were a bunch of other people piling into the car. I wouldn't be alone with him. I think that's what made people comfortable enough to take rides from him sometimes, because there were usually a bunch of people doing it. Safety in numbers, or whatever. So I climbed in, too. Michael was in the passenger seat, and that also made me feel safer. He'd tutored me for a while a few years earlier, and always seemed like a good guy."

I fought to keep my expression neutral. How many of the girls had Michael tutored?

"There were three of us in the backseat," Joyce said. "Everything seemed pretty normal at first. Raymond had the music turned up loud, and folks were laughing and talking, telling stories from the party. They dropped the girl I knew off first, since she lived closest. Then they dropped off one of their teammates on the basketball team. And then it was just me, Michael, and Raymond. I told them where I lived, and Raymond looked at me through the rearview mirror, the first time he'd acknowledged me that whole drive, and said, 'I remember. From the bus.'"

I swallowed with effort; my mouth was suddenly as dry as sand.

"He didn't say anything after that," Joyce went on. "Neither of them did. They just went strangely silent. I was relieved when Raymond finally turned onto my street. But then he drove past my house. I told him, 'My house is just there.' But he kept going. I told him he could stop and let me out anywhere. But he still didn't say anything. I thought maybe Michael had fallen asleep in the passenger seat, because he wasn't saying anything either, but I tilted my head so I could see around his headrest, and I could see the reflection of his eyes through the window. He was just gazing out of it, like nothing strange was happening. I begged Raymond to stop, to just let me out. I told them both that it wasn't funny. But they just stayed silent." Joyce held the thick collar of her cardigan to her throat.

"I got desperate," she said. "When they finally had to stop at a light, I bolted out of that car and ran as fast as I could."

"Did they chase you?" I asked.

Joyce shook her copper curls. "No. I could just hear their laughter pouring out of the open back door."

"Did you tell anyone about this?"

She shook her head and studied her shoes again. Her head was bowed, as if with shame.

"I was so embarrassed. I wasn't supposed to be at that party, and my parents would've killed me if they'd known I'd gotten into Raymond's car," she said. "And what if I'd gotten Michael into real trouble if it was all just a dumb prank? Everyone liked him. I didn't think anyone would've believed me."

All the blood in my body ran cold. "I don't think it was a prank at all," I said.

January 11, 1965

Michael has been more and more distant lately, and busy all the time. Busy with RayRay, of all people. It's starting to feel like he's putting their friendship before our relationship.

Maybe he's tiring of me, after all this time. Maybe there's some girl at Shaw he's got his eye on.

Or it might have something to do with our last conversation (fight, more like it) about where we'll go when we leave Raleigh. He said if I really loved him, I'd agree to come to Oakland over Detroit.

Why does everyone's love for me only exist under the condition that I give up my own dreams? Is that what love is supposed to look like? Why are my dreams worth less than theirs?

The last few times I've been over to Michael's, he's made up excuses to leave me there, heading out with RayRay on little errands in RayRay's car. Like he can't stand to be around me for too long. Sometimes they're gone for hours, and I'm just sitting there, twiddling my thumbs.

Is this what life would be like if I went to Oakland with him? Why would he even want me with him, if this is how it's going to be?

Where do they go off to on their drives?

TWENTY-FIVE

THAT NIGHT, IN MY DREAM, I WAS BACK IN MY AND MA-
lik's fictional future home, watching through the shut
sliding glass door as our daughter toddled around our backyard. It
looked as though she'd only recently learned to walk. She pulled
each leg—long but adorably plush with baby fat—up from the
ground with effort and wobbled when her feet returned to the earth
as though it trembled beneath her.

I smiled at the sight and sipped from a glass of iced tea. I looked
down at the glass in my hands and realized it was the same one that
Eloise, Michael's mom, had used to serve me sun tea during my
previous visit to Raleigh. I was holding the glass when she gave me
the yearbook containing the images, names, and disappearance
dates of all the missing girls.

Something about this realization caused the dream to slip off its
axis; everything began to slide precariously in the direction of a
nightmare.

When I looked up from the glass, I saw that the backyard had
suddenly morphed in that unsettlingly ephemeral manner of dreams.
Now, instead of being bordered by a line of neat shrubs, the back

edge of the yard had transformed into a giant hydrangea bush, taller than any tree in view. The bush appeared to swell as I watched, its ends stretching along the border of our yard like tentacles. Its stems probed the air like thousands of antennae.

My heart leapt into my throat as I watched our daughter begin to move unsteadily toward the pulsing, spreading plant.

"No!" I screamed, dropping my glass of tea. I banged against the door with both fists, trying desperately to get the little girl's attention. The glass shattered loudly when it hit the hardwood, sending iced tea cascading around my feet. As can happen only in a dream, the spilled tea continued to fill the room, as though from a geyser instead of a glass. It rose up my legs at an alarming speed and threatened to sweep me off my feet. I grasped the handle of the sliding glass door and struggled to pry it open, but it wouldn't budge.

I kept one hand on the door handle to maintain my balance in the now chest-high flood and continued to bang on the thick glass with the other, watching in horror as my daughter toddled closer to the hydrangeas. The flowers moved toward her on their antennae-stems, appearing to sniff her.

The sloshing tea, thick and brown as river water, licked at my chin. I hurled my body upward to grasp the top of the doorframe, struggling to pull my head farther above the surface of the liquid.

I was going to drown in my own kitchen, I realized. My eyes filled with hot, defeated tears as I continued to bang fruitlessly against the door.

Just before the liquid closed the gap between my head and the ceiling, I watched the bush wrap its stems around my daughter like rope. I couldn't hear her scream, but I could see it. Her little mouth stretched wide with terror as the plant sucked her into its dense green depths, consuming her.

I sat bolt upright in bed, panting. My T-shirt and shorts were soaked with sweat, as were the sheets tangled around my body. The dampness made me feel as though I'd actually just been rescued from my flooded kitchen. My heart thudded as I kicked the bedding from my legs and instinctively checked the sheet beneath me, and the inside of my shorts. But no, I wasn't bleeding. Just light spotting. Thank God, I thought, hoping my fertility nurse would get back to me soon. What was taking her so long, anyway?

I stumbled to the bathroom on shaking legs, peeled off my wet clothes, wrapped myself in the thick white hotel robe, and splashed my face with water.

I hadn't had a drowning nightmare since Detroit, when Sasha helped me realize what inspired them. I felt foolish to have thought they were behind me. And now an awful new layer had been added. It was incredibly cruel of my subconscious to introduce such a beautiful and tangible projection of what my future child might look like only to immediately torment me with the thought of losing her.

I took another long breath before walking back to the bedroom. I sat on the edge of the bed and picked my phone up from the nightstand.

The first thing I noticed was that it was just after 4:00 A.M. The second thing I noticed was the eight unread text messages from Malik, the latest of which read: "Please just text me in the morning and let me know you're okay."

"Fuck." Guilt crawled up my arms like ants. I'd promised to call Malik every night to tell him how the trip was going. Instead, after Stanley and Dorothy had left Barbara's house, shaken and confused, and I'd helped Barbara clean up after the guests, I went back to the hotel, ordered room service, typed up a detailed account of the day, emailed it to *The News & Observer* reporter in the hope of inspiring further investigation, and collapsed into bed. I'd gotten lost in my work. It was intoxicating, working on something that felt truly urgent and important. And it was a feeling I'd rarely experienced since I'd left the *Chronicle*. But I'd done it all over checking in with my loving, concerned husband.

I did the math in my head; it was after 1:00 A.M. in L.A. Malik was an early-to-bed, early-to-rise kind of guy. He also always kept his ringer on in case of emergencies. Calling would wake him in a panic, but he deserved more than a text.

I opened the Voice Memos app, cleared the sleep from my voice, and hit record.

"Hi, sweetheart. I'm so, so sorry I didn't call last night. I was just tired from all the driving and talking to so many people. I passed out right after I finished my room service dinner."

I fiddled with the belt on my robe for a moment before forcing myself to stop. Why was I nervous? I wasn't exactly lying; but I knew I couldn't tell Malik the whole truth without worrying him.

"Barbara's been so helpful," I went on. "I'm glad I came—there's no way I would've gotten all this information back in L.A. I hope you're having a great weekend, and I'll call you tonight. I promise. I love you."

I was far too alert to bother trying to fall back asleep, but it was too early to go anywhere, talk to anyone, or do much of anything. The Starbucks down the street wasn't even open yet.

My phone vibrated against my palm, startling me. Malik had already texted back: "I'm just glad you're all right."

I could feel the chill of his message deep in my chest. No "I love you." No kiss emojis. Either he'd been up waiting, attacking some neglected corner of our apartment with his arsenal of cleaning supplies, or he'd set his phone to max volume before retreating to bed.

"I'm really, really sorry," I replied, adding a string of sad face and heart emojis for good measure.

I walked over to the little desk facing the window and opened my laptop, deciding I might as well put my early morning energy to good use. My email window was still open, and I was surprised to see that *The News & Observer* reporter had already replied, shortly after midnight. Guilt threatened to smother me for the second time that morning; I hoped I hadn't introduced her to her equivalent of my McEwan case.

Thanks for sharing all this, Sydney—I'll take a closer look in the morning.

Are you familiar with a podcast called "The Unforgotten"?

Several of their listeners sent them the article about the missing girls, and they're considering doing an episode about them. They asked for your contact info to learn more; would you like me to share it with them?

I covered my mouth to stifle a squeal. *The Unforgotten* was my favorite true crime podcast, the podcast that got me hooked on the genre in the first place. They had built a massive audience who dubbed themselves the Unforgotten Army and supported the podcast by attending sold-out live shows, buying merch, and donating to causes championed by the hosts.

If they dedicated an episode to the girls, millions of people would hear about what happened to them. They had put enough pressure on a few cold cases that police were forced to reopen their investigations.

I typed an emphatic reply to the reporter and did a celebration dance around the hotel room, tiptoeing so I wouldn't wake the neighbors below me. This was working. All the time and effort I was pouring into this investigation, all the difficult conversations I was forcing with people from Carol's past and with my husband . . . it would all be worth it if I could help crack this case. I just had to keep pushing. I was getting so close—I could feel it.

As soon as my heart rate returned to normal, I forced myself to sit back down at my desk. I scanned the notes I'd sent to the reporter the night before, including the epiphany sparked by Joyce's harrowing story, how she flung herself from Raymond's moving car after he and Michael ignored her pleas to be released.

Michael and Raymond hunted those girls together.

It all made perfect sense now, why popular, charismatic Michael befriended creepy, friendless Raymond. It had nothing to do with kindness, or pity. Michael was drawn to Raymond because they shared the same dark, depraved proclivities, and Raymond provided the perfect cover for Michael's crimes. After all, why would anyone suspect Michael of wrongdoing with Raymond right there, given Raymond's notoriously unsettling behavior over the years?

In her final diary entry, Carol had described how Michael and Raymond would regularly step out for "little errands in RayRay's car," sometimes leaving her alone at Michael's place for hours.

Where do they go off to on their drives? Carol wondered.

Perhaps they circled Raleigh's streets, prowling for girls to offer rides to. Leveraging Michael's charm and reputation to gain their trust. Where would they have taken Joyce if she hadn't managed to break free? Would she have become yet another missing girl?

All of the girls with missing person reports—every girl except Carol—were last seen walking. Walking to or from school, or a library, or a grocery store, or an after-school job, or home. And both Geri and Sally—Barbara's and Stanley's sisters—were last seen climbing into a dark early 1950s sedan, likely a Chevy 210.

I pulled up the dates of the girls' disappearances. Marian, the first to go missing—a girl Michael tutored, though later claimed not to have known—was last seen in September 1963. Shortly after Michael would have moved out of Eloise's house and into his own place at Shaw.

Maybe he used his newfound freedom to prey on Raleigh's girls. Maybe away from Eloise's watchful eye, he allowed his evil impulses to go unchecked.

Did Carol eventually suspect what was happening? Maybe that explained Sally's bracelet—maybe Carol had found the bracelet Sally never removed at Michael's, and instantly knew. Maybe she stashed the bracelet in her trunk as evidence. Maybe she confronted Michael about what happened to Sally and the other girls and paid the ultimate price. Maybe he'd killed Carol, and thinking he might finally become a suspect this time, given his direct connection to her or the way it all went down, he filed the missing person report to throw police off the trail and later asked his sister to retract it, leading them to believe that Carol was alive and well.

I felt heartsick for Carol, though the sensation was immediately followed by a different sort of queasiness: had Sasha and I really walked willingly into the home of a serial killer?

I suddenly saw the whole experience in a different light. The odd hint of disappointment in his voice when he realized I hadn't come to Detroit alone. How his wife, Rosa, had prepared that enormous feast only to make an excuse for her and her daughter to leave, as though he'd asked to be alone with me. How he'd looked me up on Instagram prior to my visit and noticed how closely I resembled Carol. The string of Instagram notifications he later left on my account, as he scrolled far back through my photos, as if savoring them.

Michael had my home address. I'd given it to him so he could send me Carol's trunk.

A shudder racked my body.

Maybe Raymond was a victim of Michael's, too. He had apparently vanished shortly after Carol. Maybe Michael decided he no longer needed a partner. Or wanted to get rid of anyone with knowledge of what he'd done.

It all made a sick, perfect kind of sense. But how could I prove it?

I opened the digital file containing the police records and typed in Michael's name. Nothing. I went to the contacts app on my phone and looked up the address of Eloise's home, the home Michael grew up in. I plugged the address into my search bar in case police had stopped by to question Michael at some point, as they'd done with Raymond. Also nothing.

I shouldn't have been surprised; based on everything I'd heard about Michael prior to Joyce's frightening story, it didn't seem that there was any reason to suspect Michael. I thought about Joyce's reasoning for not going to the police. *I was so embarrassed . . . My parents would've killed me . . . Everyone liked him . . . I didn't think anyone would've believed me.* If anyone else had gone through what she'd been through, and survived, they might have felt similarly and kept their mouths shut.

I wasn't sure how to go about further investigating Michael. I did have a concrete tactic I wanted to try regarding Raymond, though. I was frustrated that his former property was too overgrown for me to explore. But what would be more helpful would be to talk to people who had a clear view of his land back when Raleigh's Black girls were disappearing. I had to try to talk to Raymond's old neighbors. It's what the hosts of *The Unforgotten* would do.

Anxiety flooded my lungs like icy water. I'd had to go door-to-door searching for quotes and information often back in my reporting days. It usually took hours, if not days, and frequently proved futile. I was also completely out of practice; I hadn't canvassed for quotes since the McEwan kids went missing nearly a decade ago.

I didn't have that kind of time. This was my last full day in Raleigh; I had to make every second count. I couldn't imagine Malik would be so supportive of another trip after the previous night's fuckup. I needed to narrow down my search before I ventured back into Raymond's former neighborhood. I typed his old address into Google Maps and panned around the property, jotting down the surrounding addresses. Then I looked them up on Zillow to find out when the homes were built and last sold.

The house to the right of the property was built in 1982 and last listed in 2012. I scratched it from my list. The house across the street had been purchased just last year; anyone who'd lived there while Raymond had was long gone. I was beginning to feel defeated when I plugged in the address of the house to the left of Raymond's land. According to Zillow it had been built in 1920, though clearly it had undergone a few facelifts since its original construction. It had been listed for sale once in 2016, and there had been a pending sale, but the listing was taken down after a few months.

Bingo.

TWENTY-SIX

THE CLOUDS HUNG LOW ABOVE BRANCH STREET LATER
that morning, giving the outdoors a claustrophobic feeling. I parked in front of Raymond's old property and stared beyond my window into the verdant abyss.

A vision from my nightmare tore through my mind: the terror
in my little girl's scream as she was devoured by the hydrangea
bush. My hands shot down to my abdomen reflexively, as though
protecting her.

I climbed out of my rental car and walked toward the charming
redbrick home beside Raymond's former land. There wasn't a car
in the shallow gravel driveway, though that didn't mean the house
was empty; there was plenty of street parking available. I noticed
that the front porch had been modified to accommodate a wheel-
chair ramp.

The heavy wooden door had a column of cut glass down its center. I paused on the porch, listening for signs of life, any indication
of who might be inside. But all I could hear was the sound of dry
leaves scuttling down the road behind me, briefly animated by a
gust of wind.

I pressed the doorbell and listened to it echo through the house. I listened harder as the echo subsided, waiting for the sound of footsteps. I kept an eye on the glass portion of the door to see if a shadow passed in front of it.

My heart sank as the seconds ticked by. I tried the doorbell again; more silence.

Leaving a note would be a last resort. If I left one now, and the inhabitants didn't want to talk to me, they could easily avoid answering the door for the rest of my visit. Besides, my reason for wanting to speak to them was difficult to capture on the hotel notepad I'd stashed in my tote bag, a list of questions primed and ready to go on the first page. I checked my watch; it was 8:00 on a Sunday morning. Maybe they'd gone to an early church service.

I reluctantly turned toward my car; I'd try coming back later. I was increasingly and acutely aware of how precious my remaining time in Raleigh was. My direct access to these people and places would be beyond my reach before I knew it.

As I stepped onto the gravel drive, I heard the door behind me creak open. I turned to see a tall man standing in the doorway. His tremendous muscles shifted beneath his Henley as he dried his hands with a powder blue towel the same hue as his pants. Scrubs. He looked to be around my parents' age, maybe a little younger; I wondered if he'd grown up in this house. "Hi there," he said, his voice as bass-heavy as a hip-hop beat. "Can I help you?"

"Hi," I said, smiling sheepishly, my heart skittering with nerves. "I'm sorry to bother you. This is random, but I was wondering if anyone who currently lives in this house lived here back in the early to mid-1960s?"

A ripple of surprise passed over his face. "That is random," he said with a laugh.

"I know. . . . My aunt grew up nearby. She disappeared in 1965."

His brows lifted. "There were a few girls who went missing around that time, weren't there?" he asked. I nodded. "I was real little when all that happened. Made my mama paranoid about me and my brother growing up." His childlike chuckle contrasted sharply with his booming speaking voice. "She barely let us leave the house!"

"Is your mom around, by chance?" I asked. "I'm trying to talk to a few folks in the neighborhood, get a sense of how things were back then."

His smile faded, like a thin cloud had veiled the sun. "You a reporter or somethin'?"

"No . . . I'm just trying to piece together what happened to my aunt. I don't think anyone in my family really looked for her. I want to change that."

The man nodded, his expression warming. He slung the towel over one boulder-like shoulder. "My mother passed years ago," he said. "But my pop's still around. I'm just helping him get dressed for the day."

I didn't think I physically reacted to this, but he must have picked up on a subtle change in my face. "Pop has Parkinson's," he explained. "It's getting harder for him to get around, but his mind's as sharp as ever. I'm an RN at Duke Raleigh; I come over and get him situated for the day before my shifts."

I smiled. "My grandmother was a pediatric nurse here for decades. First at St. Agnes, and then at Wake Memorial."

His brows lifted in admiration. "Whoa, St. Agnes. That's where Pop was born. Before any of the other hospitals admitted Black folks." He consulted a large watch on his large wrist. "We're just finishing up. Let me see if he's up for a chat. But your odds are good," he added with another chuckle. "Pop's a talker, and I've already heard all his stories."

I waited on the porch while the man disappeared into the house. He was back at the door in under a minute. "Come on in," he said, holding the screen open, "he'll be right out. Can I make you a cup of coffee? Or herbal tea?"

"Tea would be great."

The house smelled warm, like cinnamon and cloves, though it also carried the distinctly astringent undertone of bleach. The living room was a time capsule from the 1990s: there was a couch and love seat set covered in a faded pastel floral pattern, plush carpeting the color of sage, and a strip of floral wallpaper that ran along the top of the creamy white walls. A conspicuous exception from the feminine décor was a large reclining chair covered in worn chocolate microsuede, which the man eventually helped his father settle into.

"I just realized I never introduced myself," the younger man said. "I'm Jeremy, and this is my father, Alvin."

Alvin was nearly the same height as his son, though he was reed thin. He was dapperly attired in an argyle sweater and wool slacks. His dark skin had the crinkly texture of a leather club chair, and the color of his close-cropped hair gave him the appearance of having just walked in from a snowstorm. He whistled as he looked at me.

"My, my, my, aren't you pretty!" Alvin said. "Are you single? No, I see the ring. It's too bad, I was gonna try and set you up with my son here." He laughed, a sound that mirrored Jeremy's youthful chuckle. Any residual anxiety over my rusty interviewing skills melted away. "Don't know why he hasn't met a nice young lady of his own yet. He's a handsome fella, ain't he?"

Jeremy shook his head affectionately as he set a folded metal walker beside his dad's chair. "Please feel free to ignore him."

"She can't ignore me," Alvin called to Jeremy as his son walked into the kitchen. "I'm the person she came to see! Now," Alvin said, his expression suddenly solemn, "Jeremy tells me you're interested in learning more about when those little girls started to go missing. Said your aunt was one of them?" When I nodded, Alvin tutted. "I'm real sorry to hear that. What made you want to speak with me in particular? Can't imagine you're going round all of South Park knocking on doors."

"I've been going through old police files," I answered, pulling the hotel-branded notepad from my bag. "There isn't much to go on, but I'm trying to track down more information on some of the people mentioned in the records. One of those people was Raymond Green, who lived next door to you around that time. Police interviewed him once, shortly after Geraldine Williams went missing on July third, 1964. And a few people called in to the tip line to suggest that police look into him."

Alvin nodded slowly. "We felt bad for that kid for a long time," he said. "My wife dropped off a casserole for him and his aunt every Wednesday for weeks after his folks died in that wreck. But when he got older—especially after his aunt passed—that's another story altogether. Child, those parties!" He tutted again. "Felt like I was banging on that door every other night, telling him to turn the damn music down."

The creases around his mouth and forehead deepened. "Wait, did you say the cops talked to him about a girl who went missing right before the Fourth? In 1964?"

"That's right," I said, my pulse quickening. "Geraldine Williams. She disappeared the day before the holiday."

Alvin's slow, contemplative nod returned. "July Fourth of that year was my youngest's due date. My wife had a rough pregnancy; she'd already been in the hospital for days by the time the Fourth rolled round. Every night the doctors would shoo me away, tell me to go home until visiting hours the next morning."

Jeremy returned to the room and passed me a mug of mint tea before turning to his father. "Here, Pop," he said, handing his father a smoothie the color and texture of wet cement, along with a handful of pills. "Breakfast of champions."

Alvin took a long sip through a metal straw. "I remember the night of the Fourth real well," he said. "I was a nervous wreck, pacing the house for hours. Jeremy here was just a little tyke; either he sensed how stressed I was or he just missed his mama, 'cause he would not stop crying. Could've been the fireworks, too. The Fourth's a tough time for babies, pets, and vets, I'll tell ya! I'd often look out the kitchen window to see what all was going on over at Raymond's, since the kitchen faces right into his yard." Alvin harrumphed. "Not much to see now, just a tangle of weeds. The lot was always kinda wooded, but the yard was neat looking when his aunt was alive. Think Raymond kept it pretty well maintained too, 'cause of his parties, probably, since they tended to spill out back there."

He took another pull on the metal straw. "I remember staring out the window that night, rocking Jeremy against my shoulder. If I looked at the right angle, I could catch a bit of the fireworks out past Raymond's yard. I remember there was a really big, bright one that illuminated everything for a minute. That's when I noticed a figure in the yard, standing out by the flower bush. It was Raymond. He was doing something out there, though I couldn't quite make out what it was. He was moving in a way that told me he was catching his breath, like he was winded from something. He had a garden tool with him, and he was resting on the handle."

My blood turned to ice.

"Could've been anything, Pop," Jeremy chimed in. "Maybe I was keeping him up with all my crying so he decided to do a little late night gardening."

"Maybe," Alvin conceded. "But I remember he had on this light-colored T-shirt. And when the sky lit up, I saw that the front of his shirt was covered in these dark splotches."

"Could it have been dirt?" I asked doubtfully.

"I may have only gotten a quick view, but, Sydney . . . I was fairly certain it was blood." Alvin shook his head. "And last I checked, hydrangeas don't bleed."

TWENTY-SEVEN

As I returned to my rental car, I looked up the address of the Raleigh Police Department Headquarters, entered it into Google Maps, and began driving there before I could talk myself out of it.

All my emails to law enforcement had either gone unanswered or received some version of the same rote response they'd shared with *The News & Observer*: *There are no active investigations . . . all viable leads have been exhausted . . .* My calls were directed to voicemail boxes that either were full or went ignored. I figured it would be much harder to ignore me in person.

I pulled into the department's parking lot twenty minutes later, maneuvering past boldly labeled squad cars and subtler navy Crown Victorias until I found the guest parking area.

"You can do this," I told myself, though I clutched the steering wheel for dear life.

My phone buzzed against the plastic cup holder. I picked it up; it was a message from my fertility nurse. My heart pumped double-time as I clicked it open.

I'm so sorry about my delayed response, Sydney! Not to worry—light spotting is very normal at this stage. It often indicates that the embryo has attached to the wall of your uterus.

A wave of relief washed over me, cool and strong. "I want this baby," I said out loud, the determination in my voice reverberating against the windows of my rental car. I recalled what Barbara had told me in her living room. *I don't think most people know for sure that they're ready to have kids,* she'd said. *They just make a commitment and trust they'll figure things out along the way.* After so many years spent straddling the fence of my feelings about having children, it felt good to have both feet newly planted on one side. Even though I could see myself living a happy life without children of my own too, if I could, I wanted to experience life as the mother of the little girl from my dream. I would do my best to be the mother that little girl deserved.

I was more than capable of trying my best.

I held on to this confidence as I strolled into the lobby of the police station and sauntered up to the uniformed officer sitting behind a plexiglass barrier.

"Can I help you?" she asked, her voice distorted by the silver disk that allowed sound to pass through the partition. The words left her mouth before she peeled her gaze from her computer screen.

"I hope so," I said. I tried to endear myself to her with a self-deprecating chuckle, but her expression remained deflatingly neutral. "My aunt disappeared from Raleigh in 1965, when she was seventeen," I continued. "Five other teenage girls disappeared from the same neighborhood around the same time. I know there isn't an active investigation right now, but I have some information that could be pertinent to the case."

"Okay," the officer said, her attention returning to her computer screen. "Can you please give me your name, your aunt's name, and the names of the other missing women?"

"They were girls," I corrected her gently, "not women."

Her glacial blue eyes shot up to meet mine and held them for a moment. But then she nodded.

I listed the names, which the officer must have typed into some sort of database, because a few seconds later she said, "You're correct, there aren't any active investigations on these wo—girls—at this time. But if you tell me this information you have, I can add it to the file."

"Is there anyone on the cold case team I might be able to speak with?" I asked, keeping my voice light and hopeful. "It's just . . . I'm visiting from across the country, and I fly back tomorrow morning. My aunt's disappearance has weighed heavily on my family, and on so many of the other missing girls' families. It would mean so much if I could talk to someone who might consider reopening their cases."

The officer's expression remained impassive, though my words seemed to have an impact on a man shuffling papers a few feet behind her. He wasn't in uniform—he wore a blue dress shirt in need of a good starching, and khakis too large for his rangy frame—but I could see a badge attached to his waistband. A detective, perhaps.

The officer at the front desk shook her head. "Unfortunately, we don't have a dedicated cold case unit."

"I read on your website that your homicide detectives sometimes take a second look at cold cases," I said, louder than necessary. "I know technology has changed a lot since the girls went missing . . . maybe if their cases were reopened, someone might find something the original officers lacked the tools to uncover."

The detective continued to shuffle his papers, but something about the slow, repetitive movement made me think he was listening to our conversation.

"We do occasionally dedicate detectives to reopen cold homicide cases," the officer said on a sigh, clearly losing patience with me. "But those are homicides. These are missing person cases."

Frustration rose from my belly like bile. "Ma'am, six teenage girls disappeared sixty years ago and were never seen again. These were good girls, from good homes." I hated myself a little for that line, as though the lives of girls whose temperaments and homes were categorized as something other than "good" weren't just as precious.

"They were studying to become a doctor and an accountant and a singer and a beautician," I continued. "Girls who loved their families and friends and boyfriends. These weren't girls who would just run away." I swallowed the fact that Carol was a known flight risk; it didn't support the narrative I needed the officer to believe.

"All this time, without a word from any of them," I said. "Why should we believe that they weren't the victims of homicide?"

The detective exhaled heavily, almost comically, as he approached the plexiglass. The grooves between his brows had been carved so deep that they gave him the appearance of scowling, though his eyes looked more curious than angry.

"So, you're the one behind all the emails," he said. His voice was gravelly, as though he were recovering from a persistent case of laryngitis.

I gave him a deferential smile. "That's me."

He gave me another long look. "And you have new information?"

"I do."

After another impromptu staring contest, he moved toward a door to the left of the reception desk and propped it open. "Well, let's hear it," he said, a grudging singsong in his voice. "One less email to get back to."

I fought a triumphant smile as I walked through the door and followed him across an office space decorated in gray scale. The carpet was the color of graphite. There was an ashen undertone to the white paint on the walls. Even the detective's pupils were a blue-tinged shade of slate.

"I'm Detective Bruce Higgins," he said, abruptly breaking stride to sit behind a desk near the back of the office. He gestured toward a plastic chair beside his desk for me to sit in. "I'm homicide, but based on your emails, you seem to have figured out that I've also led a few of the department's cold case investigations."

"I'm Sydney Singleton," I said. "My aunt Carol Singleton was one of the missing girls."

"Yeah, I heard you up there," he said, leaning back in his chair, his hands folded in front of his stomach as though he was used to having a gut to rest them on. "Today must be your lucky day. I'm only around because my court appearance got canceled. Perp managed to OD in lockup."

I raised an eyebrow, casually, to let him know I wasn't fazed by this comment. "Sounds like it was just someone else's *un*lucky day," I said.

Detective Higgins snorted in reply. He struck me as the type of curmudgeon who actively embraced this role, perhaps as a way of protecting an unexpectedly soft heart. "Why don't you catch me up on this new information you have," he said.

I nodded, sitting taller in my seat. "I think you all need to take a second look at Raymond Green. He lived in the neighborhood where the girls went missing and was just a few years older than them. He was briefly questioned after Geraldine Williams disappeared, but he had an alibi—"

"Wait," Detective Higgins said, raising a hand. "How do you know all this?"

"Geraldine's younger sister was able to get copies of most of the case files, years after they went cold," I answered.

Detective Higgins gave an almost imperceptible nod. "Go on."

"Anyway, I don't think Raymond was working alone. He had a friend, Michael Hall. I couldn't find any evidence that police spoke to him. But I think he might have been involved in the girls' disappearances, too."

The detective took a deep breath, the furrows in his brow deepening in thought. "What makes you think that? Actually . . . do you mind if I record this?"

I told him everything—about Joyce's harrowing ride in the back of Raymond's car. About Carol's diary and her question about where Michael and Raymond went off to on their long drives together. About the direct connections Michael and Raymond had to the girls. About how Raymond seemingly vanished after Carol disappeared, and then the disappearances suddenly stopped. About what Alvin, Raymond's former neighbor, saw on July 4, 1964, the day after Geraldine went missing.

Detective Higgins held up a hand again, closing his eyes. "Sydney, you really should leave the questioning to police, all right?"

I shrugged. "It's not like I've been getting in the way of an active investigation."

His snort seemed to say, *Touché.*

"There's one more thing," I said, reaching into my tote bag to retrieve Sally Dunn's bracelet. I handed the cloudy plastic bag to Detective Higgins; he held it up to the light to get a better view of the contents.

"I found that behind a hidden panel in my aunt Carol's trunk, the one Michael gave me," I explained. "There's an engraving on one of the charms, 'SD.' I showed it to Sally Dunn's cousin yesterday. She was wearing a matching bracelet with her own initials. She recognized the bracelet immediately; she said Sally never took it off."

Detective Higgins lowered the bag and his eyes to his desk; I could tell that the gears were turning in his mind.

"I think it might be worth taking a closer look at Raymond's property," I pushed on. "Raymond and all the missing girls all lived along Walnut Creek. The creek goes right by Raymond's old property line and heads directly into the wetlands. So much of that land is undeveloped, and swampy, if not underwater. Those girls have been missing for so long. It just . . . it seems like the wetlands might be a good place to look, too."

"Let's not get ahead of ourselves." He tapped his thumb against his desk, considering his next move. Finally, his thumb stilled and he lifted his eyes to meet mine.

"We have nearly ninety unsolved homicides dating back to the time those girls went missing. And in those cases . . . Sorry to be insensitive, but in those cases we at least have bodies. Some hard evidence to work with."

I was suspended on a high wire, teetering between hope and hopelessness. Then Detective Higgins sighed. "I've lived in Raleigh all my life," he said quietly, almost remorsefully, "and I've never heard anything about these missing girls."

My heart leapt toward the side of hope. "I know you can't promise anything," I encouraged, "but if you could just look into it, and give these disappearances the time and attention they deserve, it would be more than their families have seen from law enforcement in decades."

Detective Higgins regarded me for a long, quiet moment. Then he hit stop on the recording app on his phone. "Let me talk to my commander. That's all I can guarantee for now."

As I walked into the lobby, I noticed a Black woman talking to a detective near the exit. She looked familiar, but I couldn't quite place her. The detective talking to her saw me coming toward them, motioned in my direction with a quick jerk of his head, and the woman turned to face me.

My stomach dropped. It was Yvonne, Michael's sister. I hadn't seen her since we met at the coffee shop by her law firm during my first visit to Raleigh, and I hadn't contacted her since she threatened to sic her lawyers on me.

She shook hands with the detective, who glared at me as he headed back toward the maze of desks. Yvonne stood there, smiling tightly at me. Waiting for me. Was she there to see *me*?

"Hi, Yvonne," I said, hoping my polite smile masked the growing sense of dread I felt. "What are you doing here? I thought you were a corporate litigator."

She shrugged. "I spent several years in the D.A.'s office. I have a lot of friends around here," she said, her index finger doing a quick twirl in the air. "What are *you* doing here?"

"I'm trying to see if the police would be willing to take another look at the missing girls' cases," I said. "Felt like I had to give it a shot since I was in town."

"Mmm," she said, her eyes narrowing. "Sounds like you're also recommending persons of interest. And not just here—my brother told me he got a call from that local reporter you've clearly been in touch with, too."

Fuck.

"I'm just sharing what I know," I said. "It's up to the police and press to decide what to do with it."

Yvonne's eyes traveled up and down my frame, as though sizing me up for a fight. "You should tread lightly, Sydney."

I balked. "Are you actually threatening me in a police station, Yvonne?"

She shook her head slowly. "It isn't a threat. If you keep this up, you're going to find yourself with a serious defamation suit on your hands."

"I'm not defaming anyone," I said, though I immediately began sifting through everything I'd said and sent to Detective Higgins, to *The News & Observer* reporter, and on the true crime chat boards for any potential wrongdoing. "I'm just searching for the truth."

Yvonne shrugged. "Can't say I didn't warn you." She turned and walked toward the exit with the slow, purposeful gait of a woman confident in her power. The sound of her heels clicking against the linoleum echoed through the sparsely furnished lobby. *Tick, tock, tick, tock.* Like the timer on a bomb.

TWENTY-EIGHT

THERE SHOULD BE A WORD FOR THE PARTICULAR TYPE OF tension a person experiences when they're in a period of prolonged waiting. "Dread" is far too negative when you're holding out hope for a favorable outcome. "Impatience" minimizes the emotion of the experience. And "anxiety" is used so often in modern parlance that its edges have grown as dull as an overworked kitchen knife.

The same word could also apply to the persistent, creeping unease I'd felt since encountering Yvonne in the lobby of the Raleigh Police Department. I'd fallen down a rabbit hole on the internet that night researching defamation cases, and the truth was, I was on thin ice.

I hadn't directly accused Michael or Raymond of killing the girls, but I'd pointedly encouraged police to look into them. And I'd implied accusation in my latest emails to *The News & Observer* reporter and the producers of *The Unforgotten*, who'd reached out earlier that day. While defamation cases were notoriously difficult to litigate, if my statements damaged Michael's reputation, and were proven false, he'd totally have grounds to sue me.

I imagined Malik and me being forced to sell the townhouse and drain our hard-earned savings to pay the legal fees I incurred, all while possibly settling into our new lives as parents. The thought made me shudder.

Was Yvonne threatening me in her role as "mama bear," protecting her younger brother because she believed he was innocent? Or because she feared he might be guilty? Or was this all an effort to prevent reputational damage to her family name and her own law career?

I considered all this while staring through the oval-shaped window beside me after I'd boarded my return flight to L.A. As the plane lurched from the runway and rose over the gold and crimson trees, I saw just how wet the Raleigh area was. The wide, muddy Neuse River wound its way through the trees, and countless creeks branched from its winding body like tentacles. White water towers sprouted from the saturated land like mushrooms from a marsh, feeding on whatever decayed belowground.

The thought sent my stomach churning.

Or was it an early symptom of pregnancy?

It was Monday afternoon; on Friday morning I'd go back to the fertility clinic for the blood draw that would determine if I'd actually get to meet the baby girl who'd been toddling through my dreams. The episode of *The Unforgotten* featuring Aunt Carol and the missing Raleigh girls would air that same day. I just had to find a way to manage my frayed nerves until then.

MALIK WAS SO EXPERIENCED AT picking me up from the maze of LAX that he had to circle only once before I made it through the doors at Arrivals. He hopped out of his Range Rover and wrapped me in an embrace that lifted me from my feet before gingerly setting me down. His hand rested apologetically on my flat abdomen, as though I already had a baby bump in danger of squashing.

"I know you've only been gone a couple days, but I've really missed you, Babygirl," he said.

After he stowed my suitcase into the trunk and navigated the labyrinth of idling Priuses that hampered our exit from the curb, I reached over to rest a hand on his leg.

"I want to apologize again for going off the grid on Saturday," I said. "It really wasn't intentional."

"It's okay, babe," Malik said. He brought my fingers to his warm lips before returning them to his lap. "It's good that we're working out these kinks before we have a little one running around that we have to keep track of together."

His tone was light, maybe even a little playful. But the subtext of the words stung.

If you want to be a good mother, you're going to have to change.

I removed my fingers from his thigh and placed them on my own.

SOMEHOW, MIRACULOUSLY, FRIDAY MORNING FINALLY dawned. I'm not sure I slept at all the night before; I was wide awake when the sky outside our bedroom window melted from a moonless, starless black to an otherworldly shade of violet.

When I turned to look at Malik I was surprised to find that he was also awake, staring vacantly at the ceiling.

"Hey," I said softly, sliding a hand onto his chest.

"Hey," he answered, offering a small smile.

"We can do this," I said. "No matter what happens."

He kissed my fingers and squeezed them tight.

Despite my optimistic words, my insides were braided with nerves. I usually felt anxious the day of the first pregnancy test, yet I'd always managed to keep some level of emotional distance from the outcome. But that was before I dreamed of the little girl with my curls and Malik's eyes. If the blood test revealed that she was just a foolish fantasy, a delusion that was never meant to be mine . . . I didn't know if I could handle it.

Malik offered to make us a quick breakfast before we headed out for our 8:30 appointment: oatmeal with fruit, because it was the suggestion that hadn't immediately turned my gnarled stomach. But I asked him for ten minutes to meditate alone in the bedroom before I came down to eat.

He blinked at me for a moment—meditation wasn't a habit of mine—before replying, "Of course. Take your time, Babygirl."

I lowered myself onto the floor, my back against the bed, and aimed my face toward the brightening light outside our window. I conjured the image of the little girl from my dreams, replaying the moment when she launched her body into my waiting arms, again and again. Savoring the memory of the feeling one more time, just in case I'd never experience it in real life.

I continued to play the memory on a loop in my mind as we drove to the fertility clinic. As we sat in the waiting room. And as the blood was drawn from my vein. I meditated on the image of our daughter extra hard then, as though if I concentrated well enough, I might actually be able to will her into existence.

MALIK AND I RETURNED HOME for yet more waiting, this time for the call that would tell me whether the hormones in my body confirmed the presence of a forming baby. There was never a scheduled time for this call—we just had to wait, my phone set at max volume, jumping and twitching at every social media notification and telemarketer call until the clinic finally reached out.

Usually we would repeat our ritual from embryo implantation day—lying on the couch watching cozy, familiar movies, attempting to create an atmosphere of calm despite our tortured nerves. But I could no longer ignore the other milestone marked by this particular day.

"I was thinking," I began tentatively as we settled onto the couch, "maybe instead of watching something, we could listen to the episode of *The Unforgotten*. It just went live."

Malik wrinkled his nose, as though smelling something foul. "I don't know, Syd. That doesn't seem like the best headspace to put ourselves in today."

My instincts told me to drop it, to claim I needed a nap and listen to the episode alone upstairs. But I thought of my Good Parent List. If I wanted our home to be a place where our little girl could

talk openly about anything, I'd have to practice talking more openly
with Malik.

"I know it isn't ideal. But this could be such a huge moment for
the girls' cases." I could sense Malik forming an argument against
my suggestion. "I've worked really hard on this," I added. "It will
be so rewarding to actually hear the results of my efforts. And to
share them with you."

Malik nodded slowly, his face softening. "Okay. Yeah. Let's
do it."

I took a deep, unsteady breath, and hit play.

*Take a moment and think of a few famous missing person cases. I
bet some familiar names will come to mind: Kristin Smart. Natalee
Holloway. Madeleine McCann. These were all stories that led to
international media attention and public outcries for information
about their disappearances.*

*Now, I'd like you to try to think of a missing person case involv-
ing a Black girl.*

I'll wait.

*There's a reason why you're probably having trouble coming up
with a name. News outlets are four times more likely to cover a
missing person story when the person is white than when they are
Black or brown.*

*Perhaps that's why I never heard about the six teenage girls who
went missing from the South Park neighborhood of Raleigh, North
Carolina, between 1963 and 1965. And perhaps that's why none of
their cases have been solved.*

*Today you will learn the names of Marian Bradbury, Bettie
Brooks, Geraldine Williams, Loretta Morgan, Sally Dunn, and Carol
Singleton. You'll also learn about the suspicious similarities that
connect their disappearances. And maybe . . . just maybe . . . we'll
be able to shed enough light on their mysterious disappearances to
help their families finally find the answers they've been searching
for for sixty years.*

This is the story of the Raleigh Six, and the Creek Killer.

It was surreal to hear the hosts' familiar voices, voices I'd listened to every week for years, dissect the story of Carol and the other missing girls. I felt as though I didn't breathe for the entirety of the episode. I had no idea if they would identify any suspects by name, and I dreaded what might happen if Michael's name was mentioned. I could still feel the sharp edge of Yvonne's gaze in the lobby of the Raleigh police station.

I was relieved when, despite name-checking Raymond, they identified Michael only as "Suspect B," a "potential person of interest and known alliance of Raymond's." Though they described him in enough detail that anyone who knew of him would know who they were talking about. Surely Yvonne would need more ammunition to sue me . . . I hoped.

My blood went cold when another familiar voice filtered through my phone's speaker. It was Joyce, the copper-haired woman from Barbara's house, who recounted the harrowing tale of her car ride with Michael and Raymond.

Before you jumped out of Raymond's car, what ran through your mind? one of the hosts asked. *What did you think was going to happen?*

I knew in my bones that they wanted to hurt me, Joyce answered. *Why else would they just go silent like that, drive right by my house, and keep the doors locked no matter how much I begged for them to let me out? There was no doubt in my mind. They wanted to hurt me. When they drove me past my house, I thought . . . maybe that would be the last time I'd ever see it.*

You thought they might try to take your life?

I didn't know for sure. But I just thought . . . I couldn't end up like those other girls.

I DISTRACTED MYSELF FOR THE next few hours by sharing the podcast episode with the true crime message boards; sending a note to Barbara, Stanley, and the family members of the other missing girls; pinging Detective Higgins with a link to the podcast, and hitting send on the emails to Raleigh press waiting in my drafts folder.

I did this all from the couch beside Malik, who was also hunched over his laptop, working. Our movie-watching ritual hadn't been completely abandoned, though. *Coming to America* played in the background, and we found ourselves laughing at all the jokes we knew by heart, despite our focus on the screens in front of us and the nervous adrenaline coursing through our bodies.

Eddie Murphy had just disarmed a shotgun-wielding Samuel L. Jackson with a broom handle when my phone rang. I had both the volume and vibration settings turned on high, and the phone skittered across the coffee table, causing both me and Malik to jump. We glanced down at the screen and gasped when we saw the words *"Beverly Hills Fertility."*

I grasped clumsily for my phone and hit the speaker button while Malik struggled to mute the TV. My voice was strangled when I answered; I covered my mouth to clear my throat.

"I have your results from earlier today," the nurse said brightly, "and I have good news."

Malik pulled me close to him. Tears immediately began to flood my vision.

"Your hCG hormone, or pregnancy hormone, is positive. It came in at 167.4, and if you remember, we were hoping to see your levels around at least fifty, or ideally over a hundred, so this is a fantastic place to start."

I heard Malik swallow a sob of joy, which only made my tears flow faster.

I'd been here before, so I knew that it wasn't wise to get my hopes up too high. But I couldn't help myself.

"Congratulations!" she said, and the sincere joy in her voice was palpable.

"She's real," I said, my words slurred with emotion. Malik hugged me tighter, and I felt his tears against my face, mingling with my own. "Our baby girl is real."

TWENTY-NINE

THE SECOND TIME I THREW UP WAS AT GELSON'S, ONE OF L.A.'s fancier grocery stores. It was Thanksgiving morning, and Malik had been in the process of preparing cornbread stuffing with oysters and sausage when he realized he'd forgotten to purchase a crucial ingredient.

"How could I have forgotten the oysters?" he'd asked himself incredulously, standing behind our kitchen island, wrist-deep in cornbread batter.

"It's no problem," I'd said, draining the freshly boiled sweet potatoes waiting to be transformed into pie. "I can run out and grab some."

"Are you sure?" He rubbed the tip of his nose absentmindedly; bits of cornmeal clung to it like beach sand. I smiled and brushed his nose clean.

"I'm sure. It won't take me long to finish this pie. And I could use the fresh air."

"Speaking of fresh, can you get fresh oysters? Shucked in the shell? I did some research—pregnant women are allowed to eat oysters if they're fresh and have been thoroughly cooked."

I kissed Malik's baking powder–freckled cheek. "You've got it."

My family was happy to order our Thanksgiving dinner from Whole Foods, but Malik had always drawn the line at stuffing, which he believed should be made only at home. Each year he tried a new rendition, and each year the preparation grew more complicated.

I couldn't let him be the only person who actually cooked, so I focused on perfecting the same sweet potato pie recipe I made every year. My mother also asked if I could bring a charcuterie plate, without knowing that I'd be the only person in attendance who wouldn't be able to enjoy it.

I'd had to go back to the fertility center for additional blood tests to confirm that my hCG levels were rising sufficiently three times in the past two weeks. Each time I spent the day clinging fiercely to the image of the little girl from my dreams, and each time the clinic called with good news. But we had a long way to go before I'd feel confident enough to begin telling anyone I was pregnant. We were scheduled for our first ultrasound the following week; then, we hoped, we'd hear our little girl's heartbeat for the first time.

The nausea had begun that Monday. It wasn't just "morning sickness" but a low-grade queasiness that persisted throughout the day. Fortunately, the first time I'd actually gotten sick I'd been at home, within running distance of my own bathroom. But the second time, I stood at the seafood counter at Gelson's waiting for Malik's oysters to be wrapped, and the smell of raw fish sent my stomach roiling.

"Excuse me," I said to the man wrapping the oysters, trying to keep my voice calm, "where's your bathroom?"

Something in my expression must have communicated the urgency of my request, because the man's face went ashen. "Just down the hall," he said, pointing. Then he lifted the packet of oysters. "I'll hold these for you."

I sprinted toward the stockroom, finding the door to the bathroom just in time to relieve myself into the garbage can. I stumbled to the sink, chest heaving, and rinsed my mouth with cold water.

This is a good sign, I reminded myself. I'd read a statistic that miscarriage rates were lower among women who experienced nausea, and I'd clung to that data point like a life jacket. I dried my face with a sandpapery sheet of paper towel, took a deep breath, and walked back out to face the man behind the seafood counter.

When I thanked him and accepted the package of oysters, he gave me a kind, knowing smile. "I double-wrapped them for you, so you shouldn't be able to smell anything," he said. When I looked at him quizzically, he leaned forward and lowered his voice. "My wife and I have four kids. I'd recognize that look on your face anywhere," he explained, chuckling cheerily.

I was so grateful for his kindness that I thought I might cry. Or maybe it was just all the hormones.

I pulled my phone from my purse as I waited in the long checkout line and hit refresh on my Google News search for "Raleigh missing girls." A week after *The Unforgotten* episode aired, the Associated Press published a story, "Popular Podcast Probes Mystery of Six North Carolina Girls Missing Since the 1960s." The article didn't reveal new information about the case, but it did call the depth of the authorities' investigation into question. And now a new story appeared in my Google searches every other day.

It was starting; the groundswell of support and outrage had spread from the true crime forums to the local press, a major podcast, and now national news. I just had to hold out hope that new information would keep the story alive and give Detective Higgins the ammunition he'd need to officially open the girls' cases.

As I continued to inch forward in the line, I saw that a new story had run the night before, this time from a local TV station. I gasped when I saw a still image of a reporter standing in front of Raymond's empty lot. I'd know that tangle of bushes and branches anywhere.

I fumbled in my bag for my earbuds, slipped them into my ears, and hit play on the video.

"Law enforcement are under increasing pressure to excavate the property, particularly the land beneath a sprawling hydrangea bush along the back edge of the lot," the reporter said, holding aside a branch so the camera operator could catch a glimpse of the browning blue flowers. "The families of the missing, Raleigh residents, and fans of the popular podcast are holding out hope that there might be enough evidence buried in this abandoned lot to thaw this decades-old cold case."

A shudder of excitement coursed through me. It wouldn't be long before police would be forced to reopen the girls' cases. I could feel it in my bones.

MALIK AND I ARRIVED AT my mother's doorstep with our prepared dishes in hand at 5:00 P.M. sharp, just as my mother requested. As was often the case in L.A., it was a nearly eighty-degree Thanksgiving, and a thin layer of sweat gathered beneath the cranberry-colored sweater dress I'd insisted on wearing.

"Happy Thanksgiving, family!" Sasha shouted over Luther Vandross's velvety tenor as she opened the door. Her long dark braids were threaded with thin festive ribbons of crimson and gold. "Come in!"

We followed Sasha into the kitchen, where our mother hovered with the nervous energy of a hummingbird. Every inch of counter space was covered with platters of food, carefully decanted from their Whole Foods cartons.

Mom greeted us distractedly with awkward sideways hugs, the dishes we'd brought still in our hands. "I'll take that cheese plate into the living room; we'll do apps out there," she said, taking the marble tray from my arms and fleeing the room. "You can put the rest down anywhere you can find space," she called over her shoulder.

My gaze caught Sasha's and we both stifled a giggle. "How is she always so stressed for a meal made by Whole Foods?" I whispered.

"Girl, you missed the part where she couldn't find the 'good napkins' and sent me on a field trip to Home Goods."

"Oooh," Malik said, picking up a bottle of Heitz Cellar cabernet. "This is a really good wine." He passed the bottle to me. "Remember when we did that private tasting at the estate, Syd? Up in Napa?"

"Um, yeah, I do," I replied, examining the label. It had been early in our relationship, back when we lived an hour outside of wine country and would spend several weekends a year exploring Napa, Sonoma, Santa Rosa, and Healdsburg. "It's way more expensive than the stuff Mom usually buys."

A cheshire grin spread across Sasha's face. "I bought it!" She plucked the bottle from my hands and placed it gingerly back on the counter, as though rescuing a family heirloom from a child's clumsy grasp. "I remembered y'all going on and on about how much you loved that winery."

"Girl, that's a sixty-dollar bottle of wine," I said.

She shrugged, her expression smug. "Pretty generous thing for me to do with a first paycheck from a new gig, huh?"

"What new gig?" I asked, laughing. "Stop being so mysterious!"

"Okay, okay. So, remember that internship I was interviewing for a while back? Well, I guess they lost their administrative assistant during the process, and my résumé made it into the pile, and they hired me. I mean, yeah, it's an assistant job or whatever, but it's actually better than the internship, 'cause I'll still be reading and tracking submissions and helping with research and all that, but I'll also get benefits. Even if I have to answer the phones—"

I interrupted Sasha with a fierce hug. "I'm so proud of you, Sis," I said, fighting back tears for the second time that day.

"Congrats, Sash. That's huge," Malik said, squeezing her shoulder.

"Thanks," Sasha said, laughing uncomfortably, awkward as always beneath a spotlight. She stroked the bottle of wine absentmindedly with a finger. "My celebratory purchases were so random," she said. "I got this bottle of wine, a fresh pair of Air Force Ones, and a DNA kit. Don't worry, I didn't spend it all. I've gotta save up for a car."

There was so much information coming at me that I wasn't sure which parts to focus on first. "Wait, why a DNA kit?"

Sasha shrugged and lowered her voice, as though afraid Mom might overhear. "All this stuff about Carol made me realize how little I know about our family," she said. "I mean, we never really got to spend much time with the folks on Mom's or Dad's side. We don't know any details about who Dad's father was. And we don't know anything about who came before our grandparents. All this research you've done about Carol and those girls kind of inspired me. Like, it's up to us to learn their stories while we can. Otherwise they could be gone forever."

I couldn't remember the last time I'd seen Sasha quite so somber. It made her seem grown up. Sasha looked at the modest-size turkey on the stove. "Our Thanksgivings have always been so small," she said. "Don't you wonder what it would be like to be in one of those big families, with a bunch of people laughing and talking over each other, and a bunch of little kids running around?"

I blinked back tears at the phrase "little kids running around" and fought the urge to blurt out that we might have a new addition at next year's Thanksgiving.

Dinner began smoothly enough; we floated on a tepid pool of surface-level conversation. It was peaceful, if tedious, making small talk as though we were all plus-ones at a stiff corporate holiday party.

"Oh, I was looking at *The Unforgotten*'s Instagram page today," Sasha whispered to me. "I didn't realize how huge they were. Like, 750,000 followers—huge! The post about the Raleigh episode alone already has over ten thousand likes."

Mom's head snapped in our direction at the word "Raleigh."

"Sasha." Mom said her name with the same clipped, warning tone she'd use when we were kids.

Sasha grimaced and cast her eyes down to her plate. "Sorry, Mom," she grumbled.

It felt as though the temperature in the room dropped twenty degrees. I looked from Sasha to Mom and back again; they both kept their eyes pointed away from mine.

"What?" I asked, trying to keep my voice neutral.

My question hovered low in the air, like wildfire smoke. Finally, no longer able to bear the tense silence, Sasha quietly spoke. "Mom didn't want us to talk about the Carol stuff today."

"The Carol 'stuff'?" I scoffed, the neutrality in my tone obliterated. "Why?"

"I just don't understand why you told all our business to that podcast, Sydney." Mom still couldn't bring herself to look at me. "Your grammy obviously didn't want people to know about that whole thing, and the second she's in the ground, you take it to some *true crime podcast* so they can use it for some morbid form of entertainment?"

I should have anticipated this reaction. Given our unofficial family motto—*what happens in this house stays in this house*—of course my mother was upset to learn that the painful story my grandmother had tried so hard to bury had been unearthed and exposed for all the world to see.

"Did you listen to the episode?" I asked.

"I don't need to. I've heard all about those true crime podcasts, and how they treat very real tragedies as if they're just spooky stories to tell around a campfire. It's disgusting."

Hot tears of shame coated my eyes, but I fought with all my strength to keep them from falling. "If you'd listened, you would have heard that the hosts don't sensationalize the criminals or their crimes; they focus on telling the stories of the victims and survivors. They try to help them and their families find justice. And the outpouring of support they've created with their episode has been incredible—it's already inspired several other news stories."

Mom made a sharp bark of disbelief. "That's just great. Our dirty laundry splashed all over the news."

"You know, Grace," Malik interjected calmly, "I've learned through all of this that cases of missing people of color are less likely to be solved than cases of missing white folks. And that's probably due in part to the fact that their cases are less likely to be covered by the press." My heart swelled with gratitude. I wasn't sure anyone had ever stood up for me against my mother in this way. "Press coverage leads to greater public awareness," he continued, "which contributes to more information coming in to police, and more pressure applied to law enforcement to find answers."

For a moment, I wondered if my argument would be more convincing if it came from sensible, measured Malik. But when my mother looked up at me, it was with an expression I could only describe as a sneer.

"You've always had a habit of sticking your nose where it didn't belong."

Wow; after all these years, she still hadn't forgiven me for committing the mortal sin of becoming a journalist.

Sasha squeezed my hand beneath the table, as if to apologize for bringing up this forbidden topic in our mother's presence. It was as though we'd been transported right back into childhood. I had to remind myself that I was a full-grown woman, a mother in the making, God willing. I'd earned the right to my voice.

"What do you mean by that, Mom?" I asked.

"You know what I mean."

A miserable montage flashed through my mind like a sepia-toned film reel. That awful night on the Pacific Coast Highway. The pictures of my father's mangled Corvette, shrouded in jacaranda petals, now even more gruesome knowing that Sasha had been his intended passenger. The time he'd launched his crystal tumbler at the wall beside my mother's head and snarled, *Maybe I should put everyone out of our misery and end us all.* How when Sasha told her how scared she was, Mom had brushed her off. *Why should you be scared?* she'd said. *None of this concerns you.*

A wave of nausea coursed through me. I closed my eyes for a moment and breathed deeply, willing my stomach to settle. I couldn't leave the table now; my mother would see it as an acceptance of defeat.

I opened my eyes and looked at her. Her lips were pulled tight against her teeth, and her eyes shimmered with rage. Something Dr. Domínguez once said returned to me in a flash: *Anger is a secondary emotion,* she'd said. *We often reach for anger to protect ourselves from experiencing more vulnerable feelings, like sadness or fear.*

Just like an optical illusion that reveals itself if you stare at it long enough, the longer I looked at my mother, the more clearly I could see evidence of her pain. I noticed how the skin around her eyes crinkled at the corners, as though she were wincing, anticipating a blow. I saw the way her shoulders caved slightly inward, as though bracing herself. The tightness in my chest slowly began to soften.

"You must have been so lonely," I said.

Mom blinked in surprise, and I continued.

"Out here in L.A., your only family outside of us gone, with an unstable husband and two little girls, trying to hold everything together and keep up appearances while doing it. I can't imagine how that must have felt."

Her lips released their hold of her teeth; I noticed the bottom one tremble slightly.

"I just wish you could try to imagine what it felt like for me and Sasha, too," I continued. "You act like we couldn't see what was going on with you and Dad. Like we couldn't hear your fights. Or didn't have to worry about what mood we'd find him in when we got home from school every day. We knew about all of it, we just didn't understand it. And that was really scary, knowing something was wrong but not being able to talk about it with you."

I struggled to swallow. I had never spoken to my mother so honestly, so directly.

"My therapist says talking about the things that scare us steals their power," I went on. "And I believe that. I also believe that's why true crime podcasts are so popular. Because through listening to them, we face some of our worst fears. When you hear about the warning signs the criminals showed before they committed their crimes, or the ways survivors saved themselves from terrible situations, it makes you feel more powerful. Like you might be able to save yourself if you ever found yourself in a similar situation."

I could feel Malik's gaze from across the table, warm and encouraging. It gave me the extra push I needed to go on.

"I have no idea how Grammy would react if she'd lived to hear the podcast," I admitted. "But I can tell you how grateful the other girls' families have been to hear the names of their loved ones again. How good it makes them feel to know there are people out there who care that their girls have never been found and are willing to help them get answers."

I tried to read my mother's stoic expression. She was so still I wasn't sure she was breathing. Finally, she took the marigold-colored napkin from her lap, patted it against her mouth, and rose from her chair.

"I have a headache," she said, her voice completely devoid of emotion. "You all . . . eat as much as you want, and just clean this up when you're done, would you? I'm going to go lie down."

She turned from us and moved silently down the hall. The only sound came from the speakers, which played Earth, Wind & Fire's cheerful "September" incongruously, as if a wedding DJ was incapable of reading the room.

SASHA, MALIK, AND I PICKED at our plates for only a few more minutes before calling it quits. We formed a silent assembly line of cleaning. As my body fell into the meditative movements of dishwashing, I allowed my thoughts to linger on those words I'd heard so often as a child—*what happens in this house stays in this house.* The statement had sounded somewhat sinister when I was a kid, but as an adult, I could understand the benign intentions behind it. It was about protecting your family's reputation. It was about preserving your pride, even in the face of an embarrassing or shameful incident. It was about protecting yourself from dwelling on events that caused you pain. It was about appearing strong, and not allowing anyone to learn your weak spots.

I knew this mentality had been passed down by my parents' own parents, who'd likely learned it from their parents, and so on. And it made sense—when you are of a race of people that has been systematically disenfranchised by the country your ancestors had been brought to against their will, and hundreds of years later you are still struggling to free yourself from the shackles that limit your access to property, opportunity, and earning potential, your family's hard-won good name might be all you have.

Yet while our motto may have limited my family's vulnerability to the outside world, it also prevented us from being vulnerable with each other.

Just then I thought I heard a sound come from Sasha's direction, a noise that sounded a lot like "I'm sorry."

"Did you say something?" I asked.

Sasha set my heavy marble charcuterie board down and turned to look at me. "I said 'I'm sorry.' For earlier. You were right about how it felt growing up with them, with Mom and Dad. I should have said something. It's not fair that she thinks you're the only one who felt that way."

I gave Sasha's shoulder a squeeze. "It's a lot easier for me to speak freely. I get to go back to my own place after this. You have to stick around and deal with the aftermath."

Sasha shrugged. "Yeah. Maybe not for much longer, though."

I tried not to show how much hope that comment gave me.

"I think it's time," she went on, gazing down at my charcuterie board and tracing a dove gray vein with a finger. "When you left for NYU, it was just me, Mom, and Dad. I've realized, as fucked up as it is, I started to think of her as my only source of safety. And then Dad died, and it was all so fucking traumatic. Even if it technically meant we were safer or whatever. You know?"

When she looked up there were tears in her eyes. "It's like it bonded us, Mom and me. And I just . . . I haven't been ready to leave yet. But now . . . I think I might be ready to try." She smiled her trademark dimpled Sasha smile. "That is, if I stop buying wine and Nikes and start putting more money away."

"If you could use help with putting down a security deposit, I c—"

"No," Sasha interrupted. "I think I need to do this on my own."

Malik walked into the kitchen carrying the tray that still held seventy-five percent of the turkey Mom had bought. His lips pulled into a confused half smile as he took in the scene by the sink. "What'd I miss?"

"Oh, nothing," I said. "I'm going to run to the restroom; be back in a sec."

It had been too long since I'd refreshed my Google News search about the missing girls; it gnawed at me like a caffeine withdrawal headache. I padded toward the entryway where my purse hung on a peg and fished my phone from its pocket.

I saw that I had a missed call notification, and a new voicemail. My heart lurched when I saw it had been left by a Raleigh phone number.

I ducked into the powder room between the entryway and kitchen, hit play on the message, and pressed the phone tight against my ear.

"Hi, Sydney, this is Detective Bruce Higgins. I know it's late on a holiday, but I thought you'd want to know—we're executing a warrant to excavate the old Green property in the morning. It'll probably be all over the news by the time you hear this message. Don't expect a play-by-play, but I'll let you know when I have more information I can share." I heard the sound of a chair squeaking, as though he'd pulled himself farther upright in his seat.

"Look, I can't promise you anything. I told you that," he said. "But I'm going to do everything I can to find out what happened here."

THIRTY

"It's like they're surgically removing all the trees and brush. Can you see?" Barbara asked.

The image came into focus. Yellow caution tape was strung along Raymond's property line like a macabre take on the holiday lights adorning neighboring yards. A swarm of uniformed staff cleared the overgrown lot as officers looked on, the word SHERIFF emblazoned on their dark jackets in the same hue as the caution tape.

They'd begun their work on Friday, the day after Thanksgiving, once police had gathered enough statements from Raymond's former neighbors and party attendees to secure a warrant. It was now Sunday, and they had more than half the yard left to go.

"I'm honestly surprised police were willing to put so much money toward this search given how little evidence they had," I said.

Barbara sucked her teeth. "They had to do something to make up for their lack of effort to date. The community's demanding it, and the sheriff is up for reelection next year. Everywhere I go—the grocery store, the beauty shop, the post office—I hear people talking about it. How shameful it all is."

I couldn't help but imagine Grammy overhearing those conversations while running errands around town. Would she have been as angry with me as my mother was on Thanksgiving? Or would all those years without a word from Carol eventually have eroded her pride?

I wondered if Carol ever haunted Grammy's dreams.

"Folks are planning to hold a vigil here tonight in honor of the girls," Barbara said.

"Oh." I felt a pang of guilt; would Carol be the only one without a loved one present? "I wish I could be there."

Barbara turned her phone around so I could see the care and concern in her eyes.

"Do you have a good picture of your aunt?" she asked. "If you send it to me, I can have it blown up and printed out for the vigil."

"Really?" The word caught in my throat. "I'd really appreciate that."

"Don't worry," Barbara said. "We'll make sure no one forgets about Carol."

I woke early the next day to scan the news for any updates from Raleigh before getting ready for work. The forensics team hadn't announced any findings, but I did find three stories about the vigil held the night before, including one TV segment.

There must have been a hundred people holding white candles that flickered in the fragile darkness of early evening. I'd expected to see some of the older members of the community in attendance, people who'd been alive when the girls disappeared. But I was surprised by the number of young people at the vigil, particularly the number of high school girls.

"I'm sixteen, same age as three of the girls who went missing," one teenager told the reporter. "It's scary to think that me and a bunch of classmates could just vanish, and no one would even try that hard to find us. Someone has to know what happened to those girls. And it's about time they speak up."

The camera panned to six blown-up pictures of the missing girls, arranged on easels along the curb in front of the caution tape. The photos were grainy and pixelated in their enlarged sizes, giving them a ghostly quality.

The camera seemed to linger on Carol's photograph, the final picture in the row. I'd given Barbara a digital scan I'd taken of Carol's final yearbook photograph, when she was in the eleventh grade. It was the most recent picture of Carol I had, and the one in which she looked the most like me. The same half-cocked smile that appeared in most of my own photographs, the same sly stare. If you looked quickly, you might think that I was the one who vanished in 1965.

BY WEDNESDAY, RAYMOND'S FORMER PROPERTY was stripped bare. Jeremy texted me photos from his father's kitchen. "No matter what police find, Dad's happy you gave him his view back," his message said.

From Jeremy's pictures, I could see clear across Raymond's yard to the creek that slithered along its edge. The investigators had cut the hydrangea bush way back, lopping off most of its bobbing blue heads. Officers streamed in and out of a canopy tent erected in a corner of the yard, its white plastic walls shielding its contents from the prying eyes of onlookers. A woman swept the yard with what I assumed to be a ground-penetrating radar device.

I wished I could set up camp in Alvin's kitchen. I'd sit at the window all day long, watching the workers' every move through powerful binoculars.

It was yet another excruciating exercise in patience, just like waiting for our ultrasound appointment to finally roll around. I felt relieved on the days when I rushed to the bathroom, overcome by a tidal wave of nausea. It felt like proof that our little girl was still growing inside me. The days I felt totally fine worried me; my hands anxiously traveled to my belly again and again, asking our daughter for a sign that she was all right.

I knew a positive ultrasound held no guarantee of a successful birth. I was just one week beyond the point in my pregnancy when I had lost our last baby that horrible Valentine's Day. Yet every ultrasound, every appointment, and every milestone gave me a concrete reason to hope.

I awoke on Friday morning to the rarest of sounds in Los Angeles—the crack and rumble of thunder. It shook our apartment like a distant earthquake. Rain pelted our bedroom window with such force that I had to check to make sure it wasn't hailing.

The city was ill-equipped for such weather. By the time Malik and I left for our 9:00 A.M. ultrasound, it had been pouring for hours. Rainwater tumbled from roofs like waterfalls and bubbled out of storm drains and onto oversaturated roads. Angelenos, treacherous drivers in the best of weather, had little opportunity to master driving in rain. Malik and I passed two accidents on our fifteen-minute trip to the fertility clinic.

We could even hear the echo of rainfall from the exam room, where we sat holding hands, waiting for our doctor to arrive. I stared at the ultrasound machine, its screen already on and projecting an abstract black-and-blue image of nothing, a placeholder for where my uterus would soon be on display. I couldn't help but think of the radar device back in Raleigh. I wondered if it would be sweeping Raymond's lawn while the ultrasound wand swept my womb, one machine searching for signs of life, the other probing for evidence of death.

I tried not to think about what might happen if law enforcement did find something on Raymond's property, the impact it might have on my emotional state. After all, it was the sight of the pulverized van holding the bodies of the McEwan family that had sent me over the edge ten years earlier.

There were two quick, perfunctory knocks on the door before Dr. Tanaka breezed into the room. As I lay down on the exam table, a large monitor mounted on the wall in front of me clicked on, projecting a larger version of what was displayed on the ultrasound screen. Dr. Tanaka positioned the wand inside me, and a small dark oval emerged in the grainy black-and-blue sea. "So here is the gestational sac," he said, using the cursor of his mouse to indicate the dark oval, "and here is your baby," he said as the cursor circled a little ball of light.

Malik squeezed my hand, hard and happy.

Dr. Tanaka zoomed in on the little ball of light, our little girl. "If you look closely, you can see a flicker," he said, his cursor hovering near her center. And there it was, a flash of light within light, like looking at a candle's flame through frosted glass. "Do you see that? That's the heartbeat."

"Oh my God," I whispered, gripping Malik's fingers.

"Let's see if we can give it a listen." Dr. Tanaka tapped a few buttons on the machine. There was a thick, staticky silence for what seemed like hours. I felt my own heart race painfully against the confines of my ribs.

Then a low rhythmic whooshing sound filled the room: *a-whoomp, a-whoomp, a-whoomp, a-whoomp.*

Malik and I muffled our own delighted cries so we could continue listening to our new favorite sound.

A-whoomp, a-whoomp, a-whoomp, a-whoomp.

"One hundred twenty-six beats per minute, exactly what we want to see." Dr. Tanaka's smile was so wide that I wondered if he was also relieved, after so many years of trying and failing to get me pregnant. "Congratulations, you two."

The doctor left the room, and Malik wrapped his arms around me before I could pull my underwear back on. "We did it." He wept into my neck, his voice thick with tears. "We actually did it. All those years of trying . . . all the sacrifices we've made . . . all the times we could've given up . . ."

"I can't believe it," I said, my own voice faltering. Malik lifted my chin and gently wiped the tears from beneath my eyes with his thumbs. Then he threw his head back and laughed like a child. "We're going to be parents!"

We held each other and cried for so long I expected someone to kick us out of the room. "Okay, wow," he said, finally extricating himself from our embrace. "I need to go to the restroom and get myself together."

"Go, go." I laughed, dabbing at my runny nose with the back of my hand. "Meet you in the lobby."

"I love you so much, Babygirl."

"I love you, Malik."

I was filled with so much joy, relief, and adrenaline that my brain no longer felt connected to my body. I pulled my clothes back on as if on autopilot, my arms and legs tingling as though they'd recently woken from a deep slumber.

She's real! Our little girl is real!

I lifted my jacket from the coat hook on autopilot. I grabbed my purse from the chair on autopilot. And I pulled my phone from my purse on autopilot.

On its screen was a new text message, delivered only moments earlier. It was from Barbara.

Sydney . . . they found something.

THIRTY-ONE

IT WAS ONLY FITTING THAT MARIAN BRADBURY, THE FIRST girl to go missing, was the first girl to be found. Of course authorities didn't immediately know that the bones buried beneath the hydrangeas were Marian's, wrapped tight in the decrepit remains of a red blanket tied shut with fraying green rope, like a gruesome Christmas gift.

It was a week before dental records confirmed the identity of the sixteen-year-old girl, who wore a three-strand pearl necklace and an elaborate updo in her final yearbook photo, which stood in stark contrast to her wide, guileless grin, as though she'd played in her mother's closet on picture day.

Forensic odontologists were still combing through vintage dental X-rays when two more sets of bones were found nestled closer to the creek line. Another week passed before we learned that one of the skeletons belonged to Sally Dunn, Stanley's little sister and Carol's friend, the aspiring beautician who was never seen without the silver charm bracelet that matched those worn by her favorite cousins.

The third set of bones were the remains of Geraldine Williams,

Barbara's beloved big sister. The reserved, bespectacled girl whose friends had dragged her to Raymond's house parties. The kind of practical teenager who dreamed of becoming a CPA when she grew up. Whose body Alvin likely saw being buried on July 4, 1964, when he glimpsed Raymond leaning on a garden tool in a flash of firework light.

It was nearly Christmas before autopsies revealed broken bones in the necks of all three girls, which, according to Google, were telltale signs of strangulation.

Despite this steady barrage of grisly discoveries, unlike in the aftermath of seeing photos of the McEwan crime scene, my grasp on reality and my emotional stability never wavered.

I was reminded of Dr. Domínguez's reassuring refrain: my history is not my destiny. Maybe the difference was that this time I didn't have the unprocessed, long-buried memory of that night on the Pacific Coast Highway lurking in my subconscious.

"I was right," Barbara said between gasping sobs when I called after learning Geraldine had been found. "All those times I rode my bike past that awful house after Geri went missing. I *knew* she was there, deep down inside. You never lose that sisterly bond, Sydney. Even if one of you is no longer living."

I couldn't help but think of Sasha. Tears welled in my eyes as I pictured myself in Barbara's position, wondering for years if her body was hidden a mere mile from home.

Stanley was stoic when we spoke. "Someone asked if this brought me some peace, knowing Geri and Sally were together back there." He scoffed. "Geri and Sally went missing seven months apart. Those girls were all alone when they died. Just them, and the monster who did that to them. Ain't no peace in that."

I tried and failed to muster a condolence commensurate with his loss. Stanley breathed deep in my silence.

"I can't say knowing where she's been all these years brings me peace either. It's like one weight's been removed from my shoulders; knowing the mystery of her whereabouts is solved. But it's been replaced with a different weight, the weight of knowing that her killer won't pay for what he did to her and the others. That bastard's been in the wind since the sixties."

It seemed clear that Raymond was involved in the girls' deaths. But as Detective Higgins confirmed when we spoke on the phone in the days following the autopsies, finding the girls' bodies on his old property wasn't enough to definitively pin their deaths on him. And there wasn't enough concrete evidence to warrant Michael's arrest.

"It's tough to get a murder conviction without a body, but it's *impossible* to convict a person in absentia," Detective Higgins said. Malik and I had been decorating our Christmas tree in the living room when he called. From the kitchen, I watched Malik meticulously place the silver and gold ornaments onto our tree while the detective and I spoke. "We're in talks with Mr. Hall, and we're going to keep doing everything we can to track Raymond down," the detective said.

So Michael knew he was officially a person of interest. I swallowed a lump of anxiety at the memory of his sister's threat, and the knowledge that the man who likely played a part in killing all those girls had my home address. "And there's no sign of Carol, Bettie, or Loretta?" I asked.

"We combed every inch of that yard," Detective Higgins said, "but we haven't found any other remains."

I picked at a stubborn fleck of gold ornament glitter on the cuff of my sweater. "It's like he rotated his burial locations," I said. "If you go in the order of their disappearances, he buried Marian in his backyard, then buried Bettie somewhere else, Geraldine in his backyard, Loretta somewhere else, Sally in his backyard, and Carol somewhere else. I wonder if it means something."

"Well, we can't confirm what happened to Bettie, Loretta, and Carol," Detective Higgins said, his tone just shy of scolding.

I returned to the living room in time to see Malik place our gold star atop the tree. He turned to face me, and his smile faded as he processed my expression. "What's wrong?" he asked.

I sighed and lowered myself onto our couch. "I don't know

where to go from here. I mean, finding Marian, Geraldine, and Sally is huge. It feels so good to help their families get some semblance of closure. But I'm starting to wonder if our family ever will. I don't feel like we're any closer to figuring out what happened to Carol. And we still don't know where Bettie and Loretta are." I rested my elbows on my thighs and massaged my suddenly throbbing temples. "It's pretty damning that three of the girls were buried in Raymond's yard, but it's not definitive proof of what happened. No one even knows where he is. That means no arrest, no trial, no answers. And there's no direct evidence tying Michael to what happened to those girls."

Malik sat beside me and rubbed my back. "I'm sure the police are looking into it. Maybe they'll find an old fingerprint on one of the blankets the girls were buried in or something."

I couldn't stop myself from rolling my eyes. "This isn't *CSI*, Malik."

"Well, I don't know. I guess what I'm saying is, maybe you've done your part, Syd. I mean, you helped police find three girls who've been missing since the sixties. You pointed them toward two key suspects. You inspired a whole wave of press attention about the missing girls. Maybe it's time to let the experts take it from here and let yourself focus on all the good things happening in your life right now."

His hand traveled from my back and found its way to my clenched fist. He gently pried my fingers open and wove them with his. "This will be our last Christmas together, just the two of us," he said, an earnest grin spreading across his face. "There's going to be a 'Baby's First Christmas' ornament on that tree next year. Our office will be transformed into a baby's room. Actually, come with me, I want to show you what I was thinking."

I gave a halfhearted laugh as he led me to the guest-bedroom-slash-office, fighting the emotional whiplash of the change in topic. "You've already got ideas for the nursery?" I asked as we walked down the hall. "Do you have a secret Pinterest board you've been keeping from me?"

He grimaced as if I'd caught him eating ice cream straight from the tub. I laughed for real that time.

"Okay," he said, releasing my hand at the doorway and walking inside. "A photographer I follow on Instagram posted this picture, and I thought it could be the perfect starting point for us to decorate around."

Malik fished his phone from his pocket, scrolled for a few seconds, and handed me the phone. I stared down at a photograph. Dozens of hot-air balloons drifted over rocky-road mountaintops against a cotton candy sky. The soft golden sunlight cast the colorful balloons in dreamy, muted hues.

"It made me think of that hot-air balloon ride we took in Temecula, over the vineyards at dawn," Malik said hopefully. "Remember how peaceful it was up there, floating above everything? Every time we're in this room we can look at that photo and remember that moment. Like it's just the three of us, floating above it all."

A sudden warmth radiated from the center of my chest. "I love that idea."

"We could put a dresser on this wall, beneath the window, and put a large print of the picture above bookshelves on that wall, and the crib would go there," he said, pointing at Carol's trunk.

"This all sounds really great," I said, staring at the faded brown leather of the trunk. "I wonder where we should put that."

"Oh yeah." Malik glanced at it as though he'd forgotten it was even in the room. "I figure we can store it in the garage."

I pictured the trunk on the shelves beneath tubs of Christmas décor and our backup supply of toilet paper. Dusty and forgotten. Again. A lump formed in my throat.

"I guess that makes sense."

Malik wrapped his arms around me. "It's time for a new start, Babygirl," he said.

I couldn't take my eyes off of Carol's trunk.

WHILE I COULD HAVE EASILY pretended to work from home like the handful of other people still on Slack on Christmas Eve's Eve, the near-empty office was the perfect place to spend hours lurking in the comments on the true crime message boards. It was beginning to feel wrong to read about such gruesome things in the presence of Malik's overpowering cheer.

Activity on the message boards had increased exponentially since the discovery of the bodies on Raymond's property hit the national news, and I didn't want to miss a single salient clue. Though the office was a ghost town, I commandeered a conference room for maximum privacy.

How does someone bury three bodies in their backyard without anyone noticing???

I wonder why he'd bury all of his sick souvenirs with Sally. Had he decided to stop murdering people?

Who could that ring have belonged to?

My breath caught in my throat. What "souvenirs" were they talking about? What ring? Was there a story I missed?

A Google search unearthed a new article from *The News & Observer* reporter that must have been published during my commute into the office: RALEIGH POLICE SEEK PUBLIC'S HELP TO IDENTIFY ITEM BURIED ALONGSIDE LONG-MISSING LOCAL TEENS.

I frantically scanned the article and learned that Sally had been buried clutching a jewelry box containing multiple items. Several of the items were identified as belonging to the missing girls: Bettie Brooks's laminated library card, Loretta Morgan's driver's license, a pair of horn-rimmed glasses matching those worn by Geraldine Williams, a necklace belonging to Marian Bradbury.

Trophies, I thought with a shudder. It was common for serial killers to hold on to belongings of their victims; seeing the items helped them relive the terrible acts they committed.

While police hadn't found Bettie or Loretta, it had to mean

something that their belongings were kept alongside those of the others. We just hadn't found their burial sites yet.

The article included photographs of the fifth and final item in the box, which police were trying to identify: a gold ring with a large rectangular stone at its center, the color of the ocean just after sunset. The words "John W. Ligon Junior-Senior High" framed the stone. It was a class ring from the school that all of them—Marian, Bettie, Geraldine, Loretta, Sally, Carol, Raymond, and Michael—had attended.

I toggled to the next image, which featured a close-up shot of the inside of the ring. It was well worn, webbed with scratches and smudges of tarnish. But the inscription it held was clear, chiseled in precise, looping script: "MEH."

My breath caught on a gasp; I immediately called Detective Higgins.

"It's Michael's," I sputtered, pacing the room, my body coursing with far too much adrenaline to stay seated. "The ring you're trying to ID. His full name is Michael Eugene Hall. It has to be his."

"Happen to have any proof?" Detective Higgins asked. "Otherwise, it's just our word against his. The jeweler that made those rings doesn't have records dating back that far."

I sifted through the mental Rolodex of photos and files I had on the case. I had to have something, or I needed to find something. This ring was the closest thing to a smoking gun we were probably going to get from a sixty-year-old crime scene. "I'm going to comb through everything I have to see if I've missed something," I said.

"All right. But, Sydney, for the love of God, do *not* ask Michael about the ring yourself. Doing so could seriously jeopardize our investigation." When I didn't speak, Detective Higgins's voice grew urgent. "Do I have your word?"

I paused for longer than I intended before replying, "You have my word."

I continued to pace the tiny glass box of a conference room, trying to make sense of it all. How did Michael's ring wind up in a box buried with Sally? It seemed deliberate; Michael would have been far too careful to simply allow his ring to slip from his finger and into a box of his victims' trophies.

Was the ring meant to serve as a vile memento from Carol's murder, since she was the only missing girl without an uncovered personal item? But Michael would never have knowingly allowed his own ring to be buried, since it would point straight back to him.

Maybe the box had belonged to Raymond. Did Raymond bury Michael's ring on purpose, in an attempt to cast suspicion onto his friend? But what would be the point of that? Nothing is more incriminating than bodies buried in your own backyard. And why would he want to point the finger at Michael, if they were indeed friends?

Sally went missing in February 1965, three months before Carol was last seen. Which meant the ring couldn't have been a trophy Raymond took from Carol's body before burying her.

Was it actually possible that Carol's disappearance wasn't connected to the others at all?

A dull pain in my mouth made me realize I'd been biting the sides of my tongue in concentration. I unclenched my jaw and turned toward my phone. I had two new texts, one from Malik, asking me about my dinner preference, and another from Sasha.

Sis, r u free for lunch? I need to talk to u.

I was going to see Sasha at another awkward family dinner two days later, for Christmas. She needed to talk about something that couldn't wait until then? She'd also never requested such an urgent in-person conversation before; texting was Sasha's preferred mode of communication.

There was only one way for me to respond:

Just tell me when and where.

* * *

AN HOUR LATER, SASHA AND I carried cafeteria trays to a corner table at a salad spot in West Hollywood.

"I have to be back at the studio in forty-five minutes, so I'm gonna make this quick," Sasha said. "Remember when I told you I ordered a DNA kit, on Thanksgiving? They have this family tree feature they create based on all the DNA they collect from other members. I was looking at it this morning, and I found something weird."

Sasha pulled her phone from her purse, fiddled with the screen, and placed it on the table facing me. On the screen was a colorful flow chart composed of circles. All the circles seemed to represent different people, connected by winding yellow lines. "So, there's me," Sasha said, zooming in on her circle. "And it shows that I came from two people whose DNA they don't have, Mom and Dad. If you scroll to the right, you can see that Mom's cousin Gladys took a test at some point, so these people over here belong to Mom's side."

"Okay . . ."

"Right, so all that makes sense. But here's the weird part." Sasha scrolled to the left side of the chart. "This must be Dad's side of the tree. So this circle is Grammy, and this one is Dad's father, whoever that was."

My mouth went dry as I stared at the screen. "There are two lines stemming from Grammy and our grandfather on Dad's side," I said, my voice quavering. "Which makes sense, one for Dad, and one for Carol. But . . ."

"You see it, right?" Sasha asked, her tone hushed and urgent. She traced a line on the screen with a long acrylic fingernail. "There's a line stemming down from Carol's branch. Because she had a kid, Sydney. And that kid—our cousin—took the same DNA test."

My heart pounded so hard it hurt. "Sasha," I croaked, zooming in on the screen so I could read the words beneath our cousin's circle, "who is Wesley Jones?"

THIRTY-TWO

When I clicked on Wesley Jones's icon on our family tree, a scant profile popped up. My eyes flicked to the words "Predicted relationship: 1st cousin."

"Some profiles have a lot of information," Sasha explained. "Wesley's page is pretty blank, and it says that he last logged in six months ago."

I scrolled back to the top of Wesley's page. Beneath his name were two buttons: Connect and Message.

Sasha's gaze followed mine. "What should we do?"

"I don't know." I picked up my phone and typed "Wesley Jones" into Google. As expected, the results numbered in the hundreds of thousands. "We don't have enough information to search for him online. He could live anywhere, be any age . . . I don't understand what this means."

"Maybe Michael found out Carol was pregnant and killed her?" Sasha theorized in a whisper, as though Michael was in earshot of our conversation.

"But how would that explain the baby?" I wondered. "Maybe

she found out she was pregnant and ran away, knowing how Grammy would have reacted to something like that?"

"But why would she run away from Michael?" Sasha asked. "It sounds like they were in love and already planned to run away together—why would she just go off on her own?"

I stared at the two buttons. Connect. Message.

"People sign up for these subscriptions because they want to learn more about their families," I said, thinking aloud. "You wouldn't share your DNA with a company if you were trying to stay hidden. I think we should reach out to him."

Sasha tapped a long nail nervously against the table. "I wouldn't know what to say."

"We'll tell the truth," I said, picking up her phone. "Well, a version of it anyway."

I clicked the Message button and began to type:

> Hi Wesley, my name is Sasha Singleton. I recently joined this service because I realized how little I know about my family, especially my father's side. He died several years ago, and his mother—my grandmother—died a few months back. I saw your branch on my family tree and wanted to learn more about you. I'm also happy to share more about what I know about my/our family.
>
> Would you be interested in chatting over email?

I handed the phone back to Sasha. She scanned the message. "Should we come out and say more?" she wondered. "Or ask about his parents?"

I shook my head. "We don't want to spook him; we want to make him curious. Make him want to talk to us. Then he'll be as invested in our conversation as we are."

Sasha lifted her eyebrows. "That's pretty smart, Sis." She glanced back at her watch. "Fuck, I've gotta go. Okay, I'm just adding my email address here, and then . . . sent. Done. I'm gonna grab a to-go box for this salad."

"Mind grabbing two? And, Sasha," I said, catching her arm before she left the table. "You may have helped us solve this entire thing."

NEWS COVERAGE OF THE RALEIGH Six and the Creek Killer trailed off considerably in the days following the grim discoveries in Raymond's yard. This was frustrating yet to be expected, since there didn't seem to be any new facts to report.

I emailed Detective Higgins on Christmas Eve to see if there were any updates, or if he'd been able to confirm whether the class ring buried in the box with Sally's body belonged to Michael. He responded less than an hour later with his usual line: "I'll let you know when I have more information to share."

Later that day, my Google News alerts got a hit on a new segment from one of the Raleigh TV stations. I waited for Malik to head out for a run before slipping into our office to pull up the clip on my laptop.

A woman with glossy blond hair and a Christmas-red parka stood in front of Raymond's bare property.

"Members of this South Park community have not seen Raymond Green since 1965, though authorities are currently seeking information on his whereabouts. While he does not appear to have lived in the Raleigh area for several decades, many local residents have vivid memories of the man who is now a person of interest in the investigation of the deaths and disappearances of the young women now known as the 'Raleigh Six.' A few of these individuals were willing to share their stories with Action News 14. We're concealing their identities out of respect for their safety and privacy."

The next shot focused on a person in silhouette sitting in an austere room. "There was one time when a few of us stayed after school for various activities—sports, choir, that sort of thing," a distorted voice said. "I was waiting for my older brother to come pick me up, but he was real late. A girl I was talking to said I should just get in with her and her friends, that they'd drop me off. Course it was Raymond behind the wheel. He dropped everyone else off first. When it was my turn, he drove in the opposite direction from where I told him to go. He drove into this swampy area, parked, and just stared at me in the passenger seat for a real long time. I kept begging him to let me go, and he just kept looking at me. Finally it was like he snapped out of a trance. He looked me in the eyes and said, 'You have a real pretty neck.' Then he drove me home, as if nothing happened."

The reporter came back on screen, but her voice faded into the background as my mind began to churn.

He drove into this swampy area . . .

I'd been so focused on Raymond's property that I'd nearly forgotten about the wetlands. I recalled the story from Carol's diary, about when Grammy sent her to retrieve my father from *that terrible swampy place.* How Michael intercepted her as she rode her bike toward the wetlands and waded into the muck in her stead, *like a knight in shining armor.*

Detective Higgins had brushed me off back in Raleigh when I pointed out that all the girls lived on Walnut Creek, which crept along Raymond's property and snaked into the wetlands. But that was before I'd helped him find three bodies.

I emailed the detective a link to the news story, and the time stamp when the woman shared her unsettling experience in a swamp.

"I still think the wetlands would be a good place to look," I wrote.

WHILE MALIK INSISTED THAT AT least some of our dishes be homemade at Thanksgiving, he fully gave in to my mother's preference to buy Christmas dinner premade from Dulan's Soul Food Kitchen every year. She even dispensed with the effort of decanting and replating every dish. Instead, we served ourselves right from the Styrofoam packaging: fried chicken, oxtails smothered in gravy, black-eyed peas, steamed cabbage, macaroni and cheese, collard greens, and mashed potatoes. A heaping portion of peach cobbler sat on my mother's kitchen island, like a guest star waiting backstage for her cue.

"I'm going to need a break before dessert," Sasha said, patting her stomach.

"Me too," Mom said, lifting her paper napkin from her lap and draping it demurely over her disposable plate. "Let's take care of this table and then we can get started on our movie. Malik, why don't you choose this year?"

Malik's lips pulled into a grimace. "That's a lot of pressure, Grace."

She stood and rested a hand on his shoulder on her way to the kitchen. "We promise to reserve judgment. Don't we, girls?" She also gave my shoulder an affectionate squeeze before she left the room.

If you'd glanced through my mother's kitchen window and glimpsed us, laughing and smiling as we tidied up after dinner, you would never have guessed how bitterly our previous holiday had ended. As expected, when Malik and I arrived at the house, Mom acted as though our Thanksgiving fight had never happened.

"Retreating may deescalate a conflict, but if the issue is never addressed, it leaves no room for true resolution," Dr. Domínguez once told me. Maybe that's why I was bothered by the sight of Mom and Sasha giggling at Malik as he struggled to uncork the next bottle of pinot. Our peace felt as brittle and tenuous as the first layer of ice on a deep lake. Superficially solid, but incapable of holding much weight.

An hour later, we were halfway through our viewing of *The Best Man Holiday,* and I was already on my third bathroom break of the film. I'd incorrectly assumed that a constant urge to pee wouldn't be something I'd need to worry about until I was much further along in my pregnancy.

When I opened the bathroom door, I was startled to find a wild-eyed Sasha standing on the other side. I yelped in surprise. Sasha put a finger to her lips, hustled me back into the bathroom and closed the door.

"What is it?" I hissed, fumbling for the light switch.

"Wesley wrote back," she whispered, pushing her phone into my hands.

Sasha, wow, it's so great to hear from you!! I totally understand what you mean. Now that I'm 60 years old, it's really starting to hit me how little I know about my family. My Ma had a tough upbringing; she doesn't like talking about her folks, so I don't know much about them. And now I can't help thinking that your grandmother who recently passed might have been my grandmother too.

I'd definitely be interested in talking more over email. I honestly don't even know where to start. What are your parents' names, and your/our grandmother's name?

Where do you live, by the way? I'm in Brooklyn.

Oh, and Merry Christmas!—Wes

A gasp escaped my lips. " 'She doesn't like talking about her folks.' That's present tense. His mother's still alive?!"

"Sixty years old . . ." Sasha said. "That means it's possible Carol was pregnant when she left Raleigh." Her eyes, incandescent with shock and excitement, lifted to meet mine. "What do we do? Should we answer his questions?"

I wrung my hands. "I'm not sure that's a good idea. What if we start exchanging a bunch of information with him, and then he confronts Carol about it, and she freaks out and disappears again?"

Sasha frowned. "Would she do that now? At her age, and with at least one kid that we know about?"

I shook my head. "I don't want to risk it. This could be our only chance to find her and get some answers." I motioned for Sasha to hand me her phone, and before I could stop to think about the consequences, I typed a reply.

> Merry Christmas, Wesley! It's great to connect with you, too. It's such a coincidence that you live in New York. My sister and I are actually heading there to ring in the new year. Could we meet for coffee while we're in town?

I returned the phone to Sasha. She read the message, and a smile spread across her face.

"Let's do it."

THIRTY-THREE

THE MORNING AFTER CHRISTMAS WAS THE FIRST TIME I struggled to fasten my favorite pair of jeans. After wrestling with the top button for a few futile moments, I rushed into the bathroom, lifted my sweater, and stared into the mirror. I hadn't developed a bump overnight; if it hadn't been for the snugness in my jeans, I wouldn't have noticed the slight thickening around my middle at all. I examined my reflection more closely, turning from side to side. My breasts were beginning to swell beyond the confines of my bra.

My heart fluttered. I'd never gotten far enough along in any of my earlier pregnancies to see my body begin to change, or to think about shopping for maternity clothes. I rested a palm on my belly. "We're really going to do this, aren't we?" I whispered.

A few hours later, when Dr. Tanaka navigated the ultrasound wand toward my womb, we found that our baby was no longer an indistinct cluster of cells. Even though she was no larger than a fig, I could clearly see her little head and the outline of her body on the black-and-blue screen. Malik and I both gasped when one of her tiny arms wiggled, as though waving at us.

"Her measurements are right on track," Dr. Tanaka said, grinning. "Looks like you three are officially ready to graduate."

"Graduate?" Malik asked.

"I specialize in getting folks to this moment right here," Dr. Tanaka said, walking to the sink to wash his hands. "Your ob-gyn will take you through to delivery."

"You're going to love Dr. Adams," I told Malik as I sat up on the exam table, the paper sheet crinkling beneath me like wrapping paper. "She's been my doctor for years."

Malik still stared at Dr. Tanaka, his mouth ajar. Dr. Tanaka laughed. "I know. We've been on quite a journey together! You're in excellent hands with Dr. Adams, but I'm also always here for you. Don't hesitate to reach out if you have any questions or if you need any additional support along the way."

Dr. Tanaka extended a hand toward Malik, though Malik only stared at it, wet-eyed, before pulling Dr. Tanaka into a bear hug. Malik stood a foot taller than the doctor and had to contort himself to bury his face into the doctor's shoulder. "Thank you, thank you, thank you," Malik sobbed.

"There, there," Dr. Tanaka said with a chuckle. He patted Malik tenderly, one hand on my husband's back, the other cradling the back of his head, consoling him like a child.

"WE SHOULD GO SOMEWHERE NICE for lunch to celebrate," Malik said as we walked hand in hand toward his Range Rover. "What are you in the mood for?"

I gave him a sheepish smile. "In-N-Out."

Malik laughed. "Not exactly the white tablecloth experience I had in mind, but hey, red meat is good for you. Helps with your iron levels."

I grimaced. Malik lifted his hands in apology. "Sorry, I can't help it. It's all the pregnancy books I've been reading."

"Maybe you can share the CliffsNotes over lunch."

"Speaking of restaurants," he said as we climbed into his SUV, "I've seriously dropped the ball on finding us a dinner reservation for New Year's—pun intended. Maybe I can find us an early seating somewhere, celebrate on Eastern Time?"

My stomach knotted as I clicked my seatbelt into place. "What if we actually celebrate on Eastern Time this year? In New York?"

Malik glanced at my stomach as though I were already huge with pregnancy. "What, like in Times Square? Now?"

I swallowed. "No, not Times Square exactly. We could visit your mom in Queens. And then . . . Sasha and I can take care of something in Brooklyn."

Malik looked at me dubiously. "Oh, so now Sasha's coming with us? What's going on, Syd?"

I filled Malik in on Sasha's discovery, and our email conversation with our likely cousin, Wesley. "I just feel like if we meet him now, in person, while we have his attention, we'll have our best chance of getting real answers," I concluded.

Malik stared blankly at the windshield for an uncomfortably long time. Then he looked at me as though finally seeing me clearly for the first time and realizing he didn't like what he saw.

"It's always going to be like this, isn't it?" he asked quietly.

"What do you mean?"

His eyes continued to search mine. "We're never going to come first."

My heart began to thud painfully. "We? You mean . . . you and our baby?"

Malik nodded slowly.

"I don't understand where this is coming from. . . . I'm pretty sure I can gestate a baby in New York."

Malik scoffed, and tears I hadn't noticed gathering in his eyes spilled down his cheeks. " 'Gestate a baby.' Jesus, Sydney . . . we just got pregnant. Newly pregnant, like it's too fragile to even tell anyone about it yet. All the years we've poured into trying for this baby . . . all the stress and appointments and needles and heartbreak. And you can't even take one afternoon to be fully in this with me. To celebrate over lunch and shop for baby clothes and savor this huge moment in our lives. Because this isn't your primary focus. It never has been, and I don't think it ever will be."

My skin burned from a cocktail of shame and indignation. "I'm sorry if I'm not exhibiting the appropriate level of maternal enthusiasm for you, Malik. I can't help the timing of all this; I can't help that Sasha uncovered that Carol might still be alive right before this appointment. It doesn't mean that I'm not as excited as you are that I'm pregnant."

Malik's eyes continued to stream. "All of this—it's starting to feel more like an obsession than a passion. There's always going to be a trip to New York, or a reason to fly to Raleigh at a moment's notice."

My indignation boiled over into rage. "Where's this magical line between passion and obsession? I didn't say anything when you spent all those late nights and early mornings getting Wealthmate off the ground, having meetings in the living room of our apartment and using our walls as your whiteboards. Why is it so wrong for me to be passionate about figuring out what happened to Carol and the girls?"

The look he gave me was as charged as a live electrical wire, and the shock it gave me was just as lethal. I knew what his look meant: *Because unlike you, I didn't wind up in a psych ward over it.*

"It's not your fault, what happened in S.F.," he said. "But it's really hard to just sit back and watch you put yourself in danger of it happening again." He gestured at my stomach. "Especially now, after all we've been through."

"You don't trust me," I croaked, losing the battle against my own tears.

"I was there the whole time, you know?" he said. "I mean, we lived together. Of course I noticed you were starting to act different, and that maybe you were more emotionally invested in that McEwan story than you should have been. But either you were great at hiding what was really going on, or I was just oblivious, because I didn't know how bad things had gotten until they put you in that ambulance."

"This isn't like then," I protested.

"From this angle, it's hard to tell."

I leaned into the leather headrest and closed my eyes. "I can't change what happened back then. But I also can't live the rest of my life walking on eggshells, worrying you might think I'm having a psychotic break every time I'm passionate about something other than you and our baby."

"That's not fair," Malik said, his voice wavering.

"Neither is this! I'm not the same person I was back in San Francisco. I'm so much stronger now. I've worked so hard to get stronger. It really hurts that you can't see that. That you still don't trust me, after all this time."

Malik reached into the glove compartment and extracted a handful of Starbucks napkins. He held a few out for me; we both dabbed our faces.

"It's not that I don't trust you," he said. "It's more like I don't trust myself. You were drowning, and I just stood by and watched you sink. What kind of partner am I to have lived in the same apartment as you, and not realized how much you needed help?"

Malik's expression took me back to that awful day in front of the Potrero Hill restaurant. I saw a flicker of the fear and confusion he had in his eyes when the paramedics secured me to the gurney. For the first time, I imagined the situation in reverse: Malik strapped to the gurney, me trying to calm him as I climbed into the ambulance. Wondering if the man I'd loved was gone for good, lost forever in a dark corner of his own mind. Wondering if there was something I could have done to prevent it.

The thought made my insides ache.

"I haven't allowed myself to think about how difficult that must have been for you," I said. "I mean, yeah, we were living together, but we hadn't been dating that long. Seeing me that way—it's not the kind of thing that inspires confidence in building a future with someone. I actually can't believe you stayed."

Malik's hand closed around mine. "I was already so in love with you," he said. "We might not have been married yet, but I was already in that in-sickness-and-health mindset. We were partners. We are partners. Partners don't quit on each other."

"Sometimes they do."

"Not me."

I looked at Malik's hopeful face. "I didn't realize you were so worried about it happening again. You never told me."

Malik shook his head. "It never seemed like the right thing to say. I think I'm also edgy because for a while I wasn't sure you wanted this anymore. Having a baby, I mean."

I felt my palm go clammy in his as I admitted the truth about my earlier doubts.

A ripple of worry moved across Malik's face. I brushed his knuckles with my fingers. "I didn't tell you this, because I was afraid of jinxing us, but right before our first blood test after the transfer, I had this super vivid dream." I told him about our adorable little girl, how happy and whole we all seemed. When I looked back at Malik, his eyes were wet again, his smile wide. "There was something about seeing us all that way. It all felt so warm and safe. I know I must have felt like that at some point when I was growing up, but if I did, I don't remember it. I wasn't sure I'd be able to create a different experience for our kids. But, seeing us all in that dream . . . it felt like it was possible. Is that silly?"

Malik shook his head. "Not at all." He smoothed the back of my hand with his thumb. "I wish you'd told me about it sooner."

"We have to do a better job of talking to each other about this kind of stuff," I said. "Even the hard stuff. Especially the hard stuff."

"I know," he replied.

"I want this baby, Malik. But that doesn't mean I'm going to give up on everything else that matters to me. I need you to trust that I can focus on other things while also doing everything I can to keep myself and our little girl healthy."

Malik stroked my fingers for a few moments, taking in everything I said. "Going to New York is really important to you, isn't it?"

I nodded. "It really is."

"Okay," Malik said, bringing my hand to his lips. "Then let's go meet this cousin of yours."

THIRTY-FOUR

I WOKE IN THE MIDDLE OF OUR FIRST NIGHT IN BROOK-lyn. I could guess the time by the unusual quiet outside the balcony door. It was late enough that even the after-hours pizza spots were empty, but early enough that the garbage trucks hadn't begun banging down the streets.

I stared at the ceiling, willing Malik's rhythmic breathing to lull me back to sleep. When my joints grew stiff and my mind grew restless, I slipped out of bed, pulled on the cashmere sweatsuit and coat I'd worn on the plane, and crept out onto the narrow balcony.

The air was cold and smelled vaguely of snow. We were staying at a hotel in Williamsburg, and the Manhattan skyline sparkled on the other side of the East River; its ripples caught the city's reflection like black diamonds. I lowered myself onto a chair and stared at the place I'd briefly called home.

I wondered if I'd unknowingly crossed paths with my first cousin during my time in the city. Had we ever sat beside each other on a subway? Stood in the same line to order a bacon, egg, and cheese? Brushed elbows in the narrow aisles of Duane Reade?

I thought about how lonely I'd felt freshman year after moving across the country to attend NYU, knowing no one. How, while I was usually relieved to have thousands of miles between me and my parents' unhappy home, I desperately missed my postschool ritual of watching *House Hunters* with Sasha. How when I'd gotten the flu sophomore year, I had to trudge out of my dorm for my own medicine, chicken noodle soup, and ginger ale. How destabilized I was after learning of my father's crash senior year, ignoring the typhoon of complicated feelings churning inside me so I could focus on getting myself back to L.A. How different it all might have been knowing I had family in the same city.

I wrapped my arms tight around my body. The city looked endless from my balcony perch, like gazing through a telescope at a neighboring universe. Had Wesley grown up in New York? And if so, did that mean Carol had also lived in the city during the four years I attended college here? Had she ever glimpsed me through a shop window and done a double take, confronted by a living memory of her own face?

Was it really possible that Carol's disappearance had nothing to do with the other missing girls? I couldn't make it make sense in my mind. She seemed so intertwined with all of it. She fit the profile of all the others—she was a Black teenage girl, a student at John W. Ligon Junior-Senior High School. She lived near Walnut Creek and went missing between 1963 and 1965. She had the closest connections to Michael and Raymond of all the girls. And the disappearances seemed to end after hers.

What if, against all odds, Carol was still alive? What did it all mean? And how would I manage to pull the truth from a woman who had so fully divested herself of her past?

BEFORE WE LEFT FOR NEW YORK, I told Malik he wouldn't be able to join me and Sasha on our coffee meeting with Wesley. From both my reporting days and my years in public relations, I knew that having too many people on the other side of an interview made an interview subject more cautious. We had only one shot at getting this first conversation right; I needed to make Wesley as comfortable as possible.

Once I assured Malik that we were meeting in a public place, he agreed to spend the day with his mother in Queens. Sasha and I would meet up with them for dinner later, and we'd all spend New Year's Eve together the next night.

There was a renewed intimacy and openness in my relationship with Malik since the heated conversation in his SUV. The rarity of our fights reminded me of the rarity of rain in Los Angeles. You get used to the persistent placidity, the unrelenting sunshine. You don't realize how badly the rain is needed until it has come and gone, when the dust you never noticed hovering in the air is cleared away, and you can smell the hint of sea salt on the breeze, see the craggy details of the mountains in the distance. When the storm passed, there was a new crispness in the air of our home, an unflinching clarity I hadn't realized we'd longed for beneath the serene surface of our marriage.

"Maybe we are related to this guy," Sasha remarked as we entered the coffee shop in Bed-Stuy that Wesley had suggested for our meeting. We took in the café's Scandinavian décor, lush green plants, and mellow lo-fi hip-hop soundtrack. "You could pick this place up and drop it in L.A., and your bougie ass would be there on the regular."

We ordered our coffees from two handsome men with meticulously coiffed beards and fluorescent beanies, and sat side by side so we could both stare at the door.

A cold flop sweat began to collect in my armpits. It was like waiting for the oddest blind date of my life.

My breath hitched when I saw a tall man approaching through the plate-glass windows. His face was heart-shaped—just like mine and Sasha's—and framed by thin shoulder-length dreads. Though he wore glasses with thick charcoal-colored frames, I could see his eyes lock on to mine before he reached the door.

Sasha grabbed my hand, and I squeezed hers back, grateful we were doing this together.

"What up, Wes," a beanie-clad barista greeted him. "Your usual?"

"Thanks, man," Wesley said distractedly as he walked toward our table, staring at me as though trying to work out a puzzle. "You have to be Sasha and Sydney."

I extended a clammy palm. "I'm Sydney."

"I don't mean to stare," he said, shaking my hand mechanically. "It's just . . . you look so much like a younger version of my ma, it's crazy."

I picked up my phone, scrolled to my photos, and found Carol's final yearbook picture. "Is this your mom?"

"Ha!" Wesley said, a sound of surprise more than amusement. "Wow . . . I've never seen a picture of her this young. But yeah. That's definitely Ma." He looked up at me, then back down at the photo. "It's trippy."

"Got your decaf honey oat milk latte, man," the barista said.

Sasha's eyes widened. "Talk about trippy. That's exactly what Syd ordered."

"I thought there must've been a glitch in the DNA app when it said I had cousins on Ma's side," Wesley said, sitting down with a steaming mug. His locs dusted the shoulders of his peacoat, making a pleasant swishing sound. "But looking at you two . . . the likeness is unmistakable."

"You didn't know your mother had a brother?" Sasha asked. When Wesley shook his head, she said, "We didn't know our father had a sister either."

"You figured it out through the app, too?" he asked.

Sasha and I exchanged a glance. "We just learned about your mother this past September, after our grandmother died," I said.

Wesley stared into the steamed-milk flower floating like a water lily on his beverage. "She told me her mother died years ago, way before I was born." His voice had grown quiet, muffled by confusion or pain. Or both.

"What else did your mother tell you about her childhood?" I ventured gently.

"Not much. Ma said that she grew up everywhere, that she and her mother moved around a lot, all over the South. She said they didn't have much money. She didn't know her father, and her mother worked as a domestic, cleaning up after rich folks. Said her mother started dragging her along to help her at work when she was really young. I guess her mother was pretty strict and sort of cruel. Ma said she left for New York as soon as she graduated from high school, built a new life for herself. Said her mother never forgave her for that, and they never spoke again."

Something about this story nagged at me, like a piece of food caught between my teeth. "Her favorite singer's mother worked as a domestic servant," I said as the memory returned to me, "and she'd sometimes bring her daughter along to help. Mary Wells — I looked up her bio after I learned how much your mother admired her."

A flicker coursed through Wesley's brow. "My ma's name is Mary. She was born Mary Wright and became Mary Jones when she married my dad."

Sasha took a deep breath, as though steeling herself on Wesley's behalf. We were about to turn his world upside down.

"Your mother was born Carol Singleton," I said slowly, giving the words time to sink in. "Her mother was Effie Singleton, and her brother was Lawrence Singleton, though most people called him Larry. It's true that she grew up without her father. They grew up in a proud Black neighborhood in Raleigh, North Carolina. They didn't have a lot of money, but as far as I know, Grammy didn't make Carol or our dad work to support the family. And Grammy was strict, but I don't think she was cruel." I looked at Sasha for confirmation; she shook her head.

"They had a stable home, from what I could tell," I continued. "They never moved. Grammy lived there up until her death." I picked up my phone and scrolled to the photograph of Grammy's house I thought I'd taken in vain, on that first visit to prepare her house for sale. I handed the phone to Wesley.

"Why would she lie about all of this?" he wondered as he gazed at Grammy's modest, well-kept home.

"Maybe the truth was too painful to tell," Sasha said.

"It doesn't sound that painful."

"What was your upbringing like?" I asked, both out of curiosity and out of a desire to lighten the mood. I wasn't sure how long I could keep Wesley talking if things stayed this grim. As I'd hoped, a smile spread across his face. I saw a glimmer of my father's smile in his expression, in the moments when he was genuinely happy.

"I had a great childhood," Wesley said. "I grew up in Harlem. Ma was a music teacher—she actually still volunteers at the middle school twice a week."

Sasha grabbed my leg beneath the table and squeezed it, hard. *Still volunteers at the middle school.*

Carol is alive.

"Pop was a history teacher at the same school before he eventually became the principal," Wesley continued. "We used to call him Mr. Congeniality. He was the kind of person who knew everyone at the grocery store by name, their kids' names, who had an ailing parent and what their ailment was." Wesley chuckled, shaking his head at the memory. "Ma's quieter and more reserved, but they made sense together. They balanced each other out. Without Ma there to pull him along, Pop would just stay at the store all day, chatting everyone up."

"Do you have any siblings?" Sasha asked.

"Nah. Now that Pop's gone, it's just me and Ma in the city, outside of my wife and kids. I have a bigger family on Pop's side, but they mostly live out in Oklahoma and Texas."

I vibrated with excitement but tried to remind myself to be calm; I couldn't risk spooking Wesley.

"Your mom still lives in New York?" I asked, as casually as possible.

Wesley nodded. "My parents bought a brownstone on a rough block back when white folks were scared to cross 125th. It's worth a fortune now, but Ma would never sell."

My heartbeat stuttered. Carol was in New York. Right now. Just a handful of miles away.

"I'd love to meet her," I said.

Wesley sat back in his chair, his lips pulled into a long, thin line.

"Ma's always been kinda private. Like, I could never just bring friends over unless we'd talked about it days in advance." He rubbed his chin. "Thing is, if I give her a heads-up about you two, it'll give her too much time to come up with a story, or an excuse not to see you." His eyes met mine, and then Sasha's. "I don't want you to get the wrong idea about her. I love my ma. It's just . . . she isn't an open person, ya know? She's guarded. You get the feeling that she thinks really hard about what she says before she says it. Like she's constantly aware of the narrative she's building around herself." He cringed. "I don't think I made her sound any better."

"We get it," Sasha said, a smile in her voice. "Our mom's actually pretty similar."

Wesley checked his watch. "School's out for winter break, and she'd be back from her yoga class at the Y by now." He took a deep breath before looking up at us. "I think we should go to Harlem before I lose my nerve. Y'all got time?"

THIRTY-FIVE

As Ella Fitzgerald famously sang, the A train was, in fact, the quickest way to Harlem. After an hour underground, Wesley, Sasha, and I emerged from the 125th Street station, blinking and disoriented. It had begun to snow while we were on the train, thick, loose flakes the consistency of cotton candy.

"Ma's place is a ten-minute walk, this way," Wesley said, raising the collar of his peacoat against the frigid wind.

The throng of pedestrians thinned as we turned onto Frederick Douglass Boulevard. We were quiet as we walked, just as we'd been on the train, absorbed in our own thoughts. I tried to use the time to formulate a plan, a list of questions to ask my long-lost aunt. But I was too numb with shock to think. I was minutes away from meeting Carol.

Carol was alive.

Eventually we turned onto a street so quintessentially New York it looked as though we'd stumbled onto a movie set. It was flanked by handsome brownstones. The tall trees scattered along each side were bare but must have provided gorgeous dappled shade when they were heavy with leaves.

"I feel like I'm on my way to visit the Huxtables," Sasha said.

Wesley snorted. "They lived in Brooklyn Heights. But I know what you mean. Most of these buildings have been broken up into apartments, but there are still a few proper townhouses here and there. Ma's is one of them." He gestured toward a brownstone with vintage-looking wooden doors and windows sheathed with white curtains. "That's hers."

My stomach flipped. Wesley paused with one foot on the lowest step, gripping the gleaming black banister, head bowed. For a moment, I worried he might have changed his mind about confronting his mother. But then he lifted his head, marched up the stairs, and rang the doorbell. My heart raced as I heard footsteps approaching and saw the curtains flutter just before the door pulled open.

It was as though someone had run her photo through an age progression app, a kind one. Her face was a bit fuller. Her long dark hair was now a toffee-colored bob. Fine lines branched from the corners of her eyes. But she was unmistakably Carol.

Carol—whose preteen photo I'd stared at every day since I'd found it buried in that forgotten drawer in Grammy's house. Whose name Grammy had forbidden me from uttering when I was roughly the same age Carol was in that photograph. Whose diary I'd pored over since discovering it in Grammy's house, searching for clues about what happened to her. Whose teenage body I'd been certain was buried somewhere in the Raleigh wetlands sixty years ago.

I felt paralyzed by the overpowering mix of relief, joy, confusion, and curiosity coursing through my body. Carol was alive. How was this possible?

She had the look and presence of a former Hollywood starlet: proud posture, meticulously arched brows, lips and cheeks stained a subtle shade of mauve. A black pearl necklace hugged her collarbones. She gave Wesley the same smile she wore in her yearbook photo, the left side of her mouth climbing slightly higher than her right.

"Wesley, what a surprise! I wasn't expecting you till to—" All the life drained from her face the moment her heavy-lidded eyes, the eyes that reminded me so much of my own, landed on me. Some-how, though, her smile remained frozen on her face. "Oh," she said breezily, her focus fixed on me. "Friends of yours?"

"These are your nieces, Ma," Wesley said, a new edge to his voice. "Sydney and Sasha Singleton."

Carol's smile twitched. Then she closed the door in our faces.

THIRTY-SIX

THE FESTIVE COTTON CANDY FLAKES QUICKLY ESCALATED into a full-on blizzard; a nor'easter that had been forecast to bypass New York now threatened to stall over the city. Wesley received the emergency weather alert on his phone as we sat at Red Rooster, commiserating over fried chicken and cornbread after Carol slammed the door on us.

Wesley had tried ringing the doorbell again and again before giving his mother a call. She stayed on the line only long enough to tell her son to go home.

I shouldn't have been surprised, I realized in retrospect. This was a woman who'd purposely hidden from her family and friends for sixty years, who'd assumed a new identity to ensure this day would never come. Of course she didn't immediately and warmly invite me and Sasha in, knowing the questions we'd surely have for her.

A terrible realization dawned on me then, all at once: if Carol was alive, she was in danger. Given all the new suspicion he was under, Michael would probably be more determined than ever to silence her for good.

In our desperate effort to find her, had Sasha and I led Michael directly to Carol's doorstep?

"I better do a grocery run in case things get bad." Wesley sighed, tossing his napkin onto the table. "Last year I had to go out for Pampers in a foot of snow."

"How old are your kids?" Sasha asked.

He beamed. "Almost three. Twin girls."

The thought warmed me. My little girl had cousins.

I remembered something Sasha said at Thanksgiving, about how small our holiday celebrations were. *Don't you wonder what it would be like to be in one of those big families, with a bunch of people laughing and talking over each other, and a bunch of little kids running around?*

Was this actually a possibility for us now?

"Listen, I'll keep trying her," Wesley said, flagging down our server for the check. "But I have to warn you . . . Ma can be pretty stubborn. When do you head back to L.A.?"

"We fly back in three days, on the second," I answered, my mind racing. I had to figure out a way to get through to Carol before we left. But this damn storm was going to make it impossible for me to camp out on her stoop like I wanted to.

"I'm sorry we barged in and blew up your family, during the holidays of all times," Sasha said.

"Nah. It's better to know the truth," he said, and I tried not to wince. There was so much that Wesley still didn't know.

He waved off my attempt at paying for our lunch, signed the check, and stood to leave.

"Hey, Wesley," I asked, speaking before the thought fully formed, "how often does your mom check her email?"

THERE WOULD BE NO DINNER with Malik's mother that night; we barely made it back to the hotel before the city suspended above-ground subway service and warned its inhabitants to avoid nonessential travel.

I was grateful for the forced confinement in our Williamsburg hotel room; it gave me plenty of time to pen the most heartrending email to Carol I could muster.

Instead of picturing the elegant woman in the brownstone, I pictured the preteen girl in the framed photograph back home in L.A. I thought of the willful, passionate, and fiercely loving teenager from the diary I'd committed to memory. The teenager who reminded me in many ways of myself. And I remembered her words about the kind of love, compassion, and absolution she'd wished she'd gotten from Grammy.

So I started my email by apologizing—for showing up at her home unannounced, realizing how unsettling that must have been for someone who'd tried so hard to remain hidden. For invading her privacy further by reading the diary she'd secreted in the crawl space above her childhood bedroom. For how badly she'd wanted to feel cherished and understood by Grammy. For Grammy and Larry's failure to look for her after she disappeared, and their refusal to acknowledge her existence once she was gone.

I also thanked Carol—it was a shared desire to figure out what happened to her that had brought me and Sasha closer than we'd been in decades. And in that closeness, we'd been able to heal deep, destructive wounds we hadn't even realized we suffered from.

I know how much you loved my father, I wrote. *As a protective big sister myself, I know you wouldn't have left without a very good reason. Sasha and I aren't here to berate you for the past. We're here to offer you the family you've had to sacrifice all these years.*

I hesitated before adding my closing line. It was a Hail Mary move; it could be either the tipping point that convinced her to come clean about what happened sixty years ago or the breaking point that convinced her to run again.

But it was a risk I'd have to take; I couldn't live with myself if I didn't warn her about what might be coming her way.

I have a feeling that you left Raleigh because you were fleeing Michael Hall, I typed. *And I think you were right to do so—he's never stopped looking for you. Now that I know you're alive, now that I've found you, I worry he may do the same.*

We need your help, Aunt Carol. Together, we can make sure Michael never hurts anyone ever again.

Sasha, Malik, and I tried to make the most of a subdued New Year's Eve dinner at the hotel restaurant the next night. The staff did their best to create a festive mood for their snowbound guests, festooning the restaurant with silver tinsel and placing paper cone New Year's Eve hats on each table, though Sasha appeared to be the only diner wearing one. I did my best not to check my email every five minutes, an act that felt increasingly hopeless.

The snow finally stopped by the morning of New Year's Day. I couldn't open our balcony door without inviting piles of drifting snow to blow into our room. When I glanced out across the East River, it looked as though someone had emptied a giant jar of Marshmallow Fluff onto the city.

We ventured back down to the hotel restaurant for breakfast, trying to find an option that we hadn't yet eaten or that hadn't been removed from the menu because of the restaurant's dwindling supplies. I was just hoping to find something that wouldn't trigger the violent heartburn that had begun plaguing me the day we saw Carol. I knew it was yet another pregnancy symptom, but the timing of its emergence seemed somehow fitting.

"Guys, I'm really sorry," I said, setting my menu down on the table. "This trip has been a total bust."

"How can you say that?" Sasha asked. "We confirmed that Carol is alive. We saw her with our own eyes!"

"Yeah, I know . . . but she won't talk to us. She hasn't even responded to Wesley's New Year's calls and texts, and we're flying home tomorrow."

Malik put a comforting arm around my shoulders. "Carol might not be ready to talk to you two yet, but she's got to talk to her own son at some point."

"I don't know." I sighed. "A few months ago, we didn't even know Dad had a sister. We didn't know we had this whole other part of our family living right here. And now we've figured out that she's still alive and is sitting in a house just an hour away, but she won't even talk to us. We've come so far, and we've gotten so close."

Tears of frustration pooled hot in the corners of my eyes. I looked at Sasha; her eyes had gone wet, too. "I'm starting to feel like there's no hope for this family," I told her. "What's the point of trying to salvage things with folks who'd rather die with their secrets than risk opening up to the people who actually love them?"

Sasha offered me a small smile. "I have more hope for this family now than I ever had before," she said, looking from me to Malik and back again. "No matter what happens with Aunt Carol."

BACK IN OUR SUITE, I began to pack my suitcase, feeling increasingly desperate. Maybe I could go back to Carol's later that day, once the city had a chance to clear some of the snow. I had to try. I had to do something.

My phone chimed then, causing my heart to skip a beat. I nearly tripped on my suitcase on the way to my nightstand to retrieve it.

I had a new email.

My fingers shook as I opened the app. It was a reply from Carol. And she'd copied Wesley.

> Hello Sydney—If you're still in New York,
> I'm willing to meet with you all at my home at 10 a.m.
> tomorrow.
> Wesley, you might as well come too.
> I don't think I'll be able to say all of this more than once.

THIRTY-SEVEN

SASHA, WESLEY, AND I ARRIVED AT CAROL'S STOOP AT TEN on the dot the next morning. Our flight was scheduled for 5:00 p.m. If our conversation ran long, Malik would pick us up from Carol's house at two with our luggage loaded into the trunk to head straight to the airport. That meant I had just four hours to pull the truth from someone who'd managed to keep her existence secret for six decades.

"Have you talked to her at all since the last time we were here?" I asked Wesley.

"Nah," he said, his dreads swishing against his shoulders. "She still hasn't answered my calls or texts. I was starting to worry, what with the storm and all, until we got that email."

Just then, Carol's front door swung open. She looked every bit as regal as she had three days prior, clad in a knit tunic and pants the color of sapphires, her black pearls still clutching her throat. But the dark circles beneath her eyes told us that she hadn't slept in days, or had cried her way through them.

"I thought I heard my son's voice out here," she said, a brave smile on her face. "Come in, it's positively glacial today."

Sasha and I exchanged a wild-eyed glance before following Wesley inside.

The entryway was a shrine to Carol's son. The framed photographs on the wall opposite the coat closet chronicled his life. Wesley as a newborn, his features soft and pliable as fresh dough. Wesley as a gangly preteen smiling on a stoop with a group of other smiling, gangly preteens. Wesley standing proudly between his parents at his high school graduation, and again at his college graduation, and again when he earned a postgraduate degree. Wesley dancing with his wife at their wedding reception, their foreheads touching tenderly. Wesley, his wife, and their twin toddlers posing in a park.

Wesley turned in to a long narrow kitchen. Carol stood facing the countertop, a large island a barrier between us. The sudden din of grinding coffee beans made me and Sasha jump.

"How do you two take your coffee?"

"Please, Ma," said Wesley. He'd retreated into the corner of the kitchen, as though trying to put as much distance between himself and his mother as possible. "Stop acting like this is normal. You have to explain all this."

Carol took her time pouring the water into the coffeemaker. She dried the bottom of the carafe with a dish towel before placing it onto the warming plate and clicking the machine on. "I know, Wesley," she said at last. "I know that. I just need a minute." She fidgeted with her gold wedding ring; it appeared too tight for her to spin on her finger, but she tried anyway, as though it was an old habit she couldn't break. "How'd you all find each other?" she asked.

"A genealogy app," Wesley croaked. "One of those services that uses your DNA to help you find your relatives."

Carol closed her eyes and nodded. "Of course."

"I thought something bad happened to you," I said, sounding strangely hurt. I cleared my throat and started again. "Up until a few months ago, I didn't know you ever existed. But right after I found out about you, I also learned that several other girls went missing from your neighborhood around the time you did. We thought whatever happened to those girls happened to you, too."

Carol's expression didn't change, but her fingers continued to fidget. "Did they ever learn what happened to those girls?" she asked. The coffee machine sputtered behind her.

"A few of them, sort of," I answered. "Police dug up Raymond Green's backyard a few weeks ago. They found Marian, Geraldine, and Sally buried there. It looks like they'd been strangled to death."

"Oh my God," Wesley murmured from the corner. Carol's eyelids slid closed.

"Sally was buried with a box of things that had belonged to the girls," I went on. "Bettie's library card, Loretta's driver's license, Geraldine's glasses, Marian's necklace. Strangely, they didn't find anything of Sally's. Not in the box, anyway. But that was probably because Sally's charm bracelet was hidden in the back of your trunk."

Carol's eyes flew open. "My . . . trunk?"

I nodded. "Michael gave it to us. When Sasha and I went to talk to him in Detroit."

Carol's hands stilled. "You . . . talked to Michael?" When I nodded, she took a shuddering breath. "I knew he'd go to Detroit."

She reached clumsily for one of the stools perched behind the island. Wesley flinched, ready to spring across the room in case she fell. But Carol caught herself, pulled out a stool, and sat. She looked around the room with watery eyes.

"I don't deserve this life," she said. "But after a few years I allowed myself to think that maybe Mary Jones did." She glanced tentatively at her son. "Maybe Wesley's mother does. Wesley deserves everything." Twin tears spilled down her cheeks.

She was breaking. I had to choose my next move carefully. I needed her to break open, and tell us what she knew, not implode into herself, sealing the truth forever.

"Those girls' families have been searching for them for sixty years," I said gently. "Sixty birthdays. Sixty Christmases. All those mothers, wondering what happened to their babies. Bettie's and Loretta's families still don't have remains to bury. We have to help them if we can. They need closure. They deserve closure."

I moved toward the island. It felt too intimate to touch her, so I lowered my clasped hands right in front of hers, close enough that I could feel the warmth emanating from her skin, and I was sure she could feel mine.

She took a long, unsteady breath. "I know where the bodies are buried," Carol said. "I helped put them there."

THIRTY-EIGHT

There was a clatter behind me. I turned to see Wesley straightening the large, brightly colored painting hanging beside him as though he'd lost his footing and crashed into it.

"Oh, son." Carol moved toward him, but Wesley threw his hands up, stopping her in her tracks. Carol's shoulders slumped. "You all should go sit down in the living room," she said. "I'll bring in the coffee."

"I'll help you," I said. I didn't want to let Carol out of my sight.

She turned to me as Sasha and Wesley left the room, a cautious smile tugging at the corner of her mouth. "Mind grabbing the water pitcher from that shelf? The glasses are right below it."

I stole glances at Carol as we moved awkwardly around her kitchen, the weight of her words choking the air between us. *I know where the bodies are buried. I helped put them there.*

Carol, the spunky dreamer from all those diary entries. The devoted big sister to my adoring father. This doting mother, this volunteer music teacher. This elegant grandmother of twins. My long-lost aunt, finally found. Could she really have played a part in killing those girls?

Once our trays of water and coffee were assembled, I followed Carol down the hall into the living room. Two cream-colored sofas faced each other across a glass coffee table. In front of the window stood a handsome vintage upright piano and matching bench, their polished oak glinting in the winter sunlight. Built-in bookshelves spanned an entire wall, though instead of books, the shelves were filled with vinyl records, standing neatly in their paperboard sleeves.

This must have been a wonderful home to grow up in, I thought. Warm, colorful, full of music. Regret flooded me when I saw Wesley crumpled in a corner of a sofa. He'd never look at his mother the same way again.

I sat beside Sasha, and Carol sat beside her son. No one touched the beverages on the coffee table.

"For a long time, I expected someone to find me," Carol said at last. She sat completely erect, like a small bird ready to take flight at a moment's notice. "I thought I'd hear a knock on my door one day, and I'd open it to find the police. Or Michael. Or my mother, ready to drag me back to Raleigh. I didn't expect you two, after all this time." She looked around the room as though trying to savor its memory, as though she might never see it again. Maybe she wouldn't; there was no statute of limitations on murder in North Carolina.

"You thought Michael would come looking for you," I said. "Is that why you didn't move to Detroit?"

"I thought it might be easier to disappear in a big city like New York."

"Um, hello?" Wesley asked, raising his hand. "Who is this Michael person you all keep talking about?"

Carol told her son all the things Sasha and I had learned from her diary, from Michael, and from the stories we'd heard from her classmates and neighbors. She told him about how she fell in love with Michael. She was just shy of fifteen when he began taping roses to her locker. Hearing her tell it, I realized the large developmental gap that stretched between fourteen and eighteen. One was firmly rooted in childhood, the other beginning a new chapter as an adult. One was too young to drive, the other was old enough to legally buy a bottle of wine in North Carolina at the time.

She told Wesley about how Michael became increasingly distant during his time at Shaw, and how he began spending more and more time with his ghoulish friend, Raymond.

"I started to wonder if maybe Michael had a new secret girl-friend or something," she explained. "But I didn't understand what that had to do with Raymond. That is, until I was at choir practice after school one day and had to step out to use the restroom. The window beside the sink had a view of the side parking lot, where the buses usually lined up. The buses were gone already, but there was a car idling at the curb. Raymond's car. And it looked like Michael was sitting in the passenger seat, talking to a girl standing on the sidewalk. She kept looking down and smiling, glancing up through her lashes. The way shy girls flirt. Before I knew it, the girl was climbing into the backseat."

Carol shook her head. "It threw me into a jealous rage. I didn't know what they were up to with that girl, but I didn't like it. They were always going off on drives together, and this time, I was going to find out where they were going. I ran out of the bathroom, out of the school, unlocked my bike, and sped after them like a bat out of hell. After a few minutes I realized how foolish I was, following them on a bike when they were in a car. But they didn't go very far. It wasn't too hard to keep up with them either, since they had to keep stopping at lights and signs along the way."

She began rubbing her palms on her legs, as if trying to soothe herself. Wesley watched this with a conflicted expression on his face, like he wanted to take her hands in his but couldn't quite bring himself to touch her.

"They were driving along this big patch of trees, maybe a mile or so away from school, on a quiet stretch of road. And then, all of a sudden, they pulled off the road and into the trees, toward this big swampy area Larry used to play in sometimes when he was young."

I felt a chill as I recalled the diary entry about how Michael swooped in and rescued Carol on her way to retrieve her brother from the "Snake Pit." How Michael's apparent care for her and Larry in that moment endeared him to her.

Carol shook her head, a faraway look in her eyes. "I'll never forget how dark it was in there. It was the middle of the afternoon, but all the trees just blotted out the light. I have no idea how they even found a trail wide enough for that car to fit through, but given how comfortable Raymond was driving through it, it was clear that it wasn't his first time. I followed them on the bike as long as I could, but it was so wet and muddy."

Her words took me back to the trails snaking from the Walnut Creek Wetlands Center. I recalled standing on the bridge over a pool of murky water, staring out at the seemingly endless expanse of trees, moss, and mud, and whispering to Sasha, *Wouldn't this be the perfect place to hide a body?*

"What happened after you followed them into the trees?" I asked.

Carol looked as though she was struggling not to be sick.

"When I couldn't get the tires through the mud any longer, I set my bike against a tree and followed them on foot," she said. "They were driving real slow by then. Pretty soon, they stopped altogether, and cut the engine. They'd come to a slight clearing. The trail widened out, and there was a large fallen tree that blocked the rest of the path. It was an old tree, covered with moss. The way its branches were splayed out, it looked like a large letter K had tipped over onto its back."

Carol's breath rattled in her chest. She closed her eyes and kept them that way as she continued her story. "Next thing I knew, that girl started screaming bloody murder. The car was rocking all over the place. I couldn't see what was happening, I didn't want to get too close. But I could hear her screaming, and this thudding sound. Like somebody was being hit. I don't know how long I stood there, hiding behind a tree. Then the car doors flew open, and Michael and Raymond climbed out. Raymond had this wild look in his eyes. Michael just seemed . . . calm. Clinical even."

Wesley glanced at me and Sasha, eyes wide. I couldn't tell if he wanted us to stop this conversation or help him make sense of what he was hearing.

"Michael was the one in control," Carol said. "All those years I'd worried about Raymond. Creepy Raymond. Yet here was Michael calling the shots. He told Raymond to tie the girl up and set her down in front of the car, in front of the headlights. I saw Raymond drag her from the backseat and pull her down into the mud. I don't know what happened next. I covered my ears and knelt down with my eyes against my knees. Like a coward."

"You were a kid," Sasha said softly. "A kid in an impossible situation. What could you have done?"

Carol snorted. "I could have tried. Something. Anything. Instead, I just cowered behind that tree until I was too afraid that they might find me there. When I peered back around the tree the girl was still lying there in front of the car, but she wasn't moving anymore. The trunk of the car was open, and Michael and Raymond were digging beside that fallen tree. Like they'd pulled the shovels from the trunk. Like they'd planned the whole thing. That's when I thought of the other girls, Marian, Bettie, and Geri. And I remembered how Marian was last seen leaving school, walking to the store where she worked. That's when I put it all together—they were the ones who took those girls."

My heartbeat pulsed loudly in my ears. I knew it. I knew Michael and Raymond were behind this, together. I ran through the names of the other missing girls in my mind.

"It was Loretta Morgan, wasn't it?" I asked. "Loretta was last seen leaving a student council meeting after school."

Carol's eyes filmed over. "I didn't know it at the time, but yes. I began to retch, listening to the mud hit the girl's body. I had to get out of there. I thought they wouldn't hear me leave with all their digging." She shook her head. "I wasn't watching where I was going and I tripped over a tree root. I fell splashing into the mud. They ran over to see who'd made all that noise. For a moment, Michael looked at me as if he might cry. And then he went all serene, like he'd expected to find me there. He said, 'Starling.' That's what he used to call me. 'My Starling. You must be here to help us.'"

Carol began to shake, a tremor that radiated down her arms and into the fingers clutching her knees. Wesley snapped out of his stupor and wrapped an arm around his mother. "It's all right, Ma," he whispered. "You're all right now."

"Michael walked me over to the shallow grave where they'd dropped Loretta, facedown in the mud. I thought they were going to drop me in on top of her. Michael handed me his shovel and said, 'Be a good girl and cover up this mess, would you?' I didn't know what else to do, so I just did as I was told. Raymond started to help me, but Michael said, 'No, let her do it.' I kept hoping that Loretta would wake up. I kept hoping that I would wake up, that it was all a terrible dream."

Carol began to cry, mascara-inked tears that she didn't bother wiping away. "The mud was so heavy. My palms were raw when Michael finally patted me on the shoulder, saying 'That's enough now.' They had a whole system. They'd lined the trunk with a tarp, and they wrapped the shovels in another tarp. Then they stripped off all their clothes and put them in a garbage bag. They made me strip down too, Raymond watching me the whole time. They kept a jug of water and rags in the car, and we used them to clean the mud from our bodies. They put on new clothes and shoes; they made me put on an extra outfit of Raymond's. It smelled sour, like him. Then they made me go into the backseat, where Loretta had been. They waited till dark to leave the tree line. When the coast was clear, we headed to Raymond's house."

Carol lifted a hand toward the water pitcher, but after noticing how violently it trembled, she lowered it back onto her knee.

"Michael only said one thing to me the entire time we sat in that car. He told me that what I'd done in those woods made me an accomplice. He said I was one of them now. And that if I didn't keep helping them, he'd finish recruiting Larry to do it."

A sinkhole opened in the pit of my stomach. "What?" Sasha and I asked in tandem.

Carol nodded miserably. "Larry had been hanging around Michael more and more. He looked up to him, and Michael had always been kind to him. Larry was fourteen; he was getting to that age where he wanted more male role models in his life, I think. What a fool I'd been, thinking Michael spent time with Larry out of the goodness of his heart, or genuine affection for my brother. Apparently Michael and Raymond had already taken him 'hunting' before, as they called it, cruising around looking for girls to offer rides to. Nothing happened while Larry was with them, thank God. But Michael said if I didn't help them, or if I told anyone, they'd make Larry the third member of their sick group, and pin everything on him. He said it would ruin my family; they'd be run out of Raleigh. It was worse than just threatening to kill me, too."

"They made you . . . continue to do this?" Wesley croaked, still holding his mother.

"Oh yes," she said. "They said it was even easier with another girl in the car. It made the girls feel safe."

I thought of Joyce, the copper-haired woman from Barbara's gathering who threw herself from Raymond's car. *I was at a party with some friends,* she'd told me. *A girl I knew said she was getting a ride home with a few people and convinced me to come with her. She didn't want me to walk home alone.*

Had that girl been Carol?

"They were selective," Carol said. "They usually went for girls Michael knew, or girls he knew had a little crush on him. Often we'd drive around for hours and they wouldn't approach a single girl. I was terrified every single time one of them got in the car. I wanted to signal to them somehow, give them a sign that they were putting themselves in danger. But every time they made me climb into that backseat, Michael threatened me. Reminded me what would happen if I betrayed them."

A cyclone of questions whirled through my mind. Did she never fear for her own life, given how closely she fit the profile of the girls they killed? Or did the fact that she knew what they were doing ruin the thrill of the "hunt" for Michael and Raymond, as they called it?

The community was well aware that their children were being preyed on by then; what must it have been like to see the families of the missing girls in town, knowing that she could not only give them the closure they deserved but also prevent other families from being destroyed?

How could she live with herself, knowing all of this?

Carol looked right at me and as though intuiting my thoughts, said, "I think I lost myself for a while there. I lost my grip on reality. I wasn't processing what was happening. It's as though I hid in a safe corner of my own mind, and walled off everything else, so it couldn't hurt me. Outside of those rides, Michael acted completely normal around me. As if nothing had happened. Sometimes I allowed myself to believe that the murders were all just an awful dream. But when I was actually able to sleep, all I'd dream about was the memory of covering Loretta's body with that thick, sticky mud."

I realized that I could relate to Carol's uncanny ability to compartmentalize. "Repression is a defense mechanism," I said, repeating what Dr. Domínguez once told me. "A self-defense tool we sometimes use to protect ourselves. It's something I've had to work through myself."

Carol nodded, a look of gratitude in her eyes. "Nothing happened for a while," she went on. "When we picked up a girl, Michael and Raymond would just drop them off wherever they'd asked them to. As if they were practicing. Or maybe they got off on knowing what they could've done to those girls if they wanted to. It went on like this for a few months. Then one day we saw Sally walking down the street."

My blood ran cold. Sally Dunn. Stanley's younger sister.

"Sally was my friend," Carol choked. The decades-old dam she'd built finally burst; tears streamed down her face, and she blotted at them with shaking fingers. "I begged them to leave her alone, but they just ignored me, as if I hadn't said anything at all. Michael rolled down his window, told her we were heading to a party at Raymond's, and invited her to come along. Sally started making excuses—she couldn't skip out on work, she'd have to go home and change first. I was relieved, but then Michael snaked an arm into the backseat, carefully, so Sally wouldn't see, and pinched my thigh, hard. I thought about telling her to run, but then I thought of my little brother's face. I imagined what would become of his life if Michael framed him for what happened to the girls. So I rolled my window down and told Sally she looked great. To just come, it would be a lot of fun." Carol choked on a sob as she said, "I was the one who convinced her to get into the car."

Wesley rose from the couch and left the room momentarily, returning with a box of tissues that he handed to his mother. I started to feel claustrophobic, too hot in my wool sweater. I ran a finger between its neckline and my throat, wiping away a layer of sweat.

"When we got to Raymond's house they asked her to come upstairs to help them bring down some things for the party," Carol said. "I locked myself in the downstairs bathroom and sat on the floor crying with my hands over my ears, though some of the screams and thuds got through. I stayed that way for hours. By the time Michael knocked on the door and I crawled out of the bathroom, it was already dark outside."

"Didn't Grammy wonder where you were all that time?" Sasha asked.

Carol's eyes flickered. "Grammy . . . I've never heard her called that." She sniffled and studied her hands. "Michael only brought me along on the days when Mama worked as a night nurse for a family in town after her day shift. She didn't even know I was gone." Fresh tears traced her face. "Mama worked that night job to put money away for college for us. Meanwhile, I was busy burying my friend by the creek in Raymond's yard." Carol's shoulders heaved. "Oh, Sally!"

Wesley held his mother's face against his shoulder as she sobbed, though his expression was gobsmacked. My heart ached for Sally, for allowing the presence of her friend to make her believe she was safe, only to have her young life taken in such a brutal and terrifying way. And my heart ached for Carol, for being manipulated into serving as an accomplice to her friend's murder, and for keeping these horrible secrets all this time.

I remembered the box authorities found, clutched in Sally's skeletal fingers.

"Did you see the box Sally was buried with?"

Carol's eyes widened. "Did the police find Michael's ring?"

I felt an inappropriate pang of pride. I knew it was Michael's ring. "They did," I replied, "though they aren't able to prove it was Michael's. Not without a witness or evidence that directly connects him to it. Both of which are difficult to come by after all this time." A series of emotions crossed Carol's face like clouds. "You put the ring there. Didn't you?" I asked.

"What happened to Sally . . . I can never forgive myself. I knew my family was in jeopardy, but I couldn't just keep playing Michael's game. I had to do something." Carol's fingers made useless twisting motions around her wedding band. "Raymond and I were digging a hole in his backyard, and Michael went back inside to grab something. I asked Raymond what he was doing, and he said Michael was 'gathering the evidence.' He told me Michael thought this should be the last time they did this. Michael was getting ready to enter his junior year at Shaw. He planned to graduate early and head west for law school. Apparently Michael thought things were getting too hot. Police had questioned Raymond a while after Geraldine went missing, so he was already on their radar. And if I'd been able to tail them on my bike, it was only a matter of time before someone else saw something that could put us all away. Raymond said Michael worried all this was going to jeopardize his real life, after he left Raleigh."

Carol made a sardonic sound. "I know it sounds insane, but up until that moment, I still believed that Michael actually loved me. We'd been together for nearly three and a half years at that point, since I was so young. He'd been the first person in my life who truly made me feel precious; I think I was holding out hope that this was all some sick phase, and after we ran away together we'd put this whole thing behind us. But Michael didn't actually love me. He wasn't actually considering my dreams of moving to Detroit. He was going to the West Coast with or without me. He was just using me until he got to go off to his 'real life,' using me as a pawn to help him kill those poor girls.

"That realization shook something loose in me," Carol continued. "Michael eventually came out of the house holding that wooden box, and they dragged Sally into the hole, and he placed the box in her hands." She shook her head. "He wanted to get rid of the girls' things so his hands would be clean, so there wouldn't be anything tying him back to the murders. I was panicking, trying to come up with something I could do. That's when we all heard a sound coming from the direction of a neighbor's house, like a window being pulled open."

I pictured Alvin, who'd glimpsed Raymond standing with a garden tool on the Fourth of July of the previous year, an unwitting witness to Geraldine's burial.

"While the two of them were distracted, I opened the box, took Sally's charm bracelet, slipped Michael's class ring from my finger, and put it in the box," she said. "He'd given me the ring for our anniversary the previous year. Before I knew . . . who he really was."

"I don't get it," Sasha said. "If Michael was so worried about all of this getting out, why did he let you live?"

"I'm not sure he planned to," Carol answered, shaking her head. "I think I may have left before he got the chance. And I don't think he worried about doing anything right away because he was confident in the power he believed he had over me. He sincerely believed I'd never betray him." Carol winced. "Apparently, he was right."

I thought about how eager Michael had been to return my first phone call. To invite me to visit him in Detroit. To send me and Sasha home with Carol's trunk as a parting gift, oblivious to the damning clue it held. These weren't acts of generosity; they were feats of unimaginable hubris.

"Sally went missing in February 1965," I pointed out, "but you didn't leave Raleigh until that May," I said. What made you decide to run then?"

Carol sighed. "I was catatonic after Sally was killed. It was like I was no longer living in my body, just going through the motions of life. Raymond was right; it was like Michael wanted to stop what we were doing. They didn't make me go hunting with them after Sally. Michael was even more distant than before; we barely saw each other. I started to think that maybe it was over, all of it. Then one afternoon I was leaving choir practice, and was about to ride my bike home, when Raymond's car pulled up. He told me Michael asked him to come get me, that he wanted to apologize for everything. The last time I saw Michael, we'd argued over Detroit versus Oakland again, as if that even mattered anymore, given everything else that happened. But for some reason I believed it, that Michael wanted to make things right. Or I wanted to believe it. So I put my bike in Raymond's trunk and got into the passenger seat."

The air in the room was staticky. I think we could all feel it, the electric tingle of intuition, our bodies screaming, *Don't get into that car.*

"I thought we were heading to Michael's apartment. It took me a while to register the quiet road we were traveling down. I didn't put it together until he turned in to the thicket of trees."

Carol shook her head. "I started crying. 'No,' I said, 'I thought we were through with all this.' Raymond didn't look at me when he responded. He said, 'I never said I was through.'"

Sasha shifted uncomfortably beside me. Wesley winced as though anticipating a blow.

"He drove down the same trail as before, stopping at the same spot where they took Loretta, in that clearing in front of the tree like a toppled over K. My brain couldn't catch up with what was happening. I asked Raymond where Michael was. Then he got this strange smile on his face and said, 'It's just you and me this time.' He told me to get out of the car. He opened the trunk, grabbed a shovel, and pushed it into my hands. Then he told me to dig."

Fresh tears spilled down Carol's cheeks. "He was going to make me dig my own grave. I understood it then. I was crying hysterically, but there was no one to hear me. It was as though the trees absorbed all the sound. I set the blade down in one spot and Raymond told me to stop. He said, 'You don't want to dig up the other one.' That's when I realized at least one other girl was down there under the mud."

Bettie, I thought, the last of the girls who were unaccounted for. Bettie and Loretta were buried in the wetlands.

"So I started to dig in a different area. After a while I stopped crying. I told myself I deserved this. I deserved to die out there, in the middle of nowhere, only a mile from home. I'd helped bury Loretta. I'd led Sally to her death. I deserved to die, too."

A tear slipped down Wesley's face.

"Raymond leaned against the car, watching me dig. I think he enjoyed that, being the one in charge instead of Michael. Watching me struggle under the weight of the mud. After a while he said that was enough, and then told me to take off my clothes."

Carol's breath went ragged. "I'd never allowed myself to think about what they might've done to those girls before killing them." She closed her eyes and steeled herself before she continued. "I told him no. I'd hit some sort of limit. I was ready to die, but I wasn't ready for him to touch me. We argued, and before I knew it, he lunged at me. I fell back into the mud, next to the grave I'd dug. I fought every way I knew how. I scratched and bit and punched. He wasn't used to having to take a girl down on his own, without Michael's help. One of my scratches caught his eye. He yelped and reared back. I'd drawn blood. I scrambled out from under him just enough to grab the shovel. I'd grabbed it awkwardly, holding the blade. I hit him with the handle as hard as I could, aiming for that wounded eye. He cried out and rolled away. It gave me time to fix my grip. I brought the blade down on his head over and over, until I knew for certain that he wouldn't ever get up again."

All of our eyes had gone wide with the horror of the story. Sasha's and Wesley's jaws hung slack.

"They'd taught me what to do next," Carol said. "I pushed Raymond into the grave I'd dug and covered his body with mud. I took the tarp from the trunk, wrapped the shovel in it and shoved it into some brush. I cleaned as much mud from my body as I could with the jug of water and rags he kept in his car. I changed into a spare pair of Raymond's old sour clothes. I waited until it was very late, and then I drove Raymond's car home. I was used to driving that car; Michael would sometimes let me when he used it to take me on dates."

I remembered Michael's story about the picnic Carol drove him to in the middle of a field. *Don't tell my wife,* he'd said, *but it's still the single most romantic thing that ever happened to me.*

My stomach churned at the thought.

"It was one of the days when Mama only worked a day shift," Carol continued, "so I had to sneak into the house through my bedroom window. I filled a bag with a bunch of things, took my piggy bank with the cash I'd saved up at my job the previous summer, and ran back out to Raymond's car."

Pain rippled across Carol's face. "When I looked back at the house, I could've sworn I saw the curtains move in Mom's bedroom. Like she saw me."

I thought about how adamant Grammy had been that Carol had run away. Maybe it wasn't a matter of stubborn denial; maybe she'd actually watched Carol leave.

"I sat in the driver's seat for a moment, watching the house," Carol said. "I told myself, if she ran out after me, I'd just give up. I'd turn myself in. But then I remembered what all of this would do to my family. Even if I owned up to it and made it clear Larry had nothing to do with the girls' deaths, it would kill our family's reputation. It would ruin everything Mama had worked so hard for. And anyway, I didn't see the curtains move again. She didn't come running out the front door, begging me to stay. So I left."

Carol dabbed at her eyes with her wad of tissue; Wesley handed her a fresh sheet. "I had no idea where I was going . . . I just drove," she said. "I headed north for a while before I realized I was still in

Raymond's disgusting clothes. I pulled off the road and changed into something I'd thrown in my bag, then I tossed his clothes into the first trash can I found. At some point it dawned on me that I couldn't keep driving a car that connected me to him. I parked it a few blocks away from a bus station near D.C. and left the keys on the driver's seat. Then I caught a bus to New York, and never looked back."

Carol reached over and took Wesley's hand. They stared at each other tearfully.

"I've had such a wonderful life," she said, gazing around her home. "I don't deserve any of this. For a long time I thought that I should have been buried in that grave I'd been forced to dig. But if that had happened, Wesley wouldn't be here." She squeezed her son's hand, then turned to look at me and Sasha. Though tears streamed from her eyes, her chin was raised, her expression resolute. "Mom's gone . . . I've known that for a while. My baby brother's gone; I googled him every year on his birthday, that's how I found out about his crash. And now you all know the truth. There's no one left to hurt with my secrets."

Something like relief cleared the air in the room, like an unexpected breeze. I felt my shoulders relax for the first time since we'd landed in New York.

"I needed time to sit with your letter, Sydney. To come to terms with all this. To come to terms with what I have to do."

My heart swelled with hope. I stood, walked around the coffee table, and sat beside her, wrapping an arm around her so she was sandwiched between me and Wesley. I felt her body shudder with tears as she leaned her head against mine.

"I don't want to go to my grave with this," she said. "I'm ready to go back to Raleigh now. I want to help those families properly bury their girls. I'm ready to pay for what we've done."

I took her hand and pulled back so I could look her square in the eye. "You're going to help us make Michael pay for what *he's* done," I said.

THIRTY-NINE

Fifteen Months Later

 YOU'D HAVE TO KNOW WHAT YOU WERE LOOKING FOR TO find it.

Angels' Clearing appeared on the trail map and on the wooden markers scattered along the paths, though its name belied the gruesome events that transpired there. It was nestled so deep in the wetlands that a new trail had to be built in order to reach it.

The trail was serene, meandering over two wooden bridges and through endless acres of greenery. Walnut Creek ran alongside the trail for much of its length, playing a gentle rhythm as it drummed against the rocks and fallen branches in its path.

The end of the trail spilled into a half-circle-shaped field. There was something miraculous about the meticulously trimmed patch of grass in the midst of such wilderness. The canopy above the field had been thinned; sunlight filtered through the leaves as if through stained glass.

A reclaimed wooden bench stood on one end of the field. It looked like a large piece of driftwood that had washed up onto a tiny beach cove. The bench had been carved from a single tree. Its surface was polished smooth, and a long seat had been scooped from its middle, though its overall shape had been preserved. A pair of large branches formed an organic backrest of sorts. If you looked at it from a certain angle, the tree looked like a letter K, tipped over onto its back.

Five young oak trees were planted at equal intervals along the edge of the field. Their trunks were circled by wildflowers, their technicolor faces tilted toward the dappled spring sunlight. A small golden plaque stood in front of each tree, each featuring an inscription: FOR MARIAN, FOR BETTIE, FOR GERALDINE, FOR LORETTA, FOR SALLY.

Angels' Clearing and the trail built to accommodate it would officially open to the public the following week, but the parks department offered the families and friends of the girls they memorialized the opportunity to christen them with a private gathering. As soon as the invitation was issued, Barbara reached out to ask if my family and I could join them.

None of this would have been possible without you, she wrote.

Once the girls' remains were released to their families, each held a memorial service sixty years overdue. When the families discussed what the Angels' Clearing event should look like, they all agreed that they didn't want another somber occasion.

There's already been too much grief surrounding our girls, Barbara wrote. *This time, we're choosing to celebrate their lives.*

Someone had compiled a playlist featuring music from the girls' favorite artists. The sounds of Martha and the Vandellas, the Supremes, the Temptations, and Sam Cooke floated from speakers on either side of the bench. A bouquet of lilac and marigold balloons was tied to each of the oak trees with cascading white ribbons. The scents of pulled pork, brisket, potato salad, collard greens, and hush puppies catered by Clyde Cooper's BBQ mingled with the smell of freshly shorn grass.

If anyone had stumbled upon our party, they would never have been able to guess at the darkness that brought us all together.

Barbara steered me around the clearing, introducing me to anyone I didn't know. "This is Sydney Singleton," she'd say, with the pride of a parent showing off a child visiting home from an Ivy League school.

I wasn't prepared for the reactions I received from the guests. An older man's grumpy resting face exploded into a toothy grin as he clasped my hand and raised it into the air, as if I were a prize-fighter who'd just delivered a knockout punch. A woman who appeared younger than me wrapped me in a tight hug. "This is what my mom would've done if she were here," she whispered into my ear. "She talked about how much she missed her sister Bettie every single day." An older woman simply burst into the sort of tears that left me and Barbara wiping our cheeks, too.

"My sister, Sasha, played an important role in all of this, too," I said again and again, pointing in her direction. Sasha spent much of the event with one headphone over an ear, holding a microphone in the air to capture ambient noise, or close to the mouth of an interview subject. "We're working on a special episode of our podcast," I explained. "We hoped this would show anyone grieving a missing loved one that there can still be joy and celebration in their future, even if it seems impossible at the moment."

After Sasha, Wesley, and I accompanied Carol to Raleigh for her interview with Detective Higgins, it was only a matter of weeks before a warrant was issued for Michael's arrest. As hard as I'd worked for that very outcome, it was difficult to see the photos of him being escorted from his handsome Detroit home, his head bowed and wrists handcuffed behind him. I couldn't shake the mental picture of his wife and daughter huddling in an upstairs room, away from the intrusive lenses of the cameras posted in their front yard, documenting the moment their lives fell apart.

"I can't believe we were in that man's house," Sasha said with a shudder during our biweekly lunch the day of his arrest. "Isn't it strange that he was so eager to have us visit? I mean, if you hadn't seen that picture of him with Raymond in his office, or found Sally's bracelet in Carol's trunk, he might have gotten away with all this forever."

I shook my head. "You'll see when you listen to more episodes

of *The Unforgotten*. It's weirdly common for killers to send taunt-
ing letters or false leads to police and press, or later be found in
pictures of memorials and volunteer searches for the people they
killed. It's like they think they're too clever to be caught. Or they
get off on seeing all the pain and mayhem they're causing. Or both."

I pushed my barely touched salad to the edge of the table. "Michael kept Carol's trunk all this time as a trophy, a physical reminder
of that time in his life. What could be more thrilling than having
flesh-and-blood nieces of Carol in his home, especially one that
looks exactly like her?"

Sasha grimaced and pushed her plate away, too.

"He let us in his home because he didn't see us as a threat."

Sasha snorted. "Joke's on him. They still have the death penalty
in North Carolina."

Thanks to Carol's firsthand account, a fair amount of circum-
stantial evidence, and a damning latent fingerprint pulled from the
lens of Geraldine's horn-rimmed glasses, it took twelve jurors only
two hours to find Michael guilty on multiple counts of kidnapping,
false imprisonment, and first-degree murder. Although he was still
awaiting sentencing, given the minimum prison time associated
with his crimes, there was zero chance that he would see freedom
again. Especially given that authorities were looking into his possible connection to several Black girls who'd gone missing from
Oakland and Detroit during the years he resided in those cities.

Marian, Bettie, Geraldine, Loretta, and Sally were the ones memorialized by Angels' Clearing, but they were only a handful of the
victims of what happened in Raleigh. Every mother, father, sibling,
friend, aunt, uncle, high school sweetheart, beloved coach, or
teacher . . . everyone left behind was a victim, too.

Among the victims of the senseless murders was Michael's family back in Raleigh. It was probably a cosmic kindness that his
mother and Grammy's friend, Eloise Hall, died just days before
Michael's arrest. His sister, Yvonne, left North Carolina before the
trial began. I couldn't blame her. It made me think of Michael's

threats to Carol about what would happen if she didn't help them, if they'd pinned their crimes on my father instead.

He said it would ruin my family; they'd be run out of Raleigh, Carol had said. *It was worse than just threatening to kill me, too.*

I wondered if Michael ever considered that the very same thing he'd threatened Carol with could befall his own family. I would never know if Yvonne tried to protect Michael from me because she believed in his innocence or in an effort to preserve her family's good name. Maybe "what happens in this house stays in this house" was a family motto of theirs, too.

In the midst of the national news frenzy that followed Michael's arrest, I received a text from the producer of *The Unforgotten* podcast:

This story would make an unbelievable podcast series.

And I think you'd be the perfect person to host it.

If this is something you'd be interested in, I'd be happy to support you in any way I can.

I didn't respond to the text for several days. Me? A podcast host? Based on what qualifications?

And yet I couldn't stop thinking about it. There was clear interest in the story, and there was clear value in its telling, in case it could help others looking for missing loved ones, too. Besides, I might not have had experience tracking down missing people, but look at all I'd been able to accomplish anyway.

The idea of taking on an entire podcast on my own was overwhelming. But when I thought about my favorite podcasts, *The Unforgotten* included, I realized they were nearly all hosted by two people. Not only had Sasha been my partner in traveling to Detroit to meet Michael, and the person who ultimately led us to find Carol, but she had relevant experience given her myriad jobs in the enter-tainment industry.

When Sasha and I met with the producer over a video call to ask her for advice, she told us she and the hosts of *The Unforgotten* were starting their own podcast network and asked if we'd be inter-ested in joining their growing roster.

We originally planned to call the podcast "We Don't Talk About Carol." But the producer suggested we name it something broader, something that gave us the ability to expand beyond Carol's story in future seasons, if we chose to do so. Eventually we landed on "Every Missing Black Girl." It was the title of *The New York Times* story that went viral following Michael's arrest. In addition to sum-marizing Michael's case, the story highlighted the disproportionate number of missing Black girls in America.

Thank goodness for the producer's advice. As we neared the final episode of our first season, we had already amassed millions of downloads and had received countless tips for stories to cover in future seasons.

Barbara and I walked over to the corner of the field where Sasha was interviewing Stanley, Sally's older brother. Sasha's face was draped in concern, the microphone pointed at Stanley as she asked, "Does it feel strange to be celebrating at the site of so much trag-edy?"

I stifled a proud smile.

Sasha poured more hours into the podcast on a weekly basis than I did, though she insisted that she was happy to do it. While she'd worked her way up from an administrative assistant to an as-sistant script editor at the film studio, Sasha found that she really enjoyed working on the production side of the podcast and thought it might be a career path she'd like to pursue instead. Unlike the Sasha of the past, however, she had no intention of immediately abandoning her steady paycheck. After all, she had to come up with her monthly contribution to the rent and utilities at the Park La Brea apartment she and her roommates shared.

It was a good thing Sasha moved out of Mom's house before we started the podcast; after we told Mom about our plans to do it, she didn't speak to us for over a month. Since then, we'd managed to settle back into a rhythm of mostly amiable monthly dinners at Mom's house.

At the last dinner before our Raleigh trip, Mom had surprised us by leaving the table and returning with two slips of paper. She handed one to each of us.

I glanced down at mine. It was a check for $10,000.

"Whoa!" Sasha cried, pushing her chair back with such force I was certain she'd slashed the rug beneath us. "What's this for?"

"It's part of the proceeds from the sale of Grammy's house," she said matter-of-factly, taking another sip of iced tea. "I put most of the rest in a trust for you girls. I offered the whole thing to Carol, since it was her mother's house, but she refused."

Mom sighed. "I wasn't sure what to do with the money for a while. Sasha, I thought you could use it to bolster your savings. And, Sydney, I thought it could make a nice contribution to Little Bit's college fund. Or . . . I don't know . . . I read that article about you all in the *Times*. Maybe you could invest it in your little podcast."

Sasha and I locked eyes across the table. We knew that was as close to praise for what we had accomplished as we were going to get from our mother.

Now, at Angels' Clearing, Stanley considered Sasha's question, the crevasse deepening between his thick brows. "I had my reservations about having a celebration on this land," he said. "But then I thought, those monsters had so much power over us all those years, hiding in the shadows. By turning this area into such a lovely, peaceful place, it's like we're taking that power back. We've decided the cemetery can be the place where we mourn, but this can be the place where we celebrate the girls' memories."

Stanley smiled at the festive scene in front of him. "It's nice to think of all the joy this area will see in the future. All the birthday parties, all the picnics. All the people who will fill this space with love, having no idea what happened here."

Barbara slid her hand into Stanley's, and he planted a wet kiss on her forehead.

"It's so good to see you two together, finally," I said, my smile giving my voice a singsong quality.

Stanley squeezed Barbara's hand. "If it's one thing all this has taught me, it's that life is entirely too short, and we can't wait until someone's gone to tell them how much we love them. All this," he said, gesturing at the festive field, "I just wish our girls could've seen this. I wish we could've done all this while they were here." His voice cracked; he looked away.

Barbara wrapped her arms around Stanley's waist. "Geri and Sally knew how much we loved them, Stan. It might sound silly, but I hope they're all up there having a picnic together too, celebrating right along with us."

Sasha and I exchanged a glance, a frequently shared unspoken agreement. *That's going in the episode.*

"Mah-muh," said a little voice behind me. It was a new milestone, one that had just begun in the last few days. It was the sweetest sound I'd ever heard, right up there with the first time I heard her heartbeat, and the first time I heard her helpless little cry in the delivery room.

Unlike the dark days of my involuntary stay at the UCSF Medical Center, Mom and Sasha were right there with me and Malik at UCLA Labor and Delivery.

"I know I probably haven't always been there for you the way you wanted me to be," my mother said when Malik and Sasha made a cafeteria run in the early hours of my labor, shocking the pain from my mind. She squeezed my hand tighter than I'd squeezed Malik's mid-contraction. "But I want to be there for this little girl. Even if I don't get it quite right all the time."

I squeezed her hand back. "You're already doing great," I told her. "You're here now, aren't you?"

I turned to see Nia grinning at me from the baby carrier Malik had strapped to his front, her huge brown eyes shining with joy. Malik's eyes. She also had his smile, only with fewer teeth. Nia pumped her pillowy legs with excitement. The baby carrier unfortunately covered much of her adorable outfit, a cream cotton dress scattered with golden suns. A matching golden headband circled her crown of curls. My curls. Nia looked every bit the miniature version of the toddler in my dreams.

"Hi, Nia," I cooed as she stretched her little arms toward me. "Can I take her for a bit?"

"Of course," said Malik, helping me unfasten her from the carrier.

"She's beautiful," Barbara fawned. I felt Nia's surprisingly strong yet deliciously squishy body press against my chest. She continued babbling my favorite song as she searched my face with her tiny hands, *mah-muh, mah-muh, mah-muh.*

Malik reached into the diaper bag he carried, extracted a muslin cloth, and wiped Nia's glossy, dribbling mouth. "Here," he said, draping the cloth over my shoulder.

"Thanks, Malik; I appreciate you."

"I appreciate *you.*"

Sasha gagged. "Couples therapy has made you both insufferable."

Malik and I gazed at each other sappily, which only made Sasha roll her eyes harder. Between starting couples therapy shortly after Carol's confession and embarking on our journey as parents, our relationship had reached a new level of honesty and understanding. It also seemed that seeing me deliver our child had shifted Malik's perception of me. Whereas he used to see me as something fragile, something in need of his protection, he now appeared to recognize that I possessed much more strength than either of us had given me credit for. Perhaps it was a combination of Nia's birth, stepping into my new role of motherhood with bravery and determination, and the fact that investigating what happened to Carol and the girls didn't make me fall apart that made us both see me differently, more clearly than ever before.

Three months before Nia arrived, Malik onboarded a new CEO to Wealthmate and assumed the role of Founder/Chief Product Officer. In addition to allowing him to focus on the work he cared about most—providing Wealthmate's members with meaningful, sophisticated personal finance tools—he was able to build additional flexibility into his life. Now he ended work at noon on Fridays and spent one-on-one time with Nia while Sasha and I worked on the podcast.

Since we no longer needed its generous fertility benefits, having decided that our family was complete with Nia, I quit my job at the trendy activewear company and took a position as a freelancer for a big PR firm. It gave me the flexibility to end most workdays at 3:30 P.M., and Fridays by midday. It wasn't glamorous or vital work, but I no longer needed it to be; the podcast was the most fulfilling work I'd ever done, and it was all the more special because I got to do it with my sister.

As Nia toyed with my necklace, I inhaled her sweet scent, the hint of coconut oil in her hair. I looked back toward the trail. The bridge was just visible through the trees. "I'll be right back."

I cooed to Nia as we walked along the trail. She pointed down to the burbling creek and up to a trilling bird in a high branch. I was eager for the day when she'd be able to tell me all the things she thought, and felt, and knew.

Carol stood on the bridge staring out into the thick layers of green but turned to smile at us as she heard Nia and me approach.

"There's my little grandniece," Carol said, giving Nia the hand-cupping wave people share only with small children and pets. Nia made a gurgling sound and reached for Carol, who pulled her gently into her arms.

The state decided not to press charges against Carol for her involvement in Sally's kidnapping and burial, the burial of Loretta, and the concealment of what happened to the other girls, given that she was a minor at the time and had also been victimized by Michael and Raymond. While killing Raymond surely would have been deemed an act of self-defense, no charges were filed against her hiding his body to conceal her crime, likely given her willingness to cooperate in building their case against Michael.

While Carol was spared jail time, her involvement in the case had taken a visible toll on her. She seemed to have aged a decade in the fifteen months since we met. The faint, fine lines that etched her face had deepened and darkened. Her limber balletic movements had stiffened and slowed. I'd never know if the heavy cloud of regret that shrouded her was new, or if it had been something she carried ever since the fateful day she followed Raymond and Michael into the wetlands.

"You sure you don't want to come see the field, and say hi?" I asked gently, reaching out to tap one of Nia's tiny feet. "I know it would be hard. But it might be cathartic?"

Carol traced Nia's smooth cheek with the back of a hand. "I can't see that place without reliving what happened there." She sighed. "I did enough of that on the stand during the trial. Took everything I had in me to make it this far into this place." Nia made the whimper warning that a full-blown meltdown was around the corner. Carol handed her to me, and I bobbed her up and down. "Besides, I know my presence would put a damper on things. Least I could do is give them the space to enjoy today."

While the families were grateful to put an end to the agonizing mystery behind the girls' disappearances, many firmly believed that Carol deserved to be in prison for the role she played. I was relieved the state recognized how much Carol had already sacrificed. Michael and Raymond had stolen Carol's innocence and robbed her of the opportunity to pursue her lifelong dream. And Michael's cruel ultimatum—along with Raymond's forcing her to fight him to the death—made Carol believe that the only way she could save her family was to sever all ties with them.

Carol rested her hands on the bridge and fidgeted with her wedding band. I lowered my hand over hers to still her fingers. "I'm sure Barbara wouldn't have invited you if the other families were against it. Maybe now that some time has passed, they're willing to forgive you. Maybe they can see that you were a victim in all of this, too."

She craned to glimpse the clearing behind me. The trees managed to absorb much of the music, but I could make out Nancy Wilson's honeyed rendition of "Our Day Will Come." Carol shook her head, her expression tranquil.

"I don't deserve their forgiveness. But that's all right." She slid her hand from beneath mine, rearranging them so hers was on top. "I've got you, and Wesley, and Sasha, and Malik, and little Nia. Your coming into my life gave me the strength to finally tell the truth, and start the process of beginning to forgive myself."

Nia babbled something that sounded hilariously similar to "That's right!" Carol and I burst into laughter.

The entire park seemed to be filled with laughter. It radiated from the celebration in Angels' Clearing. It floated on the gentle breeze from neighboring trails. Though Angels' Clearing and its new trail were its only modifications, the atmosphere of the park felt drastically different from my first visit, when I had felt suffocated by the dense verdant darkness. Maybe it was because there were no more skeletons here. Not buried beneath the mud, and not buried within my own family.

As I held Nia against my chest, felt the weight of Carol's hand covering mine, and listened to the cheerful din of the party in the clearing, I had never felt more at peace.

ACKNOWLEDGMENTS

While this novel is a work of fiction, the sobering statistics at its heart are based in fact. A disproportionate number of Black people are reported missing in America every year. According to the FBI's National Crime Information Center, of the nearly 563,400 people reported missing in America in 2023, nearly 202,100 — or 36 percent — were Black. Yet Black people make up just shy of 14 percent of the country's population, per the July 2023 estimates of the United States Census Bureau. If you have been moved by this story and want to take action, I encourage you to support the Black and Missing Foundation, a nonprofit dedicated to bringing awareness to this issue, and providing support and resources to those searching for their missing loved ones.

People often talk about how lonely and isolating being a writer can be. I am thankful to say that this has been far from my experience. I'm fortunate to have had numerous champions throughout this journey, in no small part because I was brave and vulnerable enough to invite them in along the way.

I'm so grateful to Sharon Pelletier, my brilliant and tenacious literary agent at Dystel, Goderich & Bourret, and Jenny Chen, my wise and talented editor at Bantam/Penguin Random House, for recognizing the promise and potential in this story six drafts ago. Thank you both for sometimes seeing what I was trying to accomplish even more clearly than I could, and for making the process of sharpening, polishing, and deepening this novel so collaborative, compassionate, and enjoyable.

My heartfelt thanks also go to Mimi Bark, Sara Bereta, Saige Francis, Abdi Omer, Jennifer Rodriguez, Jean Slaughter, Emma Thomasch, Samuel Wetzler, and the entire team at Bantam/Penguin Random House for the pivotal roles each of you played in making my lifelong dream of becoming a published novelist come true. And thank you to Lauren Jane Holland, my talented film and TV agent at CAA, for envisioning the possibility of bringing this story to the screen before the novel even reached its final form.

To the beloved members of my critique group, past and present—Sarah "Vandie" Van de Kamp, Samara Simmerman, Kristin Gifford, Halleta Alemu, and Susan Zieger—I am eternally grateful that you were the first readers of this novel, offering chapter-by-chapter feedback and encouragement as I found my way through my first rough drafts. While some of you have moved on, and some are newer to the team, you have all been instrumental in making this novel what it is today.

Thank you to my incredible book club crew for being such loyal and enthusiastic advocates of this novel before you read a single page. And to Chelsea Berg, Liz David, Nicole Tam Goldberg, Lausanne Miller, and Ellen Reavey, I will never forget the rainy Friday evening when you all came over to discuss an early draft of this novel. The fact that you all carved time out of your busy lives to read this manuscript (some of you with very young children at home, no less!) and provided such thoughtful feedback meant the world to me, and it made this book so much stronger. Even if this novel were never published, being a fly on the wall for a book club discussion about this story was a highlight of my life.

To my amazing husband, Hector—thank you for not only telling me how much you believed in me and in this novel but for showing your support in so many ways, every single day. From offering to take on extra dinner shifts so I could meet with my writing group, to volunteering to greet my book club friends at the door the night I hosted them for my manuscript critique, to encouraging me to adjust our weekend schedules to protect my writing time, to dropping off little snacks and beverages on my desk when I was in the middle of a drafting sprint, to happily agreeing to let me turn our hallway into a makeshift whiteboard . . . all of those loving acts of service felt like doses of faith, proof that you were as invested in the success of this novel as I was. I'm so grateful for your endless love, light, and partnership.

Thank you to my mother for always encouraging my love of reading and introducing me to the joy of spending countless cozy hours in bookstores at an early age. I sincerely appreciate all your support around this novel, and for all the insights you shared about your own experiences growing up in Raleigh. And thank you to my uncle Jimmie and my late aunt Connita for graciously hosting a private tour of Raleigh during my visit in the fall of 2022. I will cherish those memories always.

Thank you to all the teachers who have guided and nurtured my love of literature and writing over the course of my life. This includes (but is certainly not limited to) Mrs. Hayes, Mr. Pound, and Mr. Sleete at Southfield-Lathrup High School; Prof. Arlene Keizer and Prof. Ralph Williams at the University of Michigan; and novelist and instructor Merrill Feitell from the UCLA Extension Program. My sincere thanks also go to Elana K. Arnold—I don't know how I would have made it through this novel's initial revision process without your insightful, soulful, and inspiring Revision Season course. And I'm eternally grateful to Sarah Enni of the *First Draft* podcast and to Bianca Marais, Carly Watters, and CeCe Lyra of *The Shit No One Tells You About Writing* podcast for teaching me so much about the craft of writing and the business of publishing and helping me build my creative community through their Discord groups and virtual retreats.

Speaking of my creative community, thank you to Tanisha

Mathis, Ashley Jordan, Brenna Hewer-Darroch, Maddy Wolfe, Ridhima Borooah, and the talented members of my 2025 Debuts Discord group for our affirming and inspiring conversations, for graciously offering feedback on my work, and for generously sending relevant opportunities and resources my way whenever you see them. I'm grateful to have you all in my corner.

I'm fortunate to have had so much support for this novel beyond my writing community. Thank you to my best friend, MK Juric, for your love, encouragement, and faith in me throughout every step of this experience. Thank you to my sister, Carla Vaughn, for being my constant cheerleader during this journey. Thank you to Rachelle Sweeney, Sara Galerne, Chibuzo Okafo, Elissa Vazquez, and Vanessa Wiater for enthusiastically celebrating every milestone on my road to publication. And I am deeply thankful for every friend, family member, colleague, and social media connection who has offered a kind word or supportive message over the course of this process. It has meant more to me than you'll ever know.

ABOUT THE AUTHOR

KRISTEN L. BERRY is a writer and communications executive. Born and raised in Metro Detroit, Kristen graduated from the University of Michigan with a bachelor's degree in English language and literature. She has provided PR and communications expertise to leading consumer brands for nearly twenty years, all while writing in her spare time. When she isn't reading or writing, Kristen can be found lifting heavy at the gym, hiking in Malibu, eating her way through Los Angeles with her husband, or shouting at the latest Formula 1 race. *We Don't Talk About Carol* is her debut novel.

kristenlberry.com
Instagram: @kristenlberry